The History Of The First West India Regiment

by

A. B. Ellis

Double9
BOOKS

The History Of The First West India Regiment
by A. B. Ellis

ISBN: 978-93-62769-35-0

Published by

DOUBLE 9 BOOKS

2/13-B, Ansari Road
Daryaganj, New Delhi – 110002
info@double9books.com
www.double9books.com
Tel. 011-40042856

ABOUT THE AUTHOR

A. B. Ellis, a distinguished historian and military scholar, is renowned for his seminal work, "The History of the First West India Regiment." This comprehensive masterpiece offers a detailed and authoritative account of the regiment's formation, contributions, and legacy within the context of British colonial history. Ellis's meticulous research and compelling narrative style provide readers with a thorough understanding of the regiment's pivotal role in shaping the social, political, and military landscape of the West Indies and beyond. Drawing upon archival sources, firsthand accounts, and military records, Ellis skillfully traces the regiment's evolution from its inception to its participation in key historical events, including conflicts, campaigns, and social movements. Through vivid storytelling and insightful analysis, he illuminates the experiences of the regiment's officers and soldiers, highlighting their bravery, sacrifices, and struggles amidst the challenges of colonial warfare and racial prejudice. "The History of the First West India Regiment" stands as a testament to Ellis's dedication to historical scholarship and his commitment to honoring the contributions of marginalized communities in shaping the course of history. It is an indispensable resource for scholars, students, and enthusiasts seeking to explore the complex intersections of race, imperialism, and military history in the Caribbean and beyond.

CONTENTS

INTRODUCTORY CHAPTER

At the present day, when our Continental neighbours are outvying each other in the completeness of their military organisations and the size of their armies, while in the United Kingdom complaints are daily heard that the supply of recruits for the British Army is not equal to the demand, it may not be out of place to draw the attention of the public to a source from which the army may be most economically reinforced.

The principal difficulty experienced by military reformers in their endeavours to remodel the British Army on the Continental system, is that caused by the necessity of providing troops for the defence of our vast and scattered Colonial Empire. Without taking into consideration India, our European and North American possessions, a considerable portion of the army has to be employed in furnishing garrisons for the Cape Colony, Natal, Mauritius, St. Helena, the Bermudas, the West Indies, Burmah, the Straits Settlements, Hong Kong, etc.; which garrisons, though creating a constant drain on the Home Establishment, are notoriously inadequate for the defence of the various colonies in which they are placed; and the result is that, whenever a colonial war breaks out, fresh battalions have to be hurriedly sent out from the United Kingdom at immense expense, and the entire military machine is temporarily disarranged.

In size, and in diversity of subject races, the British Empire may be not inaptly compared with that of Rome in its palmiest days; and we have, in a measure, adopted a Roman scheme for the defence of a portion of our dominions. The Romans were accustomed, as each new territory was conquered, to raise levies of troops from the subject race, and then, most politicly, to send them to serve in distant parts of the Empire, where they could have no sympathies with the inhabitants. In India we, like the Romans, raise troops from the conquered peoples, but, unlike them, we retain those troops for service in their own country. The result of this attempt to modify the scheme was the Indian mutiny.

The plan of a local colonial army was, however, first tried in the West Indies. At the close of the last century, when the West India Islands, or the Plantations, as they were then called, were of as much importance to, and held the same position in, the British Empire as India does now, there was in existence a West India Army, consisting of twelve battalions of negro troops, raised exclusively for service in the West Indies.

As India was gradually conquered, and the West India trade declined (from the abolition of the slave trade and other causes), the West India Colonies, by a regular process, fell from their former pre-eminent position. Each step in the descent was marked by the disbandment of a West India regiment, until, at the present day, two only remain in existence; and it is a matter of common notoriety that those two are principally preserved to garrison Sierra Leone, the Gold Coast Colony, British Honduras, and British Guiana—colonies the climates of which, experience has shown, are fatal to European soldiers, who are necessarily in time of peace, from the nature of their duties, more exposed to climatic influence than are officers. Economy was, of course, the cause of this continued process of reduction, for, until recently, such gigantic military establishments as those of Germany, Russia, and France were unheard of; and Great Britain was satisfied, and felt secure, with a miniature army, a paper militia, and no reserve. All this is now changed, and the necessity of an increase in our defensive power is admitted.

These negro West India troops won the highest encomiums from every British commander under whom they served. Sir Ralph Abercromby in 1796, Sir John Moore in 1797, Lieutenant-General Trigge in 1801, Sir George Provost in 1805, Lieutenant-General Beckwith and Major-General Maitland in 1809 and 1810, all testified to the gallantry, steadiness, and discipline of the negro soldiers. Sir John Moore, speaking of the new corps in 1796, said "they are invaluable," and "the very best troops for the climate." To come to more recent times, in 1873 the 2nd West India Regiment bore for six months the entire brunt of the Ashanti attack, and had actually forced the invading army to retire across the Prah before the men of a single line battalion were landed. In fact, the efficiency of West India troops was, and is, unquestioned.

This being so, it may be asked, why should not the present number of regiments composed of negro soldiers be increased for the purpose of garrisoning the colonies, especially those of which the climate is most prejudicial to English soldiers? This would not be a return to the former state of affairs, for when we had twelve negro regiments they were all stationed in the West Indies, whereas the essence of the present scheme is to send them on service in other colonies. Such an augmentation of our West India, or Zouave, regiments certainly appears politic and easy. I will also endeavour to show that it would be economical.

Each West India battalion would take the place of a Territorial battalion now serving abroad. The latter would return to the United Kingdom, be reduced to the Home Establishment, and have from 300 to 400 men passed into the Reserve. Repeat this process seven or eight times, and the services with the colours of between 2000 and 3000 European soldiers are dispensed with, the Reserve being increased by that number. In addition, negro soldiers being enlisted for twelve years' service with the colours, negro regiments on foreign service would not require those large drafts sent to white battalions to replace time-expired men, transport for which so swells the army estimates; while the negro being a native of the tropics, invaliding home would be reduced to a minimum.

The pay of the black soldier is ninepence per diem, against a shilling per diem to the white, so that there would be some saving effected in that way. In fact, it has been calculated that for an annual addition to the army estimates of some £27,000, six new negro battalions, each 800 strong, could be maintained; giving, on the one hand, an addition of 4800 to our present military force, and on the other, an increased Reserve, and six more Territorial battalions in the United Kingdom, ready to hand on a European emergency. To this may be added the lives of scores of Englishmen yearly saved to their country.

By the Territorial scheme now in force in Great Britain, an attempt has been made to localise corps on the German system, irrespective of the fact that Germany has no colonies, while those of Great Britain are most numerous. In Germany, in time of peace, each army corps is located in a district, from which it never moves, and in which the Reserve men, destined to complete the regiments to war strength, are compelled to live. Thus, when a general mobilisation takes place, the men are on the spot, and join the regiments in which they have already served. France has adopted this system, with the exception that army corps are not permanently located in districts, and the army thus localised is the one for European service only. For her colonies an entirely distinct army is maintained, composed of men specially enlisted for foreign service. In Great Britain we have neither adopted the German system nor the French modification of that system; but a scheme of localisation, with the main-spring of localisation removed, has been endeavoured to be grafted upon our old system, under which the regular army is sent on service in time of peace to distant portions of the globe. Should the mobilisation of an army corps be necessary in England, the Reserve men would, in a large number of cases, find the regiments in which they had formerly served, on foreign service. It would then be necessary to draft them into regiments to which they were strangers, in which they would take no interest, and where they would be unknown to their officers.

On the other hand, should it be necessary to despatch suddenly six or seven battalions to India or the Cape, they have to be made up to a war strength from other corps, for they have been reduced to a skeleton establishment in order that men may be provided for the Reserve.

Localisation, to be effectual, must be thorough; but it and the demands of foreign service are so incompatible that they cannot be efficiently combined. At the present time, neither is said to be in a satisfactory condition, and the Reserve, which was expected to have risen to a total of 80,000 men, consists of 32,000 only.

Military reformers have long since arrived at the conclusion that if the British Army is to be maintained at such a footing as to give weight to the voice of Great Britain in the councils of Europe, we must have two distinct armies; namely, one for home service, ready for a European imbroglio, and a second to which the defence of the colonies can be entrusted. The objection to this has been, hitherto, the great expense, for it has always been taken for granted that this Colonial Army would consist of white soldiers; and the question of increased pay, supply of recruits, and periodical removal of men to the United Kingdom, over and above the cost of the Territorial Army, had to be considered. With negro troops, however, for the Colonial Army, this objection, if it does not entirely disappear, is reduced at least by three-quarters. Should it be tried on a small scale and found successful, there need be no reason why in time almost the whole of the Territorial battalions should not be withdrawn from foreign service. In this way localisation could be made a reality; and with such vast untouched recruiting grounds as our colonies offer, there can be no doubt as to the practicability of raising the negro regiments required. Such regiments might also partly compose the garrisons of Gibraltar, Malta, Cyprus, Aden, and Ceylon. There is, indeed, no reason, except the hatred of the Hindoo for the negro, why such regiments might not serve in India. As the negro would never coalesce with the natives of India, a new and entirely reliable force, indifferent to tropical heat, and not requiring a vast retinue of camp-followers, would be always at hand. Of course, negro battalions could never be employed in cold latitudes, for the negro suffers from cold in a manner which is incomprehensible even to Europeans who have passed the best part of their lives in the tropics. Instead of being braced by and deriving activity from the cold, he becomes languid and inert; and nothing but the rays of the sun can arouse him to any exertion. Even in West Africa, during the Harmattan season, natives may be observed in the early morning, hugging their scanty clothing around them and shivering with cold; while the ill-fated expedition to New Orleans showed what deadly havoc an inclement climate will play with negro troops.

Next, as to the men of whom these negro regiments would be composed. It is too much the custom in Great Britain, in describing a man of colour, to consider that all has been said that is necessary when he is called a negro; yet there are as many nationalities, and as many types of the African race, as there are of the Caucasian. No one would imagine that a European was sufficiently described by the title of "white man." It would be asked if the individual in question were an Englishman, German, Frenchman, and so on; and the same kind of classification is necessary for the negro. On the western coast of Africa, the portion of the African continent from which North and South America and the West Indies obtained their negro population, there are at least twenty different varieties of the African race, distinct from each other in features and even in colour; and these are again subdivided into several hundred nations or tribes, each of which possesses a language, manners, and customs of its own.

In the days of the slave-trade, the slave-dealers adopted certain arbitrary designations to denote from what portion of the coast their wares were obtained. For instance, slaves shipped from Sierra Leone and the rivers to the north and east of that peninsula, and who were principally Timmanees, Kossus, Acoos, Mendis, Foulahs, and Jolloffs, were called Mandingoes, from the dominant tribe of that name which supplied the slave-market. Negroes from the Gold Coast kingdoms of Ashanti, Fanti, Assin, Akim, Wassaw, Aquapim, Ahanta, and Accra were denominated Koromantyns, or Coromantees, a corruption of Cormantine, the name of a fort some sixteen miles to the east of Cape Coast Castle, and which was the earliest British slave-station on the Gold Coast. Similarly, slaves from the tribes inhabiting the Slave Coast, that is to say, Awoonahs, Agbosomehs, Flohows, Popos, Dahomans, Egbas, and Yorubas, were all termed Papaws; while those from the numerous petty states of the Niger delta, where the lowest type of the negro is to be found, were known as Eboes.

Thousands of men of these tribes, and others too numerous to mention, were carried across the Atlantic and scattered at hap-hazard all over the West India Islands. At first tribal distinctions were maintained, but in the course of years, in each island they gradually disappeared and were forgotten; until at the present day a West India negro does not describe himself as a Kossu or a Koromantyn, but as a Jamaican, a Barbadian, an Antiguan, etc. It would naturally be supposed that as the West India Islands all received their slave population in the same manner, and that as in each there was the same original diversity of nationalities, subsequently blended together by intermarriages and community of wants and language, a West India negro of the present generation from any one island would be hardly distinguishable from one from any other. Nothing, however, would be further from the truth. Since the abolition of slavery, the conditions of life in the various islands have been so different—in some the dense population necessitating daily labour for an existence, while in others large uncultivated stretches of wood and mountain have afforded squatting grounds for the majority of the black population—that, in conjunction with diversity of climate, each group of islands is now populated with a race of negroes morally distinct *per se*. The difference between a negro born and bred in Barbados and one born and bred in Jamaica is as great as between an American and an Englishman, and the clannish spirit of the negro tends to increase that difference. At the present time the negro of Jamaica does not care to enlist in the 2nd West India Regiment, which is largely recruited in Barbados; and, in the same way, the Barbadian declines to serve in the 1st West India Regiment, because it is almost entirely composed of Jamaicans.

While the negroes of the West Indies have thus lost all their tribal peculiarities in the natural course of progress and civilisation, those of West Africa have remained at a standstill; and there is to-day as much difference between the hideous and debased Eboe and the stately and dignified Mandingo, between the docile Fanti and the bloodthirsty Ashanti, as there was one hundred and fifty years ago. Civilising influences have made this contrast between the Africans and their West India descendants still more striking. The latter have, since the abolition of slavery, been living independent lives, in close contact with civilisation, and enjoying all the rights of manhood under British laws. From their earliest infancy they have known no language but the English, and no religion but Christianity; while the former are still barbarians, grovelling in fetishism, cursed with slavery, ignorant, debased, and wantonly cruel. The West India negro has so much contempt for his African cousin, that he invariably speaks of him by the ignominious title of "bushman." In fact, the former considers himself in every respect an Englishman, and the anecdote of the West India negro, who, being rather roughly jolted by a Frenchman on board a mail steamer, turned round to him and ejaculated, "I think you forget that we beat you at Waterloo," is no exaggeration.

Just as the negro races of West Africa are distinct from one another, and the West India negro from all, so are the coloured inhabitants of both those parts of the world entirely distinct from the Kaffir tribes of South Africa; and a coalition between Galeka or Zulu inhabitants and West India troops would be as impossible as the fraternisation of a Territorial battalion with the natives of India. Apart, however, from the fact that negro troops could always be safely employed alone outside the colony in which they were bred, history has shown that the fidelity of West India soldiers is beyond question. Indeed it would be difficult to say what stronger ties there could be than those of sentiment, language, and religion, and the association from childhood with British manners, customs, laws, and modes of thought. When to these are added discipline, the habit of obedience, and that well-known affection for their officers and their regiment which is so particularly an attribute of the West India soldier, it must be acknowledged that the guarantees of fidelity are, with the single exception of race, at least as good as those of the linesmen.

In India, the native army consists of men hostile to us by tradition, creed, and race, who consider their food defiled if even the shadow of a British officer should chance to fall across it, and assuredly it would be as safe a proceeding to garrison our colonies with English negroes as to garrison India with such men. Yet that is done at the present day, and excites no remark.

The English-speaking negro of the West Indies is most excellent material for a soldier. He is docile, patient, brave, and faithful, and for an officer who knows how to gain his affection—an easy matter, requiring only justness, good temper, and an ear ready to listen patiently to any tale of real or imaginary grievance—he will do anything. Of course they are not perfect; they have their faults, like all soldiers, and when they chance to be commanded by an officer who is unnecessarily harsh, or who speaks roughly to them, they manifest their displeasure by passive obedience and a stubborn sullenness. English soldiers, on the other hand, under such circumstances, proceed to acts of insubordination, and it is for military judges to say which mode of expression they prefer.

The West African negro does not appear to such advantage as a soldier. Although all the specimens, with the exception of the Sierra Leone negro, possess the first necessary qualification of personal courage, they are dull and stupid, and cannot be transformed into intelligent soldiers. It may be wondered why the Sierra Leonean, who alone among the West Africans is an English-speaking negro, should be worse than his more barbarian neighbours; but I believe the solution may be found in the fact that the large proportion of slaves landed in former days at Sierra Leone from captured slavers were so-called Eboes, from the tribes of the Niger delta; which tribes all ethnologists are agreed in describing as among the lowest of the African races, and which, it may be remarked, are even at the present day addicted to cannibalism. The West African soldier is a mere machine, who mechanically obeys orders, and never ventures, under any circumstances, to act or think for himself. Should an African be placed on sentry, he fulfils to the letter the orders read to him by the non-commissioned officer who posts him, but frequently entirely ignores their spirit. Sometimes this is productive of amusing incidents. For instance, some years ago, among the orders for the sentry posted at Government House, Sierra Leone, was one to the effect that no one was to be permitted to leave the premises after dark carrying a parcel. This order had been issued at the request of the Governor, to prevent pilfering on the part of his servants. One evening the Governor was coming out of his house with a small despatch-box, when, to his surprise, he was stopped by the sentry, an old African.

"But I'm the Governor," said the astonished administrator, "and I had that order made myself. You mustn't stop me."

"Me no care if you be Gubnor or not," replied the imperturbable African. "The corporal gib de order, and you no can pass." And Her Majesty's representative had to turn back and leave his despatch-box at home.

The greatest objection to the African, however, is the strange fact that no amount of care or attention on the part of his instructors can ever make him a good or even a fair shot. In the 1st West India Regiment there are still a few Africans remaining, most of whom have from twelve to eighteen years' service; and who have annually expended their rounds without hitting the target more than once or twice during the whole musketry course. Give these men a rifle rested on a tripod, and tell them to align the sights upon some given mark, and they cannot do it. They will frequently aim a foot or two to the right or left of an object only a few yards distant. Every possible plan has been tried to make them improve, but all have equally failed; and, in consequence, Africans are not now enlisted. Still, although on account of this failing, African troops could never, in these days of long-range firing, meet Europeans in the field, a battalion of Africans would be quite good enough for bush fighting against an enemy like the Ashanti, a still worse marksman, and worse armed; or against tribes armed with the spear or assegai.

Of course one reason of the African's dulness is that until he enlists, that is until he is from twenty-four to thirty years of age, he has never exercised his mind in any way; and the long years of mental idleness have produced a sluggishness which makes it extremely difficult for him to acquire anything new that requires thought. After enlisting, he picks up a species of unintelligible English, but that is the most that he can do. It is pitiful to see these men, some of them now old, struggling day after day, according to regulation, in the regimental school, to learn their letters. It is to them the greatest punishment that could be inflicted, and though they attend school for years, they rarely succeed in doing more than master the alphabet.

In former days, whenever the cargo of a captured slaver was landed at Sierra Leone, a party from the garrison used to be admitted to the Liberated African Yard for the purpose of seeking recruits amongst the slaves. Many of the latter, pleased with the brilliant uniform, and talked over by the recruiting party, who were men specially selected for this duty on account of their knowledge of African languages, offered themselves as recruits. If medically fit, they were invariably accepted, though it must have been well known that they could not possibly have had any idea of the nature of the engagement into which they were entering. Some fifteen or twenty recruits being thus obtained, they were given high-sounding names, such as Mark Antony, Scipio Africanus, etc., their own barbaric appellations being too unpronounceable, and then marched down in a body to the cathedral to be baptised. Some might be Mohammedans, and the majority certainly believers in fetish, but the form of requiring their assent to a change in their religion was never gone through; and the following Sunday they were marched into church as a matter of course, along with their Christian comrades. Although thus nominally christianised, they still remained at heart believers in fetish, for it is a remarkable fact that no adult West African has ever become a bonâ-fide convert, and the missionaries have long since given up attempting to proselytise grown persons, reserving all their efforts for children. Holding, as they did, in great dread all fetish, or obeah, practices; usually someone amongst them, more cunning than the rest, professed an acquaintance with the supposed diabolical ritual; and gained influence with, and extorted money from, his more timid comrades. Officers now in the 1st West India Regiment can remember the time when, there being many Africans in the regiment, the feathers of parrots or scraps of rags might be found in the neighbourhood of the orderly room. Whenever this was the case, it was known that an African was about to be brought before his commanding officer for some neglect of duty or breach of discipline; and these fetishes had been placed there to induce the colonel to deal leniently with the offender. Ridiculous as this practice must seem to every educated person, it sometimes produced the most serious effects upon the credulous Africans; and I have heard old officers speak of instances, which came within their own knowledge, of soldiers who, having found old bones, broken pieces of calabashes, or glass, placed on their beds, immediately resigned themselves to death, saying that "fetish was thrown upon them," and in nine cases out of twelve, so certain were they that it was impossible to escape the coming doom, they positively frightened or worried themselves to death. The professors of fetishism likewise drove a good trade in amulets which rendered the wearer invulnerable. On one occasion at Sierra Leone, a young African who had been recently enlisted displayed with much pride a gri-gri or amulet which he wore on his wrist, and which, he asserted, rendered him invulnerable. His West India comrades laughed at him; and the African, indignant at the doubt thrown upon the efficacy of his charm, drew his knife, and, before he could be stopped, plunged it into his thigh to prove that he spoke the truth. His eyes were opened, unfortunately, too late; for though he was at once removed to the hospital, he died from the effects of this self-inflicted wound. In West India regiments the practice of fetish was made a military crime, and was severely punished. Sufferers or imaginary sufferers from fetishism, however, rarely complained to their officers, for they believed that the occult art practised by the professor was superior to any power held by man, and consequently, culprits were but seldom detected. With the disappearance of Africans from West India regiments, the offence of fetishism has, however, also disappeared.

Military crime in West India regiments is of comparatively rare occurrence. Even when the 3rd West India Regiment was in existence, there was less in the three negro regiments than in one of the Line; while drunkenness is confined to the few black sheep who will be found in every body of men. Riots or disturbances between West India soldiers and the inhabitants of the towns in which they are quartered are unheard of, and in every garrison they receive the highest praise for their unvarying good and quiet behaviour. In fact they are merry, good-tempered, and orderly men, who do not wish to interfere with anyone; and, owing to their temperate habits, they are not led into the commission of offences by the influence of drink. Of course, the popular idea in Great Britain of the negro is that he is a person who commonly wears a dilapidated tall hat, cotton garments of brilliant hue, carries a banjo or concertina, and indulges in extraordinary cachinnations at the smallest pretext; but this is as far from the truth as the creature of imagination in the opposite extreme, evoked by the vivid fancy of Mrs. Beecher Stowe.

The bravery of the West India soldier in action has often been tested, and as long as an officer remains alive to lead not a man will flinch. His favourite weapon is the bayonet; and the principal difficulty with him in action is to hold him back, so anxious is he to close with his enemy. It is unnecessary here to refer to individual acts of gallantry performed by soldiers of the 1st West India Regiment, they being fully set forth in the following history; but of such performed by soldiers of other West India regiments the two following now occur to me.

Private Samuel Hodge, a pioneer of the 3rd West India Regiment, was awarded the Victoria Cross for conspicuous bravery at the storming of the Mohammedan stockade at Tubarcolong (the White Man's Well), on the River Gambia, on the 30th of May, 1866. Under a heavy fire from the concealed enemy, by which one officer was killed and an officer and thirteen men severely wounded, Hodge, and another pioneer named Boswell, chopped and tore away with their hands the logs of wood forming the stockade, Boswell falling nobly just as an opening was effected. Again, in 1873, during the Ashanti War—when it was reported, on the 5th of December, by natives at Yancoomassie Assin that the Ashanti army had retired across the Prah—two soldiers of the 2nd West India Regiment volunteered to go on alone to the river and ascertain if the report were true. On their return they reported all clear to the Prah; and said they had written their names on a piece of paper and posted it up. Six days later, when the advanced party of the expeditionary force marched into Prahsu, this paper was found fastened to a tree on the banks of the river. At the time that this voluntary act was performed it must be remembered that, on the 27th of November, the British and their allies had met with a serious repulse at Faisowah, through pressing too closely upon the retiring Ashantis; that this repulse was considered both by the Ashantis and by our native allies as a set-off against the failure of the attack on Abracampa; that the Houssa levy was in a state of panic, and no reliable information as to the position of the enemy was obtainable. It was under such circumstances that these two men advanced nearly sixteen miles into an (to them) unknown tract of solitary forest, to follow up an enemy that never spared life, and whose whereabouts was doubtful.

Other qualifications apart, however, West India troops have proved themselves of the very greatest value on active service in tropical climates ᐧ from the very fact that, being natives of the tropics, they can undergo fatigue and exposure that would be fatal to European soldiers. In campaigns in which both the West India and the European soldier are employed, all the hard and unpleasant work is thrown upon the former, and the publication, in general orders of the thanks of the officer in command of the force is the only acknowledgment he receives; for newspaper correspondents, naturally anxious to swell the circulation of the journals they represent, while giving the most minute details of the doings of the white soldier, leave out in the cold his black comrade, who has few friends among the reading public of Great Britain. Occasionally, facts are even misrepresented. For instance, the defence of Fommanah, on the 2nd of February, 1874, which was really effected by a detachment of the 1st West India Regiment, was, in an account telegraphed to one London daily paper, attributed to the 23rd Regiment, of which corps there were only six or seven men in the place, and those in hospital.

On the last occasion on which West India troops served with Line battalions, namely in the Ashanti War of 1873-74, West India soldiers daily marched twice and even three times the distance traversed by the white troops; and, south of the Prah, searched the country for miles on both sides of the line of advance, in search of carriers. It is not too much to say, that if the two West India regiments had not been on the Gold Coast, no advance on Coomassie would, that year, have been possible. In December, 1873, the transport broke down; there was a deadlock along the road; each half-battalion of the European troops was detained in the camp it occupied, and the 23rd Regiment had to be re-embarked for want of carriers. The fate of the expedition was trembling in the balance, and the control officers were unanimous in declaring that a further advance was impossible, and that the troops in front would have to return by forced marches. Prior to this, the want of transport had been felt to such an extent that the West India soldiers had been placed on half rations; a step, however, which was not followed by any diminution of work, which remained as hard as ever. In this emergency the two West India regiments, with the 42nd—to whom all honour be due—volunteered to carry supplies, in addition to their arms, accoutrements, and ammunition. They acted as carriers for several days, and moved such quantities of provisions to the front that the pressure was removed and a further advance made possible. Even if more carriers had been obtained from the already ransacked native villages, they could not have arrived in time, for the rainy season was fast approaching and the delay of a fortnight would have been fatal.

There was a peculiar irony of fate in the expedition being thus relieved of its most pressing difficulties through the exertions of the West India regiments. It had been Sir Garnet Wolseley's original intention to take into Ashanti territory only the Rifle Brigade, the 23rd, and the 1st and 2nd West India Regiments; and, on the arrival of the hired transport, *Sarmatian*, he wrote, on the 15th of December, that he did not propose landing the 42nd. In the course of the next three days, however, he changed his views, and, in his letter of the 18th December, gave as his reason: "I find that the one great obstacle to the employment of a third battalion of English troops, viz., the difficulty of transport, is as great in the case of a West India regiment. The West India soldier has the same rations as the European soldier, and a West India regiment requires, man for man, exactly the same amount of transport as a European regiment." The 42nd, therefore, was to be landed and taken to the front, while the 1st West India Regiment was to remain at Cape Coast Castle and Elmina as a reserve. Afterwards, when the transport failed, it was found that the West India soldier could do the work of the European on half rations, and carry his own supplies as well.

West India regiments at the present day labour under many disadvantages. Owing to the two battalions having to furnish garrisons for colonies which really require three, they are alternately for one period of three years divided into three detachments, and for the next period of three years into six. No lieutenant-colonel of a West India regiment can ever see the whole of his regiment together. The largest number that, under present circumstances, he can ever have under him at any one station is four companies; and the most he can have under his actual command at any one time is six companies on board a troopship. Thus in a regiment there are sometimes three, and sometimes six, officers vested with the power of an officer commanding a detachment; and however conscientiously they may endeavour to follow out a regimental system, every individual has naturally a different manner of dealing with men, and a certain amount of homogeneousness is lost to the regiment as a whole.

Endless correspondence is entailed, and sometimes questions have to remain open for months, until answers can be received from distant detachments. In small garrisons, also, drill becomes a mere farce; for, after the clerks, employed men, and men on guard and in hospital are deducted, there are perhaps only a dozen men or so left for parade. In spite of all these drawbacks the regiments still maintain a wonderful efficiency, and afford another proof of the soldierlike qualities of the West India negro.

Another disadvantage is that a West India regiment is never seen in England, the British public knows nothing of such regiments, has no friends, relatives, or acquaintances in their ranks, and consequently takes no interest in them. Yet they are a remarkably fine body of men, and a picked battalion of the Guards would look small beside them if brigaded with them in Hyde Park. So little is known, that I have sometimes been asked if the officers of West India regiments are also black, and it is with a view to making the regiment to which I have the honour to belong better known to the public at large, that the following history has been written. There has been no attempt at descriptive writing, facts being merely collected from official documents, so that the authenticity of the narrative may be unquestionable.

In order that the earlier chapters may be the more readily understood, it may be as well to state that, with the 1st West India Regiment, which was called into existence in the *London Gazette* of the 2nd of May, 1795, were incorporated two other corps; of which one, the Carolina Corps, had been in existence since 1779, while the other—Malcolm's, or the Royal Rangers— had been raised in January or February, 1795. It is from the Carolina Corps that the 1st West India Regiment derives the Carolina laurel, borne on the crest of the regiment.

CHAPTER I
THE ACTION AT BRIAR CREEK, 1779—
THE ACTION AT STONO FERRY, 1779

In the autumn of 1778, during the War of the American Independence, the British commanders in North America determined to make another attempt for the royal cause in the Southern States of Georgia and South Carolina, which, since the failure of Lord Cornwallis at the siege of Charlestown in July, 1776, had been allowed to remain unmolested. With this view they despatched Colonel Campbell, in November, from New York, with the 71st Regiment, two battalions of Hessians, three of Loyal Provincials,[1] and a detachment of Artillery, the whole amounting to about 3500, to make an attempt upon the town of Savannah, the capital of Georgia. Arriving off the mouth of the Savannah River on the 23rd of December, Colonel Campbell was so rapidly successful, that, by the middle of January, not only was Savannah in his hands, but Georgia itself was entirely cleared of American troops.

It was about this time that the South Carolina Regiment, the oldest branch of the 1st West India Regiment, was raised. Numerous royalists joined the British camp and were formed into various corps;[2] and the South Carolina Regiment is first mentioned as taking part in the action at Briar Creek on the 3rd of March, 1779,[3] the corps then being, according to Major-General Prevost's despatch, about 100 strong. The action at Briar Creek occurred as follows:

In the early part of 1779, General Prevost's[4] force was distributed in posts along the frontier of Georgia; Hudson's Ferry, twenty-four miles above Savannah, being the upper extremity of the chain. Watching these posts was the American general, Lincoln, with the main body of the American Army of the South, at Purrysburgh, about twenty miles above Savannah, and General Ashe, who was posted with about 2000 of the Militia of North and South Carolina and Georgia, at Briar Creek, near the point where it falls into the Savannah River.

General Ashe's position appeared most secure, his left being covered by the Savannah with its marshes, and his front by Briar Creek, which was about twenty feet broad, and unfordable at that point and for several miles above it; nevertheless, General Prevost determined to surprise him. For the purpose of amusing General Lincoln, he made a show of an intention to pass the river; and, in order to occupy the attention of Ashe, he ordered a party to appear in his front, on the opposite side of Briar Creek. Meanwhile General Prevost, with 900 chosen men, made an extensive circuit, passed Briar Creek fifteen miles above the American position, gained their rear unperceived, and was almost in their camp before they discovered his approach. The surprise was as complete as could be wished. Whole regiments fled without firing a shot, and numbers without even attempting to seize their arms; they ran in their confusion into the marsh, and swam across the river, in which numbers of them were drowned. The Continental troops, under General Elbert, and a regiment of North Carolina Militia, alone offered resistance; but they were not long able to maintain the unequal conflict, and, being overpowered, were compelled to surrender. The Americans lost from 300 to 400 men, and seven pieces of cannon. The British lost five men killed, and one officer and ten men wounded.

After this success, the British and American forces remained on opposite sides of the River Savannah, until the end of April, when General Lincoln, thinking the swollen state of the river and the inundation of the marshes was sufficient protection for the lower districts, withdrew his forces further inland, leaving General Moultrie with 1000 men at Black Swamp. By this movement Lincoln left Charlestown exposed to the British. General Prevost at once took advantage of this, and, on the 29th of April, suddenly crossed the river, near Purrysburgh, with 2500 men, among whom was the South Carolina Regiment, which had been considerably increased by accessions of loyalists and freed negroes.

General Prevost advanced rapidly into the country, the militia under Moultrie, who had considered the swamps impassable, offering but a feeble resistance, and retiring hastily, destroying the bridges in their rear. On the 11th of May, the British force crossed the Ashley River a few miles above Charlestown, and, advancing along the neck formed by the Ashley and Cooper Rivers, established itself at a little more than cannon-shot from the city. A continued succession of skirmishes took place on that day and the ensuing night, and on the following morning Charlestown was summoned to surrender.

Negotiations were broken off in the evening, much to the disappointment of the British general, who had been led to suppose that a large proportion of the inhabitants were favourable to the royal cause, and that the city would fall easily into his hands. He now found himself in a dangerous predicament. He was without siege guns, before lines defended by a considerable force of artillery, and flanked by shipping; he was involved in a labyrinth of creeks and rivers, where a defeat would have been fatal, and General Lincoln with a force equal, if not superior to his own, was fast approaching for the relief of the city. Taking all this into consideration, General Prevost prudently struck camp that night, and, under cover of the darkness, the direct line of retreat on Savannah being closed, returned to the south side of the Ashley River. From thence the army passed to the islands of St. James and St. John, lying to the southward of Charlestown harbour, and commencing that succession of islands and creeks which extends along the coast from Charlestown to Savannah.

In these islands the army awaited supplies from New York, of which it was much in need; and, on the arrival of two frigates, it commenced to move to the island of Port Royal, which at the same time would afford good quarters for the troops during the intense heats, and, from its vicinity to Savannah, and its excellent harbour, was the best position that could be chosen for covering Georgia.

Directly General Lincoln discovered what was taking place, he advanced to attack. St. John's Island is separated from the mainland by a narrow inlet, called Stono River, and communication between the mainland and the island was kept up by a ferry. On the mainland, at this ferry, General Prevost had established a post, consisting of three redoubts, joined by lines of communication; and, to cover the movement of the army to Port Royal Island, he here posted Lieutenant-Colonel Maitland with the 1st Battalion of the 71st Regiment, a weak battalion of Hessians, the North Carolina Regiment, and the South Carolina Regiment, amounting in the whole to about 800 men.

On the 20th of June, General Lincoln made a determined attempt to force the passage, attacking with a force variously estimated at from 1200 to 5000 men and eight guns. Lieutenant-Colonel Maitland's advanced posts, consisting of the South Carolina Regiment, were some distance in front of his works; and a smart firing between them and the Americans gave him the first warning of the approach of the enemy. He instantly sent out two companies of the 71st from his right to ascertain the force of the assailants. The Highlanders had proceeded only a quarter of a mile when they met the outposts retiring before the enemy. A fierce conflict ensued. Instead of retreating before superior numbers, the Highlanders persisted in the unequal combat till all their officers were either killed or wounded, of the two companies eleven men only returned to the garrison; and the British force was sadly diminished, and its safety consequently imperilled by this mistaken valour.

The whole American line now advanced to within three hundred yards of the works, and a general engagement began, which was maintained with much courage and steadiness on both sides. At length the regiment of Hessians on the British left gave way, and the Americans, in spite of the obstinate resistance of the two Carolina regiments, were on the point of entering the works, when a judicious flank movement of the remainder of the 71st checked the advance; and General Lincoln, apprehensive of the arrival of British reinforcements from the island, drew off his men, and retired in good order, taking his wounded with him.

The battle lasted upwards of an hour. The British had 3 officers and 19 rank and file killed, and 4 officers and 85 rank and file wounded. The South Carolina Regiment had Major William Campbell and 1 sergeant killed, 1 captain, 1 sergeant, and 3 rank and file wounded.[5] The Americans lost 5 officers and 35 men killed, 19 officers and 120 men wounded.

Three days after the battle, the British troops evacuated the post at Stono Ferry, and also the island of St. John, passing along the coast from island to island till they reached Beaufort in the island of Port Royal. Here General Prevost left a garrison under the command of Lieutenant-Colonel Maitland, and proceeded with the remainder of his force, with which was the South Carolina Regiment, to the town of Savannah.

The heat had now become too intense for active service; and the care of the officers was employed in preserving their men from the fevers of the season, and keeping them in a condition for service next campaign, which was expected to open in October.

FOOTNOTES:

[1] De Lancey's Corps, the New York Volunteers, and Skinner's Corps.

[2] "Annual Register," 1779, Beatson's "Memoirs," Gordon's "History of the American War," etc. etc.

[3] Beatson's "Naval and Military Memoirs," vol. iv. p. 492.

[4] Major-General Prevost had come from Florida and assumed command in January.

[5] "Return of the killed, wounded, and missing at the repulse of the Rebels at Stono Ferry, South Carolina, June 20th, 1779."

CHAPTER II
THE SIEGE OF SAVANNAH, 1779—THE
SIEGE OF CHARLESTOWN, 1780—THE
BATTLE OF HOBKERK'S HILL, 1781

At the opening of the next campaign, although General Prevost had been obliged to retire from Charlestown and to abandon the upper parts of Georgia, yet, so long as he kept possession of the town of Savannah and maintained a post at Port Royal Island, South Carolina was exposed to incursions. The Americans, therefore, pressed the French admiral, Count D'Estaing, to repair to the Savannah River, hoping, by his aid, to drive the British from Georgia. D'Estaing, in compliance, sailed from Cape François, in St. Domingo; and with twenty-two sail of the line and a number of smaller vessels, having 4800 French regular troops on board and several hundred black troops from the West Indies, appeared off the Savannah so unexpectedly that the *Experiment*, a British fifty-gun ship, fell into his hands. On the appearance of the French fleet, on September 9th, General Prevost immediately called in all his outposts in Georgia, sent orders to Lieutenant-Colonel Maitland, at Port Royal, to rejoin him at once, and exerted himself to strengthen the defences of the town of Savannah.

For the first three or four days after the arrival of the fleet, the French were employed in moving their troops through the Ossabaw Inlet to Beaulieu, about thirteen miles above the town of Savannah. On the 15th of September, the French, with a party of American light horse, attacked the British outposts, and General Prevost withdrew all his force into his works.

On the 16th, D'Estaing summoned the place to surrender. Lieutenant-Colonel Maitland's force had not yet arrived, the works were still incomplete, and General Prevost was desirous of gaining time; he consequently requested a suspension of hostilities for twenty-four hours. This was granted, and in that critical interval Lieutenant-Colonel Maitland, by the most extraordinary efforts—for one of General Prevost's messengers had fallen into the hands of the enemy, who had at once seized all the principal lines of communication—arrived with the garrison of Port Royal, and entered the town. Encouraged by this accession of strength, General Prevost now informed Count D'Estaing that he was resolved to defend the place to the last extremity. On the 17th, D'Estaing had been joined by General Lincoln with some 3000 men, which, with the French troops, raised the total besieging force to something over 8000. The besieged did not exceed 3000.

The enemy spent several days in bringing up guns and stores from the fleet, and on the 23rd the besieging army broke ground before the town. On the 1st of October, they had advanced to within 300 yards of the British works. On the morning of the 4th of October, several batteries, mounting thirty-three pieces of heavy cannon and nine mortars, with a floating battery of sixteen guns on the river, opened fire on the town. For several days they played incessantly on the garrison, and there was continued skirmishing between the negroes of the Carolina regiments and the enemy.[6]

On the morning of the 9th of October, the enemy, under a furious cannonade, advanced to storm in three columns, with a force of 3000 French under D'Estaing in person, and 1500 Americans under Lincoln. General Prevost, in his despatch to Lord George Germain, dated Savannah, November 1st, 1779, says: "However, the principal attack, composed of the flower of the French and rebel armies, and led by D'Estaing in person, with all the principal officers of either, was made upon our right. Under cover of the hollow, they advanced in three columns; but having taken a wider circuit than they needed, and gone deeper in the bog, they neither came so early as they intended nor, I believe, in the same order. The attack, however, was very spirited, and for some time obstinately persevered in, particularly on the Ebenezer Road Redoubt. Two stand of colours were actually planted, and several of the assailants killed upon the parapet; but they met with so determined a resistance, and the fire of three seamen batteries, taking them in almost every direction, was so severe, that they were thrown into some disorder, at least at a stand; and at this most critical moment, Major Glasier, of the 60th, with the 60th Grenadiers and the Marines, advancing rapidly from the lines, charged (it may be said) with a degree of fury; in an instant the ditches of the redoubt and a battery to its right in rear were cleared.... Lieutenant-Colonel de Porbeck, of Weissenbach's, being field officer of the day of the right wing, and, being in the redoubt when the attack began, had an opportunity, which he well improved, to signalise himself in a most gallant manner; and it is but justice to mention to your lordships the troops who defended it. They were part of the South Carolina Royalists, the Light Dragoons (dismounted), and the battalion men of the 4th 60th, in all about 100 men, commanded (by a special order) by Captain James, of the Dragoons (Lieutenant 71st), a good and gallant officer, and who nobly fell with his sword in the body of the third he had killed with his own hand."

After their repulse from the Ebenezer Redoubt, the enemy retired, and, a few days afterwards, the siege was raised, the Americans crossing the Savannah at Zubly's Ferry and taking up a position in South Carolina, while the French embarked in their fleet and sailed away. During the assault the French lost 700 and the Americans 240 killed. The British loss was 55, four of whom belonged to the South Carolina Regiment, who were killed in the redoubt, where also Captain Henry, of that corps, was wounded.

According to the "Journal of the Siege of Savannah," p. 39, the garrison of the redoubt in the Ebenezer Road was as follows:

28 Dismounted Dragoons.
28 Battalion men of the 60th Regiment.
54 South Carolina Regiment.
—
110

In the same work is the following: "Two rebel standards were once fixed on the redoubt in the Ebenezer Road; one of them was carried off again, and the other, which belonged to the 2nd Carolina Regiment, was taken. After the retreat of the enemy from our right, 270 men, chiefly French, were found dead; upwards of 80 of whom lay in the ditch and on the parapet of the redoubt, and 93 were within our abattis."

The strength of the South Carolina Regiment at the termination of the siege was: 1 colonel (Colonel Innes), 1 major, 4 captains, 7 lieutenants, 3 ensigns, 15 sergeants, 7 drummers, and 216 rank and file.

Nothing of note took place in Georgia and South Carolina till January, 1780, when Sir Henry Clinton arrived in the Savannah River with a force destined for the reduction of Charlestown. He had sailed from New York on the 26th of December, 1779, and, having experienced bad weather, put into the Savannah to repair damages. Sir H. Clinton selected a portion of General Prevost's force at Savannah to take part in the coming operations, and among the corps so selected was the South Carolina Regiment, which is shown in the return of troops at the capture of Charlestown as "joined from Savannah."

On the 10th of February, the armament sailed to North Edisto, where the troops disembarked, taking possession of the island of St. John next day without opposition. On the 29th of March, the army reached Ashley River and crossed it ten miles above Charlestown; then, the artillery and stores having been brought over, Sir H. Clinton marched down Charlestown Neck, and, on the night of the 1st of April, broke ground at 800 yards from the American works. The garrison of the city consisted of 2000 regular troops, 1000 North Carolina Militia, and the male inhabitants of the place.

On the 9th of April, the first parallel was finished, and the batteries opened fire; and Charlestown finally capitulated, after an uneventful siege, on the 12th of May. In the "Return of the killed and wounded" during the siege, the South Carolina Regiment is shown as having had three rank and file wounded.

Sir H. Clinton sailed from Charlestown on the 5th of June, leaving Lord Cornwallis in command. The latter meditated an expedition into North Carolina, and, for the preservation of South Carolina during his absence with the main body of the troops, he established a chain of posts along the frontier. One of these posts was at Ninety-six, and for its defence was detailed the South Carolina Regiment, under Colonel Innes, with Allen's corps, "the 16th and three other companies of Light Infantry."[7] Lieutenant-Colonel Balfour was then in command of the post, but was soon after relieved by Lieutenant-Colonel Cruger.

The garrison of Ninety-six remained undisturbed till September, 1780, when, Lord Cornwallis having moved into North Carolina and occupied Charlotte, Georgia was almost denuded of troops; and an American leader, Colonel Clarke, took advantage of this to attack the British post at Augusta. Lieutenant-Colonel Brown, who commanded there with 150 men, finding the town untenable, retired towards an eminence on the banks of the Savannah, named Garden Hill, and sent intelligence of his situation to Ninety-six. Lieutenant-Colonel Cruger, with the 16th and the South Carolina Regiment, at once marched to his relief. Colonel Clarke, who had captured the British guns and was besieging the garrison of Garden Hill, upon being informed of Cruger's approach raised the siege, and, abandoning the guns which he had taken, retreated so hurriedly that, though pursued for some distance, he effected his escape.

In the spring of 1781, Lord Cornwallis had again invaded North Carolina, and, having defeated the American general, Greene, at Guildford Court House, had continued his march towards Virginia, expecting the enemy to make every effort to prevent the army entering that state. General Greene, however, allowed Lord Cornwallis to pass on, and then, having assembled a considerable body of troops, made a sudden descent upon the British posts in South Carolina, where Lord Rawdon had been left in command. These posts were in a line from Charlestown by the way of Camden and Ninety-six, to Augusta in Georgia. Camden was the most important, and there Lord Rawdon had taken post with 900 men.

On the 20th of April, 1781, General Greene appeared before Camden, which was a village situated on a plain, covered on the south by the Wateree, a river which higher up is called the Catawba; and below, after its confluence with the Congaree from the south, assumes the name of the Santee. On the east of it flowed Pinetree Creek; on the northern and western sides it was defended by a strong chain of redoubts, six in number, extending from the river to the creek. Lord Rawdon's force was so small that the approach of Greene to Camden necessitated the abandonment of the ferry on the Wateree, "although the South Carolina Regiment was on its way to join him from Ninety-six, and that was its direct course; he had, however, taken his measures so well as to secure the passage of that regiment upon its arrival three days after."[8]

General Greene, whose force amounted to 1200 men, determined to await reinforcements before attacking, and on the 24th of April he retired to Hobkerk's Hill, an eminence about a mile north of Camden, on the road to the Waxhaws. Here Lord Rawdon resolved to attack him, and on the morning of the 25th, with 900 men, he marched from Camden, and, by making a circuit, and keeping close to the edge of the swamp, under cover of the woods, he gained the left flank of the Americans, where the hill was most accessible, undiscovered.

The alarm was given, while the Americans were at breakfast, by the firing of the outposts, and at this critical moment a reinforcement of American militia arrived. So confident was General Greene of success that he ordered Lieutenant-Colonel Washington, with his cavalry, to turn the right flank of the British and to charge them in the rear, while bodies of infantry were to assail them in front and on both flanks.

The American advanced parties were driven in by the British after a sharp skirmish, and Lord Rawdon advanced steadily to attack the main body of the enemy. The 63rd Regiment, with the volunteers of Ireland, formed his right; the King's American Regiment, with Robertson's corps, composed his left; the New York volunteers were in the centre. The South Carolina Regiment and the cavalry were in the rear and formed a reserve.[9]

Such was the impetuosity of the British that, in the face of a destructive discharge of grape, they gained the summit of the hill and pierced the American centre. The militia fell into confusion, their officers were unable to rally them, and General Greene ordered a retreat. The pursuit was continued for nearly three miles. The Americans halted for the night at Saunders' Creek, about four miles from Hobkerk's Hill, and next day proceeded to Rugeley Mills, about twelve miles from Camden. After the engagement the British returned to Camden. The American loss was 300; the British lost 258 out of about 900 who were on the field.

FOOTNOTES:

[6] "The True History of the Siege of Savannah," published 1780.

[7] "The Campaigns of 1780 and 1781, in the Southern Provinces of North America," by Lieutenant-Colonel Tarleton, London, 1787.

[8] Tarleton, p. 461.

[9] "Martial Register," vol. iii. p. 110.

CHAPTER III
THE RELIEF OF NINETY-SIX, 1781—THE BATTLE OF EUTAW SPRINGS, 1781— REMOVAL TO THE WEST INDIES

Lord Rawdon was not in a position to follow up his success at Hobkerk's Hill, and on the 3rd of May, 1781, Greene passed the Wateree, and occupied such positions as to prevent the garrison at Camden obtaining supplies. Generals Marion and Lee were also posted at Nelson's Ferry, to prevent Colonel Watson, who was advancing with 400 men, from joining Lord Rawdon, and Watson was obliged to alter his route. He marched down the north side of the Santee, crossed it near its mouth, with incredible labour advanced up its southern bank, recrossed it above the encampment of Marion and Lee, and arrived safely with his detachment at Camden on the 7th of May.

Thus reinforced, Lord Rawdon determined to attack Greene, and, on the night of the 8th, marched from Camden with his whole force. Greene, who had been informed of this movement, passed the Wateree and took up a strong position behind Saunders' Creek. Lord Rawdon followed him and drove in his outposts, but, finding the position was too strong for his small force, he returned to Camden.

Camden being too far advanced a post for Lord Rawdon to hold with the few troops at his disposal, he evacuated it on the 10th of May, and retired by Nelson's Ferry to the south of the Santee, and afterwards to Monk's Corner. In the meantime, attacks were made on the British posts in Georgia, Augusta itself being taken on the 5th of June, while the post of Ninety-six in South Carolina was closely invested by General Greene with the main American army in the Southern States.

About this time, a change took place in the South Carolina Regiment. Lord Rawdon, in a letter to Lieutenant-General Earl Cornwallis, dated Charlestown, June 5th, 1781, speaks of the difficulty which he has experienced in the formation of cavalry, and goes on to say that the inhabitants of Charlestown having subscribed 3000 guineas for a corps of dragoons, out of compliment to those gentlemen "I have ordered the South Carolina Regiment to be converted into cavalry, and I have the prospect of their being mounted and completely appointed in a few days."

On the 3rd of June, Lord Rawdon had received considerable reinforcements from England, and on the 9th he left Charlestown with about 2000 men, including the South Carolina Regiment in its new capacity, for the relief of Ninety-six. In their rapid progress over the whole extent of South Carolina, through a wild country and under a burning sun, the sufferings of the troops were severe, but they advanced with celerity to the assistance of their comrades. On the 11th of June, General Greene received notice of Lord Rawdon's march, and immediately sent Sumpter with the whole of the cavalry to keep in front of the British army and retard its progress. Lord Rawdon, however, passed Sumpter a little below the junction of the Saluda and Broad Rivers, and that officer was never able to regain his front.

In the meantime, the Americans were pushing hard the garrison of Ninety-six; they were nearly reduced to extremities, and in a few days must have surrendered; but the rapid advance of Lord Rawdon left Greene no alternative but to storm or raise the siege. On the 18th of June, he made a furious assault upon the place; but, after a desperate conflict of nearly an hour, was compelled to retire. Next day he retreated, crossing the Saluda on the 20th, and encamping at Little River.

On the morning of the 21st, Lord Rawdon arrived at Ninety-six, and the same evening set out in pursuit of Greene, who, however, retreated; and Rawdon, despairing of overtaking him, returned to Ninety-six. He now found it necessary to evacuate that position and contract his posts; and, having destroyed the works, he marched towards the Congaree. There, on the 1st of July, while out foraging, two officers and forty dragoons of the South Carolina Regiment were surrounded and taken prisoners by Lee's Legion. This blow sadly crippled Lord Rawdon, who was much in need of cavalry, and two days later he retreated to Orangeburgh.

The summer heats now coming on, Lord Rawdon proceeded to England on sick leave, leaving Lieutenant-Colonel Stuart in command of the troops in South Carolina and Georgia. The new commander at once proceeded with the army to the Congaree, and formed an encampment near its junction with the Wateree.

Towards the end of August, while Lieutenant-Colonel Stuart was expecting a convoy of provisions from Charlestown, he received information that General Greene, who had been reinforced and was now at the head of 2500 men, was moving towards Friday's Ferry on the Congaree. The American cavalry was so numerous and enterprising that the expected convoy, then at Martin's, fifty-six miles from the British camp, would inevitably fall into their hands unless protected by an escort of at least 400 men; and Lieutenant-Colonel Stuart's force being too small to admit of so considerable a body being detached without risk, he determined to retreat by slow marches to Eutaw Springs, about sixty miles north of Charlestown, and meet the convoy on the way.

General Greene followed the retiring British, and, on the 7th of September, arrived within seven miles of Eutaw Springs. Being there reinforced by General Marion and his corps, he resolved to attack next day. At six in the morning, two deserters from the American army entered the British camp, and informed Stuart of the approach of the enemy; but little credit was given to their report. At that time Major Coffin, with 140 infantry and 50 of the South Carolina Regiment, was out foraging for roots and vegetables—the army having neither corn nor bread—in the direction in which the Americans were advancing. About four miles from the camp at Eutaw, that party was attacked by the American advanced guard and driven in with loss. Their return convinced Colonel Stuart of the approach of the enemy, and the British army was soon drawn up obliquely across the road on the height near Eutaw Springs.

The firing began between two and three miles from the British camp. The British light parties were driven in on their main body, and the first line of the Americans attacked with great impetuosity. For a short time the conflicting ranks were intermingled, and the officers fought hand to hand. At that critical moment, General Lee, who had turned the left flank of the British, charged them in the rear. They were broken and driven off the field, their guns falling into the hands of the Americans, who eagerly pressed on their retreating adversaries.

At this crisis, Colonel Stuart ordered a strong detachment to take post in a large three-storey brick house, which was in rear of the army on the right, while another occupied an adjoining palisaded garden, and some close underwood. The Americans made the most desperate efforts to dislodge them from their posts; but every attack was met with determined courage. Four pieces of artillery were brought to bear on the house, but made no impression on its solid walls, from which a close and destructive fire was kept up, as well as from the adjoining enclosure. Almost all the gunners were killed and wounded; and the guns had been pushed so near the house that they could not be brought off. Colonel Washington attempted to turn the British right, and charge them in rear; but his horse was shot under him, and he was wounded and made prisoner. After every attempt to dislodge the British from their position had failed, General Greene drew off his men, and retired to the ground which he had left in the morning. This conflict had lasted nearly four hours. The Americans lost 555, the British 693. The British kept their ground during the night, and next day began to retreat. About fourteen miles from the field of battle, Lieutenant-Colonel Stuart was met by a reinforcement, under Major McArthur, marching from Charlestown to his assistance. Thus strengthened, he proceeded to Monk's Corner.

Eutaw Springs was the last engagement of importance in the southern provinces. The British soon retreated to a position on Charlestown Neck, and confined their operations to the defence of the posts in that vicinity; while in Georgia, the British force was concentrated at Savannah. The surrender of Lord Cornwallis at Yorktown, in October, 1781, and the subsequent peace negotiations, put an end to the hostilities in America.

Lieutenant-Colonel Tarleton says: "It is impossible to do justice to the spirit, patience, and invincible fortitude displayed by the commanders, officers, and soldiers during these dreadful campaigns in the Carolinas. They had not only to contend with men, and these by no means deficient in bravery and enterprise, but they encountered and surmounted difficulties and fatigues from the climate and the country, which would appear insuperable in theory and almost incredible in the relation. They displayed military and, we may add, moral virtues far above all praise. During renewed successions of forced marches, under the rage of a burning sun and in a climate at that season peculiarly inimical to man, they were frequently, when sinking under the most excessive fatigue, not only destitute of every comfort but almost of every necessary which seems essential to existence. During the greater part of the time they were totally destitute of bread, and the country afforded no vegetables for a substitute. Salt at length failed, and their only resources were water and the wild cattle which they found in the woods. About fifty men, in this last expedition, sunk under the vigour of their exertions and perished through mere fatigue."

At the cessation of hostilities, the South Carolina Regiment and the Loyal American Rangers were removed to Jamaica, and as they are shown in the Jamaica Almanack for 1782 as being then in the island, they presumably arrived there about December, 1781. The South Carolina Regiment was probably dismounted, as it is shown as being stationed at Fort Augusta in Kingston harbour. At this time, the reinforcing of the West India Islands by provincial corps was considered most important, and in a letter to Sir Guy Carleton we find the following: "The object of reinforcing those islands is so important, that His Majesty wishes to have it understood that every provincial corps embarking for the West Indies shall immediately be put upon the British Establishment." It was, probably, on some such understanding that the two corps above mentioned proceeded from South Carolina; but the promise, if made, was never fulfilled, and neither of the two ever appeared in any Army List. The following is the list of officers of the South Carolina Regiment given in the Jamaica Almanack:

Lieutenant-Colonel Commandant—Captain Lord Charles Montagu, 88th Regiment.

Major—James Balmer.

Captains—G.C. Montagu, Robert Palmer, W. Oliphant, W. Lowe.

Lieutenants.

R. Marshall.	H. Craddock.	— Odonnell.
J. Carden.	D. M'Connell.	A. Clerk.
H. Rudgley.	P. Sergeant.	J. Petrie.
M. Rainford.	J.P. Collins.	— Smith.

Ensigns.

W. Splain.	J. Kent.	B. Meighan.
— Bell.	— Farquhar.	— Thomas.
— Smith.		

The South Carolina Regiment remained in Jamaica until the general disbandment of the provincial corps in 1783. The lieutenant-colonel commandant was given an independent company, and the whites, both officers and men, were pacified with grants of land. The black troopers, however, were a source of difficulty. These troopers, some of whom were originally free, while some had been purchased by the British Government, were in those days of slavery something of a "white elephant" in a large slave-holding colony like Jamaica. The planters, fearful of the consequences of the example to their slaves of a free body of negroes who had served as soldiers, agitated for their removal from the island, but, on the other hand, no other island was willing to receive them. There is no trace of how the difficulty was finally settled, but in a letter, dated War Office, June 15th, 1783, signed R. Fitzpatrick, and addressed to Major-General Campbell, commanding in Jamaica, the receipt of his letter concerning the disbandment of the provincial troops in the island is acknowledged, and the removal of "the blacks of the South Carolina Regiment" to the Leeward command approved of.

Some time, then, in September, 1783, the black troopers were removed to the Leeward Islands, and in the "Monthly Return of His Majesty's Forces in the Leeward and Charibee Islands, under the command of Lieutenant-General Edward Mathew," we find them formed into a corps, with a body of black artificers, who had served in South Carolina at the sieges of Charlestown and Ninety-six, and thirty-three black pioneers who had been included in the surrender of Yorktown. The following is the state of this corps:

RETURN OF THE BLACK CORPS OF DRAGOONS, PIONEERS, AND ARTIFICERS

A. Captains.
B. 1st Lieutenants.
C. 2nd Lieutenants.
D. Sergeants Present.
E. Drummers and Trumpeters Present.
F. Present, fit for duty.
G. Sick in Quarters.
H. Sick in Hospital.
I. On Command.
J. Total.
K. Total of the Whole.

Where Stationed.	Companies	Officers Present.			Effective Rank and File.							
		A	B	C	D	E	F	G	H	I	J	K
Grenada	Capt. Mackrill	1	-	-	3	1	25	7	10	23	65	70
St. Vincent	Capt. Anderson	1	-	1	14	5	46	4	-	138	188	209
Grenada	Capt. Millar	1	-	-	3	-	19	4	4	19	46	50
	Total	3	-	1	20	6	90	15	14	180	299	329

The officers of this corps were, according to Bryan Edwards, vol. i. p. 386, taken from the regular army, and the companies were commanded by lieutenants of regulars, having captains' rank. Artificers, it may be as well to observe, were sappers and miners. The Royal Engineers at about this date consisted of various companies of Artificers; later on they were called Sappers and Miners; and, finally, Royal Engineers.

CHAPTER IV
THE EXPEDITION TO MARTINIQUE, 1793—
THE CAPTURE OF MARTINIQUE, ST.
LUCIA, AND GUADALOUPE, 1794—THE
DEFENCE OF FORT MATILDA, 1794

In February, 1789, all three companies of the "Black Corps of Dragoons, Pioneers, and Artificers" were stationed in Grenada, and from that date until June, 1793, they are shown in every monthly return, with a strength varying from 279 to 268, and an increase of four first lieutenants.

In February, 1793, the news of the French declaration of war was received in the West Indies, and orders were soon after transmitted from England to the Commander-in-Chief in the Windward and Leeward Islands to attempt the reduction of the French islands. Tobago was taken on the 17th of April without much trouble, the majority of the planters in that island being English; and an attack on Martinique was next meditated. The whole of the British force in the West Indies was known and acknowledged to be inadequate to the reduction of that island; but such representations had been spread throughout the army, concerning the disaffection of the greater part of the inhabitants of all the French islands towards the Republican Government lately established, as to create a very general belief that the appearance of a British armament before the capital of Martinique would alone produce an immediate surrender. Major-General Bruce, on whom the chief command of the troops had devolved, was assured by a deputation from the principal planters of the island that "a body of 800 regular troops would be more than sufficient to overcome all possible resistance."

These representations induced Major-General Bruce, in conjunction with Admiral Gardner, to undertake an expedition; and the troops having been embarked at Grenada in the men-of-war, the armament arrived off Cape Navire, Martinique,[10] on the 11th of June, 1793. There the general met the officer commanding the French Royalists, and, as the latter proposed an attack upon the town of St. Pierre, the 21st Regiment was landed at Cape

Navire on the 14th, and there posted, to enable the Royalists to concentrate in the neighbourhood of St. Pierre, where the remainder of the British force joined them on the 16th. "The British troops consisted of the Grenadiers, Light Infantry, and Marines from the fleet, with the Black Carolina Corps, amounting in all to about 1100 men."[11] The Royalists were said to number 800.

On the afternoon of the 17th, the enemy made an attack, but were driven back by the pickets, with the loss of one officer and three men killed on the part of the British. An attack on the two batteries which defended St. Pierre was planned for the morning of the 18th, but failed, owing to the want of discipline on the part of the Royalists. Major-General Bruce says: "The morning of the 18th was the time fixed for the attack, and we were to move forward in two columns, the one consisting of the British troops, the other of the French Royalists; and for this purpose the troops were put in motion before daybreak; but, unfortunately, some alarm having taken place amongst the Royalists, they began, in a mistake, firing on one another, and their commander being severely wounded on the occasion, the whole body, refusing to submit to any of the other officers, retired to the post from which they had marched."

This conduct showed the general that no reliance could be placed on the Royalists, and that the attack on St. Pierre, if carried out at all, would have to be done by the British troops alone, whose numbers were not equal to the task. He, consequently, ordered the troops to return to their former positions, and on the 19th they re-embarked. As to have left the Royalists in Martinique would only have been to leave them to be massacred by the Republicans, those unfortunate people were embarked on the 19th and 20th, and the 21st Regiment being taken on board at Cape Navire on the 21st, the expedition returned to Grenada.

It may be wondered whence came the Black Carolina Corps mentioned by Major-General Bruce, but it is evident that by that designation the Black Corps of Dragoons, Pioneers, and Artificers was locally known; for in the monthly return, dated May 1st, 1794, the "state" of the corps is headed, "Return of the Black Carolina Corps," and the title, "Black Corps of Dragoons, Pioneers, and Artificers" ceases, from that date, to be used in any official document. The strength of the corps in that return is 258 of all ranks.

The failure of Major-General Bruce's attempt on Martinique induced the British Ministers to send out an armament under Sir Charles Grey for the reduction of all the French West India Islands; and, until the arrival of this force at Barbados, in January, 1794, the Black Carolina Corps remained quietly in garrison at Grenada. The troops from the various islands— and amongst them all three companies of that corps—were collected at Barbados during the remainder of January, and, on the 4th of February, the expeditionary force, 6085 strong, set sail from Carlisle Bay. The army, in three divisions, landed at three separate points in Martinique; the first at Gallion Bay, on the northern side of the island, on the evening of the 5th of February; the second at Cape Navire, nearly opposite on the south, on the 8th of February; and the third at Trois Rivières, towards the south-east. The British were so rapidly successful that, by the 17th of February, the whole of the island, except the two fortresses of Bourbon and Fort Royal, were in their hands. The services of the Black Carolina Corps up to that date are not known in detail, but the return of killed and wounded shows the Dragoons as having had one rank and file killed.

On the 20th of February, Forts Bourbon and Fort Royal were completely invested, and the pioneers and artificers of the Carolina Corps were busily engaged on the siege works. On the north-east side the army broke ground on the 25th of February; and on the western side, towards La Caste, fascine batteries were erected with all possible expedition. By the 16th of March, the advanced batteries were pushed to within 500 yards of Fort Bourbon, and 200 yards of the enemy's nearest redoubt. On the 20th of March, the fortress of Fort Royal was carried by Captain Faulkner, of the *Zebra*; and General Rochambeau at once sent a flag from Fort Bourbon offering to capitulate. The terms were accordingly adjusted on the 23rd, and on the 25th, the garrison, reduced to 900 men, marched out prisoners of war.

Martinique being now entirely conquered, Sir Charles Grey left there, as a garrison under General Prescott, five regiments, and one company of the Carolina Corps; and proceeded, on the 31st of March, with the remainder of the force to the attack of St. Lucia. That island had no means of defence against so considerable an invading force; and, on the 4th of April, the British colours were hoisted on the chief fortress of Morne Fortune; the garrison, consisting of 300 men, having surrendered on the same terms of capitulation that had been granted to General Rochambeau. The 6th and 9th Regiments, with a company of the Carolina Corps, being left as a garrison for St. Lucia, Sir Charles Grey returned to Martinique, and commenced his preparations for an expedition to Guadaloupe.[12]

Guadaloupe really consists of two islands, separated from each other by a narrow arm of the sea, called La Rivière Salée, which is navigable for vessels of fifty tons. The eastern island, or division, which is flat and low-lying, is called Grandeterre; while the western, which is rugged and mountainous, is named Basseterre.

On the 8th of April, the troops, with the remaining company of the Carolina Corps, sailed from Fort Royal, Martinique; and, about one o'clock in the morning of the 11th, a landing was effected at Grosier Bay. Before daybreak on the 12th, the fort of La Fleur d'Épée was carried by assault, and the greater part of the garrison put to the sword. Fort St. Louis, the town of Point à Pitre, and a new battery upon Islet à Cochon being afterwards abandoned, the possession of Grandeterre was complete. The reduction of Basseterre was effected on the 21st of the same month; and the company of the Carolina Corps, with other troops, being left in garrison in Guadaloupe, the general returned to Martinique.

The British, however, were not permitted to remain long in peaceable possession of their most recent conquest; for on the 3rd of June, a considerable French armament arrived off Point à Pitre. Fort Fleur d'Épée was taken by storm, and the place not being tenable after this loss, the British crossed over to Basseterre. Several prisoners were taken by the French, and amongst them were some of the Carolina Corps, for in the return of that corps for February, 1795, dated March 1st, there is the following note: "Some of the corps are prisoners at Point à Pitre, but their number cannot be ascertained." In a later return, however, we find that they consisted of one sergeant and eight rank and file.

On the 2nd of July, the British made an ineffectual attempt to recover Point à Pitre, and soon after established their head-quarters at Berville, in Basseterre. The camp at Berville was invested in September, and on the 6th of October it was compelled to capitulate. Thus the whole of Guadaloupe, with the exception of Fort Matilda, situated above the town of Basseterre, and which was still held by a British garrison, was recovered by the French. At the surrender of Berville, 300 French Royalists, who were in the British camp, were massacred by the orders of Victor Hugues, the French commander.

Fort St. Charles, Basseterre, had been rechristened Fort Matilda by the British on its surrender on the 21st of April, 1794, and against it Victor Hugues now moved all his forces. The fort was commanded by Lieutenant-General Prescott with a garrison of 610 men, including the company of the Carolina Corps which had come to Guadaloupe. General Prescott, in his despatch, dated "On board H.M.S. *Vanguard*, at sea, December 11th, 1794," says: "To enter into a minute detail of the siege, which commenced on the 14th of October, and terminated by evacuating it on the 10th of December, would not only too much occupy your time, but might be deemed equally unnecessary. It may be sufficient to remark that on entering the fort I found it totally out of repair, the materials composing the wall-work thereof being of the worst kind, and having apparently but little lime to cement them properly. By the middle of last month the works were very much injured by the daily and frequent heavy fire of the enemy, and almost all the carriages of our guns rendered useless. These were in general in a very decayed state, but even the new ones for the brass mortars that were made during the siege gave way from the almost incessant fire we kept up; so that upon the whole, what from the nature of our defences and the small number of our garrison, we were in a very unfit state to resist the very vigorous exertions of our enemy, who began to prepare additional forces about the 20th of last month, but who, from a number of causes, and especially from heavy and continued rains, could not open their new batteries till the 6th of this month. On that day they began to fire from twenty-three pieces of cannon, four of which were thirty-six-pounders, and the rest twenty-four-pounders, and from eight mortars, two of thirteen inches and two of ten. The fire was very heavy and continued all day and night, and by it all the guns on the Gallion bastion were dismounted, and the bastion itself a heap of ruins. Every day after this grew worse until the 9th, on the evening of which day I went into the ditch accompanied by the engineer, when we were both but too well convinced of the tottering state of the works from the Gallion along the curtain, and indeed the whole, from the east to the north-east. I could not hesitate a moment about the necessity of evacuating the fort. I therefore sent off immediately to Rear-Admiral Thompson, who commanded the detachment of the squadron left for our protection, to acquaint him with the necessity of evacuating the fort next evening, and to request that he would have the boats ready to take off the garrison at seven o'clock. I kept this my design a profound secret until half-past six o'clock of the evening of the 10th, when I arranged the march of the garrison.... The embarkation continued with little or no interruption, and was happily completed about ten o'clock at night, without its being discovered by the enemy, who continued firing as usual on the fort till two or three o'clock on the morning of the 11th, as we could plainly perceive from the ships. My satisfaction was great at having thus preserved my brave garrison to their king and country."

During the siege of Fort Matilda, the Carolina Corps lost 1 killed and 3 wounded, 2 of whom afterwards died of their wounds. In the "State of the Garrison of Fort Matilda, as embarked on the 10th of December, 1794," the strength of the company of the Carolina Corps is shown as 1 captain, 1 lieutenant, 4 sergeants, and 30 rank and file. After the evacuation, this company was stationed at Martinique; so that at the close of the year 1794, two companies were in that island, and one in St. Lucia.

FOOTNOTES:

[10] See map.

[11] Major-General Bruce's despatch.

[12] See map.

CHAPTER V
ROYAL RANGERS, COMMANDED BY
CAPTAIN MALCOLM, 41ST REGIMENT

A: Capt. Commandant.
B: Captains.
C: 1st Lieutenants.
D: 2nd Lieutenants.
E: Sergeants Present.
F: Drummers Present.
G: Present fit for Duty.
H: In Hospital.
I: In Quarters.

Stations.	Commissioned Officers.				Effective Rank and File.					
					Sick and Wounded.					
	A	B	C	D	E	F	G	H	I	Total
Martinico	1	2	2	2	8	4	149	28	27	204

This officer is mentioned by Bryan Edwards, vol. iii. p. 452: "Lieutenant Malcolm, of the 41st Grenadiers, was appointed Town Major" (of St. Pierre, Martinique, in 1794) "in consideration of his distinguished conduct and active services at the head of a body of riflemen, which was composed of two men selected from each company of the 1st Battalion of Grenadiers. We shall have occasion to mention this officer afterwards."

This body of riflemen, raised during the operations in Martinique, in March, 1794, must, if the above statement of its formation be correct, have been European, for there were no black troops employed in the reduction of that island, except the Carolina Corps. The corps of riflemen is not shown in any return, and it is probable that at the termination of the active operations the men rejoined their respective battalions. The Royal Rangers, shown in the return of the 1st of May, 1795, were black; for Sir John Vaughan, in a letter dated Martinique, April 25th, 1795, which gives an account of the operations in St. Lucia in that month, says: "The flank companies of the

9th Regiment and the black corps under Captain Malcolm were the troops engaged." These Royal Rangers, then, were almost certainly entirely distinct from the "body of riflemen," and the success which had attended Captain Malcolm's efforts with the first body probably led to his being employed in raising the second, about February or March, 1795. In the month of April, 1795, one company of this corps, numbering 121 of all ranks, was in St. Lucia, and the other company, 112 strong, in Martinique.

Victor Hugues, having succeeded in ousting the British from Guadaloupe, commenced, early in 1795, active measures for the recovery of the other islands that had been wrested from France in the previous year, and the plan which was first ripened appears to have been that against St. Lucia.[13] "No official and scarcely any other accounts of the event are to be found, but the invasion of this colony appears to have been effected about the middle of February.... Nor can the strength of the invading force be now ascertained. That force was probably few in number, and stolen into the island in small bodies, and under cover of the night. Aided, however, by an insurrection of the slaves, people of colour, and democratical whites, it was sufficient to wrest from us the whole of the colony, with the exception of the two posts of the Carenage and the Morne Fortune."[14]

Affairs remained in this situation till about the middle of April, when Brigadier-General Stewart resumed active operations, in the hope of recovering the lost ground. On the 14th of that month, he suddenly disembarked near Vieux Fort, with a force consisting of a portion of the 6th and 9th Regiments, the company of the Carolina Corps which had remained in the island since its capture in 1794, and one company of the new corps of Malcolm's Rangers; and, after two days' skirmishing, that town was abandoned by the French on the 16th, and immediately taken possession of by the British, the enemy falling back upon Souffriere, their chief stronghold.

"Resolved to follow up his blow, General Stewart advanced against Souffriere. Undismayed, however, by their recent defeats, the Republicans had collected together a very formidable force, for the defence of their main position. On his march, the British general was suddenly attacked by a division which had been placed in ambush, and it was not till after a severe struggle that the enemy were driven back."

Sir John Vaughan, in a despatch dated Martinique, April 25th, 1795, says: "He was attacked by the enemy upon his march on the 20th instant, who had formed an ambuscade. The flank companies of the 9th Regiment, and the Black Corps under Captain Malcolm, were the troops engaged. The enemy, after a severe conflict, were driven back. Captain Malcolm, and Captain Nesbitt of the 9th, were wounded, after behaving in a most gallant manner."

On the 22nd of April, the troops reached the neighbourhood of Souffriere, near to which, on the mountainous ground, the attack was made. The contest continued warmly for seven hours, and though the greatest exertions were made by the British, they were finally compelled to retreat to Choiseul, with a loss of 30 killed, 150 wounded, and 5 missing. In the four days' fighting between the 14th and the 22nd of April, Malcolm's corps lost 48 out of a total of 121.[15] At Choiseul the troops embarked and returned to Vieux Fort, and thence to Morne Fortune and the Carenage, which General Stewart considered his force strong enough to hold until the arrival of reinforcements.

Two months passed away without the occurrence of any event worthy of notice. Sickness, in the meantime, was making great ravages amongst the British, one-half of whose force was generally unfit for service. The enemy, on the other hand, were daily gaining fresh accession of strength. From Guadaloupe arms and other supplies were frequently transmitted; and though some of the vessels fell into the hands of the British cruisers, many more of them reached their destination in safety. The French now began to act decisively. They first reduced Pigeon Island, and, on the 17th of June, made themselves masters of the Vigie. On this last post the communication between the Carenage and Morne Fortune depended, and the enemy now prepared for a general assault upon the latter. As, in the weak condition of the garrison, it would have been imprudent to await the meditated attack, Brigadier-General Stewart determined to evacuate the position; and, on the evening of the 18th, the whole of the troops embarked on board H.M.S. *Experiment*, undiscovered by the enemy, and proceeded to Martinique.

FOOTNOTES:

[13] Bryan Edwards.

[14] See map.

[15] Return of the killed, wounded, and missing in the actions on the following days, of the troops under the command of Brigadier-General Stewart, in the island of St. Lucia.

14th of April, 1795.

Royal Rangers—1 sergeant, 5 rank and file, wounded.

15th of April.

Royal Rangers—2 rank and file, killed; 1 sergeant, 4 rank and file, wounded.

20th of April.

Royal Rangers—6 rank and file, killed; 1 captain, 1 sergeant, and 18 rank and file, wounded.

22nd of April.

Carolina Corps—1 rank and file, wounded.
Royal Rangers—4 rank and file, killed; 5 rank and file, wounded.

Names of the Officers killed and wounded.

Captain Robert Malcolm, of the Royal Rangers, wounded.

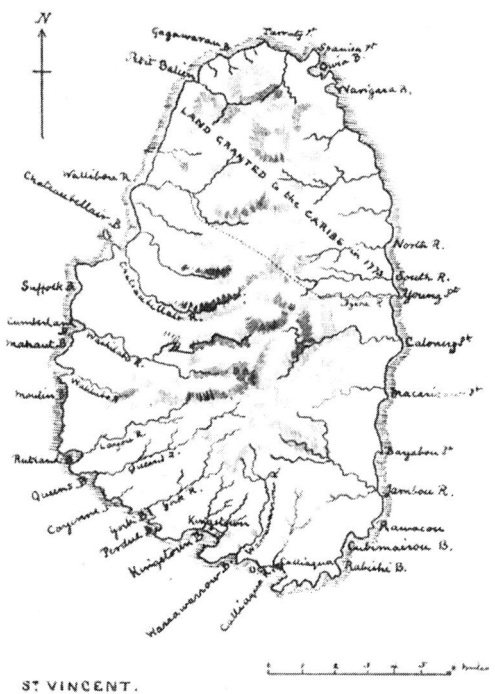

ST VINCENT.

CHAPTER VI
THE CARIB WAR IN ST. VINCENT, 1795

Some little time before the arrival, at Martinique, of the company of Malcolm's Rangers from St. Lucia, the company of that corps which had remained in the former island had been despatched, with the 3rd Battalion of the 60th Regiment, to St. Vincent. Since the month of March, 1795, that island had been devastated by a war between the Caribs, assisted by the French, and the British garrison. This war had been carried on with varying success, and the most horrible atrocities on the part of the Caribs, until the end of May, when the Commander-in-Chief, Sir John Vaughan, went over to St. Vincent from Martinique, to satisfy himself as to the state and military wants of the colony; and, finding the enemy strongly posted within a short distance of the town of Kingston itself, immediately on his return to Martinique despatched the above-mentioned reinforcement, which arrived at St. Vincent in the beginning of June.

The principal position of the enemy was at the Vigie This post was situated on a ridge, forming the south-west side of the valley of Marriaqua, and consisted of three small eminences of different heights; that nearest the sea, though the lowest, being the most extensive of them all, and that to the fortifying of which they had paid the most attention.

Lieutenant-Colonel Leighton, commanding the troops in St. Vincent, on being reinforced, determined to carry into execution a long meditated attack upon the Vigie. Accordingly, on the night of the 11th[16] of June, the troops marched through the town, and halted about ten o'clock at Warawarrow River, within four miles of the Vigie. The force was composed of detachments from the 46th and 60th Regiments, the company of Malcolm's Rangers, the St. Vincent Rangers, almost all the southern and windward regiments of the militia, and a small party of artillery. At Warawarrow River the troops were divided into three columns; and the third was further divided into small bodies to hold the passes at Calder Ridge, and prevent the escape of the enemy.

Just before daybreak, the westernmost redoubt, which overlooked the road coming from Kingston, was attacked and carried almost without opposition, the enemy retiring to their principal stronghold. The grenadiers and Malcolm's Corps had in the meantime forced their way through the bush on Ross Ridge, and being met by the light company, which had kept along the road, the whole of the British advanced against the third and strongest redoubt. At the upper end of the road a deep trench had been dug, which obstacle for some little time delayed the guns; but, by great exertions they were lifted up a bank eight or ten feet in height, and then opened fire.

For some time the enemy returned the British fire with great spirit. About eight o'clock, however, they beat a parley, and sent out a flag of truce to propose terms, which were refused. The troops were now led to the assault, and in a short time carried the works, which were defended by the French from Guadaloupe, the Caribs having retired early in the morning, and escaped to the windward portion of the island. "Never did troops display greater gallantry than did the British, militia, and rangers on this occasion."[17] The British killed and wounded amounted to 30; 250 of the enemy are said to have fallen. In the redoubts were taken three four-pounders and sixteen or seventeen swivels.

At the close of the action, Malcolm's and the St. Vincent Rangers were sent out to scour the valley of Marriaqua, and destroy the huts of the Caribs. This service they effectually accomplished before nightfall, having killed and taken prisoners many of the fugitives, and driven the remainder into Massirica.

A detachment of the 60th being left in the Vigie Lieutenant-Colonel Leighton, on the morning of the 13th of June, marched with the remainder of the troops, by several routes, towards the Carib district. So little opposition was made to their march, the enemy constantly falling back from ridge to ridge, that on the afternoon of the 16th they reached Mount Young, from which the Caribs fled with such haste that they left standing their houses, in all of which considerable quantities of corn were found. This carelessness of the enemy provided the British with a very welcome shelter. It was fortunate, also, that they had not attempted to dispute the hills and passes; for, had they done so, the troops would have suffered greatly, seven men, even as it was, having expired on the march from fatigue alone.

As soon as Mount Young was in our possession, the troops were busily employed in spreading devastation through the Carib district. In Grand Sable and other parts of the country, many houses were burned, and more than 200 pettiaugres and canoes destroyed. Several hundred slaves were also sent out, under the protection of military detachments, to dig up and destroy the provisions of the enemy. On the 4th of July, a detachment of the 46th and Malcolm's Rangers took, after a sharp action, the enemy's post at

Chateaubellair, near Walliabon, with a loss of 14 killed and 39 wounded of the 46th, and 2 killed and several wounded of Malcolm's.

The evacuation of St. Lucia by Brigadier-General Stewart was, however, as far as St. Vincent was concerned, attended by fatal consequences. The proximity of the former island enabled the French unceasingly to pour in new reinforcements to their Carib allies in St. Vincent; and, towards the end of August, a small British post which had been established at Owia was surprised by a detachment from St. Lucia, and the whole of the guns and large quantities of supplies captured.

Encouraged by this success, Victor Hugues resolved to endeavour to wrest St. Vincent from the British, as he had already wrested Guadaloupe and St. Lucia; and, in the middle of September, he landed in St. Lucia with a force of some 800 men. These, embarked in four vessels, which escaped the *Thorn* and *Experiment*, the British ships of war on the station, landed at Owia Bay, St. Vincent, on the morning of the 18th of September; and the force of the enemy was now so vastly superior to that of the British, that it became impossible for the latter to retain their advanced positions.

Orders were at once sent to Lieutenant-Colonel Leighton to abandon Mount Young without delay, and retire to the vicinity of Kingston. They were carried into execution on the night of the 19th. Having destroyed their supplies and left their lights burning in their huts as usual, to deceive the enemy, the troops were silently put in motion. They reached Biabou the next evening, and, bringing in the detachment which was there quartered, reached Zion Hill on the 21st; being then distributed among the posts in the neighbourhood.

The retreating British were speedily followed by the Caribs and French, who drove off the cattle from several estates, and finally took up a position on Fairbairn's Ridge, by which the communication was cut off between Kingston and the Vigie. The detachment of the 60th at the latter post being short of supplies, Lieutenant-Colonel Ritche, of the 60th, with 200 of that corps and 150 of the St. Vincent Rangers, was detached to escort the necessary stores. His division had nearly reached its destination when it fell in with the enemy; a sharp action ensued, victory was on the eve of declaring for the British, when, struck by an unaccountable panic, they suddenly gave way and fled in all directions. The supplies fell into the hands of the enemy, and a number of the mules were killed.

The news of this terrible disaster spread dismay through Kingston, for it was thought that the enemy would at once attack all the British posts. It was resolved to at once abandon the Vigie; and to facilitate this step, Brigadier-

General Myers, with the 46th and Malcolm's Rangers, marched from Dorsetshire Hill, and posted himself opposite the enemy, as if threatening an attack. This movement had the desired effect. The enemy called in all the detachments which invested the Vigie, and thus enabled the officer commanding that post to retreat at night through heavy rain to Calliaqua, and thence proceed to Kingston in boats.

While the troops were using the utmost exertion to strengthen the posts in the neighbourhood of Kingston, an unexpected reinforcement arrived from Martinique, on the 29th of September. It consisted of the 40th, 54th, 59th, and 2nd West India Regiments,[18] into which latter the St. Vincent Rangers were at once drafted. Major-General Irving also came over from Martinique to assume the command.

The first effect produced by the arrival of this succour, was the retiring of the enemy from their advanced position on Fairbairn's Ridge to the Vigie, where they now collected the whole of their strength. From this post Major-General Irving determined to dislodge them; and, on the night of the 1st of October, the troops marched for that purpose. One column, consisting of 750 men, under Lieutenant-Colonel Strutt, marched by the high road and took post upon Calder Ridge, on the east of the Vigie, about three in the morning. A second column, consisting of 900 men, under Brigadier-General Myers, crossed the Warawarrow River, and detached one party to proceed round by Calliaqua, and another to move up the valley, and climb the heights near Joseph Dubuc's. With this last force was Malcolm's Corps; and, to gain the point to which they were directed, it was necessary to cross a deep rivulet and ascend a steep hill covered with bushes and wood. In doing this it suffered a heavy loss, both of officers and men, from the enemy, who fired upon it almost in security under shelter of the bushes. The British, however, still pressed on, and at length arrived on the top of the Marriaqua or Vigie Ridge. During the ascent of the hill, Malcolm's Corps lost one man killed and two wounded.

In the meantime, the remainder of the second column were struggling in vain to reach the summit of the same ridge; at a point where the enemy had strongly occupied a thick wood, and thrown up a small work. Though the opposing forces were within fifty paces of each other, not an inch of ground was won on either side. Firing commenced at seven in the morning, and was kept up till nightfall. All this time the British were exposed to a violent tropical downpour of rain, which rendered the abrupt declivity so slippery that it was almost impossible to maintain a foothold on it; and, finding he could make no impression on the enemy, the general, about 7 p.m., gave orders for the troops to retire.

During the night, the enemy, from some unknown cause, abandoned the Vigie, and that so hastily that they left behind them, undestroyed, both guns and ammunition. They continued their retreat till they reached the windward part of the island, and the British in their turn advanced. For the remainder of the year, the troops were employed in circumscribing, within as narrow limits as possible, the French and their Carib allies; and, though great hardships were endured, no engagement worthy of note took place.

FOOTNOTES:

[16] Coke; Bryan Edwards says the 8th.

[17] Coke.

[18] See next chapter.

CHAPTER VII
MAJOR-GENERAL WHYTE'S
REGIMENT OF FOOT, 1795

The terrible mortality which thinned the ranks of the British troops in the West Indies, induced the British Ministers to think of reinforcing the army with men better calculated to resist the influence of the climate. The West India Governors were instructed, therefore, in 1795, to bring forward in their respective legislatures a project for raising five black regiments, consisting of 500 men each, to become a permanent branch of the military establishment. There were already several black corps in existence, for Mr. Dundas, during a debate in the House of Commons on the West India Expedition, on the 28th of April, 1795, said that "the West India Army of Europeans and Creoles consisted of 3000 militia and 6000 blacks."[19]

These black corps were distributed amongst the various islands, and were the Carolina Corps, Malcolm's or the Royal Rangers, the Island Rangers (Martinique), the St. Vincent Rangers, the Black Rangers (Grenada), Angus' Black Corps (Grenada), the Tobago Blacks, and the Dominica Rangers. Some of them, notably the Carolina Corps, Malcolm's Corps, and the St. Vincent Rangers,[20] were paid by the Imperial Government, and were consequently Imperial troops; although none of the corps appeared in any Army List, nor were appointments thereto and promotions therein notified in the *London Gazette*.

The five black regiments, now proposed to be raised, were to be in addition to those small black corps already in Imperial pay, and which were to be blended into three permanent regiments. Consequently, in the Army List dated March 11th, 1796, showing the state of the army in 1795,[21] we find the following eight corps, indexed under the heading of "Regiments raised to serve in the West Indies:"

Whyte's Regiment of Foot	(Carolina and Malcolm's Corps).

Myers'	"	"	(St. Vincent Rangers).
Keppell's	"	"	(probably the Dominica Rangers).
Nicoll's	"	"	
Howe's	"	"	
Whitelock's	"	"	} (the five new regiments).
Lewes'	"	"	
Skerrett's	"	"	

Major-General Whyte's regiment was called into existence by the *Gazette* of the 2nd of May, 1795; Major-General John Whyte, from the 6th Foot, being appointed colonel. On the 20th of May, Major Leeds Booth, from the 32nd Foot, was appointed lieutenant-colonel; and other officers were rapidly gazetted to it. On the 8th of August, Captain Robert Malcolm, of the 41st Foot, was promoted major in Whyte's regiment. The following is the list of officers appointed to the regiment in 1795:

Major-General Whyte's Regiment of Foot

Rank.	Name.	Rank in the Regt.	Army.
Colonel	John Whyte	April 24, 1795	M.G., Feb. 26, 1795
Lt.-Col.	Leeds Booth	May 20, 1795	
Major	Robert Malcolm	July 1, 1795	Lieut.-Col., Oct. 5, 1795
Capts.	James Abercrombie	" "	Major, March 1, 1794
	Edward Cotter	" "	
	Francis Costello	" "	
	Alan Hampden Pye	" "	
	Ralph Wilson	" "	

(C.)	Thomas Cunninghame	" "	
	William Powell	Aug. 24, 1795	
	Thomas Deane	Sept. 1, 1795	
	....		
	....		
	....		
	....		
Lieuts.	Ross Gillespie	July 1, 1795	Dec. 20, 1794
	Henry Ma well	" "	March 8, 1795
	David Butler	" "	
	Benjamin Chadwick	" "	
	James Reid	" "	
	James Stewart	" "	
	James Sutherland	" "	
	James Calder	" "	
	Andrew Coghlan	Aug. 24, 1795	Sept. 14, 1792
	Henry Goodinge	Sept. 1, 1795	
	Thos. Page	Sept. 16, 1795	
	....		
	(11 vacancies)		
	....		
Ensigns	William Graham	July 1, 1795	
	James Cassidy	" "	
	— McShee	" "	
	— Lightfoot	" "	
	— M'Callum	" "	
	— Froggart	" "	
	— McLean	" "	
	R.W. Atkins	" "	
	John Egan	" "	

	James Reed	" "
(Cornet)	W. Connor	" "
	— Crump	" "
	John Morrison	" "
	Donald M'Grace	" "
	William Reid	" "
	— Dalton	Sept. 1, 1795
	Thomas Byrne	" "
	C.B. Darley	Sept. 9, 1795
	Christ. Thos. Roberts	Oct. 5, 1795
	....	
	....	
Adjutant	....	
Qrmr.	— McWilliam	Nov. 18, 1795
Surgeon	— Bishop	June 10, 1795
Chaplain	....	

It was intended that each of these regiments raised for service in the West Indies should have a cavalry troop, and in the *London Gazette* are the following:

Major-General Whyte's Regiment of Foot

August 1, 1795 Lieutenant—Powell, from the 8th Foot, to be Lieutenant of Cavalry.

August 29   Lieutenant—Powell, Lieutenant of Cavalry, to be Captain of Cavalry.

July 11   Acting Adjutant—Connor, from Lieutenant-Colonel McDonnel's regiment, to be Cornet.

But this idea was soon abandoned, and in 1797 the cavalry troop disappeared.

The 1st West India Regiment (for so it was at once styled in the West Indies, although in the Army List and the *London Gazette*, the designation "Major-General Whyte's Regiment of Foot" was not discontinued until February, 1798) first appears in the "Monthly Return for the Windward, Leeward, and Caribee Islands," in September, 1795, as follows:

A: Colonel.
B: Lieut.-Colonel.
C: Majors.
D: Captains.
E: Lieutenants.
F: Ensigns.
G: Chaplain.
H: Adjutant.
I: Quarter-Master.
J: Surgeon.
K: Mate.
L: Sergeants Present.
M: Drummers Present.
N: Present, fit for duty.
O: Sick.
P: Recruiting.
Q: Total.

Regiments or Corps.	Stations.	Officers Present.											Effective Rank & File.					
		Commissioned.						Staff.										
		A	B	C	D	E	F	G	H	I	J	K	L	M	N	O	P	Q
Maj.-Gen. Whyte's	Martinico	-	-	-	3	1	5	-	-	1	-	-	6	6	43	4	4	51
Brig.-Gen. Myers'	Martinico	1	-	-	2	1	1	-	-	1	-	-	5	6	41	5	5	51
	Total.	1	-	-	5	2	6	-	-	2	-	-	11	12	84	9	9	102

and the following note is, in the same Return, appended to the state of the company of the "Black Carolina Corps," which was in Grenada; the other two companies having remained in Martinique since their removal there from St. Lucia at the end of April, 1795. "This corps has been reformed, and fifty of the men, who were fit for service, have been drafted into the 1st New West India Regiment. When the remainder of the corps can be collected together, it is possible a few more may be found fit for service."

Major-General Whyte's, or the 1st West India Regiment, remained at Martinique, without any further accession to its strength than these fifty men from the Carolina Corps, till December, 1795.

In the "Muster Roll of His Majesty's 1st West India Regiment of Foot, for 183 days, from the 25th of June to the 24th of December, 1795, inclusive," the list of officers is given as already shown. Captain James Abercrombie, Lieutenants David Butler, Benjamin Chadwick, and James Sutherland are shown as "drowned on passage," and the following note is added: "Some few of the dates of enlistments and enrolments of the non-commissioned officers and drummers may not probably be quite exact, and some others may have been engaged in England not down on the muster roll, all the regimental books, attestation papers, etc., having been left in possession of the paymaster, Brevet-Major Abercrombie (no adjutant at that time being appointed), who was lost in December or January last on board the *Robert and William* transport, No. 44, on the voyage to this country." The non-commissioned officers and drummers were Europeans, one sergeant and three corporals being shown as "sick and absent in England" in this roll; and, in the next, a drummer is similarly shown. The roll is signed by Leeds Booth, Lieutenant-Colonel; Ed. S. Cotter, Captain and Paymaster; and Thomas Holbrook, Acting Adjutant. The following is the proof table:

A: Colonel.
B: Lieut.-Colonel.
C: Major.
D: Captains.
E: Lieutenants.
F: Cornets.
G: Ensigns.
H. Adjutant.
I. Chaplain.
J. Quartermaster.
K. Surgeon.
L. Mate.
M. Sergeants.
N. Corporals.
O. Drummers.
P. Privates.

	A	B	C	D	E	F	G	H	I	J	K	L	M	N	O	P
Present	-	1	-	1	1	1	5	-	-	1	-	-	10	-	12	9
Absent	1	-	1	8	6	-	13	-	-	-	1	-	7	3	3	27
Non-effective	-	-	-	5	7	-	5	-	-	1	-	-	5	8	5	13
Total.	1	1	1	14	14	1	23	-	-	2	1	-	22	11	20	49

Although it was intended that the privates of West India regiments should be black, yet, apparently, white men were not prohibited from serving in the ranks; for, in later muster rolls, two or three privates are shown as "enrolled in England," and one of these is afterwards shown as "transferred to 60th." A volunteer, David Scott, who joined 29th May, 1797, was also promoted ensign in November of that year. These enrolments of

Europeans only occur in the first three years of the regiment's existence, and negro privates were available for promotion to, at least, the rank of corporal very early; for a Private John Lafontaine, who was promoted corporal, is shown in the muster roll terminating December 24th, 1796, as "claimed as a slave." The pay of a private in a West India regiment was then sixpence per diem.

FOOTNOTES:

[19] In the Account of the Extraordinary Expenditure of the Army, from 25th December, 1795, to 6th December, 1796, is the following:

On account of pay for sundry black corps for the year 1795,
        raised for service in the West Indies   £10,120 12 9
On account of ditto for the year 1796   60,095 10 3
                                                      — — — — —
                                                      £70,216 3 0

[20] "The military force in St. Vincent consists at present of a regiment of infantry and a company of artillery, sent from England; and a black corps raised in the country, but provided for, with the former, on the British Establishment, and receiving no additional pay from the island."—Bryan Edwards, vol. i. p. 428.

[21] The Army List for 1795 is dated January 1st.

CHAPTER VIII
THE CAPTURE OF ST. LUCIA, 1796

In January, 1796, the company of Malcolm's Royal Rangers that was at St. Vincent was moved to St. Christopher; the other company still remained at Martinique, and both, in April, 1796, were selected to take part in the expedition to St. Lucia. "That island could then muster for its defence about 2000 well-disciplined black soldiers, a number of less effective blacks, and some hundred whites, who held positions both naturally and artificially strong, and were plentifully supplied with artillery, ammunition, and stores. The post on which the Republicans chiefly confided for their defence was that of Morne Fortune. It is situated on the western side of the island, between the rivers of the Carenage and the Grand Cul de Sac, which empty their waters into bays bearing the same name. Difficult of access by nature, it had been rendered still more so by various works. In aid of this they had also fortified others of the mornes, or eminences, in its vicinity. The whole of this position, embracing a considerable extent of ground, it was of the utmost importance to invest closely, with as little delay as possible, that the enemy might not escape into the rugged country of the interior, and thus be in a condition to carry on a protracted and harassing war, which experience had already more than once proved to be highly detrimental to an unseasoned invading force.

"To accomplish this desirable purpose, the British general determined to direct his troops on three points, two of them to the north, and the third to the south of Morne Fortune. The first division was to land most to the north, in Longueville Bay, covered by several vessels, which were intended to silence the batteries on Pigeon Island. Choc Bay was the spot where the centre division was to be put on shore; and the third was to disembark at Ance la Raye, some distance to the southward of the hostile post."[22]

The fleet with the troops destined for the attack of St. Lucia, under Sir Ralph Abercromby, sailed from Carlisle Bay, Barbados, on the 22nd of April, and anchored in Marin Bay, Martinique, on the evening of the 23rd, where Malcolm's Rangers joined the force, sailing for St. Lucia on the 26th. The troops arrived off that island on the evening of the same day, and 1700 men, under the command of Major-General Campbell, composing the first division, were immediately landed in Longueville Bay; without encountering any further opposition than a few shots from the battery on Pigeon Island, the fire of which was speedily silenced by that of the ships.

A strong current had driven the transports so far to the leeward that it was not practicable to land the centre division till the following morning. Major-General Campbell was meanwhile on his march, and his progress was only feebly opposed by about 500 of the enemy, who ultimately retired from Angier's Plantation to Morne Chabot, and allowed him to effect a junction with the centre division. The current having acted still more powerfully on the vessels which conveyed the third division, under Brigadier-General Morshead, two or three days elapsed before the disembarkation in Ance la Raye could be entirely executed. The troops at length took up their appointed station, and thus held Morne Fortune invested on its southern side.

To complete the investment on the northern quarter it was necessary to obtain possession of Morne Chabot, which was one of the strongest posts in the vicinity of Morne Fortune. At midnight of the 27th, therefore, two columns, under Brigadier-Generals Moore and Hope, were despatched to attack the Morne on two opposite sides; and, by this means, not only to carry the position, but likewise to prevent the escape of the troops by which it was defended. This plan, the complete success of which would have materially diminished the strength of the Republican force, was in part rendered abortive by a miscalculation of time. The column of Brigadier-General Moore, consisting of seven companies of the 53rd Regiment, 100 of Malcolm's Rangers, and 50 of Lowenstein's,[23] advanced by the most circuitous route; while Brigadier-General Hope, with 350 men of the 57th, 150 of Malcolm's Rangers, and 50 of Lowenstein's, took the shorter road. Misinformed by the guides, Brigadier-General Moore's column fell in, an hour and a half sooner than it had expected, with the advanced picket of the enemy, who were thus put on their guard. At the moment when they were discovered, the troops, in consequence of the narrowness of the road, were marching in single file, and to halt them was impossible. In this state of things their leader resolved not to give his opponents time to recollect themselves, but to fall on them with his single division. The spirit of the soldiers fully justified the gallant resolution of their commander. Having been formed as speedily as the ruggedness of the ground would admit of, they proceeded to the assault. The Republicans made a stubborn resistance, but it was an unavailing one, as they were finally driven from the Morne with considerable loss. Nevertheless, as the second column did not arrive till the combat was over, the fugitives succeeded in making good their retreat. On the following day the victors also occupied Morne Duchasseaux, which is situated in rear of Morne Fortune.

In the hope of obtaining some advantage to counterbalance this misfortune, the enemy, on the 1st of May, made a brisk attack on the advanced post of grenadiers commanded by Lieutenant-Colonel MacDonald, of the 55th Regiment. They were, however, repulsed with much slaughter, though not till forty or fifty men, and several officers, were killed or wounded on the side of the British, among them being Captain Coghlan, 1st West India Regiment, attached to the 48th Regiment, who was wounded.

At the south side of the Morne Fortune the enemy had erected batteries, which precluded any vessels from entering into the bay of the Grand Cul de Sac. To open this bay to our fleet was an object of much importance, as at present it was necessary to convey the artillery and stores from a great distance, which could not be done without the previous labour of opening roads through an almost impracticable country. It was, therefore, resolved to make an attempt on these batteries. The principal attack was to be conducted by Major-General Morshead, whose division, in two columns, was to pass the river of the Grand Cul de Sac; the columns of the right at Cools, and that of the left at the point where the waters of the stream are discharged into the bay. To second this force, Brigadier-General Hope, on the night of the 2nd of May, was to advance from Morne Chabot with 350 men of the 42nd Regiment, the light company of the 57th, and part of Malcolm's Rangers, the whole being supported by the 55th Regiment, which was posted at Ferrands. A part of the squadron was likewise to lend its assistance, by keeping up a cannonade on the works of the enemy. Before the time arrived for putting this plan into execution, Major-General Morshead was taken ill, and the command devolved upon Brigadier-General Perryn. No change, however, took place in the arrangements which had been formed.

"At dawn of day, the division under Brigadier-General Hope began to accomplish its part of the service by carrying the battery Seche, which was situated within a short distance of the works of Morne Fortune. The assailants suffered so little in the assault, that they would scarcely have had anything to regret, had it not been for the fall of the gallant Lieutenant-Colonel Malcolm.[24] On the south side of the Morne, and at the extremity of the line of attack, Colonel Riddel, who led the column of the left, made himself master of the battery of Chapuis, and established himself there. Had the remainder of the project been as well executed, the proposed object would have been completely attained. Unfortunately, however, from some unexplained cause, the division which was the connecting link of the whole, that which was entrusted to Brigadier-General Perryn, did not perform its allotted part, by crossing the river at Cools. The consequence of this was that the victorious columns were left insulated, and would have been exposed to no trivial danger, had the enemy felt a sufficient reliance upon their own strength to incite them to act with the requisite promptitude and vigour. Painful, therefore, as it was to retire before a routed foe, the British troops were compelled to abandon the batteries which they had won, and to fall back upon their original stations. The ships at the same time returned to their former anchorage. Our loss on this occasion was 105 men; of whom only a very few were among the slain."

The Vigie was now the only post occupied by the enemy in the vicinity of Morne Fortune, and this was attacked by the 31st Regiment on the night of May 7th; the assault, however, being repulsed with a loss of 200 men. The main position was now invested by regular siege works, and the task which the British had to perform was attended with no small difficulty. "The country itself was of the most inaccessible kind, the chain of investment was ten miles in extent, all the roads that were necessary were to be made, of carriages there were none, horses were scarce, and the Republicans had been industrious in availing themselves of all the natural obstacles to our progress, and in creating as many others as their ingenuity could contrive." Malcolm's Corps rendered good service on these works, and the men being better able to stand the fatigue and exposure than Europeans, were constantly employed.

By May 16th, the first parallel was completed, and on the morning of the 24th, the 27th Regiment, supported by the 53rd and 57th, succeeded in effecting a lodgment within 500 yards of the fort. The Governor, acknowledging that further resistance was futile, demanded a suspension of hostilities; terms of surrender were agreed upon, and on May 26th, 2000 men marched out as prisoners of war. One hundred pieces of ordnance, ten vessels, and large stores of ammunition fell into the hands of the British.

Sir Ralph Abercromby sailed from St. Lucia on the 4th of June to the relief of Grenada and St. Vincent, leaving Brigadier-General Moore for the pacification of the first island with the 31st, 44th, 38th, and 55th Regiments, O'Meara's corps of Rangers,[25] and the German Yagers.

FOOTNOTES:

[22] Bryan Edwards.

[23] Lowenstein's Rangers were Europeans. They were afterwards drafted into the 60th.

[24] Return of killed, wounded, and missing, in the attack made on the enemy's batteries, May 3rd, 1796. Lieutenant-Colonel Malcolm's Rangers: 3 rank and file, killed; 2 rank and file, wounded; 2 captains, 1 lieutenant, 7 rank and file,

missing. Lieutenant-Colonel Malcolm dead of his wounds. The names of the officers of Malcolm's returned missing, not known.

[25] Raised in 1796. This corps became the 12th West India Regiment in 1799.

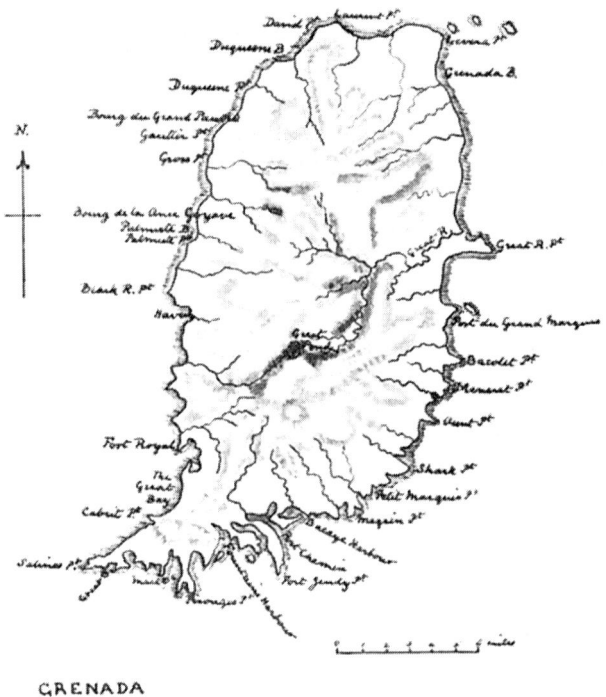

GRENADA

CHAPTER IX
THE RELIEF OF GRENADA, 1796—THE REPULSE AT PORTO RICO, 1797

Grenada, like St. Vincent, had been ravaged by the French and insurgent slaves since March, 1795, and the relief of that island was one of the first cares of Sir R. Abercromby. On leaving St. Lucia, the division of the troops intended for Grenada was ordered to rendezvous at Cariacou, one of the Grenadines; there Sir Ralph Abercromby met Major-General Nicolls, then commanding in Grenada, and arranged with him the general plan of operations. Before, however, those operations are described, it will be necessary to go back to the month of March, 1796, when a company of the Carolina Corps arrived in Grenada from Martinique, with detachments from the 8th, 63rd, and 3rd Regiments, under Major-General Nicolls.

Shortly before the arrival of this reinforcement, the French and insurgents had compelled the British to evacuate Pilot Hill, in the neighbourhood of Grenville, and had taken up a strong position at Port Royal. On the 23rd of March, Major-General Nicolls landed to the south of Port Royal; during the night the guns were got in position, and at daybreak opened on the enemy's works. The post occupied by the enemy was a hill of very steep ascent, particularly towards the summit, upon which a fort was constructed, and furnished with four six-pounders and some swivels. The first object of the British commander was to gain a position between the enemy and the open country, and thus leave them no alternative but to surrender at discretion, or precipitate themselves over a high cliff; but they had established themselves so strongly to protect their right that this failed. In the meantime two large vessels full of troops to reinforce the enemy arrived in the bay under Port Royal, from Guadaloupe; and Brigadier-General Nicolls found it necessary to storm the enemy's post without further delay. The troops employed in this service were detachments from the 3rd, 29th, and 63rd Regiments, under Brigadier-General Campbell; at the same time, 50 men of the 88th, with the company of the Carolina Corps, Colonel Webster's Black Rangers, and Angus' Black Corps, moved against the enemy's right flank, to dislodge some strong parties which were posted on the heights.

Owing to the difficult nature of the ground, it was nearly two hours before the latter column could reach the enemy, when a heavy fire commenced on both sides. The ascent was steep and difficult, encumbered with rocks and loose stones and covered with dense bush. From the summit of the ridge the enemy poured in a destructive fire, to which the British could only reply at a great disadvantage, and, after losing heavily, the column commenced to retire. Observing this retrograde movement, Major-General Nicolls sent the 8th Regiment in support and ordered Brigadier-General Campbell to proceed to the assault of the redoubt.

Repulsed at the first attempt the troops again pushed on, at length gained the summit of the ridge, drove the enemy into their redoubt and scrambled in after them through the embrasures. The enemy then fled in all directions, some threw themselves down the precipices, whilst others tried to escape down the hill through the thick underwood; but there was so heavy a fire kept up on them from above by the British that they were forced to attempt to escape along a valley, where they were charged by a detachment of the 17th Light Dragoons, and cut to pieces. The British loss consisted, in killed and wounded, of 110 Europeans and 40 of the various black corps. The Carolina Corps lost one man killed and six wounded.

Affairs were thus situated when the fall of St. Lucia enabled Sir R. Abercromby to send reinforcements to Grenada. The troops, with whom were Malcolm's Rangers, disembarked at Palmiste, on the 9th June, while Brigadier-General Campbell, with the troops already in the island, advanced from the windward side to take the enemy in rear. Captain Jossey, the commandant of the French troops at Goyave, near Palmiste, seeing that resistance must be unavailing, surrendered that post, with those of Mabouia and Dalincourt; but Fedon, the leader of the insurgent slaves, who knew he could expect no mercy, retired at the head of about 300 men to two strong and almost unapproachable positions, called Morne Quaquo and Ache's Camp, or Forêt Noir, in the mountains of the interior.

In these recesses he did not despair of being able to tire out his pursuers; but Major-General Nicolls did not give him time to throw any additional obstacles in the way of the troops. On the 18th of June he despatched against him, from opposite quarters, two divisions, under Brigadier-General Campbell and Count d'Heillemer; while Lieutenant-Colonel Gledstanes was posted with the 57th Regiment at the head of Grand Roy Valley, and the grenadiers of the 38th Regiment, with the Carolina Corps and Malcolm's Rangers, advanced against a post which the enemy had at the head of Beau Séjour Valley. The dispositions were so admirably carried into effect, that the whole of the enemy's posts were captured, nearly at the same moment, on the morning of the 19th. "Many of the blacks were slain upon the spot, and the remainder were promptly hunted down in the woods by detachments of the military. No quarter was given to these ruffians, nor was any deserved by them, their last efforts having been marked by a foul and wanton murder. When they saw that their position at Morne Quaquo, which they had regarded as impregnable, was on the eve of being forced, they led out twenty white prisoners, stripped them, tied their hands behind them, and put them to death. It was impossible, after having witnessed this act of baseness and cruelty, that anything short of their extermination should satisfy the victors."[26]

Fedon, and a number of his followers, escaped to the woods; what became of the former was never known, but the black corps were employed up to December, 1796, in hunting down and capturing the stragglers, and it was not until the end of that month that peace was entirely restored to Grenada.

Whyte's, or the 1st West India, Regiment had remained at Martinique without any addition to its strength during the operations in St. Lucia and Grenada. It had, however, according to the muster rolls for 1796, transferred, on the 24th of March of that year, four sergeants and nine corporals to Malcolm's Rangers, probably in anticipation of the speedy drafting of the whole of that corps into its own ranks. In the Monthly Returns of troops for March and April, 1796, Malcolm's Royal Rangers are shown as "under orders for drafting into the 1st West India Regiment," and in the May Return the corps ceases to be shown separately, and has no "state" of its own. As we have seen, however, it continued to act separately in St. Lucia in April and May, and in Grenada from June to December; and it was not until its return to Martinique on the 28th of December, 1796, that the drafting was finally completed. Of the Carolina Corps all the men fit for service were collected at Martinique, the remainder being formed into an invalid company at Grenada. It may be thought that the process of forming the 1st West India Regiment was being carried on very slowly, but it was more rapid than that of any other West India Regiment, except the 2nd; while the 3rd, even on the 24th of December, 1797, had no non-commissioned officers, no privates, and only two drummers.

No military event worthy of note took place in the year 1797, in which the Carolina Corps or the 1st West India Regiment took part, except the expedition to Porto Rico, in which the pioneers of the former corps were engaged. Sir Ralph Abercromby, with a force of 3000 men, sailed from Martinique on the 8th of April, and, after a delay at St. Christopher's, for the purpose of procuring pilots and guides, reached Porto Rico on the 17th and anchored off Cangrejos Point. Next day the troops disembarked, and, after a slight skirmish with the enemy, took up a position before the town. The siege continued for a fortnight without the British making any appreciable progress, while the force of the enemy, originally larger than that of the besiegers, was receiving continual accessions from various parts of the island. Sir Ralph Abercromby, therefore, determined to abandon the attempt, and the troops were accordingly re-embarked on the 30th of April.

In March, 1797, one company of the Carolina Corps that was at Martinique, 78 strong, was drafted into the 1st West India Regiment; and, on the return of the expedition from Porto Rico, the remaining company (Pioneer) was also drafted, and the Carolina Corps ceased to exist.

The following is the list of the officers who were serving in the 1st West India Regiment in 1797, and it may be observed that so many changes had taken place that, out of 43 officers who were gazetted to the regiment in 1795, only 22 were left in 1797:

Rank.	Name.	Rank in Regiment.	Army.
Colonel	John Whyte	April 24, 1795	M.-G., Feb. 26, 1795.
Lt.-Col.	Leeds Booth	May 20, 1795	
Major	Charles Miller	Nov. 30, 1796	
Captains	Edward Cotter	July 1, 1795	
	Francis Costello	July 1, 1795	
	William Powell	Aug. 24, 1795	
	A.A. Nunn	Feb. 2, 1797	November 17, 1795.
	Robert Brown	June 1, 1797	September 30, 1796.
	James Maitland	July 23, 1797	
	James Stewart	July 24, 1797	
Lieuts.	William Graham	Nov. 30, 1796	
	James Cassidy	Dec. 1, 1796	
	— M'Shee	Dec. 2, 1796	
	— Lightfoot	Dec. 3, 1796	
	— M'Callum	Dec. 4, 1796	
	— Froggart	Dec. 5, 1796	
	— M'Lean	Dec. 6, 1796	
	John Egan	Dec. 8, 1796	
	James Reed	Dec. 9, 1796	

	W.J. Speed	Jan. 11, 1797
	— Connor	March 1, 1797
	William Reid	March 2, 1796
	Thomas Byrne	March 3, 1796
	J.C. Roberts	July 1, 1796
	John C. M'Kay	July 2, 1796
Ensigns	Donald M'Grace	July 1, 1795
	— Dalton	Sept. 1, 1795
	C.B. Darley	Sept. 9, 1795
	— Horsford	July 1, 1797
	David M'William	July 2, 1797
	Morgan O'Meara	July 3, 1797
	Charles Marraud	July 4, 1797
	Niel Campbell	July 5, 1797
Adjutant	Thomas Holbrooke	April 17, 1796
Qtrmastr.	— M'William	Nov. 18, 1795
Surgeon	John Lindsay	Dec. 25, 1796

During the active operations of the year 1796 the West India colonists had offered no objection to the scheme of raising five new black regiments, but, in 1797, when the question of providing for them was brought before the various Legislatures, the plan met with the most determined opposition. When, on the 17th of January, Governor Ricketts communicated it to the House of Assembly in Barbados, and requested the concurrence of that House, the Speaker, Sir John Gay Alleyne, immediately rose and moved:

"That the design of five regiments, etc. (as expressed in the message), will, as far as such a design is likely to affect this island, prove rather the means of its destruction than its defence."

This resolution was carried, with two others, without a dissenting voice.

"The Assembly of Jamaica was no less decided and unanimous in its opposition to the measure. It refused to make any provision whatever for the subsistence of the 6th West India Regiment, which was commanded by Lieutenant-Colonel Whitelocke. In this decision it was sanctioned by the general voice of the white population. Meetings were held in almost every parish of the island, in all of which the scheme of raising black corps was heavily censured, as being, in the first place, unnecessary, the negroes being already compellable to serve in case of emergency; and, in the second place, as being of a nature to produce ultimately, and perhaps at no distant period, the most destructive effects to the persons and the property of the colonial proprietors."[27]

The British ministers were reluctant to abandon that which appeared to be a cheap and ready mode of recruiting in the western hemisphere, and consequently persevered in their project, even increasing the number of West India regiments in 1799 to twelve. That the fears of the colonists were groundless time soon showed. In 1801, at St. Martin's, the 8th West India Regiment, "composed of new negroes, who had never before faced a foe, behaved with the utmost gallantry." In 1803, the 3rd West India Regiment did good service at the capture of St. Lucia, as did the 6th at the reduction of Surinam in 1804. In 1809, at the Saintes, where the 3rd and 8th West India Regiments were engaged, "the black troops distinguished themselves by their discipline and valour." How the 1st West India Regiment remained true to its colours the succeeding chapters will show.[28]

FOOTNOTES:

[26] Bryan Edwards.

[27] Bryan Edwards.

[28] It is true that the 8th West India Regiment mutinied at Dominica, in 1802, but it was under conditions which, to a certain extent, extenuated it. For more than six months the men had been defrauded of their pay. Being utterly uneducated and all new negroes, they were ignorant of the proper methods of obtaining redress, and consequently showed their resentment by violence.

DOMINICA.

CHAPTER X
THE DEFENCE OF DOMINICA, 1805

The 1st West India Regiment remained stationed at Fort Edward, Martinique, during the whole of 1797, and up to the month of December, 1798; its strength at no time during this period being above 350 men. In December, 1798, it was removed to St. Lucia, six companies being quartered at Vieux Fort and two at Maboya, in the same island. The strength then was 343, and the "state" shows 157 as wanting to complete the establishment. The regiment remained at St. Lucia until July, 1801, when it was moved to Port Royal, Martinique. In January, 1802, two companies were detached to St. Vincent, and, in July, the remainder of the regiment, with the exception of one company that remained in Martinique, followed them to that island, from whence a company was soon afterwards detached to Antigua. In October, these detachments rejoined head-quarters, but, in April, 1803, two other companies were sent to Grenada. In May, 1804, the regiment, with the exception of one company at Grenada and another sent to St. Vincent, was moved to Dominica. In this year the establishment of West India regiments was increased from 500 to 1000 men; and in December, 1804, the strength was 618.

The rupture of the Treaty of Amiens had, in 1803, led to fresh conflicts in the West Indies, in which, however, the 1st West India Regiment had taken no share; but in the spring of 1805, while it was still stationed at Dominica, the light company being with the 46th Regiment at Morne Bruce, and the remainder of the regiment (except the two detachments) at Prince Rupert's, its turn for active service came.

On the 22nd of February of that year, the island was attacked by a French combined naval and military force, under Admiral Missiessy and General La Grange, which force had been despatched from France specially for the reduction of Dominica. The enemy's flotilla consisted of the following vessels:

	Guns.
Majestueuse	120
Magnanime	74
Suffren	74
Jemmappes	74
Lion	74
Armide	44
Gloire	44
Infatigable	44
Lynx	16
Actéon	16
	——
	580

The French regular troops employed were:

26th Regiment	1600
2nd Battalion Piedmontese	2000
Dismounted Cavalry	250
Artillery	250
Detachments of Corps	500
	——
	4600

Exclusive of the marines of the various ships.

The enemy's force sailed from Martinique on the afternoon of February 21st, 1805; and, flying the British flag, arrived off Dominica between 3 and 4 a.m. on February 22nd. The British commander-in-chief, Brigadier-General Prevost, deceived by the colours of the ships, sent the captain of the fort, an artillery officer, on board the *Majestueuse*, to conduct the supposed British admiral and his fleet to a safe anchorage.[29] Shortly afterwards the boats pushed off with the troops, and the squadron changed its colours to French.

Directly this was perceived, the grenadier company of the 46th, with the light company of the 1st West India Regiment (107 rank and file), under Captain O'Connell, and a company of militia, marched from the garrison at Morne Bruce to Point Michell, about three miles distant. At this spot the enemy concentrated, and effected a landing under a heavy fire from the fleet. Two thousand eight hundred troops having been landed at the extremity of a cape within a short distance of Point Michell, they advanced towards that place in column of subdivisions, the only formation which the restricted space would admit, the point being bounded by inaccessible heights on the right, and a broken and rugged shore on the left.

The two companies of the 46th and the light company of the 1st West India Regiment were posted behind the walls of some ruined buildings in the village of Point Michell, which afforded excellent cover, and where they were entirely sheltered from the fire of the enemy's shipping; while the French had to advance on a narrow front, entirely exposed to their fire.

The attack commenced about 5 a.m. Four times the enemy were led to the assault, and as many times they were repulsed. At about 6.30 a.m. the remainder of the 46th and some local militia arrived, and the struggle continued; but not without loss on our side, Major Nunn and Captain O'Connell, 1st West India Regiment, being wounded, the former mortally, and four men killed. At last, the enemy, finding all his endeavours to force the position were ineffectual, landed the remainder of his troops to leeward of the town of Roseau, on the British right, and attacked Fort Daniel, a small redoubt mounting a six-pounder gun, and defended by 2 artillerymen, and 1 sergeant and 5 men of the 1st West India Regiment. These were all made prisoners in the work, which the enemy had attacked with 500 men. Brigadier-General Prevost then retired with the militia to the heights of Woodbridge Estate; and, the British right being now turned, the regulars, some 200 in number, who had been so gallantly defending the left, retired to effect a junction with the garrison at Fort Rupert, commanded by Lieutenant-Colonel Broughton, 1st West India Regiment. This was effected by Captain O'Connell, although wounded, in four days, by the mountain paths, while Brigadier-General Prevost arrived at the same place by the Carib Trail.[30]

In the meantime the town of Roseau had been set on fire, and the whole of it destroyed, except a few small houses belonging to free negroes. The French, after blowing up the fortifications, embarking some guns and spiking others, re-embarked; taking with them such of their prisoners as were regulars, and levying a contribution of £5500 upon the inhabitants, and on February 27th the force set sail for Guadaloupe.

The French in their attack on Point Michell had lost over 300 men, and in selecting that spot for landing they had displayed a most astonishing ignorance of the locality, for, if a force had at once been put ashore between Point Michell and Fort Young at Roseau, the British could hardly have ventured upon a serious defence. The loss sustained by the British regulars was 21 killed, 21 wounded, and 8 prisoners. The loss of the militia is not stated, but was considerable, the French accounts fixing it at 200.

The following despatch addressed to Earl Camden, K.G., one of His Majesty's Principal Secretaries of State, by Lieutenant-General Sir William Myers, Bart., commanding the troops in the Windward and Leeward Islands, gives the official account of this affair:

"Barbadoes, *March 9th, 1805.*

"My Lord,

"I have the honour to enclose to your Lordship a copy of a despatch from Brigadier-General Prevost, dated Dominica, 1st of March, 1805. The details contained therein are so highly reputable to the Brigadier-General and the small portion of troops employed against so numerous an enemy, that I have great satisfaction in recommending that their gallant exertions may be laid before His Majesty.

"The zeal and talent manifested by the Brigadier-General upon this occasion, it is my duty to present for the Royal consideration, and at the same time I beg to be permitted to express the high sense I entertain of the distinguished bravery of His Majesty's troops and the militia of the colony employed on that service.

"The vigorous resistance which the enemy have experienced, and the loss which they have sustained in this attack, must evince to him, that however inferior our numbers were on this occasion, British troops are not to be hostilely approached with impunity; and had not the town of Roseau been accidentally destroyed by fire, we should have little to regret, and much to exult in.

"Your Lordship will perceive by the Returns that our loss in men, compared to that of the enemy, is but trifling; but I have sincerely to lament that of Major Nunn, of the 1st West India Regiment, whose wound is reported to be of a dangerous kind; he is an excellent man, and a meritorious officer.

"I have, etc.,
(Signed) "W. Myers,
"Lieutenant-General."

"Copy".   "Head Quarters, Prince Rupert's,

"Dominica, *March 1st, 1805.*

"Sir,

"About an hour before the dawn of day on the 22nd ultimo, an alarm was fired from Scot's Head, and soon after a cluster of ships was discovered off Roseau. As our light increased, I made out five large ships, three frigates, two brigs, and small craft under British colours, a ship of three decks carrying a flag at the mizen. The frigates ranging too close to Fort Young, I ordered them to be fired on, and soon after nineteen large barges, full of troops, appeared coming from the lee of the other ships, attended and protected by an armed schooner, full of men, and seven other boats carrying carronades. The English flag was lowered, and that of the French hoisted.

"A landing was immediately attempted on my left flank, between the town of Roseau and the post of Cachecrow. The light infantry of the 1st West India Regiment were the first to march to support Captain Smart's company of militia, which throughout the day behaved with great gallantry; it was immediately supported by the grenadiers of the 46th Regiment. The first boats were beat off, but the schooner and one of the brigs coming close on shore to cover the landing, compelled our troops to occupy a better position in a defile leading to the town. At this moment I brought up the grenadiers of the St. George's Regiment of militia, and soon after the remainder of the 46th Regiment, and gave over to Major Nunn these brave troops with orders not to yield to the enemy one inch of ground. Two field-pieces (an amuzette and a six-pounder) were brought into action for their support under the command of Sergeant Creed of the 46th Regiment, manned by additional gunners and sailors. These guns, and a twenty-four-pounder from Melville battery, shook the French advancing column by the execution they did.

"I sent two companies of St. George's Militia, under the command of Lieutenant-Colonel Constable, and a company of the 46th, to prevent the enemy from getting into the rear of the position occupied by Major Nunn.

"On my return I found the *Majestueuse*, of 120 guns, lying opposite to Fort Young, pouring into the town and batteries her broadsides, followed by the other seventy-fours and frigates doing the same.

"Some artillery, several captains of merchantmen with their sailors, and the militia artillery, manned five twenty-four-pounders and three eighteens at the fort, and five twenty-fours at Melville battery, and returned an uninterrupted fire; from the first post red-hot shot were thrown. At about 10 o'clock, a.m., Major Nunn, most unfortunately for His Majesty's service, whilst faithfully executing the order I had given him, was wounded, I fear mortally.

"This did not discourage the brave fellows. Captain O'Connell, of the 1st West India Regiment, received the command and a wound almost at the same time; however, the last circumstance could not induce him to give up the honour of the first, and he continued on the field animating his men and resisting the repeated charges of the enemy until about one o'clock, when he obliged them to retire from their position with great slaughter. It is impossible for me to do justice to the merit of that officer; you will, I doubt not, favourably report his conduct to His Majesty, and at the same time that of Captain James of the 46th Regiment, and Captain Archibald Campbell, who commanded the grenadiers of that corps.

"Foiled and beat off on the left, the right flank was attempted, and a considerable force was landed near Morne Daniel. The regulars, not exceeding 200, employed on the left in opposing the advance of three columns, consisting of upwards of 2000 men, could afford me no reinforcement; I had only the right wing of the St. George's Regiment of militia to oppose them, of about a hundred men. They attacked with spirit, but unfortunately the frigates had stood in so close to the shore to protect this disembarkation, that after receiving a destructive fire, they fell back and occupied the heights of Woodbridge Estate. Then it was that a column of the enemy marched up to Morne Daniel, and stormed the redoubt defended by a small detachment, which, after an obstinate resistance, they carried. On my left, Captain O'Connell was gaining ground, notwithstanding a fresh supply of troops and several field-pieces, which had been brought on shore by the enemy. I now observed a large column climbing the mountains to get in his rear.

"The town, which had been for some time in flames, was only protected by a light howitzer and a six-pounder to the right, supported by part of the light company of the St. George's Regiment. The enemy's large ships in Woodbridge Bay, out of the reach of my guns, my right flank gained, and my retreat to Prince Rupert's almost cut off, I determined on one attempt to keep the sovereignty of the island, which the excellent troops I had, warranted. I ordered the militia to remain at the posts, except such as were inclined to encounter more hardships and severe service; and Captain O'Connell, with the 46th Regiment, under the command of Captain James, and the light company of the 1st West India Regiment, were directed to make a forced march to Prince Rupert's. I then allowed the President to enter into terms for the town of Roseau; and then demanded from the French general that private property should be respected, and that no wanton or disgraceful pillage should be allowed; this done, only attended by Brigade-Major Prevost, and Deputy Quartermaster-General Hopley, of the militia forces, I crossed the island, and in twenty-four hours, with the aid of the inhabitants and the exertions of the Caribs, I got to this garrison on the 23rd. After four days' continued march through the most difficult country, I might almost say, existing, Captain O'Connell joined me at Prince Rupert's, himself wounded, and bringing in his wounded, with a few of the Royal Artillery, and the precious remainder of the 46th and the 1st West India Light Company.

"I had no sooner got to the fort than I ordered cattle to be driven in, and took measures for getting a store of water from the river and the bay. I found my signals to Lieutenant-Colonel Charles Broughton, of the 1st West India Regiment, made from Roseau soon after the enemy had landed, had been received, and that in consequence he had made the most judicious arrangements his garrison would allow for the defence of this important post.

"On the 25th, I received the summons[31] I have now the honour to transmit, from General of Division La Grange, and without delay sent the reply[32] you will find accompanying it.

"On the 27th the enemy's cruisers hovered about the Head; however, the *Centaur's* tender, *Vigilante*, came in and was saved by our guns. I landed Mr. Henderson, her commander, and crew, to assist in the defence we were prepared to make.

"As far as can be collected, the enemy had about 4000 men on board, and the whole of their force was compelled to disembark before they gained one inch of ground.

"I entrust this despatch to Captain O'Connell, to whom I beg to refer you. His services entitle him to consideration. I am much indebted to the zeal and discernment of Fort-Adjutant Gualy, who was very accessary to the due execution of my orders.

"I cannot pass unnoticed the very soldierlike conduct of Lieutenant Wallis, of the 46th Regiment, to whom I had entrusted the post of Cachecrow, or Scot's Head. On perceiving our retreat he spiked his guns, destroyed his ammunition, and immediately commenced his march to join me at Prince Rupert's with his detachment. Nor that of Lieutenant Schaw of the same corps, who acted as an officer of artillery and behaved with uncommon coolness and judgment while on the battery, and great presence of mind in securing the retreat of the additional gunners belonging to the 46th Regiment. On the 27th, after levying a contribution on Roseau, the enemy re-embarked, and hovered that day and the next about this post. This morning, the French fleet is seen off the south end of Guadaloupe, under easy sail.

"Our loss—you will perceive by the returns I have the honour to transmit—was inconsiderable when compared with that of the enemy, which included several officers of rank and about 300 others.

"I have, etc.,

(Signed) "George Prevost.

"Lieutenant-General Sir William Myers,
      "Bart., etc., etc., etc.

"P.S.—As I find I cannot spare Captain O'Connell from the duty of this garrison, I must refer you to the master of a neutral vessel, who has engaged to deliver this despatch."

Extract from Minutes of the House of Assembly, Dominica, dated Roseau, 2nd May, 1805:

"Resolved, that the Committee of Public Assembly be instructed to write to England for a monument to be erected to the memory of Major Nunn, of the 1st West India Regiment, who gallantly fell on Feb. 22nd, 1805.

"Resolved, that the thanks of this House be presented to Captain O'Connell, of the 1st West India Regiment, and that the sum of one hundred guineas be appropriated for the purchase of a sword for him.

"Resolved, that the thanks of this House be presented to the officers, non-commissioned officers, and privates of the 1st West India Regiment, for their gallant conduct on the same occasion."

Similar sentiments were expressed, and conveyed to the regiment, at a meeting held on May 23rd, 1805, at the London Tavern, Lord Penrhyn president.

Captain O'Connell was promoted to Major, 5th West India Regiment, and Lieutenant Winkler to Captain, vice O'Connell.

Return of the killed and wounded in the actions of the 22nd of February, 1805, at Point Michell, Morne Daniel, and Roseau, in the island of Dominica.

1st West India Regiment—9 rank and file, killed; 1 field officer, 1 captain, and 8 rank and file, wounded.

For its services on this occasion the 1st West India Regiment was permitted to inscribe the word "Dominica" on its colours.

FOOTNOTES:

[29] This does not appear in Brigadier-General Prevost's letter, but is mentioned in that of General La Grange.

[30] "During a continued march of four days, through an exceedingly difficult country, that brave officer (Captain O'Connell) did not leave behind even one of his wounded men."—Bryan Edwards.

[31] A summons to surrender.

[32] A refusal.

CHAPTER XI
THE HURRICANE AT DOMINICA, 1806—THE REDUCTION OF ST. THOMAS AND ST. CROIX, 1807—THE RELIEF OF MARIE-GALANTE, 1808

In 1806, Dominica was visited by a terrific hurricane, from which the 1st West India Regiment suffered some loss. On the afternoon of the 9th of September the sky became totally overcast, and masses of clouds gathered over the island. About 7 p.m. a tremendous thunderstorm commenced, accompanied by violent gusts of wind, which increased in strength, until by 10 p.m., every vessel in the harbour, to the number of sixteen, was either sunk or driven ashore. The rain fell in such torrents that the whole of the barracks on Morne Bruce, where a company of the 1st West India Regiment was stationed, and nearly the whole of those on Morne Cabot, were carried away, and three men of the 1st West India Regiment were killed, and several injured. Every house from the River Mohaut to Prince Rupert's was overthrown, and the town of Portsmouth was laid in ruins. In Roseau, 131 persons were killed or wounded, the greatest mischief being there caused by the overflowing of the river, which inundated the town in all directions, every house which obstructed its passage being swept away by the torrent. "No pen," says a witness of the scene, "can paint the horrors of that dreadful night! The tremendous noise occasioned by the wind and rain—the roaring of the waters, together with the shock of an earthquake, which was sensibly felt about midnight—the shrieks of the poor sufferers crying out for assistance—the terror of those who in their houses heard them, and dared not open a door or window to give succour, and who momentarily expected to share the same fate, formed a scene which can hardly be conceived, and is still more difficult to be described."

The regiment remained stationed at Dominica until the month of April, 1807, when it was removed to Barbados, with the exception of four companies which had been detached to Grenada and Tobago, and which soon after rejoined head-quarters at Barbados.

In this year also, the establishment of West India regiments was augmented by a second lieutenant-colonel, Major Samuel Huskisson, from the 8th Foot, being appointed the second lieutenant-colonel of the 1st West India Regiment by the *Gazette* of the 2nd of June.

A war having broken out with Denmark, the British Ministers, early in September, 1807, sent out orders to the Commander of the Forces in the West Indies, to reduce the Danish islands of St. John, St. Thomas and Saint Croix, and the 1st West India Regiment, with the other troops stationed at Barbados, embarked in men-of-war under General Bowyer, on the 15th of December, to proceed on this duty. On the 19th of December the expedition reached Sandy Point, Saint Christopher's, and receiving some troops from that garrison, sailed again the same day; arriving at St. Thomas, where it was joined by reinforcements from Antigua and Grenada, on the 21st. A summons to surrender was at once sent to the Governor, Von Scholten, the terms of which he accepted next day, and surrendered the islands of St. Thomas and St. John with their dependencies. A small garrison of the 70th Regiment being left at St. Thomas, the 1st division of the troops, in which was included the 1st West India Regiment, sailed on the evening of the 23rd for Saint Croix. The expedition arrived off the town of Frederickstadt on the 24th; and the Governor having capitulated on the 25th, the troops were landed, and the forts and batteries taken possession of, a royal salute being fired as the British colours were hoisted. Next night, the garrison and town of Christianstadt, on the other side of the island, were also occupied. The 1st West India Regiment during this expedition was commanded by Major Nathaniel Blackwell; and after the surrender of Saint Croix, it at once returned to Barbados. In January, 1808, three companies were detached from Barbados to Antigua, and one to Tobago; the detachment at Antigua rejoining head-quarters in October of the same year.

The next service seen by the regiment was at Marie-Galante,[33] in 1808. Deseada and Marie-Galante, the former a few miles to the north-east, and the latter a few miles to the south-east of Guadaloupe, had been captured by Captain Selby and a naval force in March, 1808. Deseada, the French Governor of Guadaloupe allowed to remain unmolested; but Marie-Galante was so good a privateer station, and its loss also brought the British so much more nearly in contact with him, that he determined to try to recover it.

The attempt was made on the 23rd of August, by Colonel Cambriel, who, with about 200 men in seventeen boats stole over from Guadaloupe and landed near Grand Bourg. They were preparing to attack the battery when they were espied from the *Circe*; thirty of whose seamen hurried on shore, threw themselves into the battery before the French could reach it, and gave them such a warm reception as to compel them to retreat. The enemy's boats were seized by the *Circe*, and the escape of the French being thus cut off, they retired to the centre of the island. Intelligence of their landing was forwarded to General Beckwith, at Barbados, who lost no time in sending Lieutenant-Colonel Blackwell[34] with three companies of the 1st West India Regiment against them.

The following is Lieutenant-Colonel Blackwell's report to General Beckwith:

"Grand Bourg, Marie-Galante,
"*Sept. 4th, 1808.*

"Sir,

"I have the honour to inform you that the troops which you were pleased to place under my command arrived here, in H.M. Ship *Captain*, on the 29th of August; and finding from Captain Pigot, commander of this island, that the French troops were strongly posted within three miles of Grand Bourg, I was immediately landed with the three companies of the 1st West India Regiment; and having obtained an increase of my force, of about 140 marines, and some sailors, together with a six-pounder, from the army schooner *Maria*, I lost no time in fulfilling the instructions I received from you.

"I have now much satisfaction in reporting, that after a pursuit of the enemy for five days and nights, and having during that period had four engagements with him, in each of which he was repulsed, and obliged to make most precipitate retreat, leaving behind him arms, ammunition, etc., at every different post that had been attacked, and at one place in particular, nine mariners (who had been taken prisoners on the first landing of the enemy), and at another, a brass six-pounder, which had only arrived from Guadaloupe two days, and which was found spiked; by constantly marching and harassing him, we found, on coming within one hundred yards of his front yesterday morning, that he was willing to surrender, and sending out a flag of truce, I granted the following terms: 'That the French troops might march out from the ground they then occupied with the honours of war, but that they should lay down their arms in front of the troops, and surrender themselves as prisoners of war, and that all prisoners taken since their arrival in the island should be immediately returned.' I was, however, much astonished to find that Colonel Cambriel, who had commanded the army, was not present when they surrendered, but I have since understood that he had quitted it the morning previous, and had returned to Guadaloupe, but I have some reason to imagine he is still in this island.

"The field-piece I had taken from the army schooner became useless after the first day, from the tract of the country the enemy led us over; I therefore sent it back to Grand Bourg, and at the same time I directed fifty marines to occupy the post of Delosses, three miles from town, which kept up the communication with the interior of the island.

"In our several attacks, it gives me pleasure to say that we have had only two privates wounded, one of them since dead. The loss on the part of the enemy I have not ascertained, but imagine it to have been considerable. I am sorry to mention to you that a gentleman from Antigua, of the name of Brown, being a prisoner of war, was in rear of the enemy's picket when attacked on the evening of the 2nd instant, and received a mortal wound. The force which has been brought from Guadaloupe I have not yet exactly found out, but from all accounts must have been above 200 rank and file.

"From the return I send herewith, you will find that 162 privates have laid down their arms, and there are at present many who have been sick dispersed through the country. The inhabitants that joined were very considerable. I believe their number amounted to from four to five hundred....

"I have likewise to return my best thanks to all the officers, non-commissioned officers, and privates who were under my command, for the cheerfulness with which they went through the long and harassing marches, and I think it is a duty incumbent upon me to mention to you their extreme good conduct since they have been in the field.

"I have the honour to be, etc.,
(Signed) "Nath. Blackwell,
"Lieut.-Colonel 4th W.I. Regiment."

"Return of prisoners who surrendered on the 3rd of September, 1808: 4 captains, 8 lieutenants, 162 rank and file, 1 staff.

"Return of arms, ammunition, and accoutrements taken and destroyed from 30th August to 3rd September: 1 field-piece, 450 firelocks, 200 belts and pouches, and 24 kegs of ball-cartridge.

"Ammunition for field-piece not ascertained."

On this occasion was captured the drum-major's staff of the French 26th Regiment (now in the possession of the 1st West India Regiment), bearing the motto: "La République Française une et indivisible. Battalion 26me," and surmounted by the cap of Liberty.

Of the companies of the regiment employed on this service, one was the grenadier company under Captain Cassidy, another the light company under Captain Winkler, and the third a battalion company under Lieutenant Nixon. On the return of the detachment to Barbados it was formed up on a garrison parade at St. Ann's on the right of the regiment; and Lieutenant-General Beckwith, after thanking Lieutenant-Colonel Blackwell and the officers and men engaged for their meritorious exertions, presented the former with a sword.

FOOTNOTES:

[33] See map of Guadaloupe.

[34] Major Nathaniel Blackwell, 1st West India Regiment, was, by the *Gazette* of May 24th, 1808, promoted Lieutenant-Colonel of the 4th West India Regiment, for his services at the reduction of the Danish West India Islands. At this time he had not yet joined his new corps.

MARTINIQUE

CHAPTER XII
THE CAPTURE OF MARTINIQUE, 1809[35]—
THE CAPTURE OF GUADALOUPE, 1810

The 1st West India Regiment continued doing duty at Barbados until January 27th, 1809, when eight companies joined the expedition against the Island of Martinique.

The interception, in the summer of 1808, of some despatches from the Governor of Martinique to the French Ministry asking for supplies and additional troops, and describing the condition of the island as almost defenceless, first directed the attention of the British Government to the reduction of this French colony. Preparations for the attack began at Barbados in November, 1808, the expedition assembled at Carlisle Bay, Barbados, in January, 1809, and on the 28th of that month the force sailed for Martinique.

The expeditionary force was under the command of Lieutenant-General Beckwith, and consisted of two divisions, each of two brigades, the 1st Division being commanded by Lieutenant-General Sir George Prevost, and the 2nd Division by Major-General Maitland. The 1st West India Regiment was included in the 1st Division. Six battalion companies, with the 13th and 8th Regiments, formed the 2nd Brigade under Brigadier-General Colville; while the grenadier company (Captain Winkler), with the 7th, 23rd, and a light battalion, in which latter was the light company, 1st West India Regiment, formed the 1st Brigade, under Brigadier-General Hoghton.

On the 30th of January the expedition arrived off the Island of Martinique, and on the evening of the 31st the troops disembarked, the 1st Division landing at Malgré Tout, Bay Robert, and the 2nd near St. Luce and Point Solomon on the opposite side of the island.

The 1st Division marched the same night to De Manceaux Estate. The roads were in a wretched condition from the rains, and the horses being done up from the length of time which they had been on board ship, the troops were obliged to drag the guns themselves. After a short rest the force continued its march to Papin's, which it reached at midnight. Here the main body of the 1st Division halted for the night, while the grenadier company of the 1st West India Regiment, with the 7th Regiment, pushed on to the heights on De Bork's Estate.

On the day following they were joined by the 23rd and the light infantry battalion, and advanced to the heights of Morne Bruno, the French skirmishers falling back slowly before them, while keeping up a smart fire. From this point the grenadier company, 1st West India Regiment, advanced with the 7th, the 23rd being in support, against the French position on the heights of Desfourneaux.

The enemy, under General De Hondelot, were well placed on the crest of the ridge, with a mountain torrent in their front, and a strong force of artillery drawn up on their left flank. The flank companies of the 7th were ordered to turn the French right, while the light battalion, with which was the light company, 1st West India Regiment, moved against his left, and the grenadiers of the 1st West India Regiment, with the remainder of the 7th, advanced against the centre. The troops rushed forward, fording the stream under a heavy fire, and attacking the enemy, who was greatly superior in numbers, with the bayonet, drove him from his position.

From this point, with the co-operation of the 2nd Brigade, the French were beaten back to the heights of Surirey, where they made a determined stand, but by a brilliant charge, the British carried the hill, and forced them to take shelter under the guns of their redoubts.[36]

The troops encamped for the night on the position which they had won, while the enemy took up a second position, strengthened by two redoubts connected by an entrenchment.

Next morning, February 2nd, the British made a movement to turn the French right, and, being much annoyed by the enemy's advanced redoubt, the light battalion and the 7th Regiment were ordered to take it. They were repulsed with considerable loss, but, on the following night, the 2nd division of the British having come up, the enemy abandoned the work and spiked the guns, retiring with all his force to Fort Bourbon, or Desaix.

While the 1st Division had thus been engaged at Morne Bruno and Surirey, the 2nd had been equally successful. Upon landing at St. Luce, a detachment of the Royal York Rangers took possession of the battery at Point Solomon, on the south side of Fort Royal Bay, thus securing a safe anchorage for the fleet. The same corps then pushed on and invested Pigeon Island, a small fortified island which commanded the anchorage in the upper part of the bay, and which had to be captured before any attempt could be made against the formidable fortresses of Bourbon and Fort République. Batteries were erected on Morne Vanier, from which Pigeon Island was shelled with such success that the garrison surrendered.

The way being now open for the fleet, preparations were commenced for the capture of Fort Bourbon. It was decided to attempt to take the place by storm, and on February 4th, the 1st Division, which, under Sir George Prevost, had marched over from Surirey, advanced to the assault, the grenadier companies forming the "forlorn hope." The fire from the enemy's guns was, however, so heavy and well-directed that the attempt failed, notwithstanding the most conspicuous gallantry on the part of the British, and the troops retired with a loss of 330 killed and wounded, the grenadier company of the 1st West India Regiment having suffered heavily.

General Villaret, the French commander, supposing Fort Bourbon to be impregnable, abandoned Fort République, leaving in it 4 mortars and 38 heavy guns, and collected his entire force, some 3000 in number, in Fort Bourbon. Being well supplied with food and ammunition, he resolved quietly to wait in the citadel; confident that the British army would gradually melt away from the sickness caused by the heavy rains, which had now set in and fell incessantly. On the 7th February a British force entered by night the abandoned Fort République; and, though the work was furiously bombarded from Fort Bourbon, in two days the guns which had been left in the fort were unspiked and the fire returned. In the meantime other batteries had been in course of construction, and by February 18th Fort Bourbon was completely invested.

The enemy were then summoned to surrender, but General Villaret declaring that he would rather bury himself under the ruins of the citadel, the bombardment commenced. The British batteries, six in number, opened fire simultaneously at 3.30 p.m. on Sunday, February 19th, and the fire was hotly returned. At Colville's battery, where were four companies of the 1st West India Regiment, the brushwood in front of the guns was set on fire, and was only extinguished with much difficulty, and a terrific fire was kept up on both sides. On February 20th the enemy ceased firing during the whole day, recommencing again on February 21st; but on the 22nd a shell from our batteries having blown up the magazine, the enemy sent out terms of capitulation. These were rejected, but on the 24th the place surrendered; the garrison, 2700 in number, became prisoners of war, and three eagles remained as trophies in the British hands.

The following general orders were issued during this brilliant campaign:

1. Morne Bruno, February 3rd, 1809.—"The benefit the advanced corps, under Lieutenant-General Sir George Prevost, have produced to His Majesty's service, from the gallant and successful attack made

upon Morne Bruno and the heights of Surirey, on the 1st instant, by the 1st Brigade of the army and the light battalion, under Brigadier-General Hoghton, demands from the Commander of the Forces a reiteration of his acknowledgments, and his assurance to the brigadier-general, and to the commanding officer of the Royal Fusiliers, of the Royal Welsh Fusiliers, and of the light battalion, also to the officers, non-commissioned officers, and soldiers of those regiments, that he will not fail to lay their meritorious exertions before the King. The exertions of all the corps engaged yesterday were conspicuous; and, although the state of the works possessed by the enemy did not admit of their being carried by the bayonet, which rendered it the general's duty to direct the corps employed to retire, they manifested a spirit and determination which, when tempered by less impetuosity, will lead to the happiest results."

2. February 27th, 1809.—"The grenadier company, with a detachment of the battalion of the 1st West India Regiment, who were engaged with the enemy both on the 1st and 2nd of February, 1809, having been omitted to be mentioned in the general orders of February 3rd, referring to those operations, the Commander of the Forces takes the present occasion to acknowledge their services. From the day of the regiment landing, to that of the enemy's surrender, it served with the greatest credit under all the disadvantages to which a West India regiment is exposed. The hard and severe work is generally performed by them, which the European soldiers could not undergo from the climate."

During this campaign the 1st West India Regiment was commanded by Lieutenant-Colonel Tolley; and, in token of its services, it was permitted to retain two brass side-drums and five battle-axes, which it had captured from the enemy.

The 1st West India Regiment continued to serve in Martinique till the 17th of May, 1809, when the head-quarters and six companies were removed to the Island of Trinidad. There they remained until the month of December following, when an expedition was formed for the reduction of Guadaloupe.

Since the expulsion of the British in 1794, that island had enjoyed a period of tranquility; its armament had been considerably increased under successive governors, slavery had been re-established, and its harbours swarmed with privateers, which preyed upon British commerce. The incessant annoyance and loss to our trade caused by these vessels, was a strong incentive for a descent upon the island. Added to this, it was a colony of considerable importance to France; the mother country depending, in a great measure, upon it for colonial produce.

The British army was assembled at Prince Rupert's Bay, Dominica, where, on the 22nd of January, 1810, the flank companies of the 1st West India Regiment joined. The force was under the command of Lieutenant-General Sir George Beckwith, and was thus composed:

1st Division—Major-General Hislop.

3rd Brigade— Brig.-General Maclean {	Light Companies of 1st, 2nd, 3rd, 4th, 6th, and 8th West India Regiments	500
	90th Foot	500
	8th West India Regiment	400
4th Brigade— Brig.-General Skinner {	Battalion made up of 13th and 63rd Regiments	600
	York Light Infantry Volunteers	200
	4th West India Regiment	400

2nd Division—Brigadier-General Harcourt.

1st Brigade— Brig.-General Harcourt {	Light infantry	500
	15th Foot	300
	3rd West India Regiment	400
2nd Brigade— Brig.-General Barrow {	Grenadiers of the 1st, 4th, and 8th West India Regiments	300
	25th Foot	600
	6th West India Regiment	350

Reserve.

5th Brigade— Brig.-General Wale {	Grenadiers	300
	Royal York Rangers	900
	Royal Artillery	300
	Military Artificers	100

On the 23rd of January the fleet sailed from Dominica, the 2nd Division being ordered to proceed to the Saintes, to prepare for disembarking near Basseterre, while the 1st Division and the Reserve made for the north-eastern quarter of that part of Guadaloupe which is called Cabesterre.

ISLES DES SAINTES.

The light infantry battalion of the 3rd Brigade effected its landing at 9 a.m. on the 28th of January, without opposition, at the Bay of St. Marie; and immediately possessed itself of the heights, so as to cover the disembarkation of the remainder of the 1st Division and the Reserve. The whole of the troops were landed about half-an-hour after noon, and the light infantry battalion was ordered forward as the advance guard of the division. It reached the village of Marigot about sunset, and crossing the river (called Rivière des Pères Blancs), halted in the mountains in the most advantageous position for maintaining itself during the night. The remainder of the division encamped at Marigot. The troops had marched this day with three days' cooked provisions in their havresacks. The Reserve remained at St. Marie to cover the landing of munitions and supplies.

On the 29th of January, the troops were under arms an hour before daylight, and the light battalion, being again pushed to the front, reached Bannaniers by sunset. There the division encamped for the night, while the light companies of the 1st and 3rd West India Regiments were ordered to possess themselves of the strong pass of Lacasse, above the British position.

On the same day, the 29th, the 2nd Division, after making a feint of disembarking at Trois Rivières to draw off the attention of the enemy, proceeded in the ships to the western side of the island.

On the 30th of January, at daybreak, the 1st Division again advanced. Between 9 and 10 a.m. the light battalion, which was still leading, descended the heights on the side of Trois Rivières, and coming up with the rear of a detachment of the enemy, dispersed it after a short conflict. Pursuing its march it reached the open ground, or savannah, at Loriols Trois Rivières about 11 a.m., and there halted to allow the column to come up.

The enemy's position was now in front, and consisted of a line of redoubts and entrenchments on the commanding heights of Petrizel. Major-General Hislop at once made his dispositions for an attack on the following morning; the light battalion moving to the left, and the 4th Brigade, with the remainder of the 3rd, extending along the heights to the right. In the execution of this order, the light battalion, advancing along the high road towards the enemy's position, alarmed him to such a degree as to induce him to open fire from all his batteries and entrenched lines, not only from Petrizel, but also from his post at Dolé; from which he kept up for some time an incessant fire, without doing any other injury than killing one man, and wounding another. The troops took up their positions in the meantime without further inconvenience. Towards the close of the evening numbers of the enemy were seen ascending the mountains above their works at Petrizel. The heat this day had been excessive, and the country through which the troops marched exceedingly difficult, the strong pass of Trou au Chien lying in their way. The night closed in with heavy rain.

On the 31st, at daylight, not a soul was to be seen near the enemy's works; and, it having been ascertained that they were evacuated, the light company of the 1st West India Regiment was ordered to march at noon and take possession.

The 1st Division remained halted during the 1st of February, and on the 2nd, the light battalion, as advanced guard of the 4th Brigade, was ordered to march, by a very difficult ascent, to the centre of the Palmiste heights; while the remainder of the 3rd Brigade moved to the right of the same heights, by an easier route. The troops bivouacked on the heights for the night.

While these operations had been going on, the 2nd Division had, at 10 a.m. on the 30th of January, disembarked at a bay to the northward of the village of Les Vieux Habitans and about three leagues to the north of the town of Basseterre. The troops gained the heights above the village after a slight skirmish, and encamped on the ground for the night. During the two succeeding days the 2nd Division was employed in bringing up guns to a height near Post Bellair.

By the combined movements of the two divisions, General Ernouf, the French commander, was now, by the night of the 2nd of February, hemmed in at the extremity of the island between the sea and the British army. He had judiciously chosen his position, which was naturally strong, and which he had strengthened by all the artificial means in his power. He was posted on heights, his left supported by the mountains of Matouba, and every accessible point of his line covered by abattis and stockaded redoubts. In his front was a river, the passage of which, exceedingly difficult in itself, was rendered much more so by a detachment of troops stationed behind abattis. The ground also, between the river and the heights, was bushy and full of rugged rocks, and of course highly unfavourable to the march of the assailants.

It was on the 3rd of February that the British troops were put in motion to dislodge him from his advantageous position. The 1st Division, soon after dawn, descended the north side of Palmiste, passed the river Gallion, and under a heavy fire from a battery at the bridge of Vozière, formed on the opposite heights, taking up a position so as to intercept the communication between the town of Basseterre and the enemy's camp. The 2nd Division had, during the night of the 2nd, pushed forward the grenadiers of the 2nd Brigade and a detachment of the 6th West India Regiment to occupy the ridge Beaupère St. Louis, on the upper part of which the strong post of Bellair was situated. On the morning of the 3rd the enemy perceived what had been done, and moved out in force to dislodge the British. The 1st Brigade was immediately ordered up in support; but, before it could gain the heights, a smart action had taken place, and it only arrived in time to complete the defeat of the enemy. In this engagement the grenadier company of the 1st West India Regiment lost 2 rank and file killed, Captain Cassidy and 9 rank and file wounded. During the remainder of the day the troops of the 2nd Division were moved up to Bellair, and the whole army remained on the ground during the night.

Next morning, the 4th, the British advanced to the final assault of the position. The 1st Division was charged with the operations on the right, while the task of turning the left was entrusted to Brigadier-General Wale with the Reserve. At dawn of day the light company of the 1st West India Regiment and the York Light Infantry were ordered to advance to the enemy's post at the bridge of Vozière. For some time they were unseen, but a picket of the enemy, moving along the opposite side of the ravine, discovered them; and, opening fire, a general discharge soon followed, in the face of which the British rushed forward and carried the work. Almost at the same moment, Brigadier-General Wale, who, with the Reserve, had forded the Gallion River, and under a heavy fire ascended the heights, carried the enemy's works on the left; and General Ernouf's situation had become so critical, that he at once hoisted flags of truce in the works which he still retained at Matouba.

On the 5th of February, the terms of capitulation were signed, the French marching out with military honours, and becoming prisoners of war. The British loss was 52 officers and men killed, 250 wounded, and 7 missing. The French lost 600 killed, and 2000 prisoners. Captain H. Downie, of the 1st West India Regiment, was mentioned in despatches for gallantry at the storming of the work at the bridge of Vozière.

The following general order was published, dated Beau Vallon, Guadaloupe, 6th Feb., 1810: "The enemy are now prisoners of war, to be sent to England, and not to serve until duly exchanged. Thus through the exertions and general co-operation of the fleet and the army, has been effected the important conquest of this colony in nine days from the landing of the 1st Division. The Commander of the Forces returns his public thanks to the officers of all ranks for their meritorious exertions, and to the non-commissioned officers and soldiers for the cheerfulness with which they have undergone the fatigues of a march, difficult in its nature, through the strongest country in the world, and the spirit which they have manifested upon all occasions to close with the enemy."

In this campaign, it may be observed, all the hard work had fallen to the lot of the 1st Division, and especially to that of the light infantry battalion of the 3rd Brigade, which had, by forced marches, moved across the whole breadth of the island, from St. Marie to the neighbourhood of Basseterre, over a wild and broken country, in six days.

For their services at the capture of Guadaloupe, Captains Cassidy and Winkler were appointed brigade-majors at Trinidad and Grenada respectively; and the words "Martinique" and "Guadaloupe" were inscribed on the colours of the regiment, "as a mark of royal favour and approbation of its gallant conduct at the capture of those islands in 1809 and 1810."

On the completion of this service the flank companies rejoined head-quarters at Trinidad, as did the two companies detached at Martinique and the two at Barbados. The whole regiment was then stationed in Trinidad, seven companies being at St. Joseph's and three at Orange Grove. This arrangement lasted until March, 1814, when the head-quarters and four companies were moved to Martinique, four companies to St. Lucia, and two to Dominica.

FOOTNOTES:

[35] This island had been restored to France by the Treaty of Amiens.

[36] The grenadier company of the 1st West India Regiment lost 1 rank and file, killed; 1 drummer, 18 rank and file, wounded; 1 subaltern, missing.

CHAPTER XIII
THE EXPEDITION TO NEW ORLEANS, 1814-15

In July, 1814, the 1st West India Regiment was removed to Guadaloupe, except two companies detached to St. Martin's and Marie-Galante, and remained so stationed until it was selected to take part in the expedition to New Orleans.

In June, 1812, the United States of America had declared war against Great Britain, Washington had been captured by the British on July 24th, 1813, and the war had been carried on with varying success until towards the close of the year 1814. In October of that year an expedition to New Orleans was decided upon; the force was to rendezvous at Negril Bay, Jamaica, and for that place the 1st West India Regiment embarked at Point à Prène, Guadaloupe, on November 14th, 1814. Lieutenant-Colonel Whitby, who had for the first time joined the regiment on the previous day, was then in command.

The assembly of the fleet, and the concentration of troops at a point so near to their own coast, had aroused the suspicions of the Americans; and the treachery of an official in the garrison office at Jamaica enabled them to receive positive information as to the aim and destination of the expedition. This official communicated the intelligence to an American trader residing in Kingston, and the latter at once sailed in a coasting schooner for Pensacola; where General Jackson, who commanded the United States army of the South, was on the point of marching to the relief of St. Mary's, then being attacked by a naval force under Rear-Admiral Cockburn. The American general, upon learning of the proposed expedition, at once marched to the Mississippi, concentrated a force of 13,000 men in and around New Orleans, and threw up works on either side of the river to defend the passage in the neighbourhood of the town.

On the 26th of November, 1814, the British fleet, under the command of Vice-Admiral Sir A. Cochrane, having on board a force of some 5000 men under Major-General Keane, sailed from Negril Bay and arrived off the Chandeleur Islands near the entrance of Lake Borgne, on December 10th.

"To reduce the forts which command the navigation of the Mississippi was regarded as a task too difficult to be attempted, and for any ships to pass without their reduction seemed impossible. Trusting, therefore, that the object of the enterprise was unknown to the Americans, Sir Alexander Cochrane and General Keane determined to effect a landing somewhere on the banks of Lake Borgne, and pushing directly on, to take possession of the town before any effectual preparation could be made for its defence. With this view the troops were removed from the larger into the lighter vessels, and these, under convoy of such gun-brigs as the shallowness of the water would float, began on the 13th to enter Lake Borgne."[37]

The Americans, however, being well acquainted with what was taking place, opposed the passage of the lake with five large cutters, each armed with six heavy guns, and these were immediately attacked by the smaller craft of the British. Avoiding a serious engagement, they retired into the shoal water where they could only be attacked by boats, and owing to the delay in getting together a sufficiently powerful flotilla, it was not till the 15th that they were captured, and the navigation of the lake cleared. The vessels of a lighter draught having all run aground in a vain endeavour to pass up the lake, the troops were embarked in boats to carry them up to Pine Island, a distance of thirty miles.

"To be confined for so long a time as the prosecution of this voyage would require, in one posture, was of itself no very agreeable prospect; but the confinement was but a trifling misery when compared with that which arose from the change in the weather. Instead of a constant bracing frost, heavy rains, such as an inhabitant of England cannot dream of, and against which no cloak could furnish protection, began. In the midst of these were the troops embarked in their new and straitened transports, and each division, after an exposure of ten hours, landed upon a small desert spot of earth, called Pine Island, where it was determined to collect the whole army, previous to its crossing over to the main.

"Than this spot it is scarcely possible to imagine any place more completely wretched. It was a swamp, containing a small space of firm ground at one end, and almost wholly unadorned with trees of any sort or description. The interior was the resort of waterfowl; and the pools and creeks with which it was intercepted abounded in dormant alligators.

"Upon this miserable desert the army was assembled, without tents or huts, or any covering to shelter them from the inclemency of the weather.... After having been exposed all day to the cold and pelting rain, we landed upon a barren island, incapable of furnishing even fuel enough to supply our fires. To add to our miseries, as night closed, the rain generally ceased, and severe frosts set in, which, congealing our wet clothes upon our bodies, left little animal warmth to keep the limbs in a state of activity; and the consequence was, that many of the wretched negroes, to whom frost and cold were altogether new, fell fast asleep and perished before morning."

By December 21st the whole army was collected at Pine Island, and next day it was formed into three brigades, the 1st West India Regiment with the 21st and 44th Regiments composing the 2nd Brigade. The 1st West India Regiment, which had left Negril Bay 500 strong, was now so reduced by mortality and sickness that barely 400 men were in a condition to take the field. The cold was intense, and, considering the latitude, 29° N., almost incredible. It appears that when the regiment left Jamaica no attempt was made to furnish the men with warm clothing, and their sufferings from this cause, they being all natives of the tropics, can be better imagined than described. During the voyage the regiment had been much scattered in small craft, where the soldiers were obliged to sleep on deck, exposed to the torrents of rain which fell by day and to the frosts that came on at night; and, being unaccustomed to the severity of an American winter, large numbers of them died from cold and exposure, the 5th West India Regiment suffering equally with the 1st.

On December 22nd, the 1st Brigade (1600 strong) left Pine Island in boats to proceed to Bayou Catalan, a small creek eighty miles distant, which ran up from Lake Ponchartrain, through the middle of an extensive swamp, to within ten miles of New Orleans. Next day it landed at the mouth of the creek and advanced along an overgrown footpath on the banks of a canal, its movements being concealed by the tall reeds of the swamp. After being delayed by several small streams, it finally emerged from the morass, and entering the cultivated portion of the district took up a position across the main road from Proctorsville to New Orleans, the Mississippi being on its left and the swamp on its right.

The exhausted troops, without any camp equipment, encamped for the night on the position. They were not, however, allowed to enjoy a long period of rest. Late in the evening a large schooner was observed stealing up the river, until she arrived opposite the bivouac fires around which the men were asleep; and before it could be ascertained whether she was a friend or foe, a broadside of grape swept through the camp. Having no artillery with them, and no means of attacking this formidable adversary, the troops sheltered themselves behind a bank. The night was as dark as pitch, and the only light to be seen was the flash of the enemy's guns as he continued to pour broadside after broadside into the camp. To add to the miseries of the condition of the British it began to rain heavily, and the earth, barely raised above the level of the river, became a vast puddle of slime, in which the soldiers were compelled to lie down to avoid the iron showers of grape that tore through the air.

In the meantime the 2nd Brigade, with the 1st West India Regiment, had embarked in the remainder of the boats from Pine Island, about ten hours after the departure of the 1st Brigade, and after being exposed to an incessant downpour of rain during the night of December 22nd, had arrived at the mouth of the Bayou Catalan at nightfall on the 23rd. In the stillness of the night the sound of the guns of the schooner as she opened fire on the 1st Brigade were distinctly heard, and the troops, stimulated to fresh exertions, hurried on to the assistance of their comrades. As they drew nearer to the camp, the roll of musketry was heard, for the enemy had brought up a force of 5000 men from New Orleans, thinking to overwhelm the solitary 1st Brigade in the dark, and had unexpectedly opened a semicircle of fire upon it. The 2nd Brigade pushed on, and arrived just in time to prevent the Americans turning the British right, which, owing to their local knowledge, they had partially succeeded in doing. Coming up the canal bank, the 2nd Brigade in their turn took the enemy in flank, and a hand-to-hand conflict took place along the whole line, the British fighting with the energy of despair in the darkness and depths of the wood, and trusting to the bayonet alone. At last, about 3 a.m. on the 24th, the enemy retired, beaten off at all points.

The losses in the night's engagement, and the deaths from cold and exposure that had occurred during the passage from Pine Island, had so thinned the already attenuated ranks of the 1st West India Regiment, that on the morning of the 24th, only 16 sergeants and 240 rank and file were available for duty. The officers serving with them were Major Weston, Captains Isles and Collins, Lieutenants McDonald, Morgan, Miller, Magee, Pilkington, McKenzie, and Dalomel.

Notwithstanding the repulse which the Americans had experienced, the schooner continued to annoy our troops. She had anchored in the river beyond musket range, and, from that safe distance, continued to pour round-shot and grape into the camp, which had been increased on the evening of the 24th by the arrival of the 3rd Brigade, consisting of the 93rd and the 5th West India Regiment. On December 25th, Captain Collins, 1st West India Regiment, was killed by a shot from one of her guns, and there were several other casualties in the regiment. On that day, however, Sir Edward Pakenham, who had been sent out from England to assume the command, arrived, bringing some guns with him. During the night a battery was quietly thrown up opposite the schooner, and at daybreak a heavy cannonade was opened on her with red-hot shot. Before long she was set on fire, and blew up, while another vessel, which had come to her assistance, was compelled to cut and run up the river.

The main obstacle to an advance being now removed, Sir Edward Pakenham divided the army into two columns. The right column, commanded by Major-General Gibbs, consisted of the 4th, 21st, 44th, and 1st West India Regiments; the left, under Major-General Keane, was composed of the 85th, 93rd, 95th, and 5th West India Regiments.

In the meantime the American general had occupied a position facing the British, with the Mississippi on his right, and an impenetrable morass on his left, covering New Orleans, and rendering an advance on that town impossible, until his position had been carried by a front attack. The ground thus occupied, about 1000 yards in breadth, had been fortified so as to be almost impregnable. Three deep parallel ditches had been dug across the whole front; in rear of these was a strong loop-holed palisade, and several batteries had been erected so as to bring a cross-fire to bear upon the level plain, across which the British would have to advance to the assault. The right flank of the enemy was further protected by a strong work thrown up on the right bank of the Mississippi, which effectually prevented our gunboats turning the position, should they succeed in entering the river.

The night of December 26th was spent in continual alarms. Small bodies of American riflemen would creep down upon the pickets under cover of the darkness, and, firing upon the sentries, prevent the main body from obtaining any sleep. "Scarcely had the troops lain down, when they were aroused by sharp firing at the outposts, which lasted only till they were in order, and then ceased; but as soon as they had dispersed, and had once more addressed themselves to repose, the same cause of alarm returned, and they were again called to their ranks. Thus was the night spent in watching, or at best in broken and disturbed slumbers, than which nothing is more trying, both to the health and spirits of an army."

At daybreak on the 27th, the pickets were withdrawn, and the British formed in order of attack. The right column took post near the skirts of the morass, throwing out skirmishers half-way across the plain to meet the American riflemen, while the left column drew up upon the road. It was a clear, frosty morning, and in this formation the troops advanced, the enemy's skirmishers slowly falling back before them.

After an advance of about four miles the American position was sighted, and the British were saluted by a heavy cannonade from the batteries and shipping. "Scarce a ball passed over or fell short of its mark, but all striking full into the midst of our ranks, occasioned terrible havoc. The shrieks of the wounded, therefore, the crash of firelocks, and the fall of such as were killed, caused at first some little confusion; and what added to the panic was, that from the farm-houses beside which we stood bright flames suddenly burst forth. The Americans, expecting this attack, had filled them with combustibles for the purpose; and directing against them one or two guns, loaded with red-hot shot, in an instant set them on fire. The scene was altogether very sublime. A tremendous cannonade mowed down our ranks, and deafened us with its roar; whilst two large châteaux and their out-buildings almost scorched us with the flames, and blinded us with the smoke which they emitted."

The troops having formed line, advanced to storm the enemy's works. The right column, after a sharp and victorious skirmish with an advanced body of the enemy, arrived at the edge of the marsh, through which it endeavoured in vain to penetrate. At the same time the left column reached the first ditch, or canal, and, being unable to cross it, there halted, the men endeavouring to shelter themselves from the enemy's fire in a wet ditch about knee-deep. The troops being unable to close with the enemy, Sir Edward Pakenham ordered them to retire. This was effected by battalions, the last corps moving off about noon; and by nightfall the army was encamped about two miles from the former camping-ground, and the same distance from the enemy's position.

The 28th, 29th, and 30th, were occupied in bringing up guns from the fleet, on which duty the two West India Regiments and the seamen were employed. Major Weston and Lieutenant Magee, 1st West India Regiment, died from exposure and fatigue while engaged in this work.

During the night of the 31st, six batteries, mounting in all 30 pieces of heavy cannon, were completed, at a distance of some 300 yards from the American lines, and at dawn the artillery duel commenced. During the whole of the day a heavy cannonade continued, till, towards evening, the British ammunition began to fail, and the fire in consequence to slacken. The fire of the Americans, on the other hand, increased; and, landing a number of guns from their vessels, they soon compelled the British to abandon their works. The enemy made no attempt to secure the guns, and during the night they were removed.

Sir Edward Pakenham now decided to send a portion of his force across the river to attack the fort on the right bank and turn its guns upon the main position, whilst the remainder should at the same time make a general assault along the whole entrenchment. "But before this plan could be put into execution, it would be necessary to cut a canal across the entire neck of land from the Bayo de Catiline to the river, of sufficient depth and width to admit of boats being brought up from the lake. Upon this arduous undertaking were the troops immediately employed. Being divided into four companies, they laboured by turns, day and night.... The fatigue undergone during the prosecution of this attempt no words can sufficiently describe; yet it was pursued without repining, and at length, by unremitting exertions, they succeeded in effecting their purpose by the 6th of January."

On January 1st H.M.S. *Vengeur* arrived off the Chandeleur Islands with a convoy of transports, containing the 7th and 43rd Regiments, under Major-General Lambert, and these two battalions, each 800 strong, joined the army on the evening of January 6th. Next day the final arrangements were made. Colonel Thornton, with the 85th, the marines, and a body of seamen, in all 1400 men, were to cross the river immediately after dark, seize the batteries on the right bank, and at daylight commence firing on the enemy's line, which at the same moment was to be attacked by the remainder of the army. Major-General Keane, with the 95th, the light battalion, and the 1st and 5th[38] West India Regiments, was to attack the enemy's right, Major-General Gibbs, with the 4th, 21st, 44th, and 93rd, force the left, whilst Major-General Lambert was to hold the 7th and 43rd in reserve.

In accordance with this scheme, Colonel Thornton at nightfall moved his force down to the brink of the river, but no boats had arrived. Hour after hour elapsed, and then at last only a sufficient number to transport 350 men made their appearance. With this small force Colonel Thornton determined to make the attempt, and pushed off. The loss of time which had occurred was however fatal, for day began to break before the boats had crossed the river, and though the troops carried the batteries by assault, after a short but obstinate resistance, the alarm had already been carried to the main body of the enemy, and they were thoroughly prepared for defence.

The capture of the works on the right bank had, however, really made the front attack upon the American lines unnecessary; for the passage of the river now being clear, the armed boats from the canal could have passed up the stream and taken the whole of the position in rear. Had this been done, the American general would inevitably have been obliged to abandon his defences, falling back upon New Orleans, and we should have obtained possession of his formidable position without the loss of a man. Major-General Pakenham, however, still persevered in his original intention, and ordered the assault to take place.

There had been so much mismanagement, that the advance, which should have taken place at dawn, did not commence till some time after daylight. The officer, whose duty it was to have prepared fascines for the purpose of filling the ditches, had neglected his work; and, at 2 a.m., the hour at which he had been directed to have them ready, not one was made. [39] Eventually an insufficient number were got together, but "the 44th, which was appointed to carry them, had either misunderstood or neglected their orders, and now headed the column of attack, without any means being provided for crossing the enemy's ditch, or scaling his ramparts."

"The indignation of our brave leader on this occasion may be imagined, but cannot be described. Galloping towards Colonel Mullens, who led the 44th, he commanded him instantly to return for the fascines and ladders, but the opportunity of planting them was lost; and, though they were brought up, it was only to be scattered over the field by the frightened bearers, for our troops were by this time visible to the enemy. A dreadful fire was accordingly opened upon them, and they were mowed down by hundreds while they stood waiting for orders."

The word being given to advance, the other regiments rushed on to the assault. On reaching the first ditch a horrible scene of carnage ensued; the few fascines that were thrown down floated away; there were no ladders, and the men, crowding to the edge of the ditch in the hope of closing with the enemy, fell in heaps. Many threw themselves into the water, and endeavoured to struggle across, but were shot down, or drowned. On the right, Major-General Keane's column had, though reduced to half its strength, succeeded in passing the ditches near their junction with the marsh, and pushed on desperately to the palisade. But to scale this obstacle without ladders was no easy matter. Some few, indeed, by climbing upon their comrades' shoulders succeeded in entering the works, but only to be at once shot down; while those who remained outside were exposed to a flanking fire that swept them down by scores. The two West India regiments distinguished themselves by their desperate valour, so much so, indeed, as to win encomiums from the American general, Jackson.

On the left there had been a slight success, the 21st Regiment having stormed and taken a three-gun battery; but they were not supported, and the enemy, forcing their way into the work, retook it with great slaughter. In vain was the most obstinate courage displayed, the British were beaten off at all points.

"Sir Edward saw how things were going, and did all that a general could do to rally his broken troops. Riding towards the 44th, which had returned to the ground, but in great disorder, he called out to Colonel Mullens to advance; but that officer had disappeared, and was not to be found. He therefore prepared to lead them himself, and had put himself at their head for that purpose, when he received a slight wound in the knee from a musket-ball, which killed his horse. Mounting another, he again headed the 44th, when a second ball took effect more fatally, and he dropped lifeless into the arms of his aide-de-camp."

Major-Generals Keane and Gibb were, almost at the same moment, borne off the field severely wounded. "All was now confusion and dismay. Without leaders, ignorant of what was to be done, the troops first halted and then began to retire; till finally the retreat was changed into a flight, and they quitted the ground in the utmost disorder. But the retreat was covered in gallant style by the reserve. Making a forward motion, the 7th and 43rd presented the appearance of a renewed attack, by which the enemy were so much awed that they did not venture beyond their lines in pursuit of the fugitives."

The British loss in this action was over 1000 killed; while the Americans stated their total loss to be 8 killed and 14 wounded. The 1st West India Regiment had 5 rank and file killed, 2 sergeants and 16 rank and file wounded. The following officers were wounded: Captain Isles, Lieutenants McDonald and Morgan, Ensigns Miller and Pilkington; and all, with the exception of Ensign Miller, severely so. Lieutenants McKenzie and Dalomel, the only remaining officers of the regiment with the expedition, were publicly thanked by Major-General Lambert for the courage which they had displayed, and the able manner in which they had withdrawn the remnant of their corps from the enemy's palisades.

The capture of New Orleans being now despaired of in the shattered condition of the force, a retreat was determined upon. As it was impossible, without great risk, to return to the fleet by the route by which the army had come—there not being sufficient boats to embark more than a third of the force at a time—it was decided to make a road from the firm ground to the water's edge, a distance of many miles, through the very centre of a morass, where human foot had never before trodden. The difficulties experienced in making this road were immense. Sometimes for miles together no firm soil could be found, nor trees to furnish brushwood, and all that could be done was to lay down bundles of reeds on the morass. Nor were the enemy idle; there was constant skirmishing at the outposts, and a continual fire was kept up on the camp from a six-gun battery mounted on the bank of the river.

After nine days' incessant toil the road was completed; the sick and wounded were first removed, then the baggage and stores, and on January 17th, the infantry alone remained in the camp. On the evening of the 18th it also began its retreat. Leaving the camp-fires burning as if no movement were taking place, battalion after battalion stole away in the darkness in the most profound silence. Marching all night over the fragile road of reeds, through which the men sank knee-deep into the mud, the army reached the borders of the lake at dawn. Boats were in readiness, and regiment after regiment embarked and set sail for the fleet, the only loss being the capture of a boat containing two officers and forty men of the 14th Light Dragoons.

After remaining a few days at the Chandeleur Islands, the naval commander decided, in concert with Major-General Lambert, to make an attack on Mobile, and the fleet accordingly proceeded to that place. On February 12th, Fort Bowyer, which commanded the entrance to the harbour, surrendered, and a British garrison being left in the citadel, the fleet retired to Isle Dauphin, West Florida. Hostilities were then terminated by a treaty of peace, and the 1st West India Regiment returned to Barbados, where early in March, Brigade-Majors Cassidy and Winkler rejoined from the West India staff. The former succeeded to the majority, vice Weston, deceased. [40]

FOOTNOTES:

[37] "The Campaigns of the British Army at Washington and New Orleans," by an Officer.

[38] According to Major-General Lambert's despatch to Earl Bathurst, the 5th West India Regiment was to cross the river with Colonel Thornton.

[39] This officer was afterwards dismissed the service.

[40] The British force employed in this expedition has been thus estimated:

14th Dragoons	295
Royal Artillery	570
Sappers and Miners	98
4th Foot	747
21st Foot	800
44th Foot	427
85th Foot	298
93rd Foot	775
95th Foot	276

1st and 5th West India Regiments		1040
Seamen and Marines		1200
Staff Corps		57
		— —
		6583
7th Foot	} arrived on January 6th {	750
43rd Foot		820
		— —
		8153

Out of the ten officers who accompanied the regiment on this ill-fated expedition one was killed, two died from exposure, and five were wounded.

CHAPTER XIV
THE OCCUPATION OF GUADALOUPE, 1815—THE BARBADOS INSURRECTION, 1816—THE HURRICANE OF 1817

A few months after the disastrous expedition to New Orleans, and while the 1st West India Regiment was still stationed at Barbados, an expedition was formed by Lieutenant-General Sir James Leith, commanding the forces in the Windward and Leeward Islands, against the Island of Guadaloupe, the Governor of which, Admiral Comte de Linois, a staunch Bonapartist, had thrown off his allegiance to Louis XVIII., when the news of the escape of Napoleon from Elba had reached the West Indies, and had, on June 18th, 1815, proclaimed the latter Emperor. On the formation of this expedition, Captain Winkler, 1st West India Regiment, was appointed to the staff.

The fleet with the troops from Barbados, among whom were 400 picked men of the 1st West India Regiment, under Major Cassidy, attached to the 2nd Brigade, commanded by Major-General Murray, sailed from Carlisle Bay, Barbados, on the 31st of July, while other troops from St. Lucia, Martinique, and Dominica, rendezvoused at the Saintes. The force from Barbados anchored in the Bay of St. Louis, Marie-Galante, on the 2nd of August; but it was not until the night of the 7th that the troops from the Leeward were all assembled at the Saintes.

The internal state of Guadaloupe and the season were both so critical that Sir James Leith determined to attack at once; and on the morning of the 8th the whole fleet stood towards the Ance St. Sauveur. It was the intention of the general to attack in three columns, each of one brigade, but the scarcity of boats and the heavy surf necessitated that each brigade, should disembark in succession.

A portion of the 1st Brigade being landed without opposition at Ance St. Sauveur, and ordered to drive the enemy from the broken ground and ravines about Trou au Chien and Petit Carbet, the fleet dropped down to Grand Ance, where the principal attack was to be made. There, after the enemy's batteries had been silenced by the fleet, the 2nd Brigade, with the remainder of the 1st, were landed; and after a short but sharp skirmish with a body of the enemy, advanced with the bayonet and drove him from his position at Petrizel. The approach of night put an end to further advance, and the troops bivouacked on the ground they had won.

Next morning, the 9th, at daybreak, the troops advanced in two columns. The 1st Brigade moved upon and occupied Dolé, while the 2nd Brigade marched by difficult mountain paths upon the left of Morne Palmiste, by Petrizel, and by this turning movement compelled the enemy to withdraw his posts and retreat to Morne Palmiste by noon. While this had been taking place the 3rd Brigade had disembarked in the vicinity of Bailiff, to leeward of Basseterre, and after a short struggle had occupied that capital.

In the afternoon of the 9th, the 1st and 2nd Brigades converged upon Morne Palmiste, and clambering up the rugged and bush-covered heights, compelled the enemy, after the exchange of a few shots, to evacuate his works and retire to Morne Houel, where he had eight guns in position.

While the British were still occupying the defences on Morne Palmiste, intelligence was brought to Sir James Leith that the French Commander of Grandeterre, with the whole of his available force, was moving in rear of the 1st and 2nd Brigades to endeavour to form a junction with the main body of the enemy at Morne Houel. The detachment of the 1st West India Regiment was at once despatched to reinforce the rear-guard, and to occupy in force all the passes of the Gallion, a river running through a formidable ravine at the foot of Morne Palmiste. The troops from Grandeterre being thus cut off, endeavoured to form a junction by unfrequented paths through the woods; but, being met at every point by the skirmishers of the 1st West India Regiment, who searched the woods in every direction, they were compelled to abandon the attempt and retire at dusk.

The night closed in with torrents of rain, and the British, having been told off in columns in readiness to attack the formidable position of Morne Houel at daybreak next morning, bivouacked on the ground, without shelter, and drenched to the skin. About 11 p.m., the Comte de Linois sent a messenger to propose terms of surrender; but nothing being definitely settled, the troops were put in motion at daybreak on the 10th. As they drew near to the works, however, the French hoisted the British flag on Morne Houel in token of surrender, and the position was occupied without resistance. This success put an end to the active operations.

The British loss in this, the third invasion of Guadaloupe, amounted to 16 killed and 40 wounded. The 1st West India Regiment suffered no loss.

The following general order was issued, dated Head-Quarters, Government House, Basseterre, Guadaloupe, 10th August, 1815: "The

Commander of the Forces congratulates the army on the conquest of Guadaloupe being accomplished, and desires the generals and other officers, and the troops employed on that important service, to accept his best thanks for the gallant, zealous, and active manner in which they have compelled the enemy to surrender.

"It is certainly a matter of gratifying reflection to the troops employed, not only that a colony of such importance should be placed under the British flag, but that the exertions of the army have, in two days, defeated all the preparations and force of the enemy; thus sheltering the peaceable inhabitants from a formidable and sanguinary system of revolutionary violence which had been practised against their persons and property, and which threatened the entire destruction of social order.

"Lieutenant-General Sir James Leith will not fail to represent the steadiness and good conduct of the troops to H.R.H. the Commander-in-Chief."

Guadaloupe, however, was not at once reduced to a state of tranquility. A number of French soldiers, who had deserted previous to the surrender of the island, took refuge in the woods, whence they carried on a desultory and ferocious war against the British posts. The 1st West India Regiment, being composed of men better able to support the hardships of a guerilla war, carried on in a country naturally difficult, during the height of the tropical rains, was continually employed against these insurgent bands, and several men were killed and wounded in unknown and forgotten skirmishes.

Major Cassidy and Captain Winkler were each presented with a sword of honour by the major-general; and the order of the Fleur de Lys was transmitted to them by Louis XVIII., for their services in Guadaloupe.

Major Cassidy and the detachment of the 1st West India Regiment, remained in Guadaloupe until the 10th of October, 1815, on which day they embarked for Barbados, arriving at that island on the 26th. The regiment being then very much below its strength, on account of the heavy losses which it had sustained during the expedition to New Orleans, it was determined to transfer the majority of the privates who remained to the 3rd, 4th, 6th and 8th West India Regiments, and reform the regiment from a body of some 700 American negroes, who, in the late war with the United States, had served with the British, and had been temporarily organised as Colonial Marines.

On the 14th of December, the skeleton of the regiment embarked in H.M.S. *Niobe* for Bermuda, where the Colonial Marines were then stationed, and arrived at St. George's on the 9th of January, 1816. It was only then discovered that the number of men with whom it was intended to reform the regiment, did not exceed 400; most of whom were of but poor physique, and, moreover, unwilling to engage. At first the authorities determined to force these men to enlist, but ultimately the whole plan was abandoned; and the skeleton of the regiment left Bermuda on the 18th of March to return to the West Indies. It arrived at Barbados on the 1st of April; and the men who had already been transferred being sent back to it, the corps was completed with drafts from the late disbanded Bombor Regiment.

This was effected in time to enable the 1st West India Regiment to take a very active part in the suppression of an alarming insurrection of slaves, which broke out suddenly at Barbados on Easter Sunday, the 14th of April, 1816. "The revolt broke out in St. Philip's parish, shortly after sunset, and it extended, in the two following days, to the parishes of Christ Church, St. John and St. George. A conflagration upon a high ridge of copse-wood called Bishop's Hill, in the parish of St. Philip's, was the first signal. Shortly after, the canes upon eight or nine of the surrounding estates were set on fire. Some few of the rebels were furnished with fire-arms, and a scanty supply of ammunition, and the remainder were armed with swords, bludgeons, and such rude weapons as they had been able to procure. Their approach was announced by the beating of drums, the blowing of shells, and other discordant sounds. They demolished the houses of the overseers, destroyed the sugar works, and fired the canes.... Sixty estates were more or less damaged, many of them to a considerable amount."[41]

As soon as the news reached Bridgetown, martial law was proclaimed, the 1st West India Regiment was at once ordered to march, and the militia of the island were called out. Major Cassidy, who was in command of the 1st West India Regiment, found the rebels occupying a position on the heights of Christ Church, on Grazett's Estate, a dense mob of half-armed slaves crowning the summits of the low hills. He endeavoured to parley with them, but without success; and an advance being ordered, the 1st West India Regiment stormed the heights, and at the point of the bayonet drove the rebels from their position. Not a shot was fired by the regiment on this occasion, Major Cassidy being anxious to save bloodshed as much as possible; but a large body of the slaves offered a furious resistance, closing with and aiming blows at the soldiers with their rude weapons, and endeavouring to wrench the muskets from their hands, so that a considerable number of the insurgents were thus killed and wounded. This resistance only lasted for a few minutes, and the slaves, broken and dispirited, fled in all directions; only to be hunted down and fired upon by the militia all over the disaffected portions of the island. The 1st West India Regiment took no part in the pursuit and the capture or slaughter of the fugitives, this duty being left to the European militia, who, if the author of "Remarks on the Insurrection in Barbados"[42] may be believed, were guilty of many excesses.

By the planters this revolt was attributed to the introduction of the Slave Registry Bill into the British Parliament, and it was discovered that several free men of colour, who had for several months previous attended nocturnal meetings of slaves on the estates where the insurrection began, had told the slaves that a law was being passed in England to make them free, and that as the King was giving them their freedom the King's troops would not be employed against them.

Amongst other articles taken from the rebels by the 1st West India Regiment was a flag bearing the figure of a general officer (supposed to be intended for the King), placing a crown in the hands of a negro who had a white woman on his arm. Beneath these figures was the following motto: "Brittanie are happy to assist all such friends as endeavourance." In the struggle on Christ Church heights the regiment lost one man killed and seventeen wounded.

The following general order was issued, dated August 26th, 1816: "Colonel Codd, in communicating the following letters conveying the thanks of the Members in Council and House of Assembly at Barbados to himself and the officers, non-commissioned officers, and men employed during the late insurrection of slaves, feels it his duty to specify the commanding officer and corps whose good conduct on that occasion he has already reported in his official despatch to the Commander of the Forces, namely, Major Cassidy and the 1st West India Regiment."

In November, 1816, the regiment was removed from Barbados and distributed amongst the following islands:

Head-quarters. The Grenadier, Light, and 1 Company at Antigua	= 3
2 Companies at St. Christopher	= 2
1 Company at Montserrat	= 1
2 Companies at St. Lucia	= 2
2 Companies at Dominica	= 2
	—
	10

Lieutenant-Colonel Whitby commanded at head-quarters.

Nothing of note occurred till October, 1817, when, on the 21st of that month the Island of St. Lucia was visited with a most violent hurricane in which the Governor, Major-General Seymour, was so severely injured that he died a few days afterwards; and Brevet-Major Burdett, 1st West India Regiment (then commanding the garrison), together with his wife, child, and servants, was killed by the fall of his house and buried under its ruins. The distress that the troops endured was great. The whole of the buildings on Morne Fortune and Pigeon Island, with the exception of the magazine and tanks, were levelled with the ground, and the fragments, together with the men's clothing and equipment, carried off by the wind to the woods about Morne Fortune. The hurricane had struck the island so rapidly that, although an order to evacuate the barracks was given at once, the men had barely time to escape from the buildings before they fell with a crash. The town of Castries was laid in ruins, and twelve vessels that were in harbour were driven ashore. When the hurricane abated, the killed and wounded were moved under the parapet of Fort Charlotte and temporary shelter erected from the ruins.

In January, 1819, when Lieutenant-Colonel J.M. Clifton retired, the second lieutenant-colonelcy in the regiment was abolished. In May of that year the head-quarters and three companies were moved to Barbados, two companies remaining at Antigua, two at St. Lucia, two at Dominica, and one at Tobago.

FOOTNOTES:

[41] Bryan Edwards.

[42] Published in London in 1816.

CHAPTER XV
THE DEMERARA REBELLION, 1823

On the 25th of October, 1821, the establishment of the 1st West India Regiment was reduced from ten to eight companies, which were thus distributed:

> Head-quarters and 3 Companies at Barbados.
> 1 Company at Demerara.
> 1   "   " St. Lucia.
> 1   "   " Dominica.
> 1   "   " Antigua.
> 1   "   " Tobago.
> —
> 8

No change took place in this distribution until 1823, when the light company rejoined the head-quarters at Barbados, from Tobago.

In August, 1823, an alarming insurrection broke out among the slaves in the district of Mahaica, on the east coast of Demerara. The first notice of the impending rising was communicated, on the morning of the 18th of August, by a mulatto servant, to Mr. Simpson, of Plantation Reduit (now Plantation Ogle), a place distant some six miles from Georgetown. The servant stated that all the negroes on the coast plantations would rise that night; and Mr. Simpson at once proceeded with the intelligence to Georgetown, warning the various planters at their habitations *en route*. The Governor appeared to doubt the reliability of the information, but called out a troop of burgher horse, and proceeded with a portion of it to Plantation Reduit. There a considerable body of negroes, armed with cutlasses, sticks, and a few muskets, was met; and, after a short parley with them, which led to no result, the Governor returned at once to Georgetown, and called upon the officer commanding the troops for assistance.

A detachment of the 21st Regiment, and No. 8 Company of the 1st West India Regiment, the whole being under the command of Captain Stewart, of the latter corps, at once marched up the coast; while the militia of Georgetown was called out and patrolled the town. A body of the rebels, who had with them as prisoners several Europeans, was met near Wittenburg Plantation. On the approach of the troops the slaves opened a desultory fire, which did no damage, and a volley being returned, they dispersed in all directions. The force under Captain Stewart then proceeded further up the coast, encountering and dispersing other parties of slaves.

Next day, the 19th of August, martial law was proclaimed, for nearly all the negroes employed upon the coast estates had risen and were overrunning the country, capturing every European they met. Continually dispersed by the troops, they reassembled again, and, after being repulsed by a detachment of the 21st in an attack upon the post of Mahaica, a body of some 2000 of the better-armed slaves collected together and began to advance on Georgetown. By this time another detachment of the 21st Regiment had come up from Georgetown, under the command of Lieutenant-Colonel Leahy of that corps, who joined the troops already in the field, and moved with his whole force against this more formidable body of insurgents. Proceeding past pillaged houses and destroyed bridges, the troops at last fell in with the rebels, and Lieutenant-Colonel Leahy, after reading a proclamation that had been issued by the Governor, warned them that if they did not disperse the men would open fire. After waiting for some time, the order to advance was given, and the slaves at once commenced firing. This was returned by the troops, and after a conflict of a few minutes' duration the rebels fled in all directions.

This was the last occasion on which the slaves assembled in any considerable force, but a constant skirmishing was kept up along the whole line of the coast; and two companies of the 1st West India Regiment, which were despatched from Barbados when the news of the insurrection reached there, and arrived at Demerara on the 26th of September, were actively employed in assisting to restore tranquility in the colony and in the apprehension of the ringleaders of the rebellion. Captain Chads, Lieutenants Strong and Lynch, and Ensign Brennan were the officers who were serving with these two companies.

The following general order was published, dated Head-quarters, Camp House, 17th December, 1823:

"Major-General Murray has great satisfaction in communicating to the troops and militia within this colony the following extracts from letters from Lord Bathurst, and the Commander of the Forces, Sir Henry Ward, the former conveying the approbation of His Majesty, and the latter that of His Royal Highness, the Commander-in-Chief, for their conduct during the late insurrection. The Commander-in-Chief takes this opportunity of again returning his thanks to the officers and troops for the uniform support he has received from the former, and for the good conduct of the latter, during the late operations; by these means alone have those services been accomplished which have occasioned His Majesty's flattering marks of approbation."

Extract (No. 1) of a letter from the Right Honourable Lord Bathurst, to His Excellency Sir John Murray:

"Downing Street, 23rd October, 1823.

"I have received your several despatches, as per margin, reciting the series of events that had occurred from the first intimation received by you on the 18th of August last, of a disposition towards insurrectionary movements on the part of the slave population in the District of Mahaica, and concluding with an account of the general termination of the revolt, which had yielded to the prompt and judicious measures of remonstrance and resistance offered by you, and which you represent to have been so admirably enforced by the civil and military authorities under your command. With respect to those measures, I have laid them before His Majesty, and they have received his most gracious approbation, which you will convey to the officers, both civil and military, who have so distinguished themselves on this occasion."

Extract (No. 2) of a letter from His Royal Highness the Commander-in-Chief, to Sir Henry Ward, K.C.B., commanding the Windward and Leeward Islands:

"I have received your further despatch reporting to His Lordship the issue of this revolt, so satisfactorily and judiciously terminated by the prompt and vigorous measures taken by Major-General Murray, and the exemplary zeal, discipline and good conduct of the 21st Regiment, the 1st West India Regiment, and the Militia, which entitle officers and men to the greatest credit."

Ensign Miles, of the 1st West India Regiment, the only officer serving with No. 8 Company under Captain Stewart, died a few days after the termination of the rebellion, of fever produced by fatigue and exposure in hunting down the rebel leaders.

In February, 1824, the Court of Policy passed a vote of thanks, and conferred a gift of 200 guineas on the regiment, to be expended in the purchase of plate, as a mark of the high estimation in which the inhabitants of the colony held the services of Captain Stewart and his detachment.

"King's House, Demerara,
"19th July, 1824.

"Sir,

"I have the honour to enclose to you for the information of Captain Stewart and the detachment of the 1st West India Regiment, which served with so much credit to itself under his command during the late revolt in this Colony, the accompanying resolution of the Honourable Court of Policy, expressive of the sense entertained by the Court of that officer's conduct, and that of the officers and men placed under him during that distressing period.

"I have, etc.,
"John Murray,
"Major-General.

"To Major Capadose,
"Commanding Detachment, 1st West India Regiment."

"Extract from the Minutes of the Proceedings of the Honourable Court of Policy of the Colony and dependant Districts of Demerara and Essequibo, at an extraordinary and adjourned meeting held at the Court House, George Town, Demerara, on Tuesday, the 13th of January, 1824.

"The Court of Policy, feeling anxious to mark its sense of the eminent service performed, in the late unhappy revolt, by the troops composing the garrison, as well as by the Militia of the United Colonies, take the opportunity afforded it by the cessation of Martial Law, to express its highest approbation of, and to return its warmest thanks to His Excellency the Commander-in-Chief for the able and judicious measures adopted by him, which succeeded in putting a speedy termination to a Revolt, in its nature most serious and alarming....

"The steady and soldierlike conduct of the detachment of the 1st West India Regiment commanded by Captain Stewart, the Court cannot too highly estimate; and it begs, as a testimony of its lasting regard, to be allowed to present to the Mess, through Captain Stewart, the sum of two hundred guineas, to be laid out in plate."

On the 25th of October, 1824, the three companies stationed at Demerara were removed to Barbados, where they arrived on the 2nd of November. The following brigade order was published at Demerara prior to the embarkation of the detachment:

"The detachment of the 1st West India Regiment under Major Capadose, will embark on board the *Sovereign* at half-past six on Monday morning, the

25th instant, and the transport will proceed to Barbados with the evening tide of that day.

"The Major-General commanding the district cannot allow these excellent troops to embark without expressing to them his approbation of their excellent conduct and discipline, and his cordial wishes for their health and good fortune. The unremitting attention of Major Capadose in the command of the detachment, and of Brevet-Major Gillard, Captain Hemsworth, and Lieutenant Strong, in that of their respective outposts, have given the Major-General unqualified satisfaction, and he requests those officers to accept his thanks."

The distribution of the regiment was now as follows: 5 companies at Barbados, 1 at St. Lucia, 1 at Dominica, and 1 at Antigua, and this was continued till the 21st of February, 1825, when the head-quarters, with 4 companies, embarked on board the *Sovereign* transport, and proceeded to the Island of Trinidad, to relieve the 3rd West India Regiment, ordered to be disbanded. The head-quarters landed at Port of Spain, Trinidad, on February 23rd, and were quartered at Orange Grove Barracks, being removed to San Josef Barracks on May 1st, 1828.

In April, 1826, a second lieutenant-colonelcy was re-established in the regiment, Major Henry Capadose being promoted Lieutenant-Colonel, without purchase, on the 22nd of that month.

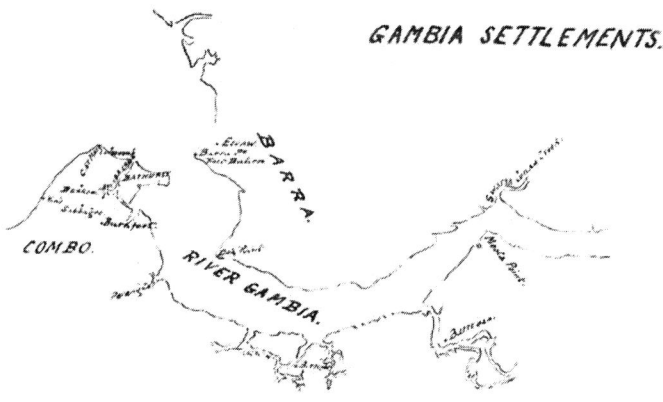

The History Of The First West India Regiment | 115

CHAPTER XVI
THE BARRA WAR, 1831—THE HURRICANE
OF 1831—THE COBOLO EXPEDITION, 1832

In 1826, owing to the difficulty found in obtaining a sufficiency of recruits in the West Indies, it was decided to send a company of the 1st West India Regiment to Sierra Leone, there to be stationed as a recruiting company, the recruits to be sent to the head-quarters of the regiment as opportunities occurred. The recruiting company embarked at Trinidad on the 17th of April, 1826, in the *Duke of York* brigantine, and proceeded to Dominica, where it was transhipped to the *Jupiter* transport. Captain Myers proceeded in charge of it to England, where it was inspected by Major-General Sir James Lyon, and it finally arrived at Sierra Leone on August 16th, 1826. Captain Myers having obtained sick leave in England, Captain Stewart, Lieutenant Brennan, and Ensign Russell, were the officers who had charge of the company.

The recruiting was so successfully carried on, that on July 9th, 1827, 73 recruits joined the head-quarters of the regiment at Trinidad; on December 27th, 1828, 182; and on February 28th, 1829, 39; the last being volunteers from the Royal African Corps. In 1829, Captain Evans and Lieutenant Montgomery proceeded to Sierra Leone to join the recruiting company.

The recruiting company continued being occupied with its peace duties until the year 1831, when the Barra War broke out. Towards the end of September, 1831, the Lieutenant-Governor of the Gambia Settlements sent an urgent despatch for assistance to the Governor of Sierra Leone. The news arrived at the latter place on October 1st, and on the 4th a force under Captain Stewart, 1st West India Regiment, consisting of detachments from the recruiting companies of the 1st and 2nd West India Regiments, from the Sierra Leone Militia, and from the Royal African Corps, sailed for the Gambia in H.M. brig *Plumper*, and the *Parmilia* transport. The events which led to this movement were as follows:

In August, 1831, disturbances having occurred amongst the Mandingoes[43] living in the neighbourhood of Fort Bullen, Barra Point, Ensign Fearon, of the Royal African Corps, by direction of Lieutenant-

Governor Rendall, had proceeded with thirty men of his corps and a few pensioners, on the night of August 22nd, to the stockaded town of Essaw, or Yahassu, the capital of Barra, to demand hostages from the king. At Essaw this small force was attacked by a large body of Mandingoes, and compelled to retire to Fort Bullen, to which place the victorious Mandingoes advanced, completely investing it on the land side. The day following, Ensign Fearon, having lost twenty-three men out of his little force, evacuated the work, which was in an almost defenceless condition, and retired across the river to the town of Bathurst. After this defeat the chiefs of the neighbouring Mohammedan towns sent large contingents of men to the King of Barra; several thousand armed natives were collected at a distance of three miles only from Bathurst, and that settlement was in such imminent danger that the Lieutenant-Governor was compelled to send to Sierra Leone for assistance.

On November 9th the reinforcements arrived in the Gambia, and found Fort Bullen still in the hands of the natives, who fortunately had confined themselves to making mere demonstrations, instead of falling upon the settlement, which lay entirely at their mercy. On the morning of November 11th a landing was effected at Barra Point by the force, consisting of 451 of all ranks, under cover of a heavy fire from H.M. brig *Plumper* (Lieutenant Cresey), the *Parmilia* transport, and an armed colonial schooner. The enemy, estimated at from 2500 to 3000 strong, were skilfully covered from the fire of the shipping by the entrenchments which they had thrown up, and from which, as well as from the shelter of the dense bush and high grass, they poured in a heavy and well-sustained fire upon the troops who were landing in their front. Notwithstanding all disadvantages, however, the British pushed on, and, after an hour's hard fighting, during which the enemy contested every inch of ground, they succeeded in driving them from their entrenchments at the point of the bayonet, and pursued them for some distance through the bush. The British loss in this action was 2 killed, 3 officers[44] and 47 men wounded.

The next few days were occupied in landing the guns, and placing Fort Bullen in a state of defence; and at daybreak on the morning of November 17th the entire force marched to the attack of Essaw, the king's town, leaving the crew of H.M. brig *Plumper*, under Lieutenant Cresey, in charge of Fort Bullen.

On approaching the vicinity of the town the troops deployed into line, and, the guns having been brought to the front, a heavy fire was opened on the stockade. This was kept up for five hours, and was as vigorously returned by the enemy from their defences, with artillery and small arms. The rockets were brought to bear as soon as possible, and the first one thrown set fire to a house in the town; but the buildings being principally composed of "swish," and the natives having taken the precaution of removing the thatched roofs of the greater number, the rockets produced but little effect, as they could do no injury to the walls. Towards noon some of the enemy were observed leaving the rear of the town, and shortly afterwards a very superior force of natives appeared in the bush on the British right, threatening an attack in flank. A second body was also observed making a lengthened detour on the left, apparently with the intention of attacking the British rear. The men's ammunition being almost exhausted, and the artillery fire, though well sustained, having produced no effect upon the strong stockades which surrounded the town, it was deemed prudent to retire, and the force was accordingly withdrawn to Benty Point, having suffered a loss during the day of 11 killed and 59 wounded. Lieutenant Leigh, of the Sierra Leone militia, and 5 men subsequently died of their wounds.

On December 7th, Lieutenant-Colonel Hingston, Royal African Corps, arrived with reinforcements and assumed the command. Immediately upon this accession to the British strength, the King of Barra notified his desire to open negotiations, and, terms being proposed which he accepted, a treaty was finally concluded and signed at Fort Bullen on January 4th, 1832. The detachment of the recruiting company, 1st West India Regiment, returned to Sierra Leone on the conclusion of the war.

In the West Indies, the detachment of the 1st West India Regiment stationed at Barbados, had, in 1831, suffered from a violent hurricane which visited that island on the 10th of August of that year. The barracks and hospitals at St. Ann's were completely ruined, 36 men of various corps were killed, and a commissariat officer, with three of his children, and his entire household, entombed in the ruins of his house.

An officer of the garrison, who gives an account of this hurricane,[45] says: "Describe the appearance of our barracks, I really cannot. This I can say, in truth, that in no part of the world, a more beautiful range of buildings, or on a more liberal scale or appropriate site, could have been found. The establishment was complete in all respects for every branch of a small army. It was the depôt of our West India military possessions. Well—in two hours during this awful night almost every building in the garrison was destroyed.... What a moment was that, when, thanks be to Heaven, the gale in some degree abated. The officers crept out one after the other, and the scene that followed can be compared only to that which one sees and feels after an action—who has escaped?—who is dead?... The first person I found wounded was Mrs. Brocklass, the lady of an officer of the 1st West India Regiment, who, with three fine children, finding the roof over them falling, hastened from under it. She had the misfortune to be knocked down by some shingles, received a blow on the head, and had two or three ribs broken; the children fortunately escaped: her husband was on duty in a most perilous situation.... The huts which were the quarters of the married people of the 1st West India Regiment were blown to pieces, and four men and one woman severely injured. The north building of the men's new barracks accommodated the left wing of the 36th Regiment, besides which a detachment of the 1st West India Regiment was quartered on the ground floor. None of the latter were hurt, but two men of the 36th were killed. The greater part of the spacious galleries was carried away, some of the arches that supported them fell, and many were very much broken. None of the roof remains that will ever be of service."

Towards the end of the year 1832, numerous complaints were made by native traders who were in the habit of trading to the Sherbro and the adjacent territories, that they were molested and their goods plundered by a marauding party of Mohammedan Acoos, who had established themselves in the vicinity of the Ribbie River. These Acoos were liberated Africans, that is, slaves who had been set free from captured slavers at Freetown, Sierra Leone, and had, contrary to the regulations then in force, clandestinely left the Colony.

A party of volunteers, having been despatched to gather information concerning these rebels, ascertained that they had been joined by other parties of marauders, and had established themselves at a place called Cobolo, on the northern bank of the Kates, or Ribbie River. The manager of the Waterloo District also reported various outrages and depredations committed by this band.

On December 13th, 1832, the Hastings company of volunteers, with that of Waterloo, marched from the village of Waterloo towards Cobolo, distant by road some thirty miles, with orders to capture and bring in the leaders of the rebels. Next morning, as this force was approaching Cobolo, the Acoos, who were concealed in the bush, fired upon the head of the column, and the volunteers at once, and without firing a shot, turned and ran in the greatest confusion; nor did they recover from their panic till they had reached Waterloo. The Acoos pursued the fugitives for some little distance, and killed seven of their number.

The rising, originally trivial, had now, through the shameful behaviour of the volunteers, become serious. The news of the defeat spread with great rapidity among the unruly tribes on the frontier of the Colony; and a Mohammedan priest, proclaiming himself a prophet, placed himself at the head of the movement. The Governor acted with promptitude; and recognising the great danger of delay, despatched, on December 17th, all the available men from the garrison of Sierra Leone, under Lieut.-Colonel

Hingston, Royal African Corps. The recruiting company of the 1st West India Regiment accompanied the force, under the command of Lieut. W. Montgomery, 1st West India Regiment.

The troops proceeded to Waterloo in boats, and were there joined by the Wellington company of the Sierra Leone militia, and the Hastings company of volunteers. At the same time, H.M. brig *Charybdis* (Lieut. Crawford) was sent with the York company of volunteers to the mouth of the Ribbie River, with orders for the seamen and marines to ascend the river in boats, co-operate with Lieut.-Colonel Hingston's column, and cut off the retreat of the rebels.

Lieut.-Colonel Hingston's force marched from Waterloo on December 18th, and, halting for the night at Bangowilli, about twenty miles from the former village, advanced towards Cobolo next morning at daybreak. The march was unusually fatiguing, and for many miles the troops had to move through rush beds and mangrove swamps, frequently up to the hips in mud and water. On emerging upon the dry ground near Cobolo the report of fire-arms was heard in front, and scouts being thrown forward, it was learned that the Kossoos, which tribe had suffered most from the predatory propensities of the rebels, had taken up arms and were then engaged in attacking Cobolo. The troops at once pushed on, and a few minutes after their arrival on the scene, the Acoos, completely routed, fled in all directions, many being killed and a great number drowned while endeavouring to escape across a neighbouring creek.

The British force remained at Cobolo for four days, daily sending out small parties in pursuit of the dispersed rebels. By one of these parties Oji Corri, the leader of the movement, was shot down; and the rebellion being at an end the troops returned to Freetown, Sierra Leone, on December 28th; a detachment of the 2nd West India Regiment, under Lieutenant Lardner, being left at Waterloo to watch the movements of the Mohammedan Acoos in the neighbouring villages.

Lieutenant Montgomery, 1st West India Regiment, died at Freetown of fever, on April 9th, 1833, and this event left the recruiting company without an officer of the corps until the arrival in Sierra Leone of Captain Hughes on November 29th, 1834.

In the West Indies one company had been removed from the head-quarters at Trinidad to Tortola in May, 1834, and this detachment was, in January, 1836, moved to St. Vincent.

FOOTNOTES:

[43] The Mandingoes are a warlike Mohammedan tribe, inhabiting the territory inland from the Gambia River to Sierra Leone.

[44] Captain Berwick, Royal African Corps; Lieutenant Lardner, 2nd West India Regiment; and Captain Hughes, Gambia Militia.

[45] An account of the fatal hurricane by which Barbados suffered in 1831, published at Bridgetown, Barbados, 1831.

"Detachment 1st West India Regiment.

"Return of the men killed and wounded during the late hurricane, 15th August, 1831:

"Killed—Henry Read, private.

"Wounded—4 privates.

(Signed)   "H. BROCKLASS, Lieut., 1st W.I. Regt."

CHAPTER XVII
THE MUTINY OF THE RECRUITS
AT TRINIDAD, 1837

On April 1st, 1836, the 1st West India Regiment was increased from eight to ten companies, and recruits being obtained with difficulty, the Government commenced the injudicious practice of enrolling the slaves, disembarked from captured slavers, in the West India regiments. In September of that year the slaves from two slavers which had been captured off Grenada by H.M.S. *Vestal*, 112 in number, were drafted into the 1st West India Regiment. Similarly, in January, 1837, 109; on May 20th, 112; and on May 21st, 93 slaves, recently disembarked from slavers captured by H.M.S. *Griffon* and *Harpy*, were sent to the regiment. Thus, in the years 1836-7, 426 such slaves were received, 314 of them in the year 1837 alone.

The formality of asking these men whether they were willing to serve was never gone through, many of them did so unwillingly; and it must be remembered that they were all savages in the strictest sense of the word, entirely unacquainted with civilisation, and with no knowledge of the English language. The majority of them were natives of the Congo and of Great and Little Popo, two towns on the western frontier of Dahomey; and it may be here remarked that the negroes of these districts have maintained their reputation for ultra-barbarism even to the present day.

The only result to be anticipated from such a wholesale drafting of savages into a regiment was a mutiny, and every inducement to mutiny appears to have been afforded them. Instead of dividing them proportionately between the head-quarters and the detachments, they were nearly all kept at the former; and but three weeks before the actual rising, as if to further remove all check, 100 rank and file, all old soldiers, were sent from Trinidad and distributed between St. Lucia and Dominica. Thus, on June 18th, 1837, the day of the mutiny, with the exception of the band, officers servants, and mess-waiters, all the men at San Josef's barracks, Trinidad, were slaver recruits. The ringleader of the movement was one Dâaga, or Donald Stewart, and the following account of him, and of the mutiny, is taken from Kingsley's "At Last":

"Donald Stewart, or rather Dâaga, was the adopted son of Madershee, the old and childless king of the tribe called Paupaus,[46] a race that inhabit a tract of country bordering on that of the Yarrabas.[47] These races are constantly at war with each other.

"Dâaga was just the man whom a savage, warlike, and depredatory tribe would select for their chieftain, as the African negroes choose their leaders with reference to their personal prowess. Dâaga stood six feet six inches without shoes. Although scarcely muscular in proportion, yet his frame indicated in a singular degree the union of irresistible strength and activity.... He had a singular cast in his eyes, not quite amounting to that obliquity of the visual organs denominated a squint, but sufficient to give his features a peculiarly forbidding appearance; his forehead, however, although small in proportion to his enormous head, was remarkably compact and well formed. The whole head was disproportioned, having the greater part of the brain behind the ears; but the greatest peculiarity of this singular being was his voice. In the course of my life I never heard such sounds uttered by human organs as those formed by Dâaga. In ordinary conversation he appeared to me to endeavour to soften his voice—it was a deep tenor: but when a little excited by any passion (and this savage was the child of passion) his voice sounded like the low growl of a lion, but when much excited it could be compared to nothing so aptly as the notes of a gigantic brazen trumpet.

"Dâaga having made a successful predatory expedition into the country of the Yarrabas, returned with a number of prisoners of that nation. These he, as usual, took bound and guarded towards the coast to sell to the Portuguese. The interpreter, his countryman, called these Portuguese 'white gentlemen.' The white gentlemen proved themselves more than a match for the black gentlemen; and the whole transaction between the Portuguese and the Paupaus does credit to all concerned in this gentlemanly traffic in human flesh.

"Dâaga sold his prisoners, and under pretence of paying him, he and his Paupau guards were enticed on board a Portuguese vessel: they were treacherously overpowered by the Christians, who bound them beside their late prisoners, and the vessel sailed over 'the great salt water.'

"This transaction caused in the breast of the savage a deep hatred against all white men; a hatred so intense that he frequently, during and subsequent to the mutiny, declared he would eat the first white man he killed; yet this cannibal was made to swear allegiance to our sovereign on the Holy Evangelists, and was then called a British soldier.

"On the voyage the vessel on board which Dâaga had been entrapped was captured by the British. He could not comprehend that his new captors liberated him: he had been overreached and trepanned by one set of white men, and he naturally looked on his second captors as more successful rivals in the human, or rather inhuman, Guinea trade; therefore, this event lessened not his hatred for white men in the abstract.

"I was informed by several of the Africans who came with him, that when, during the voyage, they upbraided Dâaga with being the cause of their capture, he pacified them by promising that when they should arrive in white man's country he would repay their perfidy by attacking them in the night. He further promised that if the Paupaus and Yarrabas would follow him, he would fight his way back to Guinea. This account was fully corroborated by many of the mutineers, especially those who were shot with Dâaga; they all said the revolt never would have happened but for Donald Stewart, as he was called by the officers; but Africans who were not of his tribe called him Longa-longa, on account of his height.

"Such was the extraordinary man who led the mutiny I am about to relate.

"A quantity of captured Africans having been brought hither from the islands of Grenada and Dominica, they were most imprudently induced to enlist in the 1st West India Regiment. True it is, we have been told they did this voluntarily; but it may be asked, if they had any will in the matter, how could they understand the duties to be imposed on them by becoming soldiers, or how comprehend the nature of an oath of allegiance, without which they could not, legally speaking, be considered soldiers? I attended the whole of the trials of these men, and well know how difficult it was to make them comprehend any idea which was at all new to them by means of the best interpreters procurable.

"To the African savage, while being drilled into the duties of a soldier, many things seem absolute tyranny which would appear to a civilised man a mere necessary restraint. To keep the restless body of an African negro in a position to which he has not been accustomed; to cramp his splay feet, with his great toes standing out, into European shoes made for feet of a different form; to place a collar round his neck, which is called a stock, and which to him is cruel torture; above all, to confine him every night to his barracks— are almost insupportable. One unacquainted with the habits of the negro cannot conceive with what abhorrence he looks on having his disposition to nocturnal rambles checked by barrack regulations.

"Formerly the 'King's man,' as the black soldier loved to call himself, looked (not without reason) contemptuously on the planter's slave, although he himself was after all but a slave to the State; but these recruits were enlisted shortly after a number of their recently imported countrymen were wandering freely over the country, working either as free labourers, or settling, to use an apt American phrase, as squatters; and to assert that the recruit, while under military probation, is better off than the free Trinidad labourer, who goes where he lists and earns as much in one day as will keep him for three days, is an absurdity. Accordingly, we find that Lieutenant-Colonel Bush, who commanded the 1st West India Regiment, thought that the mutiny was mainly owing to the ill-advice of their civil, or, we should rather say, unmilitary countrymen. This, to a certain degree, was the fact; but, by the declaration of Dâaga and many of his countrymen, it is evident that the seeds of the mutiny were sown on the passage from Africa.

"It has been asserted that the recruits were driven to mutiny by hard treatment of their commanding officers. There seems not the slightest truth in this assertion; they were treated with fully as much kindness as their situation would admit of, and their chief was peculiarly a favourite of Colonel Bush and the officers, notwithstanding Dâaga's violent and ferocious temper often caused complaints to be brought against him.

"On the night of the 17th of June, 1837, the people of San Josef were kept awake by the recruits, about 280 in number, singing the war-song of the Paupaus. This wild song consisted of a short air and chorus. The tone was, although wild, not inharmonious, and the words rather euphonious. As near as our alphabet can convey them, they ran thus:

"Dangkarrée
Au fey
Oluu werrei
Au lay.

which may be rendered almost literally by the following couplet:

"Air by the chief: 'Come to plunder, come to slay.'
"Chorus by followers: 'We are ready to obey.'

"About three o'clock in the morning, their war-song (highly characteristic of a predatory tribe) became very loud, and they commenced uttering their war-cry. This is different to what we conceive the Indian war-whoop to be; it seems to be a kind of imitation of the growl of wild beasts, and has a most thrilling effect.

"Fire was now set to a quantity of huts built for the accommodation of African soldiers to the northward of the barracks, as well as to the house of a poor black woman called Dalrymple. These burnt briskly, throwing a dismal glare over the barracks and picturesque town of San Josef, and overpowering the light of the full moon, which illumined a cloudless sky. The mutineers made a rush at the barrack-room and seized on the muskets and fusees in the racks. Their leader, Dâaga, and a daring Yarraba named Ogston, instantly charged their pieces—the former of these had a quantity of ball cartridges, loose powder, and ounce and pistol balls, in a kind of gray worsted cap. He must have provided himself with these before the mutiny. How he became possessed of them, especially the pistol balls, I never could learn; probably he was supplied by his unmilitary countrymen; pistol balls are never given to infantry. Previous to this Dâaga and three others made a rush at the regimental store-room, in which was deposited a quantity of powder. An old African soldier, named Charles Dixon, interfered to stop them, on which Maurice Ogston, the Yarraba chief, who had armed himself with a sergeant's sword, cut down the faithful African. When down, Dâaga said in English, 'Ah, you old soldier, you knock down.' Dixon was not Dâaga's countryman, hence he could not speak to him in his own language. The Paupau then levelled his musket and shot the fallen soldier, who groaned and died. The war-yells, or rather growls, of the Paupaus and Yarrabas now became awfully thrilling as they helped themselves to cartridges; most of them were fortunately blank, or without ball. Never was a premeditated mutiny so wild and ill-planned. Their chief, Dâaga, and Ogston, seem to have had little command of the subordinates, and the whole acted more like a set of wild beasts who had broken their cages, than men resolved on war.

"At this period, had a rush been made at the officers' quarters by one half (they were more than 200 in number), and the other half surrounded the building, not one could have escaped. Instead of this they continued to shout their war-song, and howl their war-notes; they loaded their pieces with ball cartridge or blank cartridge and small stones, and commenced firing at the long range of white buildings in which Colonel Bush and his officers slept. They wasted so much ammunition on this useless display of fury that the buildings were completely riddled. A few of the old soldiers opposed them and were wounded, but it fortunately happened that they were, to an inconceivable degree, ignorant of the right use of fire-arms— holding their muskets in their hands when they discharged them, without allowing the butt-end to rest against their shoulders or any part of their bodies.[48] This fact accounts for the comparatively little mischief they did in proportion to the quantity of ammunition thrown away.

"The officers[49] and sergeant-major[50] escaped at the back of the building, while Colonel Bush and Adjutant Bentley came down a little hill. The colonel commanded the mutineers to lay down their arms, and was answered by an irregular discharge of balls, which rattled amongst the leaves of a tree under which he and the adjutant were standing. On this Colonel Bush desired Mr. Bentley to make the best of his way to St. James's Barracks[51] for all the disposable force of the 89th Regiment. The officers made good their retreat, and the adjutant got into the stable where his horse was. He saddled and bridled the animal while the shots were coming into the stable, without either man or beast getting injured. The officer mounted, but had to make his way through the mutineers before he could get into San Josef, the barracks standing on an eminence above the little town. On seeing the adjutant mounted, the mutineers set up a thrilling howl, and commenced firing at him. He discerned the gigantic figure of Dâaga (alias Donald Stewart), with his musket at the trail: he spurred his horse through the midst of them; they were grouped, but not in line. On looking back he saw Dâaga aiming at him; he stooped his head beside his horse's neck, and effectually sheltered himself from about fifty shots aimed at him. In this position he rode furiously down a steep hill leading from the barracks to the church, and was out of danger. His escape appears extraordinary: but he got safe to town, and thence to St. James's, and in a short time, considering it is eleven miles distant, brought out a strong detachment of European troops; these, however, did not arrive till the affair was over.

"In the meantime a part of the officers' quarters was bravely defended by two old African soldiers, Sergeant Merry and Corporal Plague. The latter stood in the gallery near the room in which were the colours; he was ineffectually fired at by some hundreds, yet he kept his post, shot two of the mutineers, and, it is said, wounded a third. Such is the difference between a man acquainted with the use of fire-arms and those who handle them as mops are held.

"In the meantime Colonel Bush got to a police station above the barracks, and got muskets and a few cartridges from a discharged African soldier who was in the police establishment. Being joined by the policeman, Corporal Craven, and Ensign Pogson, they concealed themselves on an eminence above, and, as the mutineers (about 100 in number) approached, the fire of muskets opened on them from the little ambush. The little party fired separately, loading as fast as they discharged their pieces; they succeeded in making the mutineers change their route.

"It is wonderful what little courage the savages in general showed against the colonel and his little party, who absolutely beat them, although but a twenty-fifth of their number, and at their own tactics, *i.e.* bush fighting.

"A body of mutineers now made towards the road to Maraccas, when the colonel and his three assistants contrived to get behind a silk-cotton tree, and recommenced firing on them. The Africans hesitated, and set forward, when the little party continued to fire on them; they set up a yell, and retreated down the hill.

"A part of the mutineers now concealed themselves in the bushes about San Josef Barracks. These men, after the affair was over, joined Colonel Bush, and, with a mixture of cunning and effrontery, smiled as though nothing had happened, and as though they were glad to see him; although, in general, they each had several shirts and pairs of trousers on, preparatory for a start to Guinea, by way of Band de l'Est.

"In the meantime the San Josef militia were assembled to the number of forty. Major Giuseppi and Captain and Adjutant Rousseau, of the second division of militia forces, took command of them. They were in want of flints, powder, and balls; to obtain these they were obliged to break open a merchant's store; however, the adjutant so judiciously distributed his little force as to hinder the mutineers from entering the town or obtaining access to the militia arsenal, wherein there was a quantity of arms. Major Chadds and several old African soldiers joined the militia, and were by them supplied with arms.

"A good deal of skirmishing occurred between the militia and detached parties of the mutineers, which uniformly ended in the defeat of the latter. At length Dâaga appeared to the right of a party of six at the entrance of the town; they were challenged by the militia, and the mutineers fired on them, but without effect. Only two of the militia returned the fire, when all but Dâaga fled. He was deliberately reloading his piece, when a militia-man, named Edmond Luce, leaped on the gigantic chief, who would have easily beat him off, although the former was a strong young man of colour, but Dâaga would not let go his gun; and, in common with all the mutineers, he seemed to have no idea of the use of the bayonet. Dâaga was dragging the militia-man away, when Adjutant Rousseau came to his assistance, and placed a sword to Dâaga's breast. Doctor Tardy and several others rushed on the tall negro, who was soon, by the united efforts of several, thrown down and secured. It was at this period that he repeatedly exclaimed, while he bit his own shoulder, 'The first white man I catch after this I will eat him.'

"Meanwhile about sixteen of the mutineers, led by the daring Ogston, took the road to Arima, in order, as they said, to commence their march to Guinea; but fortunately the militia of that village, composed principally of Spaniards, Indians, and Sambos, assembled. A few of these met them and stopped their march. A kind of parley (if intercourse carried on by signs could be so called) was carried on between the parties. The mutineers made signs that they wished to go forward, while the few militia-men endeavoured to detain them, expecting a reinforcement momently. After a time the militia agreed to allow them to approach the town; as they were advancing they were met by the Commandant, Martin Sorzano, Esq., with sixteen more militia-men. The Commandant judged it imprudent to allow the Africans to enter the town with their muskets full-cocked, and poised ready to fire. An interpreter was now procured, and the mutineers were told that if they would retire to their barracks the gentlemen present would intercede for their pardon. The negroes refused to accede to these terms; and while the interpreter was addressing some, the rest tried to push forward. Some of the militia opposed them by holding their muskets in a horizontal position, on which one of the mutineers fired, and the militia returned the fire. A mêlée commenced, in which fourteen mutineers were killed and wounded. The fire of the Africans produced little effect: they soon took to flight amid the woods which flanked the road. Twenty-eight of them were taken, amongst whom was the Yarraba chief, Ogston. Six had been killed, and six committed suicide by strangling and hanging themselves in the woods. Only one man was wounded among the militia, and he but slightly, from a small stone fired from a musket of one of the Yarrabas.

"The quantity of ammunition expended by the mutineers, and the comparatively little mischief done by them, was truly astonishing. It shows how little they understood the use of fire-arms. Dixon was killed, and several of the old African soldiers were wounded, but not one of the officers was in the slightest degree hurt.

"I have never been able to get a correct account of the number of lives this wild mutiny cost, but believe it was not less than forty, including those slain by the militia at Arima, those shot at San Josef, those who died of their wounds (and most of the wounded men died), the six who committed suicide, the three who were shot by sentence of the court-martial, and one who was shot while endeavouring to escape (Satchell).

"A good-looking young man, named Torrens, was brought as prisoner to the presence of Colonel Bush. The colonel wished to speak to him, and desired his guards to liberate him; on which the young savage shook his sleeve, in which was a concealed razor, made a rush at the colonel, and nearly succeeded in cutting his throat. He slashed the razor in all directions until he made an opening; he rushed through this: and notwithstanding that he was fired at, and, I believe, wounded, he effected his escape, was subsequently retaken, and again made his escape with Satchell, who after this was shot by a policeman.

"Torrens was retaken, tried, and recommended to mercy. Of this man's fate I am unable to speak, not knowing how far the recommendation to mercy was attended to.[52] In appearance he seemed the mildest and best-looking of the mutineers, but his conduct was the most ferocious of any. The whole of the mutineers were captured within one week of the mutiny, save this man, who was taken a month after.

"On the 19th of July, Donald Stewart, otherwise Dâaga, was brought to a court-martial. On the 21st, William Satchell was tried. On the 22nd, a court-martial was held on Edward Coffin; and on the 24th one was held on the Yarraba chief, Maurice Ogston, whose country name was, I believe, Mawee. Torrens was tried on the 29th.

"The sentences of these courts-martial were unknown until the 14th of August, having been sent to Barbados in order to be submitted to the Commander-in-Chief. Lieutenant-General Whittingham, who approved of the decision of the courts, which was that Donald Stewart (Dâaga), Maurice Ogston, and Edward Coffin, should suffer death by being shot; and that William Satchell should be transported beyond seas during the term of his natural life. I am unacquainted with the sentence of Torrens.

"Donald Stewart, Maurice Ogston, and Edward Coffin were executed on the 16th of August, 1837, at San Josef Barracks. Nothing seemed to have been neglected which could render the execution solemn and impressive; the scenery and the weather gave additional awe to the melancholy proceedings. Fronting the little eminence where the prisoners were shot was the scene where their ill-concerted mutiny commenced. To the right stood the long range of building on which they had expended much of their ammunition for the purpose of destroying their officers. The rest of the panorama was made up of an immense view of forest below them, and upright masses of mountains above them. Over these, heavy bodies of mist were slowly sailing, giving a sombre appearance to the primeval woods which, in general, covered both mountains and plains. The atmosphere indicated an inter-tropical morning during the rainy season, and the sun shone resplendently between dense columns of clouds.

"At half-past seven o'clock the condemned men asked to be allowed to eat a hearty meal, as they said persons about to be executed in Guinea were always indulged with a good repast. It is remarkable that these unhappy creatures ate most voraciously, even while they were being brought out of their cell for execution.

"A little before the mournful procession commenced, the condemned men were dressed from head to foot in white habiliments trimmed with black; their arms were bound with cords. This is not usual in military executions, but was deemed necessary on the present occasion. An attempt to escape on the part of the condemned would have been productive of much confusion, and was properly guarded against.

"The condemned men displayed no unmanly fear. On the contrary, they steadily kept step to the Dead March which the band played; yet the certainty of death threw a cadaverous and ghastly hue over their black features, while their singular and appropriate costume, and the three coffins being borne before them, altogether rendered it a frightful picture; hence it was not to be wondered at that two European soldiers fainted.

"The mutineers marched abreast. The tall form and horrid looks of Dâaga were almost appalling. The looks of Ogston were sullen, calm, and determined; those of Coffin seemed to indicate resignation.

"At eight o'clock they arrived at the spot where three graves were dug; here their coffins were deposited. The condemned men were made to face to westward; three sides of a hollow square were formed, flanked on one side by a detachment of the 89th Regiment and a party of artillery, while the recruits, many of whom shared the guilt of the culprits, were appropriately placed in the line opposite them. The firing party were a little in advance of the recruits.

"The sentence of the courts-martial and other necessary documents having been read by the fort adjutant, Mr. Meehan, the chaplain of the forces, read some prayers appropriated for these melancholy occasions. The clergyman then shook hands with the three men about to be sent into another state of existence. Dâaga and Ogston coolly gave their hands; Coffin wrang the chaplain's hand affectionately, saying, in tolerable English, 'I am now done with the world.'

"The arms of the condemned men, as has been before stated, were bound, but in such a manner as to allow them to bring their hands to their heads. Their nightcaps were drawn over their eyes. Coffin allowed his to remain, but Ogston and Dâaga pushed theirs up again. The former did this calmly; the latter showed great wrath, seeming to think himself insulted; and his deep, metallic voice sounded in anger above that of the provost-marshal, as the latter gave the words, 'Ready! present!' But at this instant his vociferous daring forsook him. As the men levelled their muskets at him, with inconceivable rapidity he sprang bodily round, still preserving his squatting posture, and received the fire from behind; while the less noisy, but more brave, Ogston, looked the firing-party full in the face as they discharged their fatal volley.

"In one instant all three fell dead, almost all the balls of the firing party having taken effect.[53] The savage appearance and manner of Dâaga excited awe. Admiration was felt for the calm bravery of Ogston, while Edward Coffin's fate excited commiseration.

"There were many spectators of this dreadful scene, and amongst others a great concourse of negroes. Most of these expressed their hopes that after this terrible example the recruits would make good soldiers."

The foregoing account is identical with that in the regimental records, with the exception that the Yorubas are not in the latter credited with so large a share in the mutiny. According to Colonel Bush's account, the greater majority of the mutineers were Popos, Congos, and Eboes; the Yorubas who took part in it being very few in number. On the other hand, both Sergeant Merry and Corporal Plague, who defended the officers' quarters against the recruits, were Yorubas.

It is, perhaps, needless to add, that after this no more wholesale draftings of slaves into the regiment took place.

FOOTNOTES:

[46] Now spelt Popos.

[47] The Yorubas are a warlike Mohammedan tribe living in and around Lagos. The Houssa Constabulary is largely recruited from them.

[48] This is the manner in which West African savages usually fire, and it is dictated by motives of sound prudence, for the Birmingham muskets with which they are supplied by British traders are so unsafe (the barrel not uncommonly being made of old iron piping), and the charges of powder used are so immense, that the bursting of a piece is looked upon as an ordinary occurrence; and when firing they like to keep their muskets as far removed from their bodies as possible. The majority of the mutineers fired in this manner, because, having been less than three weeks in the regiment, they had not yet been drilled with arms.

[49] All young ensigns just arrived from England to join the regiment.

[50] Sergeant-Major D. Cantrell. He had been the first to give the alarm.

[51] Eleven miles distant from San Josef.

[52] Torrens was sentenced to death, but, at the intercession of Colonel Bush, the sentence was commuted to imprisonment for life.

[53] The firing party was furnished by the 1st West India Regiment.

CHAPTER XVIII
THE PIRARA EXPEDITION, 1842—CHANGES IN THE WEST AFRICAN GARRISONS— THE APPOLLONIA EXPEDITION, 1848

On the 7th of December, 1837, the head-quarters of the 1st West India Regiment embarked at Trinidad for St. Lucia, leaving one company at St. James' in the former island; and, after a detention of ten days in quarantine at Pigeon Island, landed on the 24th of December at Gros Islet, St. Lucia, and occupied Morne Fortune Barracks and Fort. The detachments were stationed in Tobago, Demerara, and St. Vincent.

In the early part of the year 1839, the strength of the regiment being very much above its establishment, owing to the large drafts of recruits from Sierra Leone, Lieutenant-General Sir S.F. Whittingham issued an order, dated February 1st, authorising an augmentation to twelve companies. On the 1st of July of the same year the regiment was further increased to thirteen companies, it being notified at the same time that it was to be considered only a temporary arrangement, as the surplus over 1000 men were eventually to form another corps.

On December 7th, 1839, the head-quarters of the regiment proceeded from St. Lucia to Demerara, to relieve the 76th Regiment, which was suffering heavily from the prevailing epidemic of yellow fever, arriving at the latter colony, under the command of Lieutenant-Colonel Capadose, on December 13th. The distribution of the regiment was then: Head-quarters and 2 companies at Demerara, 3 companies at Barbados, 1 at Trinidad, 1 at Tobago, 1 at St. Lucia, 1 at St. Vincent, 1 at Grenada, 1 at Dominica, and 1 at Antigua.

By Horse Guards order of the 1st of July, 1840, the Royal African Corps and the three supernumerary companies of the 1st West India Regiment were formed into one corps, and designated the 3rd West India Regiment; the 1st West India Regiment remaining at the ordinary establishment of ten companies.

New colours were presented to the regiment at Demerara on May 24th, 1841.

In September and October of the same year a violent epidemic of yellow fever broke out in Demerara, and the mortality amongst the men of the 52nd Regiment was so alarming that that corps was moved to Berbice, and the entire duties of the garrison fell upon the 1st West India Regiment. The whole of the officers of the 52nd Regiment occupying the west wing of the Georgetown Barracks fell victims to this dreadful scourge, as did Captain French and Lieutenants de Winton and Archdale of the 1st West India Regiment.

On the 11th of January, 1842, a detachment of the regiment, consisting of two lieutenants (Bingham and Wieburg), two sergeants and twenty-seven rank and file, left Georgetown, Demerara, by direction of the Under-Secretary of State for the Colonies (Lord John Russell), to proceed to Pirara, on the south-western frontier of British Guiana, and expel a party of Brazilians who had for some time encroached on British territory. The country through which the party had to pass was unexplored and almost unknown, and the duties were most arduous. It was intended to reach Pirara by ascending the Essequibo and Rypumani Rivers, and, to effect this, a particular description of boat, locally called *corials*, had to be built, each capable of holding eight men, including the Indians who paddled. During the journey seventy-three rapids or falls were crossed, in most instances the *corials* being unladen and the stores carried above the falls; and it was not until February 12th that Lieutenant Bingham's party reached a point on the Rypumani, eleven miles from Pirara. Next day they took possession of the village of Pirara, which they found occupied by a detachment of Brazilian troops who had been quietly sent over the border. Having selected and fortified a position, and raised temporary shelter for his men, Lieutenant Bingham—as the Brazilian commander declined to withdraw—despatched Lieutenant Bush, 1st West India Regiment, who had accompanied the party as a volunteer, to Georgetown for further instructions. That officer arrived there on March 11th, and on April 19th he again started with a small reinforcement under Ensign Stewart. This second party reached Pirara on May 21st, and found the detachment all well, but half-starved, as the Brazilians refused to sell them anything, and the stores had been some time exhausted. However, on the arrival of the reinforcement the Brazilian troops considered it advisable to withdraw across the frontier; and, with the exception of a few occasional night forays made by half-breeds and Indians in the pay of the Brazilians, the detachment met with no further opposition.

In 1843 it was decided to make an alteration in the system under which the West Coast of Africa was continuously garrisoned by the 3rd West India Regiment, and to remove that corps to the West Indies. The West African garrisons were to be composed of two companies from each of the three West India regiments; and, in accordance with this scheme, two companies of the 1st West India Regiment, under Captain L.S. O'Connor, embarked at Barbados for Sierra Leone on March 22nd, 1843, arriving at the latter place in the month of May of the same year. Early in 1844 the 3rd West India Regiment left West Africa for the Bahamas, and the two companies of the 1st West India Regiment, with one of the 3rd West India Regiment, composed the garrison of Sierra Leone, while that of the Gambia consisted of two companies of the 2nd West India Regiment and one of the 3rd. This arrangement was almost at once upset by the necessity of furnishing a garrison for the Gold Coast, over which the Crown had, in 1843, resumed jurisdiction, as it was suspected that the Government of the merchants, which had been established at Cape Coast Castle since 1831, connived at the maintenance of the slave trade; and, in January, 1844, one captain, two subalterns, and 100 men of the 1st West India Regiment left Sierra Leone for the Gold Coast.

In the same year, two companies of the regiment, under the command of Captain Robeson, proceeded from Demerara to Jamaica, disembarking there on June 1st. This was the first occasion on which any portion of the corps was stationed in that island.

On the 25th of February, 1845, the head-quarters, with the Grenadier and No. 8 Companies, embarked at Demerara in the *Princess Royal* transport, and sailed for Jamaica, to relieve the head-quarters of the 2nd West India Regiment ordered to Nassau, disembarking at Port Royal on March 6th. The distribution of the regiment was then as follows: The Grenadier, No. 1, No. 8, and the Light Company in Jamaica,[54] No. 5 at Demerara, No. 2 at Trinidad, No. 3 at Dominica, No. 6 at Grenada, No. 4 at Sierra Leone, and No. 7 at Cape Coast Castle. During the last six months of this year (1845) over 300 recruits joined the head-quarters from West Africa.

In 1846, No. 5 Company was removed from Demerara to Tobago, and the detachments at Dominica and Grenada rejoined head-quarters in Jamaica, where No. 2 and No. 5 Companies also rejoined on the 16th of December, 1847.[55]

In the beginning of the year 1848, the King of Appollonia, a state on the western frontier of the Gold Coast Colony, closed the roads leading to Cape Coast Castle, stopped all trade, and maltreated several British subjects.

Messengers were sent to him by the Lieutenant-Governor demanding explanation and redress, with no other result than the detention and imprisonment of the messengers; and matters were at last brought to a crisis by the murder of the French Commandant of Assinee and his boat's crew, the pillaging of Dutch canoes at Axim, and the capture of some Dutch subjects.

The only force Mr. Winniett, the Lieutenant-Governor of the Gold Coast, had at his disposal was No. 7 Company of the 1st West India Regiment, then commanded by Lieutenant E.H. Bingham; but, with the assistance of some influential merchants, he succeeded in raising an expeditionary force of from 4000 to 5000 natives. On the 24th of March, 1848, the Lieutenant-Governor marched, with half the native levies and the company of the 1st West India Regiment, from Cape Coast Castle to the then Dutch settlement of Axim, 120 miles distant from Cape Coast and about twenty miles from Atemboo, or Attaambu, the King of Appollonia's chief town and residence. By the 3rd of April the whole force was concentrated at Axim, and on the 6th, at 5 a.m., it moved onwards towards Appollonia.

The country consisting of impenetrable forest, the force had to march from Axim to Appollonia along the sandy beach; and there were the mouths of two considerable rivers to be crossed. The first river, the Ancobra, was reached at 6 a.m.; and, although a very heavy sea was breaking on the bar, the passage of the stream was commenced in canoes, which had been brought from Axim for that purpose. The first detachment consisted of the native allies, and, as soon as the canoes gained mid-stream, several hundred armed Appollonians appeared on the further bank, and opened fire on them as they came within range. Several natives were struck, and three of the canoes being upset the remainder returned to the bank they had just left.

It being found impracticable to induce the native auxiliaries to make a further attempt to force the passage, this duty devolved upon the company of the 1st West India Regiment, which the Lieutenant-Governor had originally intended holding in reserve; and, under cover of a fire from two rocket-troughs, it crossed the river in the canoes, driving the Appollonians, in spite of a smart resistance, into the bush. The remainder of the force then passed over, several natives being drowned in the surf during the passage; and at 10 a.m. they pushed on, reaching the Appollonian village of Asantah about 1 p.m. This place was found to be deserted, and here the force encamped for the night.

Next morning at daybreak a further advance was made, and about 6 a.m. the Abmoussa River—or, rather, Lagoon—was reached. A very heavy and dangerous surf was breaking on the bar, and the dense bush on the further bank, which grew close down to the water's edge, was observed to be full of armed men.

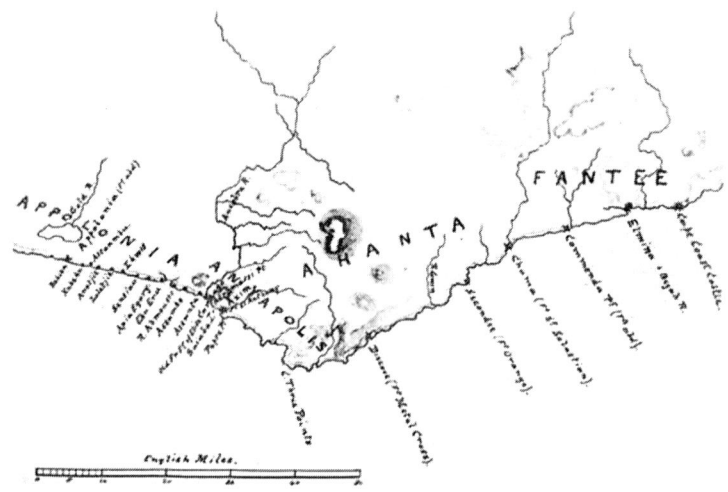

The company of the 1st West India Regiment was again called upon to lead the way, and the men, embarking in the canoes, paddled out into the breakers. A continued and furious fusillade was at once opened by the concealed enemy upon the men, who were unable to reply, as their attention was entirely occupied in keeping the canoes from capsizing. Fortunately, the Appollonians fired wildly, and their powder was of bad quality; for, although almost every man of the detachment was struck by slugs or fragments of iron, only eleven were wounded, and those slightly. A canoe was, however, unhappily upset, and two men beaten against the rocks and drowned. The company formed up on landing, and advanced steadily through the bush against the enemy, who offered but a feeble resistance and soon retired altogether. One man was shot dead while stepping ashore, an ambushed native firing at him at the distance of a few feet only. The native allies now passed over, and the march was continued. Parties of the enemy were observed hovering round the flanks, but no attack was made, and at 3 p.m. a halt was ordered at the village of Barcoo.

The force was here divided into two parts, of which one, consisting entirely of natives, was to move through the bush and prevent the king escaping inland; while the other, consisting of the company of the 1st West India Regiment with the remainder of the native allies, was to march along the beach and attack the town in front. This movement would probably have been successful, had the division of natives performed the duty allotted to them; but, being fired upon by some ambushed Appollonians, they refused to proceed further, and when the company of the 1st West India Regiment reached Atemboo, they found it entirely deserted.

The success which had so far attended the expedition, however, produced such an effect upon the native mind that, on March 9th, the principal chiefs of Appollonia came in to Atemboo to make submission; and, as it was reported that the king was in hiding in the immediate neighbourhood, parties were sent out in search of him. On the 18th his wives and family were captured to the westward, near the old fort, and the day following, a party of the 1st West India Regiment brought in a body of 121 men, all heavily manacled with irons weighing from fifty to ninety pounds, and who had been intended to be sacrificed at an approaching "custom." Two of these men thus unexpectedly saved from a horrible death volunteered to point out where the king was concealed, and some men of the regiment being sent out under their guidance, succeeded in capturing him in his hiding-place, in the midst of a mangrove swamp.

The object of the expedition being accomplished by the capture of the king, the force moved back to Axim, on the 21st of March, and, on the evening of the same day, the Lieutenant-Governor, with the captive king and the company of the 1st West India Regiment, embarked on board the merchant brig *Governor*, arriving at Cape Coast Castle on the 24th.

Lieutenant-Governor Winniett in his despatch says: "I cannot speak too highly of the detachment of the 1st West India Regiment. During its march of more than 120 miles, sometimes through very bad roads, and under the powerful rays of the sun, the crossing of five rivers, and other circumstances of disadvantage, no complaints were heard, neither was a man seen in a state of intoxication during the campaign. Mr. Bingham, the officer commanding the detachment, was most active in executing all orders entrusted to his care, and I have great pleasure in bringing him under your Lordship's notice."

FOOTNOTES:

[54] The companies in Jamaica were detached thus: No. 1, No. 8, and Grenadier Company at Up Park Camp. The Light Company between Port Antonio and Montego Bay.

[55] The distribution in Jamaica then was:

Grenadier, Light, No. 2, and No. 5 Companies at Up Park Camp.
No. 1, at Spanish Town.
No. 8, at Port Royal.
No. 3, at Falmouth   } To

occupy posts vacated

No. 6, at Lucea   }   by the 38th
Regiment.

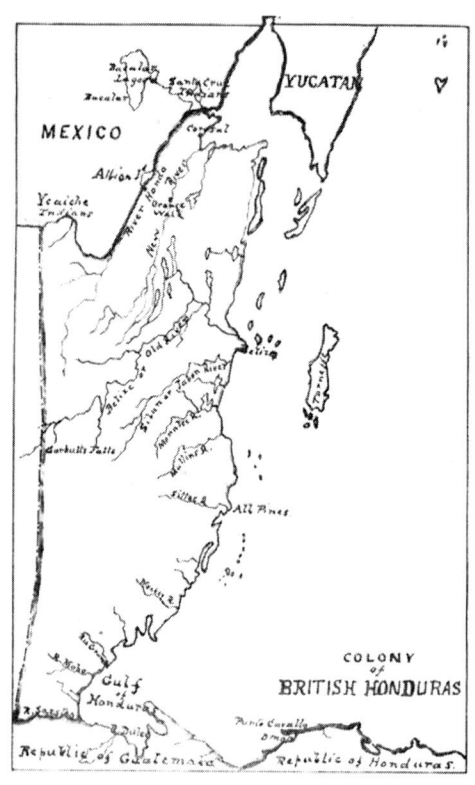

CHAPTER XIX
INDIAN DISTURBANCES IN HONDURAS, 1848-9—THE ESCORT TO COOMASSIE, 1848—THE SHERBRO EXPEDITION, 1849—ESCORT TO RIO NUNEZ, 1850

While No. 7 Company had thus been engaged on the Gold Coast, the quinquennial relief for the West African garrisons had sailed from the West Indies, No. 2 and No. 5 Companies, 1st West India Regiment, having embarked at Jamaica on February 21st, 1848. They arrived at Sierra Leone in April, and No. 5 Company being there landed to relieve No. 4, No. 2 proceeded to Cape Coast Castle to relieve No. 7. The two relieved companies rejoined the head-quarters at Jamaica on July 2nd, 1848. No. 8 Company having been sent to Nassau in February, and the light company in July, while No. 1 had been despatched to Honduras in May, the distribution of the regiment in August, 1848, was as follows: 2 companies in West Africa, 2 at Nassau, 1 in Honduras, and 5 in Jamaica.

No. 1 Company had been sent to Honduras in reply to an urgent appeal for a reinforcement from the Honduras Government, that colony being threatened with the horrors of an Indian war. In 1847 a war broke out between the Yucatecans and the Indians, and caused much anxiety to the British colony, whose strict neutrality satisfied neither of the contending parties. The Yucatecans, being driven out of the southern portion of Yucatan, took refuge in our territory, and raids and reprisals were frequent between them and the Santa Cruz Indians. In 1848 the town of Bacalar, situated on the shores of a lake, about twenty miles from the northern frontier of British Honduras, was captured by the Indians, and the fugitives, streaming into the colony, spread alarm amongst the colonists. It was at this time that reinforcements were applied for, and No. 1 Company, under Major Luke Smyth O'Connor, despatched from Jamaica.

On arriving at Belize the company was at once moved up to the Hondo, and towards the end of May a portion of it proceeded on escort duty with a British commissioner to Bacalar to endeavour to arrange a peace. That town had been the scene of the most frightful atrocities, and the streets were found strewn with the dead bodies of men, women, and children. Negotiations failing, the escort returned to the Hondo.

Collisions now became frequent between the Yucatecans and the Indians, and our northern border became a rallying point for both sides. The small British force was continually harassed by alarms and forced marches taken to prevent violation of British territory, until towards the close of 1848, it being rumoured that the Indians intended to cross the Hondo and sack Belize, it was withdrawn from the north for the protection of that town. Additional reinforcements were now asked for, and on March 29th, 1849, No. 4 Company, under Captain Meehan, embarked at Jamaica for Honduras.

In January, 1849, No. 1 Company had again advanced to the Hondo, and were within a few miles of Chac Creek on that river, when the sanguinary struggle between the Yucatecans and Indians took place. Hearing the sound of firing the troops marched to the spot, and finding the Indians employed in roasting the dead bodies of the defeated Yucatecans, were only with the utmost difficulty restrained from attacking them. But the most strict orders had been given for the preservation of British neutrality, and nothing could be done. Indeed, the Indians were themselves well aware of the advantages which they derived from our neutrality, and were exceedingly careful not to come into contact with the British; even going so far as on one occasion to shoot a chief and flog six men, who had been accused of committing an outrage across the Hondo.

In March, 1849, Major O'Connor visited Bacalar to endeavour to make peace, but without success; and the two companies of the regiment remained stationed on the Hondo, amid the same scenes of horror, until February, 1852, when they rejoined head-quarters at Jamaica.

To return to the companies in West Africa. In September, 1848, Mr. Winniett, the Lieutenant-Governor of the Gold Coast, received instructions from the Secretary of State for the Colonies to proceed on a mission to Coomassie, the capital of the Ashanti kingdom, for the purpose of establishing friendly relations between Great Britain and that power. Captain Powell, 1st West India Regiment, was then in command of No. 2 Company, stationed at Cape Coast Castle, and he, with forty-eight men of the regiment, accompanied the Lieutenant-Governor as an escort.

The mission left Cape Coast Castle on the 28th of September, 1848, crossed the River Prah on October 4th, and on the 8th reached the village of Karsi, about two miles from Coomassie. There the party halted to prepare for the entry into the capital, and, at noon, the King's messengers having informed them that everything was in readiness for their reception, they proceeded towards Coomassie.

Captain Powell says: "At a distance of about a mile from the town, a party of messengers with gold-handled swords of office, arrived with the king's compliments. After halting for a short time, we proceeded to the entrance of the first street, and then formed in order of procession, the escort leading. Presently a party of the king's linguists, with four large state umbrellas, ensigns of chieftainship, came up to request us to halt for a few minutes under the shade of a large banyan tree in the street, to give the king a little more time to prepare to receive us. After a brief delay of about twenty minutes, during which a large party of the king's soldiers fired a salute about a hundred yards distant from us, we moved on to the market-place, where the king and his chiefs were seated under their large umbrellas, according to the custom of the country on the reception of strangers of distinction. They, with their numerous captains and attendants occupied three sides of a large square, and formed a continuous line about 600 yards in length, and about ten yards in depth. After we had passed along about three-fourths of the line, we found the king surrounded by about twenty officers of his household, and a large number of messengers with their gold-handled swords and canes of office. Several very large umbrellas, consisting of silk velvet of different colours, shaded him and his suite from the sun. These umbrellas were surmounted by rude images, representing birds and beasts, overlaid with gold; the king's chair was richly decorated with gold; and the display of golden ornaments about his own person and those of his suite was most magnificent. The lumps of gold adorning the wrists of the King's attendants, and many of the principal chiefs, were so large that they must have been quite fatiguing to the wearers. We occupied about an hour in moving in procession from the banyan tree, where we had rested on entering the town, to the end of the line prepared for our reception; after which we proceeded to an open space at some distance from the market-place, and there took our seats. At 3.15 p.m. the chiefs commenced moving in procession before us, and this lasted until 6 p.m. Those whom we had first saluted in the market-place passed us first. Each chief was preceded by his band of rude music, consisting chiefly of drums and horns, followed by a body of soldiers under arms, and shaded by a large umbrella. The king was preceded by many of the officers of his household, and his messengers with the gold-handled swords, etc. etc. When he came opposite the governor, and received our military salute, he stopped, and approaching him took him cordially by the hand. After the king, other chiefs, and a large body of troops, passed in due order; and at 6 p.m. the ceremony closed."

At 9.30 a.m. on October 26th, 1848, the mission left Coomassie on its return journey to the coast, and arrived at Cape Coast Castle on November 4th. This was the first occasion on which a British Governor, or a body of regular troops, had ever visited Coomassie.

In March, 1849, a further change took place in the distribution of the regiment in the West Indies, No. 7 Company, under Captain R. Hughes, proceeding to Nassau from Jamaica. There were thus the head-quarters and 3 companies in Jamaica, 3 in Nassau, 2 in Honduras, and 2 in West Africa.

In June, 1849; the Acting Governor of Sierra Leone found that the state of affairs in Sherbro, a low-lying tract of country some seventy-five miles to the southward of Sierra Leone, imperatively called upon the British to take steps for putting an end to the war which for a long time had been carried on between the rival chiefs of the Caulker family, and had utterly paralysed trade. H.M.S. *Alert* and *Adelaide* were to be employed, but as a military force was required to proceed with the naval one, the under-mentioned force embarked in the Colonial steamer *Pluto* on the 18th of June: Captain Grange, Lieutenant Jones, and 45 men of the 1st West India Regiment, and 44 men of the 3rd West India Regiment. The expedition arrived at Yawrey Bay, at the mouth of the Cockboro River, on the 19th of June, when a stockaded fort was shelled and destroyed by the *Adelaide*. The expedition then proceeded to Bendoo, and after some delay, owing to the difficulty in inducing the chiefs to come in, returned to Yawrey Bay on the 29th, where negotiations were held and a treaty of peace between the Government and rival chiefs signed. The detachments rejoined at Freetown, Sierra Leone, on July 7th.

On the 29th of November, 1849, Lieutenant Tunstall and 34 men of No. 2 Company of the 1st West India Regiment, left Cape Coast Castle and proceeded to Appollonia in canoes, in aid of the civil power. After an absence of three weeks, during which they endured great hardships from exposure and fatigue, they rejoined their detachment at Cape Coast.

In the beginning of the year 1850, the Rio Nunez was in such a disturbed state as to necessitate the Governor of Sierra Leone taking steps for the protection of British subjects there. Some influential chiefs of the river having also besought the intervention of the Government to restore peace, commissioners were appointed, and as war was actually being carried on at the time, a military force was detailed to accompany them. This force consisted of Lieutenant Searle and 33 men of the 1st West India Regiment and Captain Prendergast and 34 men of the 3rd West India Regiment, and it embarked in H.M.S. *Teazer* on the 22nd of February, 1850. The *Teazer* arrived at the Rio Nunez on the 24th, and proceeded up the river to Ropass, a town some distance up the stream, where the commissioners landed with the escort. A "palaver" was held at this place on March 1st, the rival chieftains being attended by large bodies of armed men, but no satisfactory arrangement was arrived at, and next day the commissioners and troops proceeded to Walkariah, a town higher up the river. Here matters were finally amicably settled, and the party returned to Sierra Leone on March 9th.

In the West Indies there had been little change since 1849, except that on the 13th of February, 1851, the head-quarters and two companies were removed from Up Park Camp to Spanish Town; and a detachment consisting of half a company, under Ensign Cave, was sent to Turk's Island in December, 1851. This latter rejoined head-quarters in Jamaica in January, 1852; and in February, No. 1 and No. 4 Companies, under Captain Robeson, rejoined from Honduras. In the same year, however, they again went on detachment: No. 1, under Captain Grange, to St. Christopher's, and No. 4, under Lieutenant Imes, to Barbados. The distribution of the regiment in September, 1852, was thus: the Grenadier, No. 3 and No. 6 Companies, at Jamaica; the Light, No. 7 and No. 8 Companies, at Nassau, No. 4 at St. Christopher's, No. 1 at Barbados, No. 5 at Sierra Leone, and No. 2 at Cape Coast Castle.

In February, 1852, Major L. Smyth O'Connor, 1st West India Regiment, had arrived at Sierra Leone and assumed command of the troops in West Africa, and finding in May that the company on the Gold Coast was reduced by deaths to only 50 rank and file, he recommended that it should be recalled to Sierra Leone, the Gold Coast Corps, then almost completed, being quite sufficient for the garrison of the Gold Coast.

In September, 1852, Major O'Connor was appointed Governor of the Gambia, and as by Horse Guards letter of September 20th, 1852, "it was considered expedient that he should continue invested with the command of the troops on the West Coast of Africa, and move the head-quarters to the Gambia," this was done in October, 1852.

The War Office having approved of Major O'Connor's recommendation, No. 2 Company, 50 strong, arrived at Sierra Leone from Cape Coast Castle on March 20th, 1853.

CHAPTER XX
THE STORMING OF SABBAJEE, 1853—THE RELIEF OF CHRISTIANSBORG, 1854

On March 23rd, 1853, No. 3 and No. 6 Companies, under Captain A.W. Murray and Lieutenant Upton, embarked at Port Royal, Jamaica, in the troopship *Resistance*, for the relief of the West African garrisons. On May 17th, the *Resistance* arrived at the Gambia with four out of the six companies forming the relief for the detachments of the three West India regiments, and reinforcements being urgently required for the suppression of a hostile movement amongst the Mohammedans at Sabbajee, they were landed.

On the 25th of May, Lieutenant-Colonel O'Connor prepared to take the field with a force of 603 men, consisting of 463 of the 1st, 2nd, and 3rd West India Regiments, 35 pensioners, and 105 of the Gambia Militia. A field battery, consisting of 2 six-pounder field-guns and 2 howitzers, was also organised. On the 30th May, the brigade marched from Bathurst to Josswung, a distance of eight miles, where a camp was formed; and on June 1st, the force advanced to the attack of Sabbajee.[56]

Sabbajee was one of the oldest Marabout towns in Combo, and boasted the possession of the largest mosque in that portion of Africa. The town, more than a mile in circumference, was surrounded by a strong stockade, double ditches, and outward abattis; and the inhabitants, who could muster 3000 fighting men, were, from their predatory and warlike habits, the dread of the surrounding country.

On approaching the town, a strong body of the enemy was observed stationed round the mosque, while the stockade was lined with men. A portion of the stockade presented the appearance of having been removed, but had in reality only been laid lengthwise, so as to form a very formidable obstacle; while a deep trench dug in rear was crowded with men, who, in perfect security, could fire upon the advancing British, should they fall into the trap which had been laid for them, and attempt to carry the town at this point.

The force was drawn up in three divisions: the 1st West India Regiment, under Captain A.W. Murray, forming the centre division; the 2nd West India Regiment, under Captain Anderson, the right; and the 3rd West India Regiment, under Captain Brabazon, the left. At about four hundred yards from the stockade the field battery opened fire, and with such precision that after a few rounds the roof of the mosque and those of the adjacent houses were in flames. Observing the disorder caused amongst the enemy by the burning of their sacred building, Lieutenant-Colonel O'Connor determined to seize the opportunity, and storm.

The right and left divisions extended in skirmishing order, the centre remaining in column, and the whole advanced to the assault. The enemy kept up a heavy fire from the loop-holes of their stockade, over which the green flag was flying; but at the same moment the three divisions, which had in advancing formed a crescent, rushed at the stockade at three different points, and, clambering over, got at the enemy with the bayonet. This was more than they could stand, and abandoning their stockade, they fled down the streets and escaped through sally-ports in the rear of the town.

A strong body of fanatics, however, still held the mosque, the fire in the roof of which they had succeeded in extinguishing, and, amid the beating of war-drums and cries of "Allah" from the priests, kept up a smart fire upon the troops as they entered the large central square in which the mosque stood. To have stormed the building would have involved great sacrifice of life; the men, therefore, were directed to occupy the houses enclosing the square, and open fire, until the rockets could be brought into play.

The second rocket fired whizzed through the roof of the mosque, the defenders of which, however, only increased their drumming and shouts of defiance, for they were secure in their belief of the local tradition, which said that the mosque was impregnable and indestructible. In a very few minutes flames began to appear on the roof, and, though the enemy worked hard to extinguish it, it rapidly increased, until the mosque was untenable. Dozens of the fanatics blew out their brains rather than surrender, while others threw themselves out of the windows and passages, and rushed sword in hand, in a state of frenzy, upon the British. The coolness and steadiness of the troops was, however, more than a match for the mad rage of the Mandingoes, who were shot down one after another, until the whole of the defenders of the mosque were killed or made prisoners. The remainder of the enemy, who fled at the storming of the stockade, had taken refuge in the neighbouring woods, and, the object of the engagement being accomplished by the capture of the town, they were not pursued.

The stockade and mosque being destroyed, the force left Sabbajee on June 4th, and returned to Josswung, where, by an arrangement with the King of Combo, a portion of that kingdom, including the town of Sabbajee, was ceded to the British.

The mosque was a singularly strong building, and for a day and a half resisted every effort to pull it down, being eventually reduced to ruins by blasting the walls with bags of gunpowder. It consisted of a large central hall, with walls made of baked clay, three feet in thickness, and an external corridor running round the whole circumference of the inner apartment. The roof, conical in shape, was supported by six masonry pillars.

As the Gambia was still in an unsettled state, Lieutenant-Colonel O'Connor deemed it prudent to increase its garrison at the expense of that of Sierra Leone. No. 6 Company of the 1st West India Regiment was therefore detained at Bathurst, and on June 8th, No. 3 Company, under Captain Murray, proceeded in the *Resistance* to Sierra Leone. On arriving at that station, on June 17th, Captain Murray assumed the command of the troops.

No. 2 Company embarked at Sierra Leone for Jamaica on June 22nd, arriving at Kingston on August 5th. On October 18th the *Resistance* returned from the West Indies with the remaining companies destined for the quinquennial relief, and No. 5 Company, embarking in her on October 22nd, reached Jamaica on November 25th. The West African garrisons were now as follows: At the Gambia, one company of the 1st West India Regiment, two of the 2nd, and one of the 3rd; at Sierra Leone, one of the 1st West India Regiment, and one of the 3rd.

In the West Indies the following changes had taken place: Nos. 7 and 8 Companies had been moved in August from Nassau to Barbados and Dominica respectively, and, in July, the light company had proceeded from Nassau to Jamaica. In December, 1853, the distribution of the regiment was then as follows: 4 companies at Jamaica, 2 at Barbados, 1 at Dominica, 1 at St. Christopher's, 1 at Sierra Leone, and 1 at the Gambia.[57]

In September, 1854, the inhabitants of Christiansborg, a Danish settlement on the Gold Coast four miles from Accra, which had been recently purchased by the British, rose in rebellion against the Colonial authorities. The only armed force then on the Gold Coast consisted of the Gold Coast Artillery, recruited from amongst the Fanti tribes, and this body the rebels blockaded in the Castle of Christiansborg. On the outbreak of the rebellion, the Lieutenant-Governor of the Gold Coast at once sent to Sierra Leone for assistance; and, on the 12th of October, the following detachments embarked at Sierra Leone in H.M.S. *Britomart* and *Ferret*: Lieutenant Strachan and 33 men of the 1st West India Regiment, Captain Rookes and 46 men of the 2nd West India Regiment, Lieutenant Haneahan and 31 men of the 3rd West India Regiment. From the Gambia were also despatched in the Colonial steamer *Dover*, on the 24th of October: Ensign Anderson and 25 men of the 1st, Captain Mockler and 70 men of the 2nd, and Lieutenant Hill and 23 men of the 3rd West India Regiment.

The troops from Sierra Leone and the Gambia arrived at Christiansborg on the 27th of October and the 7th of November respectively. Several small skirmishes had taken place between the Gold Coast artillery and the rebels without either side gaining any material advantage; but, on the arrival of the reinforcement from Sierra Leone, the siege was raised, and the natives retired inland to some villages on the plain behind Christiansborg. There, like all undisciplined bodies, they gradually melted away; the chiefs, finding their followers abandoning them, were compelled to ask for terms; and directly negotiations were opened, the detachments of the three West India regiments re-embarked to return to Sierra Leone, sailing from Christiansborg on the 12th of November.

FOOTNOTES:

[56] See map.

[57] This year, 1853, appears to have been particularly unhealthy in the West Indies, to judge from the following inscription, taken from an intramural monument in Kingston Cathedral Church:

TO THE MEMORY OF THE FOLLOWING:

Capt. Robt. Mostyn, 3rd W.I.R., died of yellow fever, at Nassau, Bahamas, 23rd July, 1853, æt. 27.

Ensign John Alex. Gordon Pringle, 3rd W.I.R., died of yellow fever at Kingston, Jamaica, 31st July, 1853, æt. 21.

Assist.-Surg. Walter William Harris, 1st W.I.R., attached to 3rd W.I.R., died at Up Park Camp, of yellow fever, 4th Aug., 1853, æt. 24.

Lieut. John Maryon Wilson, 3rd W.I.R., died at Up Park Camp, of yellow fever, 13th Aug., 1853, æt. 22.

Eliza Chancellor Wilson, wife of the above, died at Up Park Camp, of yellow fever, 5th Sept., 1853, æt. 22.

Cath. Elizabeth, wife of Lieut. Wm. Hen. Wilson Hawtayne, 3rd W.I.R., died of yellow fever at Nassau, Bahamas, 9th Aug., 1853, æt. 23.

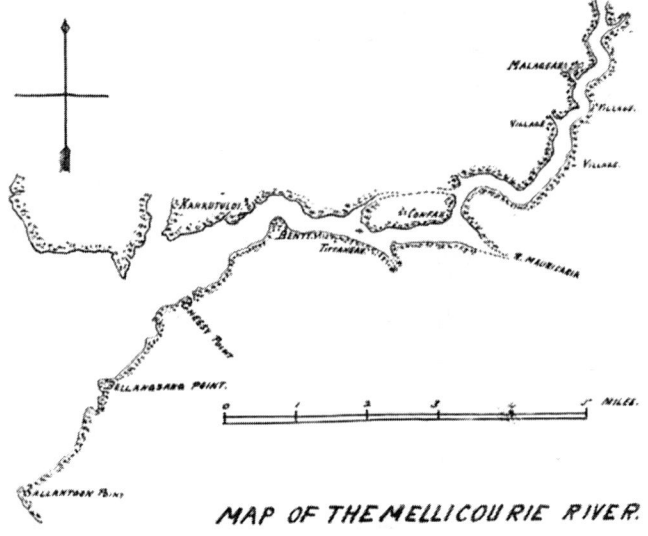

MAP OF THE MELLICOURIE RIVER.

CHAPTER XXI
THE TWO EXPEDITIONS TO
MALAGEAH, 1854 AND 1855

The troops that had been despatched from Sierra Leone and the Gambia for the relief of Christiansborg, returned to Sierra Leone, in H.M.S. *Prometheus*, on the 25th of November, 1854, and in consequence of the hostile attitude assumed by the chiefs of the Mellicourie and Scarcies Rivers, and the outrages committed by natives on mercantile factories in those rivers, the Governor of Sierra Leone decided to detain the contingent which had been sent from the Gambia, in order to have a sufficient force to overawe the chief of Malageah, the principal offender, and compel him to sign a treaty of trade. With this view, accordingly, detachments of the 1st, 2nd, and 3rd West India Regiments, numbering in all 401 officers and men, under the command of Captain Rookes, 2nd West India Regiment, embarked in H.M.S. *Prometheus* and *Dover*, on the 2nd of December, and sailed for the Mellicourie River, on which the town of Malageah is situated. The officers of the 1st West India Regiment who accompanied the expedition were Captain R.D. Fletcher, Lieutenant Connell, Lieutenant Strachan, and Ensign Anderson.

On December 4th, the expedition arrived off Malageah, and the river-banks having been reconnoitred, Captain Heseltine, of H.M.S. *Britomart*, who had been appointed diplomatic agent with powers to negotiate, directed a landing to be made. The troops disembarked, and meeting with no opposition, advanced on the town, seizing and occupying the mosque and the king's house, while a second body took possession of all the approaches to the town. By these means, a party of some 200 chiefs and Marabouts, who filled the mosque, were surrounded.

In the meantime, the 1st Division, under Captain R. D'Oyley Fletcher, 1st West India Regiment, had proceeded to a creek to the eastward of the town, which they ascended in the boats of the *Britomart*, and then crossing by bye-paths through the swamp and bush to the back of the town, where they dispersed a body of 150 natives armed with rifles and muskets, they joined the main body before the mosque.

Negotiations were opened by the diplomatic agent, and continued for about half-an-hour; when, as it was noticed that the Marabouts were gradually leaving the mosque and all going in one direction, a reconnoitring party of ten men, under Lieutenant F.J. Connell, 1st West India Regiment, was sent to the northern side of the town. Lieutenant Connell, on reaching the town gate, found from 1800 to 2000 natives armed with fire-arms, spears, bows and arrows, formed in a semicircle, from eight to ten deep, facing the small picket that had been there posted. The whole of the main body, with the seamen and marines, was at once ordered up, and took up a position on the plateau to the north of the town, facing the natives, while a detached party occupied the walls and gates. At first there was a disposition on the part of the natives to resist this movement, but it was so rapidly executed that they were taken by surprise, and, losing cohesion, they soon after gradually dispersed.

The king, Bamba Mima Lahi, now signified his desire to come to terms, promised to comply with all demands, and to pay one thousand dollars as a fine for his offences. The force accordingly re-embarked, the object of the expedition having been effected without bloodshed, and returned to Sierra Leone on December 6th. The following letter may be of interest:

"H.M.S. Britomart,
"*Sierra Leone, December 6th, 1854.*

"Sir,

"In bringing back the troops that have been embarked on board the *Prometheus* and landed at Malageah, and who, whilst afloat, have been under my command, I beg to bear testimony to their quiet, orderly, and zealous conduct, both afloat and ashore, where, had it not been for the above good qualities, collision would have been inevitable.

"To Captains Rookes, Mockler, and Fletcher, and the officers of the force, I beg to return my sincere thanks for their zealous and active co-operation; further comment on my part would be presumptuous.

"A. Heseltine,
"Commander and Senior Naval Officer.

"Lieutenant-Colonel Foster,
"Commanding troops."

On the 14th of December, the Gambia contingent sailed for the Gambia in the Colonial steamer *Dover*, and the garrison of Sierra Leone remained at its ordinary strength of three companies.

In May, 1855, as the King of Malageah had not observed the stipulations of the treaty that had been forced upon him, and had not paid the fine of one thousand dollars, the Acting Governor of Sierra Leone, a gentleman of colour, determined to take steps for his punishment. On the 21st of May, accordingly, he sent for Captain R. D'Oyley Fletcher, 1st West India Regiment, who was then in command of the troops, and informed him that it was his intention to send a force of 150 men, that very day, to burn the town of Malageah, and, if possible, capture the king. He added that the troops would proceed in H.M.S. *Teazer*, then lying in the harbour.

Captain Fletcher, in reply, said that he could not approve of the proposed arrangements; that since a force of 400 men had been deemed necessary to extract a promise from the king, it was, to say the least, injudicious to endeavour to force him to fulfil that promise with only 150 men. He stated that at the last expedition more than 2000 armed natives had been seen, and he considered it inadvisable to proceed to actual hostilities without a force proportionate to the duty to be performed. He further suggested that the expedition should be delayed for two or three days, so that the detachments of the 2nd West India Regiment might be brought in from Waterloo and the Banana Islands, and the whole garrison employed on the duty. The Acting Governor overruled these objections, insinuated that Captain Fletcher was actuated by fears for his personal safety, and finally peremptorily ordered the force he had mentioned to embark.

In consequence, on the evening of May 21st, Captain Fletcher, Lieutenant Strachan, Lieutenant Wylie, and 69 men of the 1st West India Regiment, with Lieutenants Keir and Beazley and 79 men of the 3rd West India Regiment, embarked on board the *Teazer*. Lieutenant Vincent, 2nd West India Regiment, was attached to the 1st for duty, and Deputy-Assistant-Commissary-General Frith and Surgeons Marchant and Bradshaw accompanied the troops.

The *Teazer* arrived off Benty Point, at the mouth of the Mellicourie River, on the morning of May 22nd, and, after a delay of a few hours, in consequence of the difficulty in crossing the bar, the expedition arrived off Malageah.

Lieutenant-Commander Nicolas, of the *Teazer*, and Mr. Dillet, the Acting Governor's private secretary, had been appointed commissioners, and, by their direction, the troops disembarked about 10 a.m. A flag of truce was flying on the king's house, and, as he showed a disposition to come to terms, the commissioners determined to depart from their instructions, and make an attempt to settle the affair without having recourse to force. They accordingly informed the king that if he would pay the fine his town would be spared; and they granted him one hour for this purpose, warning him that if at the expiration of that time the money was not forthcoming, the town would be shelled.

Two hours having passed without any communication having been received from the king, the *Teazer* at noon opened fire, and the troops advanced on the town, covering their flanks with skirmishers. This advance would have been unnecessary had the *Teazer* been supplied with rockets; but there being none, the men were obliged to set fire to the houses. It would be difficult to imagine a worse-planned expedition.

The troops gained the central square of the town, and, in compliance with the written instructions, set fire to the mosque, the king's house, and other principal buildings; and ultimately the whole town appeared to be in flames. The left division, under Lieutenant Vincent, was exposed to a desultory fire, during the whole of these operations, from the enemy concealed in the bush; and large numbers of natives were observed gathering on the plateau to the north of the town. As it seemed impossible that any portion of the town could escape the conflagration, and as the heat from the burning buildings was intense, the troops retired to the river bank, and embarked in the *Teazer's* boats. Scarcely had the seamen dipped their oars into the water, to pull out into the stream, than a volley was poured into the boats from the dense bush which grew close down to the edge of the water; and the ambushed enemy then commenced firing rapidly, but fortunately with so little precision that the troops succeeded in reaching mid-stream with a loss of only five wounded.

The boats continued their course to the ship, and the troops re-embarked. The town was still in flames, but they were gradually subsiding, and before nightfall were entirely extinguished, leaving a considerable portion of the town still unconsumed. The commissioners, upon this, decided, as it was too late to land again that day, to drop down the river as far as Benty Point for the night, and to return next morning to complete the work of destruction. Captain Fletcher then objected to any second landing being made, pointing out that the whole country was now alarmed, and that the people of Malageah would be reinforced by those of Fouricariah (a populous town further up the river), and that quite enough had been done to punish the king. The commissioners agreed with his views, but decided that their orders were so peremptory that they could not, without running the risk of censure, leave the river until the entire town had been destroyed.

At 5.30 a.m. on May 23rd, the *Teazer* left Benty Point, and steaming up the river, anchored off Malageah, in which the ruins were still smouldering. The vessel was so ill-provided with munitions of war that hardly any shell remained from the previous day. What little there was, was thrown amongst the houses to endeavour to fire them, and the attempt being unsuccessful, it became necessary to land the men. The dense bush around the town having been well searched with grape and canister to clear it of any lurking enemy, the troops, 135 in number, were landed on the bank of the mangrove creek running inland towards the town, and no enemy appearing, they advanced to set fire to the buildings that had hitherto escaped destruction.

The advanced guard of thirty men, with whom were Lieutenant-Commander Nicolas and Mr. Dillet, who had landed to point out which houses it was most important to thoroughly destroy, had only advanced some two hundred yards from the bank of the creek, when they were received with a murderous discharge of musketry from the enemy concealed in the bush. Almost the whole of the advanced party were shot down in this one volley, twenty men being killed on the spot, and Lieutenant-Commander Nicolas and Mr. Dillet severely wounded. The main body, seventy-five in number, under Captain Fletcher, at once hurried up to prevent the wounded falling into the hands of the barbarous natives, and behaved with great gallantry, for though falling thick and fast under the tremendous fire which the concealed enemy—to the number of several hundreds—poured into them from a distance of ten or twelve yards, they held their ground until the wounded had been safely conveyed to the boats.

Scarcely had this been accomplished than the rear-guard of thirty men, under Lieut. Keir, 3rd West India Regiment, was attacked by a large number of natives who had moved through the bush, and actually succeeded in cutting off our men from the boats. The enemy advanced with great determination into the open, thinking to overwhelm this small party, and they were only driven back into the bush by repeated volleys and a final charge with the bayonet.

By this time fully one-third of the men who had landed having been killed, and a great number wounded, the order was given to retire, which was done steadily, the ground being contested inch by inch. At this time Company Sergeant-Major Scanlan, of the 3rd West India Regiment, and six men who were covering the retreat, fell, the former mortally wounded; and some of the bolder of the natives, rushing out of their concealment, seized Deputy-Assistant-Commissary Frith, and dragged him away into the bush, where he was barbarously murdered in cold blood. Scanlan was lying in the narrow path, his chest riddled with bullets, when the chief fetish priest of the place, to encourage the natives to make further efforts, sprang upon a ruined wall in front of him, and began dancing an uncouth dance, accompanying it with savage yells and significant gestures to the dying man. He paid dearly for his rashness, however, for Scanlan, collecting his strength for a last supreme effort, seized his loaded rifle, which was fortunately lying within reach, and discharged it at the gesticulating savage, who threw up his arms and fell dead. The next moment Scanlan was surrounded by a horde of infuriated barbarians, and his body hacked into an undistinguishable mass.

The troops, sadly diminished in number, at last reached that portion of the mangrove creek where they had left the boats. Of these there had been originally but two, and one having at the commencement of the action been used to convey Lieutenant-Commander Nicolas and Mr. Dillet, under the charge of Surgeon Bradshaw, to the ship, one only remained for the men to embark in. The tide having fallen, this was lying out near the entrance of the creek, separated by an expanse of reeking mud from the shore. The men, seeing their last chance of safety cut off, threw themselves into the mud, in which many sank and were no more seen. Some few, however, succeeded in floundering along, half wading and half swimming, until they reached her, and climbed in. She was, however, so riddled with bullets, that she filled and sank almost immediately.

Captain Fletcher, Lieutenant Wylie, Lieutenant Strachan, and Lieutenant Vincent, with some thirty men, endeavoured to make a last stand upon a small islet of mud and sand, near the left bank of the creek; but Lieutenant Wylie was shot dead almost at once, and Lieutenant Vincent, being shot through the body, jumped into the water, to endeavour to swim to the ship. In a few seconds seventeen men had fallen out of this devoted band, and the survivors, plunging into the creek, swam down towards the river. The natives lined the banks in crowds, keeping up a heavy fire upon the men in the water; and Captain Fletcher and Lieutenant Strachan, who were the last to leave the shore, only reached the *Teazer* by a miracle, they having to swim more than half a mile to reach her.

As the last of the survivors gained the vessel, the natives, between two and three thousand in number, lined the banks of the river, brandishing their weapons and uttering shouts of defiance; and the heads of several of the killed, horribly mutilated, were held out towards the ship on spears, amidst cries of exultation. All the ammunition for the *Teazer's* guns having already been expended in shelling the town and clearing the bush, it was impossible to reply to the enemy, and the vessel proceeded slowly down the river, returning to Sierra Leone next day.

The casualties of this day were as follows: The 1st West India Regiment, out of 62 men who landed, lost 38 killed and 3 wounded. The 3rd West India Regiment, out of 73 men who landed, lost 46 killed and 8 wounded. Total, 95 killed and wounded, out of a force of 135 men.

The casualties amongst the officers were nearly equally heavy. Out of the ten Europeans who were under fire, three, namely Lieutenant Wylie, 1st West India Regiment, D.A.C.G. Frith and C.S.M. Scanlan were killed; and three, Lieutenant Vincent, 2nd West India Regiment, Lieutenant-Commander Nicolas, and Mr. Dillet, severely wounded.

It was learned afterwards that the reason so large a force was assembled at Malageah was that it was the time for the annual gathering of the river tribes, to hear the laws read by the Alimani. This circumstance ought of course to have been known to the Acting Governor, who was well acquainted with the customs of the people. The Imperial Government held him responsible for this defeat, and, in November, 1855, he was relieved of his post, and charged "with having, when Acting Governor, on the 21st of May, 1855, without authority, and upon insufficient grounds, sent an expedition against the Moriah chiefs in the Mellicourie River, beyond the Colony, with orders to burn or destroy the town of Malageah, planned without foresight or judgment, disastrous in its termination, and disgraceful to the British power," and was suspended from his office of Queen's Advocate and from his seat at the Council Board.

CHAPTER XXII
THE BATTLE OF BAKKOW, AND
STORMING OF SABBAJEE, 1855.[58]

The company of the 1st West India Regiment stationed at the Gambia was the next to see active service, but fortunately under circumstances less disastrous than had fallen to the lot of the company at Sierra Leone.

In June, 1855, the inhabitants of Sabbajee again began to exhibit signs of lawlessness; and, early in July, an influential Mohammedan of that town, named Fodi Osumanu, sent an armed party to the British settlement at Josswung to seize a woman, whose husband he had already placed in confinement in Sabbajee itself. In consequence of this outrage a warrant was issued for the apprehension of Fodi Osumanu, and, as a precautionary measure, the constables despatched to put the warrant in force were accompanied by a small party of the 2nd West India Regiment, under Lieutenant Armstrong, 3rd West India Regiment.

They arrived at Sabbajee on the morning of July 16th, and at first Fodi Osumanu offered no opposition to his arrest; but, on gaining the central square of the town, he endeavoured to break away from the police, and, upon this signal, the Mandingoes rushed upon the British from every street and alley. Nothing but the coolness and steadiness displayed by both officers and men, saved the whole from destruction. Forming square, they retreated steadily out of the town, repulsing the repeated attacks of the natives, and retired in good order to Josswung, and thence to the military post at Cape St. Mary's. In effecting this, two men were killed, and the Queen's Advocate, Lieutenant Davis, 2nd West India Regiment, and Lieutenant Armstrong were wounded, the latter so severely as to render amputation of the right arm necessary.

Intelligence of this occurrence being carried to Bathurst in a few hours, the Governor, Lieutenant-Colonel L. Smyth O'Connor, 1st West India Regiment, at once called out all the available force of the Colony; and, aware that every half-hour was of importance, as the inhabitants of Sabbajee were receiving reinforcements from the disaffected Mandingo towns of Jambool, Burnfut, and Cunju, and had already burned and pillaged Josswung, he marched the same day. The force consisted of 120 men of the 1st, 2nd, and 3rd West India Regiments, with 120 of the Royal Gambia Militia; and, on arriving at Cape St. Mary's, on the evening of July 16th, it was joined by 26 pensioners of the West India regiments. The officers of the 1st West India Regiment present were Lieutenant-Colonel O'Connor, Lieutenant E.F. Luke, and Lieutenant Henderson.

Early next morning the whole force marched towards Sabbajee, meeting with no resistance until it arrived at the wood of Bakkow. To reach Sabbajee it was necessary to pass through this wood, a jungle of dense tropical vegetation, only traversable by a single bush path some five feet in breadth, and, before entering this defile, Colonel O'Connor wisely ordered rockets to be thrown amongst the trees, with a view to ascertaining if they covered any concealed enemy.

Hardly had the first rocket fallen than the wood appeared alive with men, who, from every bush and tree, opened a destructive fire upon the British. This was promptly and steadily replied to by the detachments of the 1st, 2nd, and 3rd West India Regiments, which were in the van, and the action became general. The militia were drawn up in two bodies, one acting as a support to the regulars, and the other as a reserve; and the latter, shortly after the commencement of the engagement, retreated without orders, and without firing a shot. The party of militia in support, as soon as they observed the flight of the reserve, fell back hurriedly in great confusion, nor could their officers nor the Governor himself succeed in stopping them, and both parties of militia retired upon Cape St. Mary's, abandoning their wounded.

The detachments of the West India regiments still held their ground; but at the end of half an hour, as it was manifestly impossible, with the now greatly reduced numbers, to force the passage of the wood, and as the enemy were observed extending in large numbers round both flanks so as to threaten the line of retreat, the order was given to retire upon Cape St. Mary's. This was effected in good order, the victorious natives following the retreating force for more than two miles, and keeping up an incessant fire. The combined detachments suffered in this affair a loss of twenty-three killed and fifty-three wounded. Lieutenant-Colonel O'Connor was himself severely wounded in the right arm and left shoulder.

The news of this repulse was received with the greatest consternation at Bathurst, which was entirely denuded of troops and quite at the mercy of the rebellious Mandingoes. Preparations for defence were at once undertaken, all the reliable natives, principally persons in the employ of the Government or of the merchants, in all some 200 in number, were armed, and a vessel was despatched to the neighbouring French settlement of Goree to seek assistance. The Mandingoes, fortunately, made no attempt to follow up their success, and the chiefs of British Combo having volunteered their aid to the Government, a number of their men were armed, and on July 29th some sharp skirmishing took place between them and the Mandingoes in the neighbourhood of Bakkow, in which the Combos lost twenty-five killed, but without reaping any success.

On the afternoon of July 30th, the French brig-of-war *Entreprenant*, Captain Villeneuve, arrived, bringing with her eighty men, which was all the disposable force the French Governor of Goree had at his command; and all preparations being completed by the night of August 3rd, the combined British and French force marched from Cape St. Mary's next morning at daybreak. The French had brought with them three twelve-pounder field-guns, which, with a 4-2/5-inch howitzer, and three rocket-troughs in the possession of the British, were formed into a battery under the command of Lieutenant Morel, of the French marine artillery. The force was further increased by an irregular contingent of some 600 loyal natives.

As on the former occasion, no opposition was encountered until arriving at the wood of Bakkow, where the enemy showed in great force, and opened a heavy fire from the shelter of the forest. The irregular contingent, supported by the detachments of the 1st and 2nd West India Regiments, replied to the enemy's fire in a most effective manner; but so determined was the resistance, that the Mandingoes, when silenced in our front, taking advantage of the cover afforded by the high grass and clumps of monkey-bread trees, made repeated attacks on the flanks, and even at one time threatened the rear. Shell and rockets were thrown into the wood, and the village of Bakkow, which was occupied by the enemy, was burned; but it was not until after two hours' obstinate fighting, in the course of which the detachments of the 1st and 2nd West India Regiment had four times to repulse flank attacks with the bayonet, that the passage could be forced.

The wood being traversed, the force debouched upon the plain of Sabbajee, a sandy level, covered with a scanty growth of Guinea grass and dotted with clumps of dwarf palm. The guns were at once placed in position for breaching the stockade, and fire was opened with wonderful precision. A few rounds only had been expended, when a large body of natives from the disaffected and neighbouring town of Burnfut made a sudden and determined onslaught on our flank, charging furiously forward with brandished scimetars. This was met by a party of French marines and the detachments of the 1st and 2nd West India Regiments, who, after firing a volley at a very close range, charged gallantly with the bayonet and speedily routed the enemy, who took refuge in a neighbouring copse. Being ordered to dislodge them from this cover, the detachments of the 1st and 2nd West India Regiments advanced in skirmishing order, and after a short but sharp conflict, drove them out on the further side.

After a bombardment of an hour and a half, seeing that the enemy extinguished the thatched roofs of their houses as fast as they were ignited, and that the ammunition was becoming exhausted, Lieutenant-Colonel O'Connor determined to carry the stockade by storm. The detachments of the West India regiments formed up in the centre, a division of French marines being on either flank, and the whole dashed forward to the assault in the face of a tremendous fire of musketry that was opened throughout the entire length of the loop-holed stockade. In a few seconds the troops were under the stockade, which was composed of the stout trunks of trees, standing some eighteen feet high, and braced on the inner side by cross-beams. A temporary check was here experienced (the men having no ladders for escalading), during which the Mandingoes kept up a close fire from their upper tier of loop-holes, while others crouching in the ditch in rear hewed and cut at the feet and legs of the troops through the apertures in the stockade on a level with the ground. The check was, however, of short duration, for the British opened fire on the enemy through their own loop-holes, and drove them back, while others, clambering over the rough defences, effected an entrance.

After this, the Mandingoes offered but a feeble resistance, and soon fled into the open from the further side of the town. Here they were pursued and shot down by the irregular contingent, who had been sent to cut off their retreat as soon as it was seen that the stockade was carried. The enemy's loss during the assault was exceedingly heavy, the ditch in rear of the stockade, and in which they were principally sheltered, being full of dead. The loss of the combined force, exclusive of irregulars, was seventeen killed and thirty-one wounded.

Inside the stockade the 1st West India Regiment captured two kettledrums, of which one was a war-drum, and the other a death-drum, that is to say, a drum that is only beaten when an execution is taking place. These drums, consisting of polished hemispherical calabashes, of a diameter of about thirty inches at the drum-head, are now in the possession of the regiment.

The following letter, referring to these operations, which terminated with the capture of Sabbajee, was published in general orders at the Gambia, on the 26th of October, 1855:

"Horse   Guards, "

Sept. 6th, 1855.

"Sir,

"The General Commanding-in-Chief having had before him the despatches which were addressed to the Adjutant-General on July 30th and 6th ultimo, giving an account of the proceedings, from the 16th July to the 4th August last, of the force under your command against the Mohammedan rebel town of Sabbajee, which was eventually taken by assault at the point of the bayonet, I am directed to assure you of Lord Hardinge's satisfaction at the perusal of those despatches, and that he considers the gallantry and steadiness displayed by the troops on this occasion, and the judgment with which they were directed by you, to be deserving of high praise.

"His Lordship further desired that the expression of his sentiments might be communicated accordingly to yourself and to all the troops concerned.

"I have, &c.,
(Signed)   "C. Yorke,
"Military Secretary.

"Lieut.-Colonel O'Connor,
"1st West India Regiment,
"Commanding troops, Western Coast of Africa."

In the West Indies nothing of importance had occurred, and no change of station had taken place, since December, 1853. In this year, however (1855), No. 8 Company rejoined head-quarters at Jamaica from Dominica, and No. 1 was moved from St. Christopher to Demerara. The distribution, then, at the close of 1855, was: No. 2, No. 5, No. 8, the Grenadier and Light Companies at Jamaica, No. 7 and No. 4 at Barbados, No. 1 at Demerara, No. 3 at Sierra Leone, and No. 6 at the Gambia.

FOOTNOTES:

[58] See map.

CHAPTER XXIII
CHANGES IN THE WEST AFRICAN GARRISONS, 1856-57—THE GREAT SCARCIES RIVER EXPEDITION, 1859—FIRE AT NASSAU, 1859

In January, 1856, it was determined to make a further change in the mode of garrisoning the settlements on the West Coast of Africa, and the following letter was issued on the subject:

"Horse Guards,
"2nd January, 1856.

"In obedience to orders from the Secretary of State, War Department, the Field-Marshal Commanding-in-Chief is pleased to direct that instead of the detachments to the western coast of Africa being furnished, as at present, by two companies from each of the West India regiments, the settlements in that part will be garrisoned by a wing composed of six companies, to be furnished in succession by each of the West India regiments.

"At the next relief the 1st West India Regiment will furnish six companies accordingly, each company made up and kept effective to 100 rank and file, the force to be distributed as at present, viz.:

"Gambia   3 Companies.
"Sierra Leone   3 Companies.

"The remaining four companies of the 1st West India Regiment will be stationed at Jamaica, as a depôt to receive and train recruits, and maintain the efficiency of the companies on the coast of Africa."

In anticipation of this change, and as recent events at the Gambia and Sierra Leone had shown the necessity for an increase in the strength of the detachments, No. 2 Company of the 1st West India Regiment, under

Captain W.J. Chamberlayne, embarked at Jamaica for Africa in the *Sir George Pollock* on February 19th, 1856. It arrived in the Gambia on April 1st, and detachments to McCarthy's Island, 179 miles up the River Gambia, and to Fort Bullen, were at once furnished from it.

No other change in the distribution of the regiment took place in this year, with the exception that No. 5 Company, under Captain R. Hughes, was moved from Jamaica to Barbados in December.

In January, 1857, No. 1 Company from Demerara, and Nos. 4 and 7 from Barbados, embarked on board the troopship *Perseverance*, for Africa, under the command of Brevet Lieutenant-Colonel Clarke, and Captains Hughes and Macauley, arriving at Sierra Leone on February 28th.

Nos. 1 and 7 Companies were there disembarked, and the *Perseverance* then proceeded to the Gambia, where No. 4 Company was landed. In accordance with the scheme that the remaining four companies of the regiment should be stationed at Jamaica, No. 5 Company rejoined there from Barbados on April 17th; but, two months later, the scheme was again revised, and, on June 4th, the head-quarters and four companies embarked for Nassau, New Providence, under Lieutenant-Colonel F.A. Wetherall.

The detachments on the West Coast of Africa were very much subdivided, that of the Gambia furnishing garrisons for Fort Bullen, Cape St. Mary, and McCarthy's Island; and that of Sierra Leone a garrison for Waterloo. In April, 1857, the garrison of Fort Bullen was reinforced by No. 2 Company under Captain Chamberlayne from Bathurst, in consequence of disturbances having broken out between the King of Barra and one of his principal chiefs named Osumanu Sajji, and was withdrawn in May, on tranquility being restored.

In August, 1858, the natives of Sherbro threatened to plunder the British factories that had been established on Sherbro Island, and stopped the trade, and for the protection of the lives and property of the Consul and British subjects, a detachment of the 1st West India Regiment, under Captain R. Hughes, proceeded in H.M.S. *Spitfire* to Sherbro Island on September 1st. They there landed and remained until October 2nd, when, all fears of an attack being at an end, they returned to Sierra Leone. In January, 1859, however, another attack was threatened by the Mendis, and a detachment of the 1st West India Regiment, under Captain Luke, was sent for the protection of the factories in H.M.S. *Trident* on January 15th, returning to Sierra Leone on February 18th.

In September and October, 1858, Captain Luke, 1st West India Regiment, who was then on leave of absence on the Gold Coast, served with the expeditionary force against the rebel Krobo stronghold of Krobo

Hill. Captain Cochrane, Gold Coast Artillery, commanding the force, in concluding his despatch of October 26th, 1858, says: "It is not too much to say that all who have joined the expedition have done their best to further its interests, but I beg especially to call your Excellency's notice to the voluntary services of Captain F.H. Luke, of the 1st West India Regiment, whose energy, zeal, and disinterestedness, have been warmly commended by every officer here, and are deserving of honourable mention."

In February, 1859, the town of Porto Lokkoh, distant some forty miles from Sierra Leone, and on the Sierra Leone River, was burned and pillaged by a body of Soosoos who had, for some time back, established themselves at Kambia, on the Great Scarcies River. For previous outrages committed by them, Kambia had been bombarded by a naval squadron under Commodore Wise on February 1st, 1858, after which the Soosoos had entrenched themselves in a stockaded work, or war fence, near Kambia. There they had been suffered to remain, but the destruction of Porto Lokkoh, the chief *entrepôt* of the Sierra Leone trade, necessitated further measures being taken against them.

Consequently, on March 20th, 1859, the Governor of Sierra Leone, Colonel Stephen Hill, proceeded with a force of 203 men of the 1st West India Regiment, under Major A.W. Murray, in H.M.S. *Vesuvius, Trident,* and *Spitfire,* to the Great Scarcies River, where they arrived at daybreak on the 22nd. The officers of the regiment serving with the expedition were Major Murray, Brevet-Major Pratt, Lieutenants Fitzgerald, Mackay, and Mawe, Ensigns Ormsby and Temple. Colonel Hill, in his despatch, says:

"The troops having landed to the right of the town, I formed the detachment of the 1st West India Regiment, under Major Murray, into four divisions; and the marines formed, under the command of Captain Hill, 2nd West India Regiment, A.D.C., another division. A party of the former corps, acting as gunners, accompanied the Marine Artillery, who took charge of two mountain howitzers.

"Having extended one division in skirmishing order, I advanced; and, finding the first stockade deserted I passed on to the furthest one, which was then occupied by the sailors of the second division of boats under Commander Close. I then proceeded to the extreme left of all the defences, and halted in clear ground to await the arrival of our native allies. Shortly afterwards Commodore Wise sent to inform me that the enemy, who had retired before us with some loss, were in the jungle to our left at the head of some rocks, on which they could cross the river at low water. I immediately extended two divisions of the 1st West India Regiment as skirmishers, with the marines supporting one, and a division of the 1st West India the other, leaving one division in reserve in charge of the howitzers, after having first fired some rounds of shell into the jungle.

"Our advance was most difficult, the bush being almost impenetrable. However, we persevered, and, having reached a high point overlooking the country around, and not seeing any enemy, I ordered a halt, and, after some time, we retired unmolested, the Soosoos never having allowed us to close with them. The Commodore then sent me a second message to the effect that he had seen about 500 men, who had, on our advance, retired across the river, over the rocks, and disappeared in the bush on the opposite side.

"The detachment of the 1st West India Regiment, under Brevet-Major Pratt, kept the ground during the night; and our allies having arrived, and been placed in possession of the stockades, the troops were re-embarked on the 24th, and we proceeded on our return to Sierra Leone, where we arrived on the 26th.

"I have much pleasure in stating that all the officers and men under my orders performed their duties in an exceedingly zealous and satisfactory manner, exhibiting a cheerful obedience, and only anxious to close with the enemy. None but those present could form a just estimate of the difficulty attending our advance, and the consequent physical exhaustion. The heat was intense; a great part of the jungle had been fired, and the bushes and the high grass formed a network through which we were obliged to cut our way."

On January 8th, 1860, the men of the companies of the 1st West India Regiment stationed at Nassau specially distinguished themselves at an alarming fire that there broke out at Fort Charlotte, and the following Garrison Order was published on the subject:

"Lieutenant-Colonel Bourchier takes the earliest opportunity in his power of expressing his thanks to Major R. D'O. Fletcher, the officers, the non-commissioned officers, and the men of the 1st West India Regiment, for the prompt manner in which they turned out and lent their efforts to avert the extension of the late fire at Fort Charlotte.

"Such occasions as this test the discipline of a corps in a high degree, the more so when, as in the present instance, the danger of an explosion from the proximity of the flames to the magazine was imminent.

"Where all were zealous, the conduct of Ensign Bourke, 1st West India Regiment, was most conspicuous, who, assisted by Company Sergeant-Major Mason and a party of four men of the regiment, placed wet blankets on the most exposed portion of the roof of the magazine, which was then actually ignited; and it will be most gratifying to Lieutenant-Colonel Bourchier to bring the circumstance under the notice of H.R.H. the General Commanding-in-Chief."

At the Gambia nothing of moment had occurred since 1807, with the exception that a violent epidemic of fever broke out at Bathurst in September, 1859, to which one officer and several men of the regiment succumbed.

CHAPTER XXIV
THE BADDIBOO WAR, 1860-61

The next active operations in which the 1st West India Regiment was engaged, took place at the Gambia, where the King of Baddiboo, an important Mohammedan state up the river, had in August and September, 1860, plundered the factories of several British traders, and afterwards refused to pay compensation. The Governor of the Gambia, Colonel D'Arcy, resolved to blockade the kingdom of Baddiboo, in the hope that the enforced suspension of trade would compel the king to come to terms, and, on October 10th, 1860, the gunners of the companies of the 1st West India Regiment stationed at Bathurst embarked in the barque *Elm* and the schooner *Shamrock*, to close all the Baddiboo river ports. On November 3rd additional gunners were sent in the schooner *Hope*, and the blockade was strictly enforced, the natives not being allowed to export any articles of produce or import anything.

While the blockade was still in force, the wing of the 2nd West India Regiment, which had been wrecked in the troopship *Perseverance* at Maio, one of the Cape Verde Islands, while on its way to relieve the wing of the 1st West India Regiment, arrived in West Africa in various vessels, three companies at the Gambia and three at Sierra Leone; and as in January, 1861, the blockade had manifestly failed in its object of inducing the King of Baddiboo to indemnify the plundered merchants, Governor D'Arcy determined to take advantage of the presence of an unusual number of regular troops to organise a formidable expedition; which step was rendered necessary from the fact that the numerous Mohammedan tribes around the settlement and on the banks of the river were narrowly watching events, and had, owing to the long delay in punishing the King of Baddiboo, already commenced to show signs of lawlessness.

On January 12th, 1861, the hired transport *Avon* arrived at the Gambia to convey the wing of the 1st West India Regiment to the West Indies, and Colonel D'Arcy proceeded in her to Sierra Leone to make arrangements for the services of a portion of the garrison of that settlement. On February 2nd, he returned to the Gambia in the *Avon* with three companies of the 1st West India Regiment and one of the 2nd West India Regiment.

The expeditionary force now consisted of six companies of the 1st West India Regiment, under Lieutenant-Colonel A.W. Murray, and four of the 2nd West India Regiment, under Major W. Hill; the Gambia Militia were called out, and the West India detachments at McCarthy's Island, Cape St. Mary's, and Fort Bullen replaced by pensioners.

Everything being in readiness, the Governor decided to make one last endeavour to arrive at a peaceful solution of the difficulty (although the king's people had recently, on several occasions, fired on the schooners blockading the river), and despatched H.M.S. *Torch* with a flag of truce to Swarra Cunda Creek. Commander Smith returned with the intelligence that the natives had prepared stockaded earthworks, were assembled in large numbers, and had refused to hold any communication with the ship.

On February 15th, the expedition left Bathurst, and steaming up to Swarra Cunda Creek, some forty miles up the river, anchored there for the night. The troops were under the command of Lieutenant-Colonel Murray, 1st West India Regiment, and were thus distributed:

The gunners of the 1st and 2nd West India Regiment on board H.M.S. *Torch*.

Nos. 1 and 7 Companies, 1st West India Regiment, on board the Colonial steamer *Dover*.

Nos. 2 and 3 Companies, 1st West India Regiment, on the schooner *Elizabeth*.

Nos. 4 and 7 Companies, 2nd West India Regiment, on the schooner *Margaret*.

The *Dover*, after distributing her contingent amongst the other three vessels lying in the creek, returned to Bathurst the same night to bring up Nos. 4 and 6 Companies of the 1st West India Regiment and two companies of the 2nd West India Regiment.

On February 16th, the whole force being collected, the *Torch* and the *Dover* steamed up the creek to the trading landing-place of Swarra Cunda, towing the schooners. The earthworks were observed to be full of armed men, who shouted and brandished their weapons, amid a tremendous beating of war-drums. The *Torch* anchored about 180 yards from the earthworks, the two schooners lying above her and the *Dover* below, in such positions as to be able to bring a cross-fire to bear. The Governor, being still anxious to avoid bloodshed, hailed the enemy through his interpreter, calling upon them to surrender. They replied with yells of defiance, and were then informed that if they did not abandon their works the ships would open fire in half-an-hour.

The half-hour having elapsed without any result, except a considerable accession to the enemy's strength, fire was opened from the guns of the *Torch* and *Dover*, while the troops poured in a destructive storm of musketry. The enemy replied with great spirit; and, although the sixty-eight-pounder shell were crushing through the earthworks and carrying away large portions of the parapets, some of the warriors continued calmly up and down in full view on the most exposed portions of the works, to encourage the others; and it was not until this terrible fire of shell and musketry had lasted for three hours, that the natives began to abandon their works, retiring even then very gradually. This movement being observed, a landing was at once ordered; and the boats, which had been collected together under cover of the *Torch*, pulled in rapidly for the landing-place. Before, however, they reached the shore, some 800 natives, who had occupied the extreme right of the earthworks, which had not suffered from our fire as much as the other portions, rushed down to oppose them.

The landing was effected in the teeth of all opposition, the troops wading ashore and attacking the enemy with the bayonet. Colonel D'Arcy in his despatch says:—"Nothing could exceed the gallantry of the landing on the part of the officers and men of the 1st and 2nd West India Regiments; and now commenced a smart skirmish with a numerous enemy, in which our black soldiers evinced a gallantry and a determination to close which I felt proud to witness."

While this stubborn and hand-to-hand conflict was at its height, a shrill cry was suddenly heard in rear of the enemy, and at once, as if by a preconcerted plan, those natives who were disputing the landing broke and fled, while, at the same moment, a body of some 300 cavalry debouched from the shelter of a clump of dwarf palms, and came down at full gallop on the troops, who were already somewhat scattered in pursuit of the retreating enemy. The men at once formed rallying squares, and in a moment the Mandingo horsemen were amongst them, brandishing their scimetars and discharging matchlocks and pistols. The fire from the squares was so steady and well sustained, that, with one exception, the enemy could effect nothing. They rode round and round the squares for a few minutes, uttering shouts of defiance and endeavouring to reach the men with their spears; and finally, a good many saddles having been emptied, galloped off as rapidly as they had come, their long robes streaming out behind in the wind. The one exception referred to was that of a group of three men of the 1st West India Regiment and two of the 2nd, who, having advanced too far in pursuit, had become separated from their comrades, and, on the sudden appearance of the cavalry, had not time to reach any of the squares. They stood back to back, surrounded by the enemy, until overwhelmed by force of numbers and ridden down, being afterwards found lying where they had stood, surrounded by eleven dead Mandingoes whom they had shot or bayoneted.

This cavalry charge was the last hope of the enemy; and no sooner was it repulsed than they withdrew in great disorder. The troops pursued for a short distance, but as it was not deemed advisable to scatter the small force, especially as the day was beginning to close, they were soon recalled, and the men bivouacked on the ground they had so ably won, the bivouac being so arranged that the guns of the *Torch* could sweep the front and one flank. Wells were dug, the dead buried, and the night passed without further disturbance.

Next morning, the 17th, the Gambia Militia Artillery, with 400 native allies, arrived and landed, and in the afternoon the 1st and 2nd West India Regiments, under Lieutenant-Colonel Murray, after a short resistance, took and destroyed the stockaded town of Carawan, situated to the right of the position. Encouraged by this success, the native allies and the Gambia Militia Artillery advanced to the town of Swarra Cunda, to the left of the position, and finding it abandoned, destroyed it also.

During the ensuing night, H.M.S. *Arrogant*, Commodore Edmonstone, arrived in the Gambia River, and early next morning the *Dover* brought the Commodore, with a naval brigade of seamen and marines, up to Swarra Cunda Creek. This unlooked-for accession of strength determined Lieutenant-Colonel Murray to advance into the interior, and strike a blow that would bring the war to a conclusion. Cattle were obtained for the field-guns, which were then landed, and about noon on the 18th, the force marched inland, four companies of the 1st West India Regiment forming the right division, four of the 2nd West India Regiment the left division, and two of the 1st the reserve, with the guns on the flanks.

The country through which the advance was made was a level sandy plain, covered with tall grass, and dotted here and there with clumps of baobab and dwarf palm. Occasionally a few clearings for the cultivation of the ground nut were met, but as a rule the march was made through grass more than waist high. The enemy showed in force, but made no serious opposition to the advance; and, though large bodies of cavalry were observed hanging about the flanks and rear, they showed no disposition to close, and the towns of Kinty-Cunda and Sabba were destroyed without loss on our side, and very small loss, if any, on the part of the enemy.

The 19th and 20th were devoted to changing the camping ground, and arranging a plan of campaign against Indear, the king's town, in which the shipping might be used as a base; but, on the afternoon of the latter day, a slave-girl, who came into the camp to claim British protection, reported that the king's warriors, having been largely reinforced, had come down from Indear, and had erected a stockade on the ruins of Sabba. Although it did not suit Lieut.-Colonel Murray's plans to return to Sabba, he did not consider it advisable to leave this unexpected challenge unanswered; and, on the morning of February 21st, the force again marched for Sabba.

On approaching that town it was ascertained that a double stockade had been built, which appeared to be full of armed men, while detached parties were observed partially concealed in the long grass to the left of the stockade, and facing our right. The troops were halted and formed for attack, the Naval Brigade, consisting of seamen and marines from H.M.S. *Arrogant*, *Falcon*, and *Torch*, being in the centre, four companies of the 1st West India Regiment on the right, four of the 2nd on the left, and two of the 1st in reserve. The howitzer battery at once opened on the stockade, and, after a few rounds, the centre advanced to within effective rifle range and commenced firing. Directly this movement took place, the detached parties of Mandingoes on our right approached skirmishing through the tall grass, and attacked the four companies of the 1st West India Regiment, while large bodies of cavalry simultaneously appeared on the left, threatening the flank of the 2nd West India Regiment. While the 1st West India Regiment was hotly engaged on the right, the field-guns of the Gambia Militia Artillery, under Colonel D'Arcy, who was present as a volunteer and honorary colonel of that corps, were hastily brought up, and opened fire on the stockade, to breach it. As it was apparent that this would be a work of some time, the timber of which the stockade was built being quite stout enough to withstand for some time the fire of light guns, Lieutenant-Colonel Murray directed the Commodore to storm. In an instant the seamen extended, and, advancing at a sharp run, clambered over the stockades, and, attacking the enemy with the bayonet, soon carried the place. Acting in concert with this forward movement of the centre, the right (1st West India Regiment) closed on the natives with whom they had been engaged, and, cutting them off from the stockade, killed or wounded the entire force on this side, with a loss to themselves of one officer (Lieutenant Bourke) and twenty-two men severely wounded, besides slight casualties. The cavalry on the left, seeing the turn affairs had taken, withdrew without making any attack. The Naval Brigade lost Lieutenant Hamilton, of the *Arrogant*, and three men killed, and twenty-two wounded.

Ensign Garsia, of the 1st West India Regiment, had a narrow escape. Shortly before the Naval Brigade had advanced to storm, he had been despatched by Lieutenant-Colonel Murray with an order to Major Hill, commanding on the left, and, in crossing the front of the stockade under a heavy fire, both he and his horse were shot and rolled over together, Ensign Garsia being very severely wounded. While thus lying at a distance of some seventy yards from the stockade, a Mohammedan, dressed in yellow—a colour only assumed in this part of the world when the wearer is engaged in some desperate enterprise—climbed over the stockade and ran towards the wounded man with a drawn scimetar in his hand. He escaped numerous shots that were fired at him, reached Ensign Garsia, and had actually raised his scimetar to strike off his head, when a wounded sailor, who was lying on the ground, shot him dead, with his cry of exultation on his lips.

No sooner was the enemy dispersed and in full retreat, than messengers arrived from the King of Jocardo, whose territory is separated from Baddiboo by the Swarra Cunda Creek, begging an interview with the Governor, and promising that, if he would grant a three days' armistice, he would bring together all the chiefs of the Baddiboo towns, who were now anxious for peace, but afraid to come in. The Governor acceded to these terms, but, in case of negotiations failing, Lieutenant-Colonel Murray proceeded with his preparations for an advance on Indear on the morning of the 25th. On the 24th, the Governor received another message from the King of Jocardo, begging him to extend the armistice for another day, the distance to the different towns being so great. This was granted, and at 6 a.m. on the 26th, the King of Baddiboo came to terms, promising to pay a considerable sum to the Government as a fine for his past misdemeanours, and leaving hostages in the Governor's hands.

The officers of the 1st West India Regiment who took part in this expedition were Lieutenant-Colonel A.W. Murray, Captains H. Anton, J.A. Fraser, J. Fanning, and G.H. Duyer, Lieutenants A. Temple, J. Moffitt, R. Brew, T. Edmunds, J. Bourke, and Ensigns M.C. Garsia and T. Nicholson. Lieutenant-Colonel Murray was awarded the C.B. for his services.

CHAPTER XXV
THE ASHANTI EXPEDITION, 1864

The head-quarters and four companies of the 1st West India Regiment had been removed from Nassau to Barbados in the hired transport *Avon*, before that vessel sailed for West Africa, and on the 3rd of March, 1861, the six companies of the regiment embarked in her at the Gambia for the West Indies. During the four years' tour of service which they had just completed, five officers had fallen victims to the fatal West African climate, Lieutenant Kenrick having died at Sierra Leone, in August, 1857; Lieutenant Leggatt, in February, 1859; Brevet-Major Pratt, in July, 1859; and Captain Owens, in July, 1860; while Lieutenant E. Smith had died at the Gambia, in September, 1859.

On the arrival of the wing from West Africa, the regiment was distributed in the West Indies as follows: The head-quarters, with Nos. 5, 7, and 8, the Grenadier and Light Companies at Barbados; Nos. 1 and 2 at St. Lucia; No. 3 at Trinidad; and Nos. 4 and 6 at Demerara. Towards the close of the year the practice of selecting men for flank companies was forbidden by Horse Guards General Order, and the grenadier and light companies became Nos. 9 and 10.

The regiment remained thus stationed until December, 1862, when the three existing West India Regiments were called upon to furnish two companies each for the formation of a new 4th West India Regiment, and Nos. 9 and 10 Companies of the 1st West India Regiment were transferred. In the same month, No. 1 Company rejoined head-quarters from St. Lucia. The establishment of the regiment was now eight instead of ten companies as formerly.

On the 23rd of December, 1862, a detachment of three companies (Nos. 5, 7, and 8) embarked in the troopship *Adventure*, under Lieutenant-Colonel Macauley, and proceeded to Honduras, arriving there on January 3rd, 1863. A war of reprisals between the Santa Cruz and Ycaiché Indians was then raging on the frontier, and the greatest vigilance was necessary to prevent violation of British territory, the detachments of the regiment at the outposts of Orange Walk and Corosal being continually employed.

In March, 1863, the whole of the southern side of Belize was destroyed by fire, and the detachment of the 1st West India Regiment there stationed received the thanks of the Legislative Assembly for the assistance it had rendered in preventing the conflagration spreading, a sum of $200 being voted for the men, "as an acknowledgment of the valuable services rendered by them." In this, or the preceding year, companies were designated alphabetically instead of numerically; No. 1 becoming "A," No. 2, "B," and so on.

On the 31st of October, 1863, A Company, with the head-quarters, embarked at Barbados on board the troopship *Megæra*, which had arrived the day before from Demerara with D and F Companies. The vessel then proceeded to St. Lucia, where B Company was embarked, and all four went to Nassau. The distribution of the regiment was then: 4 companies at Nassau, 3 in Honduras, and 1 in Trinidad.

In 1863 occurred what is usually called the Second Ashanti War. It was caused, as almost every Ashanti war or threat of invasion has been caused, by the refusal of the Governor of the Gold Coast to surrender to the Ashanti King fugitives who had sought British protection. In revenge for this refusal an Ashanti force made a raid into the Protectorate, and reinforcements were at once asked for by the Colonial Government. In December, 1863, B Company, 1st West India Regiment, under Captain Bravo, embarked at Nassau in H.M.S. *Barracouta* for Jamaica, and proceeded, towards the end of February, 1864, to Honduras, in the troopship *Tamar*. There E and G Companies embarked, and all three, under the command of Major Anton, sailed for Cape Coast Castle on the 2nd of March, arriving there on the 9th of April. The officers of the regiment serving with these companies were Major Anton, Captains Bravo and Hopewell Smith, Lieutenants J.A. Smith, Gavin, Roberts, Smithwick, Lowry, Barlow, Allinson, and Ensign Alt.

On the arrival of the detachment of the 1st West India Regiment at Cape Coast Castle, the strength of the expeditionary force was as follows:

	Officers.	Men.
1st West India Regiment	11	300
2nd West India Regiment	6	170
3rd West India Regiment	6	170
4th West India Regiment	30	850
5th West India Regiment	4	10
	—	—
	57	1,500

The rainy season—the most unhealthy period of the year on the Gold Coast—was then commencing, and the Government appear to have had some idea of making an advance upon Coomassie at its close—about the month of June or July. In order to have everything in readiness for the forward movement, depôts of stores and munitions of war had been established at Mansu and Prahsu, and at Swaidroo in Akim, detachments of troops being stationed at these places for their protection. These detachments the Colonel commanding the troops on the Gold Coast determined to maintain during the rainy season, and it fell to the lot of B and G Companies of the 1st West India Regiment to be detailed for the fatal duty of relieving the detachment then encamped at Prahsu.

Towards the end of the month of April these two companies, under Captains Bravo and Hopewell Smith, started amidst continuous torrents of rain on their march of seventy-four miles to the Prah. They had, since their arrival, been encamped with E Company on the open space to the west of the town known as the parade ground, there being no accommodation for them in the Castle; and owing to the unsanitary condition of the site and the want of proper shelter, had already begun to suffer from the effects of the climate.

On arriving at the Prah they encamped at the ford of Prahsu, at a point where the river, making a sudden bend, enclosed the encampment on three sides. Here in the midst of a primeval forest, on the banks of a pestilential stream, without proper shelter or proper food, they remained for nearly three months. The sickness that ensued was almost unparalleled. Before they had been a month encamped, four officers and 102 men were sick out of seven officers and 214 men who had marched out of Cape Coast; and the hospital accommodation was so bad that the men had to lie on the wet ground with pools of water under them. The rains were unusually severe, the camp speedily became a swamp, the troops had worse food than usual, and, above all, were compelled to remain inactive. The small force had no means of communication with the coast, and no expectation of a reinforcement; and, had the enemy made an appearance, the troops were hardly in a fit state to defend themselves. Day after day torrents of rain fell; it was impossible to light fires for cooking purposes except under flimsy sheds of palm branches; and night after night officers and men turned into their wretched and dripping tents hungry and drenched to the skin. Neither was there any occupation for the mind or body, and universal gloom and despondency set in. It was no unusual thing for two funerals to take place in one day, and the unfortunate soldiers saw their small force diminishing day by day, apparently forgotten and neglected by the rest of the world.

By a general order published at Cape Coast Castle, on the 30th of May, 1864, the garrison at Prahsu was, on account of the sickness there prevailing, reduced to 100 men; and on the 6th of June, G Company, under Captain Hopewell Smith, marched from the Prah and proceeded to Anamaboe, a village on the sea-coast some thirteen miles to the east of Cape Coast Castle. B Company still continued to suffer severely, and on the 18th of June, 57 men were in hospital out of a total strength of 100.

At last the Imperial Government resolved to put a stop to the waste of life that was taking place, and sent out instructions to the Colonial Government that all operations against the Ashantis were to cease, and the troops to be withdrawn. The welcome intelligence reached Prahsu on the 26th of June, but the work of burying the guns and destroying the stores and ammunition, which had been collected there at such great labour and expense that the Government did not care to incur it again in their removal, occupied several days, and it was not until the 12th of July that the detachment marched out of the deadly camp on the Prah.

On the 27th of July, the hired transport *Wambojeez* arrived at Cape Coast Castle, to remove the detachments of the 1st and 2nd West India Regiments to the West Indies, and on the 30th they embarked. The day before their embarkation the following general order was issued:

"(General Order, No. 285.)

"Brigade Office, Cape Coast Castle,
"28th July, 1864.

"Paragraph 3.—The Lieutenant-Colonel commanding feels great pleasure in publishing, for the information of the officers and soldiers of the 1st and 2nd West India Regiments about to embark for the West Indies, the following handsome testimony of their soldierlike conduct while employed on the late expedition, by His Excellency Governor Pine, in which feelings and kind sentiments the Lieutenant-Colonel fully concurs, adding his own thanks to Major Anton and Captain Reece for the ready and cheerful manner in which they co-operated with him in carrying out the duties of the command, and to the officers and men under their respective orders.

"It is a pleasing duty to the Lieutenant-Colonel to have to announce to these corps that, from the day they took the field until this hour, not a complaint has been brought by an inhabitant against any of the men, so excellent has the conduct of all been.

"It is also gratifying to Lieutenant-Colonel Conran to see so few men on the sick list when about to embark, considering the large numbers that were reported sick on their return from the front."

"Government House, Cape Coast,
"27th July, 1864.

"Sir,

"On the eve of the departure of the detachments of the 1st and 2nd West India Regiments, which have been annexed to your command on my requisition since April last, I request that you will be pleased to permit me, through you, to record my thanks as Governor of these settlements for the services they have performed conjointly with yourself and regiment.

"I feel that I have been the means of imposing upon Her Majesty's troops a laborious, ungracious, and apparently thankless duty; but my intentions and motives have been so fully, and I trust, satisfactorily discussed throughout Great Britain, that I dare hope that the officers and men will believe that I invited them to participate in a constitutional measure, which I felt convinced would add to their military reputation and honour.

"To the decision of Her Majesty's Government as to its altered policy we are all compelled to bow, and it only remains for me to express my regret to every officer and man of the 1st and 2nd West India Regiments, for the natural and laudable disappointment which they have experienced in not being engaged in more active military operations, and to tender my heartfelt thanks for the prompt and ready obedience with which they responded to my call on behalf of our Royal Mistress, and for their patience and endurance under extraordinary trial.

"Major Anton I have served with, and marked with admiration his display of fortitude, moral courage, and disinterested kindness during the fearful epidemic of 1859 in the Gambia. Captain Bravo, as second in command in the Gambia, was my esteemed friend, and enjoyed the respect of all who knew him.

"This hasty and imperfect notice I trust you will not deem unworthy of being communicated to the highest military authority, and I shall esteem myself fortunate indeed if I shall be instrumental in the remotest degree in their advancement.

"I have, etc.,

(Signed)   "Richard Pine,

"Governor and Commander-in-Chief, Gold Coast.

"The Hon. Colonel Conran,
"Commanding the troops on the Gold Coast."

The *Wambojeez* arrived at Barbados on the 3rd of September; there the detachment of the 1st West India Regiment embarked by companies in H.M.S. *Pylades*, *Greyhound*, and *Styx*, for Jamaica, and disembarked at Port Royal on the 15th of September. H and C Companies rejoining at Jamaica soon after from Honduras and Trinidad, the distribution of the regiment was as follows: head-quarters and three companies at Nassau, five companies in Jamaica.

> Note.—Out of the 11 officers and 300 non-commissioned officers and men who landed at Cape Coast Castle on the 9th April, only 6 officers and 269 non-commissioned officers and men re-embarked on July 30th, 5 officers having been invalided, and 31 men having died during their short stay of three months and a half.

CHAPTER XXVI
THE JAMAICA REBELLION, 1865

In October, 1865, a rebellion broke out amongst the black population of Jamaica. On the 7th of that month, at the Petty Sessions at Morant Bay, a prisoner, who had been convicted of an assault, was rescued from the police, and on the 9th a warrant was issued for the apprehension of two persons named Bogle and several others, who were stated to have taken an active part in the riot of the 7th. Six policemen and two rural constables proceeded, early on the morning of the 10th of October, to execute this warrant at Stony Gut, about five miles from Morant Bay, where Paul Bogle and some other of the alleged rioters lived. They found Bogle in his yard, and told him that they had a warrant for his apprehension. He desired to have the warrant read to him, which was done. He then said that he would not go, and upon one of the policemen proceeding to apprehend him, he cried out: "Help, here!" At the same time, a man named Grant, who was with him, and who was addressed as "Captain," called out, "Turn out, men." Almost immediately a body of men, variously estimated at from 300 to 500, armed with cutlasses, sticks, and pikes, rushed out from a chapel where Bogle was in the habit of preaching, and from an adjoining cane-field, and attacked the policemen.

THE COUNTY OF SURREY
JAMAICA.

The police were, of course, overpowered. Some of them were severely beaten. Three of their number were made prisoners and detained for several hours, being ultimately only released upon their taking an oath that they would "join their colour," and "cleave to the black."

So far, perhaps, the disturbances might have been considered to be nothing more than an ordinary riot; but the proceedings of the rioters on the following day soon put their intentions beyond all reasonable doubt.

On the 11th of October the Vestry, consisting of certain elected members and magistrates, assembled in the court-house at Morant Bay about noon, and proceeded with their ordinary business till between three and four o'clock, when notice was given that a crowd of people was approaching. The volunteers were hastily called together, and almost immediately afterwards a body of men, armed with cutlasses, sticks, bayonets, and muskets, after having attacked the police station and obtained possession of such arms as were there deposited, were seen entering a large open space facing the court-house, in front of which the volunteers had been drawn up. The Custos, Baron Ketelhodt, went out to the steps, and called to the people to know what they wanted. He received no answer, and his cries of "Peace! peace!" were met by cries from the crowd of "War!"

As the advancing mob drew near, the volunteers retired till they reached the steps of the court-house. The Custos then began to read the Riot Act. While he was in the act of reading it stones were thrown at the volunteers, and Captain Hitchins, who commanded them, was struck in the forehead. The captain, having received authority from the Custos, then gave the word to fire. The order was obeyed, and some of the rioters were seen to fall. The volunteers were soon overpowered, and the court-house, in which refuge was sought, was set on fire. Many people were barbarously murdered while trying to escape. Eighteen persons, including the Custos, two sons of the rector, the Island Curate of Bath, the Inspector of Police, the captain, two lieutenants, a sergeant, and three privates of volunteers were killed. Thirty-one persons were wounded.

After this the town remained in possession of the rioters. The gaolers were compelled to throw open the prison doors, and fifty-one prisoners who were there confined were released. Several stores were attacked, and from one of them a considerable quantity of gunpowder was taken. An attempt was made to force the door of the magazine, where about 300 stand of arms were stored. Fortunately the endeavour was not successful.

Major-General L.S. O'Connor, commanding the troops in Jamaica, was inspecting the left wing of the 1st West India Regiment, under Major Anton, at Up Park Camp, on the morning of the 11th of October, when the news of the riot at Stony Gut on the 10th arrived, with a requisition from Governor

Eyre for 100 men in aid of the civil power. In less than an hour Captain Ross's company paraded and marched to Kingston, where they embarked in H.M.S. *Wolverine*. Unfortunately, it not being supposed that there was any necessity for urgency, the *Wolverine* did not leave Port Royal for Morant Bay until daybreak on the 12th. At about noon on the 12th the news of the massacre of the magistrates reached Port Royal, where Major-General O'Connor was inspecting the detachment of the 1st West India Regiment, under Captain Luke. In two hours from the receipt of the intelligence, the company embarked on board H.M.S. *Onyx*, and landed at Morant Bay on the morning of the 13th.

Captain Ross, on arriving at Morant Bay, had found the town deserted by all the Europeans, except Mr. Georges, who was severely wounded with three musket balls in his leg. The bodies of the unfortunate magistrates, many of which were barbarously mutilated, were buried by this company. This duty performed, the men patrolled the roads in the neighbourhood, and many ladies, whose husbands had been murdered or taken prisoners, and who had fled with their children, on the approach of the rioters, to bamboo thickets or other shelter, hearing the sound of the bugles, came in for protection. Numbers of them had passed the night in copses, from which, trembling with terror, they had seen their houses pillaged.

On the 12th of October, large parties of the rebels, armed with guns and cutlasses, marched in military order through Bath and other contiguous districts. Stores were pillaged, and property taken or destroyed. Blue Mountain Valley Estate, Amity Hall, Monklands, which is sixteen miles from Morant Bay, and Hordley Estate, were all attacked by the insurgents, the occupiers barely escaping with their lives. At Blue Mountain Valley and Amity Hall, barbarous murders were perpetrated.

On the 13th of October, martial law was proclaimed throughout the county of Surrey (except the county and city of Kingston), and Major-General O'Connor immediately took steps to hem in the disturbed districts. On the 15th of October, a detachment of the 1st West India Regiment was sent to Port Antonio; and at mid-day, Captain Hole, of the 6th Regiment, with 40 men of his own corps, and 60 of the 1st West India Regiment, under Ensign Cullen, marched from that place to Manchioneal, twenty miles eastward of Port Antonio. On the same day, 120 men of the 6th Regiment, under Colonel Hobbs, occupied (as head-quarters) Monklands, in the district of the Blue Mountain Valley, about sixteen miles from Morant Bay. Captain Strachan's company of the 1st West India Regiment proceeded to Spanish Town, whence Lieutenant Allinson, with 31 men, was sent on to Linstead, where a repetition of the Morant Bay massacre was apprehended. A detachment of the 6th was sent to Buff Bay to protect some valuable sugar estates.

On the 13th and two succeeding days the insurgents continued their course through Port Morant northward to Manchioneal, and on to Mulatto River and Elmwood; the last of which places is situated in the most northerly part of St. Thomas-in-the-East, where that parish abuts upon Portland. As they advanced with the cry of "colour for colour" they were joined by a considerable number of negroes, who readily assisted in the work of plundering. The houses and stores were sacked. The intention also of taking the lives of the whites was openly avowed, and diligent search was made for particular individuals. But in each case the imperilled person had timely notice, and sought safety in flight.

Elmwood was the point furthest from Morant Bay to which the disturbances extended; the arrival of the troops at Port Antonio, on the 15th, putting a stop to the further progress of the insurgents northwards. Thus in the course of four days the rebels had spread over a tract of country extending from White Horses, a few miles to the west of Morant Bay, to Elmwood, at a distance of upwards of thirty miles to the north-east of that place.

In the meantime, detachments of troops were rapidly converging upon the disturbed districts. As the rebels were reported to be occupying Stony Gut, an almost impregnable ravine three miles in length, a detachment of the 6th Regiment was sent to dislodge them. Captain Luke, 1st West India Regiment, by a rapid and judicious movement of his company towards Cuna Cuna Gap, rescued from the hands of the insurgents upwards of eighty Europeans and influential people of colour, who had, with their wives and children, been in hiding for three or four days in the woods and mountains, and conveyed them to a place of safety. Captain Hole moved towards Bath from Manchioneal, and, in a despatch to Brigadier-General Nelson, he mentions "a meritorious act of three privates of the 1st West India Regiment deserving commendation. The three men got separated from their party, and proceeded as far as the Plantain Garden River, where a great number of rebels are lurking. The soldiers encountering the rebels, shot several—among them three of the murderers of Mr. Hire—and brought back with them two cartloads of plunder, among which was some of Mr. Hire's clothing, and other property."

Kingston, as has been said, was exempted from martial law, and consequently became the refuge of the most disaffected people. Arrests were made hourly, and upwards of two hundred political prisoners were confined in the military custody of the 1st West India Regiment at Up Park Camp, which was under martial law. Threats were daily circulated that the city would be fired in various places, and the streets were patrolled by day and night. Sunday, the 22nd of October, was said to be fixed for a massacre of the loyal inhabitants while at church, and such universal panic prevailed, that every place of worship was on that day empty.

The insurgents gradually dispersed as the troops advanced, numbers being captured. On the 23rd of October, Paul Bogle, the ringleader, was taken; and, on the 24th, was tried and hanged. On the same day, George William Gordon, a coloured member of the House of Assembly, who had been tried by a court-martial on the 21st, and found guilty of complicity in the rebellion, was hanged at Morant Bay. All the insurgents taken in arms were put to death, and the houses of those who were known to have taken part in the insurrection were burned. By these vigorous measures all outward signs of resistance were crushed, and the movement prevented from becoming general; though reports were constantly received from various parts of the island, of disloyalty and seditious intentions.

On the 29th of October, letters D and F Companies of the 1st West India Regiment, with Major McBean, Captains Ormsby and Smithwick, Lieutenants Lowry, Niven, Hill, and Bale, and Ensign Cole, arrived from Nassau. Detachments were at once sent to Port Maria under Captain Ormsby, to Savannah la Mar under Lieutenant Hill, and to Vere under Lieutenant Bale. The 2nd West India Regiment, arriving from Barbados, was stationed along the north-western coast of the island.

From evidence subsequently obtained it was evident that the rising had been long planned, and that the outbreak at Morant Bay was premature. It is clear that meetings took place, where bodies of men were drilled, oaths administered, and the names of persons registered. The insurgents were so confident of ultimate success that the crops were uninjured, and the buildings for the most part preserved; they openly avowing that they intended taking them for themselves, when the whites were expelled. The rebels appear to have expected that the Maroons would join them, but that people remained faithful to their allegiance, and assisted in the suppression of the disturbances.

Although all the rebels in the field were taken or dispersed before the end of October, the island was not entirely quiet for some time after; and as late as the 14th of December, a detachment of the 1st West India Regiment, under Captain Ross, was sent from Black River to Oxford Estate, thirty miles distant, that place being reported to be disaffected.

Major-General O'Connor, in his despatch reporting the restoration of order, says: "The men employed in the field, exposed to the tropical sun, heavy rains, constant and long marches by day and night, have all (the 2nd 6th Regiment, and the 1st West India Regiment) highly distinguished themselves by their patience, perseverance, and general good conduct." He might have added that the fidelity of the black soldiers of the 1st West India Regiment could hardly have been put to a more crucial test. Nine-tenths of those men were Jamaicans, born and bred, and in the work of suppressing the rebellion they were required to hang, capture, and destroy the habitations of not only their countrymen and friends, but, in many instances, of their near relatives. Yet in no single case did any man hesitate to obey orders, nor was the loyalty of any one soldier ever a matter for doubt.

Governor Eyre having, by his prompt and vigorous measures, saved the colony of Jamaica from a repetition of those horrors which devastated the French West India Islands in the early part of the century, was subjected to a most vindictive and ungenerous attack on the part of the Exeter Hall party in England. By that party the judicial executions of the rebels were stigmatised as "atrocities," while the massacre at Morant Bay and the murders of the planters were only spoken of as "unfortunate occurrences." Owing to their clamour, a commission was sent out from England to inquire into the state of affairs in the colony. The commission arrived at the following conclusion: "That though the original design for the overthrow of constituted authority was confined to a small portion of the parish of St. Thomas-in-the-East, yet that the disorder, in fact, spread with singular rapidity over an extensive tract of country, and that such was the state of excitement prevailing in other parts of the island, that had more than a momentary success been obtained by the insurgents, their ultimate overthrow would have been attended with a still more fearful loss of life and property."

Many of the disaffected negroes, finding that they were being backed up by an influential party in England, preferred the most unfounded charges against several of the officers who had been most active in the suppression of the rebellion. Amongst others, Ensign Cullen, of the 1st West India Regiment, was charged with having had three men wantonly shot at Duckinfield Suspension Bridge, on the 21st of October, while on the march from Manchioneal to Golden Grove; and Staff-Assistant-Surgeon Morris, who had been in medical charge of Ensign Cullen's detachment, was charged with shooting a fourth man.

After these charges had been allowed to hang over these officers' heads for nearly a year, they were given an opportunity of clearing themselves before a general court martial, which assembled at Up Park Camp on the 2nd of October, 1866, and terminated its proceedings on the 4th of December. It is needless to say that both were acquitted.[59]

For the valuable and efficient services rendered by the regiment during this rebellion, the House of Assembly in Jamaica voted the sum of £100 to be expended in plate.

In March, 1866, all being quiet in Jamaica, Captain Smithwick's company returned to Nassau in H.M.S. *Sphynx*, being followed by Captain Ormsby's company, in August, in H.M.S. *Barracouta*.

FOOTNOTES:

[59] The following was the composition of the court:

Lieutenant-Colonel R.T. Farren, C.B., Depôt Battalion—President.

Major	W.R. Williamson,	48th	Regiment	} .	
"	J.H. Campbell,	71st	"		
Captain	F.D. Walters,	44th	"	}	
"	J.G. Day,	28th	"		Members
"	J.A. Barstow,	89th	"	}	
"	J.L. Seton,	102nd	"		
"	C.V. Oliver,	66th	"	}	
"	J.T. Ready,	66th	"		

Captain Maclean, Rifle Brigade—Officiating Judge Advocate.

Brevet Lieutenant-Colonel C.F.J. Daniell, 28th Regiment—Prosecutor.

CHAPTER XXVII
AFRICAN TOUR, 1866-70

In August, 1866, it again became the turn of the 1st West India Regiment to furnish a portion of the garrisons of the Western Coast of Africa. The system of these garrisons had again been changed, and now consisted of one battalion divided between Sierra Leone and the Gambia, and half a battalion distributed between the Gold Coast and Lagos. At this time the left wing of the 2nd West India Regiment was garrisoning the two latter colonies, and the 1st West India Regiment was to garrison the two former.

On the 29th of August, 1866, four companies under Major Anton embarked at Jamaica in H.M.S. *Simoom*, and proceeded to Africa; two being landed at the Gambia on the 28th of September, and two at Sierra Leone on the 6th of October. The *Simoom*, returning to the West Indies, embarked the remaining company at Jamaica in November; and proceeding to Nassau, the head-quarters and three companies there stationed were also embarked, the whole arriving at Sierra Leone, under Captain Bravo, on the 31st of December. The distribution of the regiment now was: Head-quarters, with A, B, D, E, F, and G Companies at Sierra Leone; C and H Companies at the Gambia. Major Anton was in command at the latter station, and on the 25th of May, 1867, Lieutenant-Colonel Yonge arrived at Sierra Leone and assumed command there.

In the beginning of August, 1867, a disturbance of a serious character occurred on the Gold Coast at Mumford, a town situated half-way between Cape Coast Castle and Accra; and Lieutenant H.F.S. Bolton, 1st West India Regiment, who, being temporarily in the employ of the Colonial Government, was Civil Commandant of the latter town, was despatched with a party of the 2nd West India Regiment to establish order. The cause of the disturbance was an old-standing quarrel between two of the native companies at Mumford, and a conflict had taken place, resulting in a large number of killed and wounded. On the arrival of the troops the principal offenders were arrested, and order was restored.

Since the arrival of the regiment in Africa, small detachments had been furnished from Sierra Leone to Sherbro, Songo-town, and the island of Bulama, at the mouth of the Jeba River. In September, 1867, the troops were withdrawn from the latter station.

In October, 1867, Lieutenant Bolton was employed in arresting some recalcitrant chiefs at Pram-Pram, near Accra, Lieutenant Ness, 2nd West India Regiment, with a detachment of that corps, acting under his orders. The service was attended with considerable difficulty and some danger, and the following general order was published on the subject, dated Cape Coast Castle, January 15th, 1868:

"The officer commanding the troops has much gratification in publishing in orders an extract of a letter received from the Horse Guards, expressing the approval of His Royal Highness the Field-Marshal Commanding-in-Chief, of the manner in which the difficult duties were carried out by the officers and troops employed in the recent expedition to Pram-Pram.

"'The attention of the Field-Marshal Commanding-in-Chief having been drawn to a despatch, received at the Colonial Office, from the Administrator-in-Chief of the West Africa settlements, containing a very favourable account of the conduct of Lieutenant H.F.S. Bolton, of the 1st West India Regiment, and Lieutenant (now Captain) Ness, of the 4th West India Regiment,[60] and of the troops under their command, on a recent expedition to some chiefs at Pram-Pram and Ningo, on the Gold Coast; I am directed to acquaint you that His Royal Highness considers the report to be highly satisfactory, and I have to request that you will express to the officers and troops employed on the service in question, His Royal Highness's approval of the manner in which they carried out the very difficult duties they had to perform.'"

On the 9th of August, 1868, at the request of the Governor-in-chief, the garrison of the 2nd West India Regiment on the Gold Coast being much below its allotted strength, E Company, 1st West India Regiment, 100 strong, proceeded to Cape Coast Castle, under Lieutenant C.J.L. Hill, and, in consequence of this reduction of the Sierra Leone garrison, the Songo-town detachment was withdrawn.

In January, 1869, a company under Captain K.R. Niven, with Ensign W.A. Broome, was despatched to Sherbro Island for the protection of British subjects, an invasion of that island being hourly expected. The presence of the troops soon produced the desired effect, and the detachment returned to Sierra Leone on the 27th of February.

In April, 1869, in consequence of the difficulty experienced by the Colonial Government in arresting certain rebellious chiefs at the Amissah River, about twenty miles to the east of Cape Coast Castle, the police having been attacked and driven off, the Acting Administrator, Mr. W.H. Simpson, applied for a military party to aid in establishing the authority of the Government over the people of that place; and, on the 7th of that month, Lieutenant E.G. Macdonald, 1st West India Regiment, with twenty-five non-commissioned officers and men of letter E Company, marched for Anamaboe, leaving that place next morning for Amissah River. On arriving there the chiefs were captured with some little difficulty, and the party returned to Cape Coast next day.

On the 1st of April, 1869, the 4th West India Regiment was disbanded, and the three remaining West India regiments were each augmented by one company; the detachment of the 4th West India Regiment at Jamaica being formed into the ninth, or letter "I," Company of the 1st West India Regiment. On the 30th of September, 1869, it embarked for Honduras in the brigantine *W.N.Z.*, under Major McAuley, arriving at its destination on the 14th of October.

In May, 1869, the Gambia was visited by a severe epidemic of cholera. Owing to the sanitary measures adopted by Major W.W.W. Johnston, 1st West India Regiment, commanding the troops, the regiment escaped with only eighteen deaths out of the 200 men there stationed between the 5th of May and the 6th of June, the period when the epidemic was at its height; while in the town there were more than 1500 deaths, out of a population of some 5000.

In 1870 the three years' tour of service of the regiment on the West Coast of Africa expired. The 3rd West India Regiment having been disbanded, a considerable reduction in the West African garrisons became necessary, and it was intended that the relief for the eight companies of the 1st West India Regiment should consist of four companies of the 2nd. On the 24th of May, the head-quarters, with A, B, and F Companies, under Captain Samson, embarked at Sierra Leone in H.M.S. *Orontes*, which, proceeding to the Gambia, took on board the two companies there on the 29th. The head-quarters, with the three companies from Sierra Leone, landed at Jamaica on the 27th of June, and the *Orontes* then sailed for Nassau, where the two companies from the Gambia were disembarked. On the return of the troopship to the West Coast of Africa with the four companies of the 2nd West India Regiment, the company of the 1st West India Regiment at Cape Coast Castle was embarked on the 24th of August, and the remaining two at Sierra Leone on the 27th. All three proceeded to Jamaica, under the command of Captain J.A. Smith, and landed at Kingston on the 3rd of October. The distribution of the regiment was now as follows: head-quarters and six companies at Jamaica, two at Nassau, and one at Honduras. On the 15th of November, F Company, under Captain Butler, embarked at Jamaica for Honduras; thus making up the detachment at that station to two companies.

During the West African tour of 1866-70, two officers succumbed to the influence of the climate, Lieutenant Gavin having died at Sierra Leone on the 22nd of February, 1869, and Lieutenant Maturin on the 7th of December of the same year.

FOOTNOTES:

[60] By the Gazette of September 25th, 1867, Lieutenant R.E.D. Ness, 2nd West India Regiment, was promoted Captain, by purchase, in the 4th West India Regiment.

CHAPTER XXVIII
THE DEFENCE OF ORANGE WALK, 1872

On the 1st of September, 1872, a most determined attack was made by the Ycaiché Indians on the outpost of Orange Walk, British Honduras, which was garrisoned by thirty-eight men of the 1st West India Regiment, under Lieutenant Joseph Graham Smith.

Orange Walk is situated on a deep and sluggish stream in the northern district, named the New River,[61] at a distance of some thirty-three miles from its mouth, and, in 1872, contained a population of about 1200 souls, the majority of whom were either Indians or Hispano-Indians, and indifferent to British rule. The business portion of the town, and most of the shops or stores, were on hilly ground, considerably above the river-bed, and built here and there, without an attempt at order or regularity. About midway between the river and this upper portion of the town was the barrack, consisting of one large room, sixty feet by thirty feet, the two ends of which were partitioned off, leaving the central part for the men's quarters. The partitioned portion at the south end was used as a guard-room. The walls of the building were constructed of *pimentos*, or round straight sticks, varying from half-an-inch to three inches in diameter, driven firmly into the ground, in an upright position, as close together as possible, and held in their places by pine-wood battens. The roof was composed of palm-leaves, or "fan-thatch." The floor was boarded.

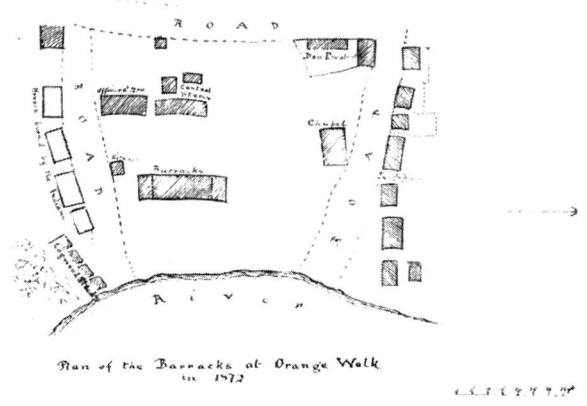

Plan of the Barracks at Orange Walk
in 1872

On the south-eastern side of the barrack, the ground fell towards the river, which was about fifty yards distant. About ten yards from the water's edge was a large quantity of logwood, packed in piles four feet high, and some little distance from each other. Across the road, on the southern side, were several native houses; to the east, and about forty yards distant, was a group of four small buildings consisting of commissariat stores and the officers' quarters; while the nearest building on the north was the Roman Catholic Church, about eighty yards off.

How or when the invaders crossed the Rio Hondo, the northern boundary of the colony, has not been ascertained; but it is a significant fact, suggestive of strong suspicions against the loyalty of the Indian and mixed Spanish-Indian population, whose small settlements were dotted here and there on the line of march of the invaders, that no information was conveyed, either to the district magistrate at Orange Walk, or to the officer commanding the small detachment, that an enemy was at hand, prepared, as the settlers must have known, to attack and plunder the town.

The Indians, consisting of about 180 braves, or fighting men, and 100 camp followers, led by Marcus Canul, chief of the Ycaiché, approached the town about 8 a.m. on Sunday, the 1st of September. They were divided into three sections, each of 60 men, and they entered the town at three different points; one attacking the upper portion, and pillaging and setting fire to the houses and stores, the other two marching directly upon the barracks, but from opposite sides. Of these latter two, one took up a position behind the stacks of logwood, thus commanding one side and one end of the barrack; and the other established itself close to the officers' quarters, under cover of a stone building, which commanded the other side of the barrack and the end already commanded from the stacks of logwood.

So sudden and unexpected was the attack, that Lieutenant Graham Smith and Staff-Assistant-Surgeon Edge, who were both at the time having their morning baths, barely had time to escape to the barracks; Lieutenant Smith, with nothing on but his trousers, and Dr. Edge in a state of nudity; while the first notice the men in the barrack had of the approach of the enemy, was the shower of lead which rattled on the building.

Lieutenant Graham Smith says: "At about 8 a.m. on September 1st, I was bathing, when I heard the report of a gun and the whizz of a bullet along the road running past the south end of the barrack-room. I looked out of the door of my house facing the barracks, and saw the corporal of the old guard, which had just been relieved, running towards me. He said, 'The Indians have come.' I repeated this to Dr. Edge, who was living in the same quarters with me, then put on my trousers, ran across to the barrack-room, and got the men under arms as quickly as possible."

Before Lieutenant Graham Smith had reached the barracks, the two divisions of the enemy had taken up their respective positions, and were pouring in unceasing discharges of ball, which penetrated the pimento sticks and raked the building from end to end. The guard, the only men who had ammunition in their possession, returned the fire, and at this moment Lieutenant Smith arrived with Dr. Edge.

Sergeant Belizario, coming forward and asking for ammunition to serve out, reminded Lieutenant Smith that he had left the key of the portable magazine, in which the ammunition was kept, in his quarters. The open space between his quarters and the barrack-room was swept with an unceasing shower of lead; but there was no help for it, and the key had to be fetched. Accompanied by Sergeant Belizario, Lieutenant Smith ran over to his house, seized the key, and ran back. Most marvellously both escaped injury, though the ground all around them was cut up by bullets. The portable magazine was kept in the partitioned end that served as a guard-room, and there was no door of communication between the central portion, where the men lived, and this room. Sergeant Belizario therefore ran out of the barrack-room, along the side of the building, into the guard-room, and endeavoured to drag the portable magazine back with him. He succeeded in moving it outside the guard-room and a little way along the wall, but further he could not drag it. All this time he was exposed to a heavy fire, and every musket-barrel from the stone building on the eastern side of the barrack was pointed at his body. Finding that all his efforts to move the magazine were fruitless, Sergeant Belizario unlocked it, and, taking out the ammunition, passed packet after packet to the men inside, through the opening under the eaves left for ventilation, between the thatched roof and the top of the pimento wall, till the magazine was emptied. This done, he returned to the barrack-room. He seemed to have borne a charmed life, for he was untouched, while the portable magazine was starred with the white splashes of leaden bullets.

A hot fire was now opened by the soldiers, and Lieutenant Graham Smith, taking a rifle, placed himself at the west door of the barracks to try and pick off some of the most daring of the Indians. Whilst there he was struck in the left side, and, at the same instant, Private Robert Lynch, who was standing next him, fell dead, pierced by two shots.

Notwithstanding his wound, which was very severe, the ball penetrating the left breast a little above the heart, and passing nearly through him, finally lodging under the left shoulder-blade, Lieutenant Smith continued directing and encouraging his men; and finding that the whole interior was swept by the missiles of the enemy, against which the frail pimento-sticks were no protection, he ordered the men to turn down their cots, and, lying on their beds, to fire over the iron heads of the cots. In this position they were tolerably well sheltered, though the Indians were so close that several of the iron heads were shot through.

In this place it will be proper to refer to a soldier who, all this time, was outside the barrack. This was Private Bidwell, who, when the Indians arrived, had just been posted sentry on a commissariat store close to the officers' quarters. The occupation of one of this group of buildings cut him off from the barrack-room; so, after bayoneting one Indian, he ran over to an enclosure belonging to Don Escalente, situated to the north of the store. From the shelter of the fence of this enclosure he fired into the Indians in the stone building till his ten rounds of ammunition were exhausted. He then said to Don Escalente, "I am going over to the barracks for more cartridges," and, before he could be dissuaded, ran out from the shelter and endeavoured to cross the open space to the barrack. On the way he received a mortal wound, but succeeded in joining his comrades.

The Indians, impatient at the delay caused by the obstinate resistance of the soldiers, now vacated the houses on the further side of the road, opposite the southern end of the barracks, and set fire to the thatched roofs, hoping to involve the barracks in a general conflagration. The houses burned fiercely, and the flames spreading across the road, caught a small kitchen situated not ten yards from the barracks. The Indians raised yells of triumph, for they considered it certain that their foes would now be driven from their shelter and then easily overpowered by force of numbers. Indeed, it is difficult to understand how the dry palm-thatch of the barracks did fail to ignite, but it did so fail, and the kitchen, after blazing up violently for a few minutes, fell in and burned itself out harmlessly.

By the destruction of these buildings the position of the soldiers was improved, the Indians now having no cover immediately opposite the south end of the barrack, and being compelled consequently to concentrate behind the stacks of logwood. A party, however, of them made a circuit and appeared on the north-west corner of the barrack, from whence they commanded the road bounding the north side of the building.

After the firing had continued for an hour and a half, Mr. Price, and another American gentleman from Tower Hill Rancho, about four miles from the barracks, having heard what was taking place, mounted and rode towards the scene of the conflict. Creeping up the river bank unperceived through the thick woods, they suddenly rode into and fired upon the Indians who were in rear of the stacks of logwood. The latter, taken by surprise, and not knowing by what unexpected force they were attacked, left their cover for a moment and appeared on the side nearest to the barracks. The soldiers perceiving this movement, and thinking that the Indians were going to attempt to rush the building, fixed bayonets, and some ran to the doors to defend the entrances. Mr. Price and his companion, taking advantage of this and the momentary surprise of the Indians, rushed forward and threw themselves into the barracks.

The enemy's fire redoubled after this, and it was hotly kept up until about half-past 1 o'clock; it then began to slacken, and by 2 o'clock had ceased altogether. For some time no one stirred, it being suspected that the cessation of the attack was only an Indian ruse; but after a quarter of an hour had elapsed, Sergeant Belizario was sent out with a party to reconnoitre. He reported that the enemy was in full retreat, and was sent to follow them up and watch their movements. No pursuit could be attempted. Lieutenant Graham Smith was, by this time, incapable of further action, and out of the detachment of thirty-eight men, two had been killed and fourteen severely wounded.

The attack lasted altogether six hours. The Indian loss was about fifty killed; the number of their wounded could not, of course, be ascertained, but amongst them was Marcus Canul himself, who was mortally wounded, and died before recrossing the Hondo. Of the civilians, the son of Don Escalente, a boy fourteen years of age, was killed, and seventeen were wounded. While the Indians had been occupied in their attack on the barracks, the European women and children had escaped from the scene of the outrage and crossed the river in boats. Thence they had made their way through the dense forest to the village of San Estevan, about seven miles below Orange Walk. Over 300 bullet-holes were counted in the walls of the barrack-room, and in many places the palmettos were shot away in patches.

On the morning following the attack, a rumour reached the barracks that the Indians were again in force near the town, and preparing to renew the attack. Every preparation for giving them a warm reception was made; but Sergeant Belizario and a small party, who went out to reconnoitre, found that the rumour was false, although several Indians were seen in the bush and fired upon.

In the meantime the news of the invasion had reached Corosal and Belize, and Captain F.B.P. White, with Lieutenant Bulger and twenty men, arrived at Orange Walk at midnight on the 4th, being followed next day by a further reinforcement of fifty-three officers and men, under Major W.W.W. Johnston, but the Indians had already retired beyond the frontier.

A colonist, in a letter to *The Times* on this affair, says:

"Concerning the conduct and proceedings of the military during and subsequent to the late invasion and attack, I have nothing to say but what redounds to their credit and high character as British soldiers; and if medals and crosses were distributed among the dusky warriors of Her Majesty's land forces in this part of her dominions as freely as among other branches of the service, all I can say is that every one of the brave fellows, who held with such determined valour and tenacity the barracks at Orange Walk on that memorable Sunday morning against such fearful odds, would be entitled to a medal at least."

The following general order was issued: "The Colonel commanding the forces in the West Indies has received with much satisfaction an account of the successful defence of the post of Orange Walk, British Honduras, by a detachment of the 1st West India Regiment, under the command of Lieutenant J. Graham Smith, against an assault of a large force of Indians.

"He has much pleasure in recording his high approbation of the gallant conduct of Lieutenant Smith, who, severely wounded at the outset of the attack, maintained the defence of his post, and retained command as long as his strength enabled him to do so; it was then successfully maintained under the direction of Staff-Assistant-Surgeon Edge, and Sergeant Belizario, 1st West India Regiment, to whom also great praise is due for their conduct and exertions; the gallant conduct of Lance-Corporals Spencer and Stirling, Privates Hoffer, Maxwell, Osborne, Murray, and W. Morris, has also been favourably mentioned.

"The Colonel commanding will have great pleasure in bringing the conduct of these officers and soldiers to the favourable notice of His Royal Highness the Field-Marshal Commanding-in-Chief, and also the judicious and energetic measures taken by Major W.W.W. Johnston, 1st West India Regiment, commanding the troops in British Honduras, who proceeded in person to the post which had been assailed, and followed up the retreating enemy."

In reply to the report made by Colonel Cox, C.B., commanding the troops, the following letter was received, and ordered to be embodied in the records of the regiment:

"Horse Guards, War Office, S.W.,
"*15th November, 1872.*

"Sir,

"Having had the honour to receive and submit to the Field-Marshal Commanding-in-Chief, your letter of the 23rd September last, with its several enclosures, containing a detailed account of the exemplary and gallant conduct of a detachment of the 1st West India Regiment, in repelling an attack of Indians on the Orange Walk outpost of the Colony of British Honduras, together with a letter on the same subject addressed to this department by the officer commanding the 1st West India Regiment:

"I have it in command to acquaint you that His Royal Highness, after consultation with the Secretary of State for War on the subject, has decided that the following recognition shall be at once made of the services of the officers and men employed on that occasion, viz.:

"That Lieutenant Smith, late 1st West India Regiment, who was gazetted to the 57th Regiment in August last, shall be immediately promoted to a Company in the 97th Foot.

"That Staff-Assistant-Surgeon Edge shall be promoted to the rank of Surgeon, as soon as he has qualified for the higher position, and a notification to this effect will be published in the London Gazette, hereafter.

"That Sergeant Edward Belizario shall receive the distinguished conduct medal, with an annuity of £10, to be given at once, in excess of the vote, until absorbed on the occurrence of a vacancy.

"That Lance-Corporals Spencer and Stirling shall be granted the distinguished conduct medal without annuity, and promoted to the rank of Corporal, to be borne supernumerary till absorbed.

"I am also to request that the men of the detachment specially named in the margin[62] may be commended for their good conduct, and the commanding officer of the regiment requested to record their claims, and give such recognition of them regimentally as may be possible from time to time.

"That you will publish these, His Royal Highness's decisions, in your general orders.

"And that a copy of this letter may be furnished to the officer commanding the 1st West India Regiment, for the purpose of being entered in the Regimental Records.

"I have, etc.,
(Signed)   J.W. Armstrong, D.A.G."

In consequence of the attack on Orange Walk, and on the application of the Governor of Honduras, Captain Gardner, Lieutenant Bale, and fifty men of the regiment, embarked at Jamaica, on the 25th of September, in H.M.S. *Fly*, as a reinforcement for Honduras.

FOOTNOTES:

[61] See Map.

[62] Privates Hoffer, Maxwell, S. Osborne, Murray, R.A. Morris, and W. Tell.

CHAPTER XXIX
THE ASHANTI WAR, 1873-4

On the 9th of December, 1872, the King of Ashanti despatched from Coomassie an army of 40,000 men to invade the British Protectorate on the Gold Coast. This army crossed the Prah in three divisions on January 29th, 1873, and spread itself slowly over the country, ravaging as it advanced. In August, 1870, the garrisons on the West Coast of Africa had been reduced to four companies, two at Sierra Leone, and two at Cape Coast. This reduction, no doubt, was one of the principal causes which led to the invasion, for at that time there were only 160 soldiers of the 2nd West India Regiment to defend 160 miles of territory.

In June, 1873, the head-quarters of the 2nd West India Regiment being ordered from Demerara to Cape Coast Castle, A Company of the 1st West India Regiment embarked at Kingston, Jamaica, on the 10th of that month, and proceeded to Demerara to garrison that place. In September, the native levies that had been raised on the Gold Coast to resist the Ashantis being found utterly worthless, it was decided to send three battalions from England and the 1st West India Regiment from Jamaica, to invade in turn the Ashanti territory and dictate terms of peace at Coomassie.

On the 15th of November, the two companies (C and H) from Nassau, under the command of Major Strachan, arrived at Jamaica, and, on the 3rd of December, the head-quarters and five companies (B, C, E, G and H), under the command of Lieutenant-Colonel Maxwell, embarked at Kingston on board the hired transport *Manitoban*. Proceeding to Barbados, A Company, which had been moved from Demerara, was embarked on the 9th of December, and the same evening the regiment sailed for the Gold Coast, arriving at Cape Coast Castle on the 27th, and disembarking on the 29th, 575 strong. The officers serving with the expeditionary force were Lieutenant-Colonel Maxwell, Major W.W.W. Johnston, Captains Sampson, Butler, Niven, J.A. Smith, Steward, and Shearman, Lieutenants Allinson, C.J.L. Hill, Bale, Molony, Cole, Bell, Clough, Elderton, Beale-Browne, and Barne, and Sub-Lieutenants Harward, Spitta, Hughes, Burke, Edwardes, Tinkler, and Ellis.

The regiment on landing was encamped on Prospect and Connor's Hills, two heights overlooking the town of Cape Coast, and Colonel Maxwell assumed command of the garrison in the Castle.

Sir Garnet Wolseley having already driven the Ashantis out of the Protectorate after the actions at Dunquah and Abracampa in November, and having garrisoned the various stations between Cape Coast and the Prah, had, a few days before the regiment landed, gone on to Prahsu with his head-quarter staff. The *Himalaya* and *Tamar*, with the 23rd Royal Welsh Fusiliers and the 2nd Battalion Rifle Brigade, which had been cruising about outside for sanitary reasons, now came into the roadstead, where the *Sarmatian*, with the 42nd Highlanders, was already lying, and everything was ready for the advance on Coomassie.

Accordingly, before daybreak on the 1st of January, the right half-battalion of the Rifle Brigade landed and commenced its march to the front, followed the next morning by the other half-battalion. On the mornings of the 3rd and 4th the two half-battalions of the 42nd landed, and passed to the front in a similar manner.

The Fantis had shown so much disinclination to act as carriers, and so few had been obtained, that the advance of these two battalions had exhausted all the available carriers, and there were none for the 23rd Fusiliers. It was necessary to adopt stronger measures, unless the expedition was to fall through, and on the 4th of January the 1st West India Regiment was posted in a cordon of sentries around the town of Cape Coast, while the armed police seized all the able-bodied men in the town, except those employed as canoe-men. This step was entirely successful, and on the morning of the 5th the right half-battalion of the 23rd landed and marched to the front, being followed next morning by C Company of the 1st West India Regiment.

The difficulty with the carriers had in the meantime increased instead of diminishing. Numbers had deserted, abandoning their loads, and the transport was almost in a moribund condition, the 23rd Regiment being even re-embarked for want of carriers. Sir Garnet Wolseley in this emergency called upon the West India regiments for assistance, saying that the fate of the expedition was hanging in the balance; and in response to his appeal, they both volunteered to carry supplies, in addition to their arms, accoutrements, and ammunition.

Accordingly, on the 7th of January, the head-quarters of the regiment, under Colonel Maxwell, with A and E Companies, marched to Inquabim, the first stage; being followed the next morning by G and H Companies, under Captain Butler; while B Company remained at Prospect Hill to furnish the necessary garrison guards at Cape Coast Castle.

The head-quarters arrived at Dunquah on the 8th, where C Company had been halted by Colonel Colley, who was in charge of the transport and communications, and had already been actively engaged driving in carriers and furnishing escorts for the convoys of provisions.

On the 9th, at 1.30 a.m., A Company, under Captain Shearman, paraded and marched into the Ecumfie district for the purpose of driving in carriers from that neighbourhood, and, at the same hour, the head-quarters and E Company continued their march to Mansu, where they arrived the same evening.

Provisions being now urgently required at the stations immediately in front of Mansu, 78 men of E Company, being all that were available, and 140 of the 42nd Highlanders, started at three o'clock in the morning of the 12th, as carriers, each man with a load of 50 lb. weight, besides his arms and accoutrements. On the evening of the same day Captain Butler, with H Company, arrived at Mansu.

The carriers continued deserting by whole tribes, and the need of them had become so urgent, that orders were issued to shoot any attempting to desert, while parties of the regiment were continually passing backwards and forwards between Dunquah and Mansu as guards over the convoys. To relieve the pressure, 94 men of G and C Companies left Dunquah on the 13th with ninety-four 50-lb. loads, and, reaching Mansu the same day, started next morning at daybreak for the Prah.

On the 17th, Captain Butler marched with H Company to Essecooma, a place about twenty miles due east from Mansu, to drive in carriers, and a similar party was sent out next day from Dunquah, under Lieutenant Roper, to Adjumaco and Essiaman.

During all these arduous duties, and since the 8th of January, so great was the scarcity of provisions at the front, that the non-commissioned officers and men of the regiment were placed upon half rations of salt meat and biscuit, without the grocery ration.

On Sunday, the 18th of January, the transport being now in sufficient order, owing to the number of carriers driven in from the surrounding districts by the regiment, the advance of the army commenced, and the head-quarters of the 42nd Regiment marched from Mansu; their left wing, and 100 men of the 23rd Fusiliers, moving up from Yancoomassie Fanti, and occupying their lines for the night. The Rifle Brigade moved simultaneously to the front from the stations ahead.

Next morning, E Company, under Captain J.A. Smith, marched with the left wing of the 42nd for the Prah, and G Company, under Captain Steward, came up to Mansu from Dunquah, leaving A and C Companies, under Captains Niven and Shearman, at Dunquah and the Adjumaco district.

On the 23rd, orders were received from the front by telegram, that the head-quarters and 200 men were to march for the Prah at once, there to receive further orders. Captain Butler, who had been ordered in with H Company from Essecooma, two days before, arrived at Mansu the same evening, and the next morning, the head-quarters and G Company marched for the Prah, H Company following on the 25th. Halting at Sutah and Yancoomassie Assin, the head-quarters arrived at Prahsu on the 27th, and on the morning of the 28th, the 200 men required crossed the Prah and marched to Essiaman. During this march the men had been obliged to carry their *tentes d'abri*, blankets and waterproof sheets, and seventy rounds of ball ammunition, in addition to their field kits and arms and accoutrements. On arriving at Essiaman, E Company, which, under Captain J.A. Smith, had crossed the Prah a day or two before, was found occupying an important post at the cross roads.

A few minutes after reaching this village, urgent orders were received to push on as quickly as possible to the summit of the Adansi Hills, and again proceed to the front with all speed, leaving fifty men at Fommanah, the capital of Adansi. On the 29th, the head-quarters were at Accrofumu; on the 30th, they crossed the Adansi Hills, and halted at Fommanah for the night, leaving E Company, under Captain Smith, at the cross-roads at the foot of the hills, in accordance with later orders that had been received, and Lieutenant Spitta with twenty-five men at the summit. The men were now becoming much exhausted from their long marches, marching, as they did, double stages every day. Their burdens were unusually heavy for troops, and they were still kept on half rations.

At Fommanah a very pressing letter was received from the chief of the staff, asking at what hour next day the regiment might be expected to join the head-quarters of the army at Insarfu, what numbers it could put into the field, and whether the boxes of small-arm ammunition ordered up from Prahsu had arrived with it. A considerable action was considered imminent on the morrow.

At daylight on the morning of the 31st, the head-quarters marched to Ahkankuassie, leaving Captain Steward and Lieutenant Hughes with fifty men at Fommanah. At about eight o'clock the sound of heavy and sustained musketry was heard, and the men, eager to join in the first battle fought on Ashanti soil, pushed on. At Adadwasi a large number of carriers, with reserve ammunition, who had halted there, frightened at the sound of the firing, were found, and were at once taken on, arriving at Insarfu about 1.30 p.m.

The firing, which had ceased for a short time, now recommenced, the Ashantis making one of their favourite flank attacks on Quarman, the next village in front. The situation appeared grave, the town being crowded with terrified carriers and wounded men, and Lieutenant Hill with a half-company was sent out to act with the 2nd West India Regiment and skirmish.

After a time, however, the musketry ceased, and the carriers, with the reserve ammunition, were pushed on hurriedly under the escort of a company of the Rifle Brigade, the 1st and 2nd West India Regiments being directed to hold Insarfu. Scarcely had the carriers started than the firing again commenced, the ambushed Ashantis having attacked the convoy, which fell back upon Insarfu. After a short delay, a second attempt was made to get the ammunition through to the front, and this time it proved successful. It was now dark, and Captain Buckle, R.E., who had been killed that morning, was buried outside the town, the firing party of the 1st West India Regiment being employed as skirmishers to protect the funeral party, instead of in the usual manner.

The next morning, orders were received for the 2nd West India Regiment to proceed to Amoaful, and hold it until the return of the army from Coomassie; while the 1st West India Regiment was directed to hold Insarfu, in which was the 2nd field hospital with 120 wounded officers and men. The work was arduous in the extreme, the men, when not on sentry or patrol, being employed in clearing the thick bush round the town, and endeavouring to strengthen the post. While the engagement at Amoaful, Quarman, and Insarfu was going on, a party of the 1st West India Regiment, which was escorting treasure from Fommanah to Dompoassi, was fired upon by some ambushed Ashantis about one hundred yards from the latter village. The escort promptly returned the fire, but the carriers all dropped their loads and ran away. After firing a few desultory shots the Ashantis retired, and the escort remained with the scattered boxes of specie, which were too numerous for them to carry on themselves. Fortunately the fugitive carriers, running headlong into Fommanah, spread the alarm, and Captain North, of the 47th Regiment, immediately marched with a party of the 1st West India Regiment, under Lieutenant E. Hughes, and a few men of Russell's Regiment, to Dompoassi, near which he found the treasure quite safe, it having, with the exception of one box, which had been dropped by its bearer some three hundred yards down the road, away from the rest, and where a turn in the path hid it from sight, been collected together by the escort. No trace was found of the enemy, and the party of the 1st West India Regiment returned to Fommanah.

On the morning of the 2nd of February, the head-quarters of the army advanced from Amoaful to march on Coomassie. There were, notwithstanding the defeat on January 31st, still large numbers of Ashantis on the flanks of the road, in the neighbourhood of Quarman and Insarfu. During the day succeeding the battle, they concentrated lower down the road, and, on the morning of the 2nd of February, made a desperate attempt to sever our line of communications by attacking the post of Fommanah.

"The post was in command of Captain Steward, 1st West India Regiment, who had a garrison of 1 officer and 38 non-commissioned officers and men, 1st West India Regiment; and Lieutenant Grant, 6th Regiment, with 102 of the Mumford Company of Russell's Regiment. There were also present two transport officers—Captain North, of the 47th Regiment, and Captain Duncan, R.A.—three surgeons, and two control officers; and in the palace, which was situated in the main street of the long straggling town, and used as a hospital, were 24 European soldiers and sailors, convalescents. The pickets had reported Ashantis in the neighbourhood early in the morning, and had been reinforced; but the village was far too large to be capable of defence by this small garrison; and when, about 8.30 a.m., the place was attacked from all directions by the enemy, they were able to penetrate into it. Captain North, in virtue of his seniority, assumed the command, but while at the head of his men was shot down in the street of the village, and was obliged by severe loss of blood to hand over the command to Captain Duncan, R.A.

"The enemy, as has been said, penetrated into all the southern side of the village, which they set on fire; meanwhile the sick from the hospital were removed to the stockade at the north end of the village, which was cleared as rapidly as possible, the houses being pulled down by the troops and labourers acting under Colonel Colley's order.[63]

"At half-past two, Colonel Colley reported as follows: 'We have now cleared the greater part of the village, preserving the hospital and store enclosure. Difficult to judge of numbers of the Ashantis; they attack on all sides, and occasional ones creep boldly into the village, but generally keep under cover of the thick bush, which in places comes close to the houses.' The firing ceased about 1 p.m.; but on a party going down for water an hour later, they were hotly fired upon. No further attack was made upon the post.

"This attack on Fommanah seriously interfered with the transport arrangements. Hitherto, though a few shots had been fired at different convoys, the panics and difficulties had always been overcome by the energy of the transport officers; but the vigour and strength of this attack frightened the carriers so thoroughly that it was impossible to move them for some days." In this affair the 1st West India Regiment lost one sergeant and five privates wounded, and Russell's irregulars three men wounded.

The Ashantis, although repulsed, still remained in the neighbourhood of Fommanah, and on February 3rd, an escort over a convoy of carriers, consisting of a sergeant and three men of the 1st West India Regiment, was fired upon between Dompoassi and Fommanah, the sergeant and one private being wounded.

The European Brigade pushed on to Coomassie, after several days' hard fighting, entered the Ashanti capital on the evening of the 4th of February, burned it and marched out on the 6th, and arrived at Insarfu on the downward journey on the 9th. Lieutenant-Colonel Johnston, commanding the head-quarters of the 1st West India Regiment at Insarfu, was directed to break up his post, burn the town as soon as all the troops had passed through, and then to follow to Fommanah, where Sir Garnet Wolseley intended remaining a few days, in order to endeavour to arrange a treaty with the Ashantis.

The head-quarter staff left Fommanah on February 14th for Cape Coast, and the European troops being ordered to push on, on account of the commencement of the rains, the 1st West India Regiment was detailed to relieve the 42nd as the rear-guard of the army. On it fell the duty of destroying the fortified posts to the north of the Prah, and the removal of the sick and wounded and stores. Carriers were still so scarce that it was not until the 20th that Essiaman was cleared out and the stockade destroyed, and the three rear companies of the regiment marched into the bridge-head at Prahsu—which, during the advance to Coomassie, had been held by C Company, under Captain Niven—on the 21st. On the 23rd they crossed the Prah, and the bridge was then destroyed.

By the 27th of February all the European regiments had embarked for England, the 2nd West India Regiment was under orders for the West Indies, and upon the 1st West India Regiment fell the duty of garrisoning the colony. Two hundred men were left at Prahsu, where a strong redoubt had been constructed, fifty at Mansu, and the remainder at Cape Coast. On the departure of Sir Garnet Wolseley, on the 4th of March, Colonel Maxwell, of the 1st West India Regiment, administered the government of the Gold Coast.

Previous to the departure of the General the following general order was published:

"(General Order No. 43.)

"Head-Quarters, Cape Coast Castle,
"*3rd March, 1874.*

"Before leaving for England the Major-General commanding wishes to convey to the soldiers of the 1st and 2nd West India Regiments his appreciation of their soldierlike qualities, and of the manner in which they have performed their duties during the recent campaign. Portions of the 2nd West India Regiment have been in every affair in the war, and the regiment generally has undergone fatigue and exposure in a most creditable manner.

"When, owing to the desertion of carriers, the transport difficulties became serious, the men of both these regiments responded most cheerfully to the call made upon them, and, by daily carrying loads, helped to relieve the force from its most pressing difficulties.

"In saying 'good-bye,' the Major-General assures them he will always remember with pride and pleasure that he had the honour of commanding men whose loyalty to their Queen, and whose soldierlike qualities, have been so well proved in the war now happily at an end."

The rains having set in at the Prah, and much sickness prevailing, it was decided to relieve the posts between that river and the coast. In fact, the mortality that had occurred at Prahsu in 1864 showed that West India troops should not be encamped there without urgent necessity; and no such necessity now existed, as the King of Ashanti had agreed to the treaty, which had been left unsettled up to Sir Garnet Wolseley's departure. Captain J.A. Smith, with fifty men of the regiment, escorted the Ashanti chiefs sent down by the king, and arrived at Cape Coast on the 12th of March. On the 18th, H Company marched in from Prahsu, and embarked on the 20th for Sierra Leone in the transport *Nebraska*, which vessel also conveyed the 2nd West India Regiment to the West Indies. C Company was the last withdrawn from the Prah, arriving at Cape Coast on April 2nd.

It had been most disappointing to the two West India regiments to have been prevented from entering Coomassie, within some twenty-five miles from which their head-quarters were halted. West India regiments rarely have opportunities of seeing active service elsewhere than on the West Coast of Africa; and, although the duties assigned to them in the second phase of the war were most important, holding, as they did, the detached posts from the Prah up to the front, keeping open the communications, protecting the convoys, sick and wounded, and constantly furnishing patrols and escorts, yet they felt it rather hard to have been deprived, in their solitary field for distinguishing themselves, of the honours of fighting beside their European comrades at Amoaful and Ordahsu.

On the return of the regiment from the bush, the fatigues and exposures of the campaign began to have their effect upon both officers and men. In ordinary years, in times of peace, Europeans who are seasoned to tropical service, can serve for twelve months in the deadly climate of West Africa without suffering much loss; but any unusual exposure or hardship is at once followed by an alarming increase of sickness. The 1st West India Regiment was the only corps which, after enduring all the fatigues of a campaign in the most deadly climate in the world, did not enjoy the advantage of a change to a healthier station. Added to this, the season proved to be unusually unhealthy, and that variety of African fever known as "bilious remittent," which can only be distinguished from yellow fever by the fact of its not being contagious, broke out. Sub-Lieutenant L. Burke succumbed to this scourge on March 1st, Lieutenant T. Williams on April 9th, Lieutenant W.S. Elderton on May 10th, and Sub-Lieutenant E.W. Huntingford on June 12th, while Lieutenant-Colonel Maxwell, Lieutenant Clough and Lieutenant Roper, being invalided, died on passage to England, and Captain Butler after arriving in England. In addition to these deaths, eight other officers were invalided, and out of twenty-six officers who were serving with the regiment on the 28th of February, only ten were left in West Africa on the 30th of June.

FOOTNOTES:

[63] Colonel Colley had arrived at the northern side of the village, from Ahkankuassie, soon after the command had devolved upon Captain Duncan.

CHAPTER XXX
AFFAIRS IN HONDURAS, 1874—THE SHERBRO EXPEDITION 1875—THE ASHANTI EXPEDITION, 1881

While the regiment had thus been engaged on the Gold Coast, the detachment left at Orange Walk had, in January 1874, had a narrow escape of a brush with the Santa Cruz Indians. On the 2nd of that month, in accordance with a requisition from the magistrate at Orange Walk, Captain F.B.P. White and Lieutenant J.R.H. Wilton, with forty men of the 1st West India Regiment, left that station about noon for Albion Island, in the River Hondo, distant about twelve miles, to demand the restitution of a woman who had been abducted by an armed party of Santa Cruz Indians from a place called Douglas, in British territory. The Hondo was reached about 4.30 p.m., and Captain White, finding a number of Santa Cruz Indians cutting bush, as if for an encampment, on the British side of the river, directed them to accompany him; and crossing to the island in their boats, sent them to tell the chief that he had a message to deliver to him.

On landing on Albion Island it was found that the public ball-room of San Antonio, a large, open, shed-like building peculiar to these Spanish-Indian towns, which was situated on a small hill, was occupied by an armed force of the Indians, about seventy strong. Opposite to them, on the nearest rising ground, the detachment was at once formed up, partly covered by a chapel.

After some time the chief of the Santa Cruz came over to Captain White's party, and inquired what was wanted of him; when he was told that no message could be delivered to him as long as he had an armed party on British soil, and that he must surrender his arms. After some little discussion the chief agreed to do so, provided that they were returned when his men left the island; and, on these terms, ten or eleven rifles were brought in; but while this was being done, a trumpet sounded in the public ball-room, and the Santa Cruz, quickly gathering together, began to load their rifles. The chief, being asked for an explanation of this sudden change, replied that his braves were only cleaning their guns, but at the same moment a sub-chief came up, and loudly declared that the Santa Cruz would not give up their arms.

The troops were rapidly posted in advantageous positions, and Captain White then informed the chiefs that if their men would not lay down their arms they must leave San Antonio at once, first handing over the woman who had been abducted. Some discussion ensued, but Captain White remaining firm, the chiefs agreed to go, and moved their men down to the boats. At the last moment, however, it was discovered that the woman, who was the cause of the expedition, was in one of the boats, and their departure was stopped until she was landed, and given in charge of the troops.

The Santa Cruz now refused to stir, but remained in their boats, which were moored to the bank. It being feared that the Indians were only delaying for reinforcements, thinking to overpower the British in the darkness, Captain White sent Lieutenant Wilton with ten men to give them a peremptory order to push off within a quarter of an hour. The Indians received the message with laughter, asking, "What will you do, if we do not go?" It was now rapidly becoming dark, and the country, wild and savage in itself, was entirely strange to both officers and men. After ten minutes had elapsed, without the Indians giving any sign of departure, Captain White had the "close" sounded, drew in his sentries, and descended towards the boats with fixed bayonets. Upon this the Indians pushed off, and were soon lost to sight in the darkness. The detachment remained under arms all night at San Antonio, and next morning, it having been ascertained that the Indians had retired across the frontier, the troops returned to Orange Walk.

The following letter was forwarded upon this subject:

"Horse Guards, War Office,
"*17th March, 1874.*

"Sir,

"The Field-Marshal Commanding-in-Chief has perused the report which you forwarded to the Adjutant-General on the 29th of January, of the proceedings of the troops at Orange Walk, in British Honduras, who were called out in aid of the civil power against a band of Santa Cruz Indians in January last, and I am to request that you will cause Captain White, 1st West India Regiment, by whom they were commanded, to be informed that His Royal Highness considers that the discretion and firmness displayed by him in the performance of this difficult duty is very commendable to that officer.

"I have, etc.,

(Signed)   "R.B. Hawley,

"Asst. Mil. Sec."

In July, 1874, the head-quarters of the regiment were moved from the Gold Coast to Sierra Leone, one company being left in garrison at Cape Coast Castle, and one at Elmina. As in June the two companies stationed in Honduras had, with the one left in Jamaica, been removed to Demerara, the distribution of the regiment in July, 1874, was: Head-quarters and four companies (A, B, C, and H) at Sierra Leone, two (E and G) on the Gold Coast, and three (D, F, and I) in Demerara.

In July, 1875, disturbances once more broke out in British Sherbro. The inhabitants of the town of Mongray, on the river of the same name, in that month made a raid upon Mamaiah, a town on the British frontier, plundered several factories there, and carried off thirty-three British subjects as slaves. Fresh outrages were committed later on, and, on the 8th of October, 1875, Lieutenant-Governor Rowe, C.M.G., with forty men of the 1st West India Regiment, under Sub-Lieutenant G.V. Harrison, and sixty armed police, left Sierra Leone in the colonial steamer *Lady of the Lake*. The detachment was landed at Bendoo in Sherbro next day. Negotiations were at once opened with the Mongray chiefs, resulting in the surrender of the captives on the 15th, and on the 25th the party returned to Sierra Leone.

Almost immediately after, fresh disturbances broke out in another portion of Sherbro, on the Bargroo River, and, on the 15th of November, Lieutenant-Governor Rowe left Freetown in the colonial steamer *Sir A. Kennedy*, with Captain A.C. Allinson, Lieutenants J.H. Jones, and A.S. Roberts, and ninety men of the 1st West India Regiment, fifty armed police, a 4-2/5-inch howitzer, and a rocket-trough. The disturbance arose from a raid of Mendis upon villages in British territory, thirteen of which they plundered and destroyed, afterwards erecting a "war-fence" at a place called Paytaycoomar, in British Sherbro. Here the Commandant of Sherbro, Mr. Darnell Davis, attacked them with a few policemen, and was repulsed with a loss of three killed and several wounded, himself severely.

The expedition, on arriving at Sherbro, established a camp at Tyama Woroo in Bargroo, and all preparations for an advance being completed by the 27th of November, the troops marched on that day, occupying Mosangrah on the 30th. On the 3rd of December, Lowarnar, a town to the eastward, was entered, and on the 5th a move was made on the stockaded town of Gundomar, which was abandoned by the enemy on the approach of the force. The dead body of one of the captives taken from British Sherbro, recently strangled, was found in the stockade, and the town was accordingly burned.

On the 6th the force advanced on Moyamba, which was also found to be evacuated by the enemy, and was burned. On the 9th the troops left Moyamba and marched to Yahwi-yamah, which was also destroyed, with the outlying stockaded villages of Mocorreh, Bettimah and Mangaymihoon. On the 10th Modena was destroyed, and the force marched through Mowato and Geeavar to Sennehoo, arriving there on the 16th. To this latter town several of the chiefs came in to treat, bringing 212 of the captives with them, and on the 18th a treaty of peace was arranged, the Mendis promising to pay a fine of 10,000 bushels of rice. The troops returned to Sierra Leone on the 24th of December.

The country through which the detachment of the 1st West India Regiment had marched was most difficult. It consisted of dense forest, through which the only advance could be made along narrow paths, wide enough only for the passage of men in single file, and obstructed by fallen trees, swamps, and unbridged streams. Numerous swamps, black and full of malaria, had to be crossed, and, though the noon-day sun was excessively hot, the nights, owing to excessive damp, were very cold. Heavy showers of rain fell almost daily, and from sunset till an hour after sunrise the whole country was buried in an impenetrable fog.

The stockades were of the same character as those found at Mongray, but were here in some instances further fortified by mud walls, fifteen feet high, and about twelve feet thick at the base. Inside the walls were ditches about six feet wide and eight feet deep. In some of the towns, machicoulis galleries had been constructed over the gates, and the entrances further protected by semicircular mud bastions.

In March, 1877, the 1st West India Regiment was relieved on the West Coast of Africa by the 2nd West India Regiment, E and G Companies embarking in H.M.S. *Simoom*, at Cape Coast Castle, on the 24th of February, and the head-quarters, with A, B, C, and H Companies, at Sierra Leone on the 3rd of March. On arriving at the West Indies the regiment was thus distributed: Head-quarters, with A, D, E, and I Companies, at Jamaica, C and F at Honduras, G and H at Barbados, and B at Nassau.

During its three years' tour of West African service the regiment had suffered very heavy loss amongst the officers. In addition to the eight deaths that occurred in 1874, directly after the Ashanti war, Captain W. Cole died in Ireland of fever contracted on the Gold Coast; Lieutenant-Colonel Strachan and Sub-Lieutenant Turner in England; and Sub-Lieutenants S.B. Orr and G.V. Harrison at Sierra Leone in 1876.

The regiment remained without change in the West Indies until December, 1879, when the head-quarters and six companies embarked in H.M.S. *Tamar* for West Africa, leaving D, E, and I Companies at the depôt at Demerara. The head-quarters and four companies disembarked at Sierra Leone on the 17th of January, 1880, and the two remaining companies proceeded to Cape Coast Castle.

In February, 1880, there being some slight disturbance in the neighbourhood of the Ribbie River, a small party of the 1st West India Regiment proceeded thither as an escort to the Governor, with Lieutenants Madden and Tipping. The whole returned to Sierra Leone without any casualty, after an absence of a few weeks.

On the 28th of January, 1881, news was received at Sierra Leone that the Ashanti king, Mensah, had threatened an invasion of the Gold Coast Colony, and a reinforcement was urgently demanded. In consequence, Captain H.W. Pollard, 1st West India Regiment, commanding the troops on the West Coast of Africa, despatched to Cape Coast Castle next day in the mail steamer *Cameroon* letter B Company, under Captain Ellis, and letter H Company, under Lieutenant Garland. These two companies arrived at their destination on the 2nd of February, and on the 9th the former proceeded to Anamaboe. This rapid arrival of reinforcements induced the king to repudiate the action of his envoys, but affairs were still in a very critical situation, and much alarm prevailed in the colony. Early in March, Lieutenant-Colonels Niven and Smith and Major White arrived from England, bringing with them letter A Company from Sierra Leone. On the 18th of March, five companies of the 2nd West India Regiment arrived in the hired transport *Humber*. Negotiations were protracted till April, when an embassy arrived from Coomassie, and the difficulty was finally settled. On the 2nd of May, the head-quarters, with A, F, and G Companies, returned to Sierra Leone, leaving B, C, and H at Cape Coast Castle and Anamaboe. In February, 1882, C Company also proceeded to Sierra Leone.

It was intended at the termination of the African tour of the regiment, in January, 1883, to reduce the garrisons in West Africa from six to three companies, and the steamship *Bolivar* was chartered to carry out the relief in two trips. That vessel, however, was wrecked off the Cobbler's Reef, at Barbados, and H.M.S. *Tyne* was sent in her place. The latter embarked H Company at Cape Coast Castle on the 6th of February, 1883, and F and G Companies at Sierra Leone on the 14th, all three proceeding to Jamaica under the command of Major C.J.L. Hill. On the return of the *Tyne* to West Africa with three companies of the 2nd West India Regiment, the head-quarters and remaining three companies of the 1st West India Regiment, at Cape Coast Castle and Sierra Leone, were embarked on the 1st and 11th of April respectively, and sailed for Jamaica under the command of Captain Ellis, arriving at their destination on the 28th of April. On the 5th of May, B, G, and F Companies embarked in the *Tyne*, the first two for Honduras and the third for Nassau. On the conclusion of the inter-island trooping, the *Tyne* proceeded with the head-quarters and three companies of the 2nd West India Regiment to West Africa, the Government having, in consequence of threatened complications with Ashanti, abandoned their scheme of reducing the African garrisons.

The distribution of the 1st West India Regiment is now (May, 1883): Head-quarters and three companies (A, C, and H) at Jamaica, two (B and G) in Honduras, one (F) in Nassau, and three (D, E, and I) in Demerara.

APPENDIX

Succession of Honorary Colonels.

Major-General John Whyte	24th April, 1795.
Lord Charles Henry Somerset	5th January, 1804.
Sir Peregrine Maitland, K.C.B	22nd February, 1830.
Major-General the Hon. Sir Henry King, K.C.B.	19th July, 1834.
Lieutenant-General Sir William Nicolay, K.C.H.	30th November, 1839.
Lieutenant-General Sir Henry F. Bouverie, K.C.B., G.C.M.G	13th May, 1842.
Lieutenant-General Sir G.H. Bromley Way	21st November, 1843.
General Sir George Thomas Napier, K.C.B.	29th February, 1844.
Lieutenant-General Sir George Bowles, K.C.B.	9th September, 1855.
General Sir Arthur Borton, K.C.B	2nd May, 1876.

Succession of Lieutenant-Colonels.

1. Leeds Booth	23rd May, 1795	From Brevet-Major, 32nd Foot.
2. George Rutherford	30th Dec., 1797	From Major, 27th Foot, vice Booth to 87th Regiment.
3. James Maitland	22nd April, 1803	From 60th by purchase, vice Rutherford, who retires.
4. Alexander Cumine	20th March, 1804	From 75th Foot, vice Maitland, who exchanges.

5. C.D. Broughton	21st April, 1804	By purchase, vice Cumine, who retires.
6. Samuel Huskisson	2nd June, 1807	From Major, 8th Foot, without purchase, on establishment of a second Lieutenant-Colonelcy.
7. Benjamin D'Urban	29th Sept., 1807	From 9th Garrison Battalion, vice Huskisson, who exchanges.
8. John Irving	9th Jan., 1808	From 2nd West India Regiment, vice D'Urban, who exchanges.
9. George H. Duckworth	16th Jan., 1808	From Major, 67th Foot, by purchase, vice Irving, who retires.
10. Henry Tolley	27th Feb., 1808	From Major, 71st Foot, without purchase, vice Broughton, cashiered.
11. W.S. Wemyss	18th June, 1808	From 48th Foot, vice Duckworth, who exchanges.
12. Joseph Morrison	2nd Dec., 1809	From Major, 89th Foot, with purchase vice Tolley, appointed to 16th Foot.
13. Jonathan Yates	21st July, 1810	From Major, 47th Foot, by purchase, vice Wemyss, who retires.

14. Clement Whitby	16 July, 1811	From Major, 17th Foot, with purchase, vice Morrison, appointed to 89th Foot.
15. J.M. Clifton	10th Sept., 1814	Without purchase, vice Yates, appointed to 49th Foot.

(Lieutenant-Colonel Clifton retired, Jan. 23rd 1819, and the second Lieutenant-Colonelcy was abolished.)

16. James Cassidy	12th Dec., 1822	By purchase, vice Whitby, who retires.
17. Francis Frye Brown	12th Jan., 1824	From half-pay, 6th West India Regiment, vice Cassidy, who exchanges.
18. Richard Doherty	6th Dec., 1827	From half-pay, vice Brown, who retires.
19. William Bush	4th Sept., 1835	From half-pay, vice Doherty, appointed to 89th Foot.
20. Henry Capadose	22nd April, 1836	Without purchase, on re-establishment of a second Lieutenant-Colonelcy.

21. Edward Rowley Hill	1st Jan., 1847	Without purchase, vice Bush, appointed Inspecting Field Officer of a recruiting district.
22. Robert Hughes	14th April, 1848	Vice Capadose, deceased.
23. Fred. Aug. Wetherall	1st May, 1855	From Major, 3rd West India Regiment, by purchase, who retires.
24. Luke Smyth O'Connor	21st Sept., 1855	Without purchase, vice Hill, appointed to a Provisional Depôt Battalion.
25. Edward Last	24th Nov., 1857	From Brevet Lieutenant-Colonel, 99th Foot, vice Wetherall, deceased.
26. Henry Dunn O'Halloran	23rd March, 1858	From Brevet Lieutenant-Colonel, Depôt Battalion, vice Last, appointed to 21st Foot.
27. Augustus William Murray	16th March, 1860	Without purchase, vice O'Halloran, retired upon full pay.
28. Bowland Moffatt	4th March, 1862	From half-pay, vice O'Connor, who retires upon half-pay.

29. James Travers	4th March, 1862	Without purchase, vice Murray, who retires upon half-pay on being appointed Deputy-Adjutant-General, Windward and Leeward Islands.
30. James Shortall Macauley	29th July, 1862	Without purchase, vice Travers, retired on full pay.
31. William M'Bean	18th Dec., 1866	By purchase, Moffatt, who retires.
32. G. Nigel K.A. Yonge	3rd April, 1867	From half-pay, late 67th Foot, vice Macauley, who retires on half-pay.
33. Henry Anton	8th June, 1867	Without purchase, vice M'Bean, who retires.
34. James Maxwell	17th Aug., 1870	From half-pay, late 34th Foot, vice Yonge, who retires on half-pay.
35. J.M. M'Auley	4th Oct., 1871	Vice Anton, deceased.
36. W.W.W. Johnston	24th Dec., 1873	Vice M'Auley, who retires.
37. W.H.P.F. Strachan	15th April, 1874	Vice Maxwell, deceased.
38. Knox Rowan Niven	24th March, 1877	Vice Strachan, deceased.
39. Joseph Alexander Smith	29th Jan., 1879	Vice Johnston, retired.

| 40. F.B.P. White | 4th March, 1882 | Vice Niven, retired. |

Stations of the 1st West India Regiment from June, 1795, to June, 1883.

1795 (June).

Head-quarters and 8 companies at Martinique.

1798 (December).

Head-quarters and 6 companies at Morne Fortune, St. Lucia.

2 companies at Maboya, St. Lucia.

1801 (July).

Head-quarters and 8 companies at Martinique.

1802 (January).

Head-quarters and 6 companies at Martinique.

2 companies at St. Vincent.

1802 (July).

Head-quarters and 6 companies at St. Vincent.

1 company at Martinique.

1 company at Antigua.

1802 (October).

Head-quarters and 8 companies at St. Vincent.

1803 (April).

Head-quarters and 6 companies at St. Vincent.

2 companies at Grenada.

1804 (May).

Head-quarters and 6 companies at Dominica.

1 company at St. Vincent.

1 company at Grenada.

1807 (January).

Head-quarters and 6 companies at Barbados.

3 companies at Grenada.

1 company at Tobago.

1807 (November).

Head-quarters and 10 companies at Barbados.

1808 (January).

Head-quarters and 6 companies at Barbados.

3 companies at Antigua.

1 company at Tobago.

1808 (October).

Head-quarters and 9 companies at Barbados.

1 company at Tobago.

1809 (February).

Head-quarters and 8 companies at Martinique.

2 companies at Barbados.

1809 (June).

Head-quarters and 6 companies at Trinidad.

2 companies at Martinique.

2 companies at Barbados.

1809 (August).

Head-quarters and 10 companies at Trinidad.

1814 (March).

Head-quarters and 4 companies at Martinique.

4 companies at St. Lucia.

2 companies at Dominica.

1814 (July).

Head-quarters and 8 companies at Guadaloupe.

1 company at Marie-Galante.

1 company at St. Martin's.

1814 (December).

Head-quarters and 10 companies at New Orleans.

1815 (February).

Head-quarters and 10 companies at Barbados.

1815 (August).

Head-quarters and 6 companies at Barbados.

4 companies at Guadaloupe.

1815 (December).

Bermuda.

1816 (March).

Head-quarters and 10 companies at Barbados.

1816 (November).

Head-quarters and 3 companies at Antigua.

1 company at Montserrat.

2 companies at St. Christopher's.

2 companies at St. Lucia.

2 companies at Dominica.

—

10

==

1819 (January).

Head-quarters and 3 companies at Barbados.

2 companies at Antigua.

2 companies at St. Lucia.

2 companies at Dominica.

1 company at Tobago.

—

10

==

1821 (October).

Head-quarters and 3 companies at Barbados.

1 company at Demerara.

1 company at Tobago.

1 company at St. Lucia.

1 company at Dominica.

1 company at Antigua.

—

8

==

1823 (May).

Head-quarters and 4 companies at Barbados.

1 company at Demerara.

1 company at St. Lucia.

1 company at Dominica.

1 company at Antigua.

—

8

==

1823 (September).

Head-quarters and 2 companies at Barbados.

3 companies at Demerara.

1 company at St. Lucia.

1 company at Dominica.

1 company at Antigua.

—

8

==

1824 (October).

Head-quarters and 5 companies at Barbados.

    1 company at St. Lucia.

    1 company at Dominica.

    1 company at Antigua.

    —

    8

    ==

    1825 (February).

Head-quarters and 4 companies at Trinidad.

    1 company at Barbados.

    1 company at St. Lucia.

    1 company at Dominica.

    1 company at Antigua.

    —

    8

    ==

    1826 (February).

Same as in 1825, with the addition of a recruiting company at Sierra Leone.

    1827 (January).

Head-quarters and 3 companies at Trinidad.

    1 company at Barbados.

    1 company at St. Lucia.

    1 company at Dominica.

    1 company at Antigua.

    1 company at Grenada.

    1 company at Sierra Leone.

—

9

==

1834 (May).

Head-quarters and 2 companies at Trinidad.

1 company at Barbados.

1 company at St. Lucia.

1 company at Dominica.

1 company at Antigua.

1 company at Grenada.

1 company at Tortola.

1 company at Sierra Leone.

—

9

==

1837 (December).

Head-quarters and 5 companies at St. Lucia.

1 company at Trinidad.

1 company at Tobago.

1 company at Demerara.

1 company at St. Vincent.

1 company at Sierra Leone.

—

10

==

1839 (December).

Head-quarters and 2 companies at Demerara.

3 companies at Barbados.

1 company at Trinidad.

1 company at Tobago.

1 company at St. Lucia.

1 company at St. Vincent.

1 company at Grenada.

1 company at Dominica.

1 company at Antigua.

1 company at Sierra Leone.

—

13

==

1840 (September).

Head-quarters and 2 companies at Demerara.

2 companies at Barbados.

1 company at Trinidad.

1 company at Tobago.

1 company at St. Vincent.

1 company at Grenada.

1 company at Dominica.

1 company at Sierra Leone.

—

10

==

1843 (November).

Head-quarters and 5 companies at Demerara.

2 companies at Sierra Leone.

1 company at Grenada.

1 company at Tobago.

1 company at St. Vincent.

—

10

==

1844 (June).

(Head-quarters) Grenadier, No. 8 and No. 5 at Demerara = 3 companies.

Light and No. 1 at Jamaica   = 2

No. 2 at Trinidad   = 1

No. 3 at Dominica   = 1

No. 4 at Sierra Leone = 1

No. 6 at Grenada   = 1

No. 7 at Cape Coast   = 1

—

10

==

1845 (March).

(Head-quarters) Grenadier, Light, No. 1 and No. 8 at Jamaica = 4 companies.

No. 5 at Demerara   = 1

No. 2 at Trinidad   = 1

No. 3 at Dominica   = 1

No. 4 at Sierra Leone = 1

No. 6 at Grenada   = 1

No. 7 at Cape Coast   = 1

—

10

==

1846 (June).

(Head-quarters) Grenadier, Light, Nos. 1, 3, 6, and 8 at Jamaica = 6 companies.

No. 2 at Trinidad = 1

No. 4 at Sierra Leone = 1

No. 5 at Tobago = 1

No. 7 at Cape Coast = 1

—

10

==

1847 (December).

(Head-quarters) Grenadier, Light, Nos. 1, 2, 3, 5, 6, and 8 at Jamaica = 8 companies.

No. 4 at Sierra Leone = 1

No. 7 at Cape Coast = 1

—

10

==

1848 (August).

(Head-quarters) Grenadier, Nos. 3, 4, 6, and 7 at Jamaica = 5 companies.

Light and No. 8 at Nassau = 2

No. 1 at Honduras = 1

No. 5 at Sierra Leone = 1

No. 2 at Cape Coast = 1

—

10

==

1849 (March).

(Head-quarters) Grenadier, No. 3 and No. 6 at Jamaica = 3 companies.

Light, No. 7, and No. 8 at Nassau = 3

No. 1 and No. 4 at Honduras = 2

No. 5 at Sierra Leone = 1

No. 2 at Cape Coast = 1

—

10

==

1852 (September).

(Head-quarters) Grenadier, No. 3, and No. 6 at Jamaica = 3 companies.

Light, No. 7, and No. 8 at Nassau = 3

No. 1 at St. Christopher's = 1

No. 4 at Barbados = 1

No. 5 at Sierra Leone = 1

No. 2 at Cape Coast = 1

—

10

==

1853 (December).

(Head-quarters) Grenadier, Light, No. 2, and No. 5 at Jamaica = 4 companies.

No. 4 and No. 7 at Barbados = 2

No. 1 at St. Christopher's = 1

No. 8 at Dominica = 1

No. 3 at Sierra Leone = 1

No. 6 at the Gambia = 1

—

10

==

1855 (December).

(Head-quarters) Grenadier, Light, Nos. 2, 5, and 8 at Jamaica = 5 companies.

No. 4 and No. 7 at Barbados   = 2

No. 1 at Demerara   = 1

No. 3 at Sierra Leone   = 1

No. 6 at the Gambia   = 1

—

10

==

1856 (December).

(Head-quarters) Grenadier, Light, and No. 8 at Jamaica = 3 companies.

Nos. 4, 5, and 7 at Barbados = 3

No. 1 at Demerara   = 1

No. 3 at Sierra Leone = 1

No. 2 and No. 6 at the Gambia = 2

—

10

==

1857 (June).

(Head-quarters) Grenadier, Light, No. 5 and No. 8 at Nassau = 4 companies.

Nos. 1, 3, and 7 at Sierra Leone = 3

Nos. 2, 4, and 6 at the Gambia   = 3

—

10

==

1861 (April).

(Head-quarters) Grenadier, Light, Nos. 5, 7, and 8 at Barbados = 5 companies.

No. 4 and No. 6 at Demerara = 2

No. 1 and No. 2 at St. Lucia = 2

No. 3 at Trinidad   = 1

—

10

==

1862 (December).

(Head-quarters) Grenadier, Light, and No. 1 at Barbados = 3 companies.

Nos. 5, 7, and 8 at Honduras = 3

No. 4 and No. 6 at Demerara = 2

No. 2 at St. Lucia   = 1

No. 3 at Trinidad   = 1

—

10

==

1863 (July).

(Head-quarters) A at Barbados = 1 company.

B at St. Lucia = 1

C at Trinidad   = 1

D and F at Demerara   = 2 companies.

E, G, and H at Honduras = 3

—

8

==

1863 (November).

(Head-quarters) A, B, D, and F at Nassau = 4 companies.

E, G, and H at Honduras = 3

C at Trinidad = 1

—

8

==

1864 (April).

(Head-quarters) A, D, and F at Nassau = 3 companies.

B, E, and G on the Gold Coast = 3

C at Trinidad = 1

H in Honduras = 1

—

8

==

1864 (October).

(Head-quarters) A, D, and F at Nassau = 3 companies.

B, C, E, G, and H in Jamaica = 5

—

8

==

1865 (November).

(Head-quarters) A at Nassau = 1 company.

B, C, D, E, F, G, and H in Jamaica = 7 companies.

—

8

==

1866 (August).

(Head-quarters) A, D, and F at Nassau = 3 companies.

B, C, E, G, and H in Jamaica = 5

—

8

==

1867 (January).

(Head-quarters) A, B, E, F, D, and G at Sierra Leone = 6 companies.

H and C at the Gambia = 2

—

8

==

1868 (August).

(Head-quarters) A, B, D, F, and G at Sierra Leone = 5 companies.

C and H at the Gambia = 2

E at Cape Coast = 1

—

8

==

1870 (November).

(Head-quarters) A, B, D, E, and G in Jamaica = 5 companies.

C and H at Nassau = 2

F and I in Honduras = 2

—

9

==

1874 (January).

(Head-quarters) A, B, C, E, G, and H on the Gold Coast = 6 companies.

F and I in Honduras = 2

D in Jamaica = 1

—

9

==

1874 (July).

(Head-quarters) A, B, C, and H at Sierra Leone = 4 companies.

E and G at Cape Coast = 2

D, F, and I at Demerara = 3

—

9

==

1877 (April).

(Head-quarters) A, D, E, and I at Jamaica = 4 companies.

C and F in Honduras = 2

G and H in Barbados = 2

B at Nassau   = 1

—

9

==

1880 (February).

(Head-quarters) A, B, H, and F at Sierra Leone = 4 companies.

C and G at Cape Coast = 2

D, E, and I in Demerara = 3

—

9

==

1881 (March).

(Head-quarters) A, C, G, and H at Cape Coast = 4 companies.

B at Anamaboe = 1

F at Sierra Leone = 1

D, E, and I in Demerara = 3

—

9

==

1881 (June).

(Head-quarters) A, F, and G at Sierra Leone = 3 companies.

B, C, and H at Cape Coast = 3

D, E, and I in Demerara = 3

—

9

==

1882 (March).

(Head-quarters) A, C, F, and G at Sierra Leone = 4 companies.

B and H at Cape Coast = 2

D, E, and I in Demerara = 3

—

9

==

1883 (March).

(Head-quarters) A and C at Sierra Leone = 2 companies.

B at Cape Coast = 1 company.

F, G, and H in Jamaica = 3 companies.

D, E, and I in Demerara = 3

—

9

==

1883 (June).

(Head-quarters) A, C, and H in Jamaica = 3 companies.

B and G in Honduras = 2

D, E, and I in Demerara = 3

F at Nassau = 1

—

9

==

INDEX

TO THE

NAMES OF OFFICERS, NON-COMMISSIONED
OFFICERS, AND PRIVATES

OF THE

FIRST WEST INDIA REGIMENT,

MENTIONED IN THE FOREGOING PAGES

Bidwell, *Pte.*,

Bingham, E.H.,

Bishop, *Surg.*,

Blackwell, N.,

Bolton, H.F.S.,

Booth, Leeds,

Borton, *Sir* A.,

Bourke, J.,

Bouverie, *Sir* H.F.,

Bowles, *Sir* G.,

Bravo, A.,

Brennan, *Ensign*,

Brew, R.,

Brocklass, H.,

Broome, W.A.,

Broughton, C.D.,

Brown, F.F.,

— —, R.,

Bulger, C.O.,

Burdett, G.S.,

Burke, L.,

Bush, *Lieut.*,

— —, W.,

Butler, D.,

— —, F. le B.,

Byrne, T.,

Calder, J.,

Campbell, N.,

— —, W.,

Cantrell, D. *Sergt. Major*,

Capadose, H.,

Carden, J.,

Cassidy, J.,

Cave, *Ensign,*

Chads, *Major,*

Chadwick, B.,

Chamberlayne, W.J.,

Clarke, *Bt. Lieut.-Col.,*

Clerk, A.,

Clifton, J.M.,

Clough, H.T.,

Coffin, E. *Pte.,*

Coghlan, A.,

Cole, W.,

Collins, F.,

― ―, J.P.,

Connell, F.J.,

Connor, W.,

Costello, F.,

Cotter, E.,

Craddock, H.,

Craven, *Corporal,*

Crump, *Corporal,*

Cullen, *Ensign,*

Cumine, A.,

Cunninghame, T.,

Dalomel, *Lieut.,*

Dalton, *Lieut.,*

Darley, C.B.,

Deane, T.,

De Winton, *Lieut.,*

Dixon, C. *Pte.,*

Doherty, R.,

Downie, H.,

Duckworth, G.H.,

D'Urban, B.,

Duyer, G.H.,

Edmunds, T.,

Edwardes, C.G.W.E.,

Egan, J.,

Elderton, W.S.,

Ellis, A.B.,

Evans, *Capt.*,

Fanning, J.,

Farquhar, *Ensign*,

Fitzgerald, C.L.,

Fletcher, R. D'O.,

Fraser, J.A.,

French, *Capt.*,

Froggart, *Lieut.*,

Gardner, D.,

Garland, V.J.,

Garsia, M.C.,

Gavin, *Lieut.*,

Gillard, *Bt. Major*,

Gillespie, R.,

Goodinge, H.,

Graham, W.,

Grange, *Capt.*,

Harris, W.W.,

Harrison, G.V.,

Harward, *Sub. Lieut.*,

Hemsworth, G.,

Henderson, *Lieut.*,

Henry, *Capt.*,

Hill, C.J.L.,

— —, E.R.,

Hoffer, *Pte.*,

Holbrook, T.,

Horsford, T.,

Hughes, E.,

— —, R. *Lieut.-Col.*,

— —, R.,

Huntingford, E.W.,

Huskisson, S.,

Innes, *Colonel*,

Irving, J.,

Isles, E. Ellis,

Johnston, W.W.W.,

Jones, J.H.,

— —, *Lieut.*,

Kenrick, *Lieut.*,

Kent, J.,

King, *Sir* H.,

Lafontaine, J. *Corporal*,

Last, E.,

Leggatt, *Lieut.*,

Lightfoot, *Lieut.*,

Lindsay, J.,

Lowe, W.,

Lowry, A.G.,

Luke, E.F.,

Lynch, *Lieut.*,

— —, R. *Pte.*,

Macauley, *Capt.*,

— —, J.S.,

McAuley, J.M.,

McBean, W.,

M'Callum, *Ensign*,

M'Connell, D.,

McDonald, A.,

Macdonald, E.G.,

M'Grace, D.,

M'Kay, J.C.,

Mackay, *Lieut.*,

McKenzie, *Lieut.*,

Mackrill, *Capt.*,

McLean, *Lieut.*,

McShee, *Lieut.*,

McWilliam, D.,

— —, *Lieut.*,

Madden, G.C.,

Magee, *Lieut.*,

Maitland, J.,

— —, Sir P.,

Malcolm, R.,

Marraud, C.,

Marshall, R.,

Mason, *Sergt.-Major*,

Maturin, *Lieut.*,

Mawe, T.G.,

Maxwell, H.,

— —, J.,

— —, *Pte.*,

Meehan, *Capt.*,

Meighan, B.,

Merry, *Sergt.*,

Miles, *Ensign*,

Millar, *Capt.*,

Miller, C.,

— —, *Lieut.*,

Moffatt, B.,

Moffitt, J.,

Molony, C.A.,

Montagu, C.,

— —, G.C.,

Montgomery, W.,

Morgan, *Lieut.*,

Morris, W. or R.A. *Pte.*,

Morrison, John,

— —, Joseph,

Murray, A.W.,

— —, *Pte.*,

Myers, *Capt.*,

Napier, *Sir* G. T,

Nicholson, T.,

Nicolay, *Sir* W.,

Niven, K.R.,

Nixon, L.,

Nunn, A.A.,

O'Connell, *Capt.* ,

O'Connor, L.S.,

Odonnell, *Lieut.*,

Ogston, M. *Pte.*, et seq.

O'Halloran, H.D.,

Oliphant, W.,

O'Meara, M.,

Ormsby, W.,

Orr, S.B.,

Osborne, S. *Pte.*,

Owens, *Capt.*,

Page, T.,

Palmer, R.,

Petrie, J.,

Pilkington, *Lieut.*,

Plague, *Corporal*,

Pogson, *Ensign*,

Pollard, H.W.,

Powell, *Capt.*,

— —, W.,

Pratt, *Bt. Major*,

Prendergast, *Capt.*,

Pye, A.H.,

Rainford, M.,

Reed, J.,

Reid, J.,

— —, W.,

Roberts, A.S.,

— —, C.T.,

— —, J.C.,

— —, *Lieut.*,

Robeson, *Capt.*,

Roper, J.,

Ross, W.J.,

Rudgley, H.,

Russell, *Ensign*,

Rutherford, G.,

Samson, A.M.W.,

Satchell, W. *Pte.*,

Scott, D.,

Shearman, F.,

Smith, E.,

— —, Hopewell,

— —, J.A.,

— —, J.G.,

— —, *Lieut.*,

— —, *Ensign*,

Smithwick, W. FitzW.,

Somerset, *Lord* C.H.,

Speed, W.J.,

Spencer, *Lce. Corpl.*,

Spitta, H.H.,

Splain, W.,

Steward, C.B.,

Stewart, *Capt.*,

— —, *Ensign*,

— —, J.,

Stirling, *Lce. Corpl.*,

Strachan, W.H.P.F.,

Strong, *Lieut.*,

Sutherland, J.,

Tell, W. *Pte.*,

Temple, A.,

Thomas, *Ensign*,

Tinkler, J.,

Tipping, C.W.G.,

Tolley, H.,

Torrens, *Pte.*,

Travers, J.,

Tunstall, *Lieut.*,

Turner, J.M.S.,

Upton, *Lieut.*,

Way, *Sir* G.H.B.,

Wemyss, W.S.,

Weston, R.,

Wetherall, F.A.,

Whitby, C.,

White, F.B.P.,

Whyte, J.,

Wieburg, *Lieut.*,

Williams, T.,

Wilson, R.,

Wilton, J.R.H.,

Winkler, J.,

Wylie, *Lieut.*,

Yates, J.,

Yonge, G.N.K.A.,